EXTRAORDI... ...ERIZING
NO...

"Marianne Willm... ...ds of suspense, the mystical, and pure romance." —*Romantic Times*

12/98

THE LOST BRIDE

"A beautifully mystical journey of love, loss and triumph. Romance gilded with magic shimmers in *The Lost Bride*. Marianne Willman once again guides the reader through the light and shadows of the heart." —Nora Roberts

"A mysterious bride, a treasure hidden in plain sight, a brooding artist, and a perfectly sensible woman—what more could you want in a romance? A delicious atmosphere haunts this unique tale of dreams and redemption." —Susan Wiggs

THE MERMAID'S SONG

"A lyrically woven tale that glows with romance, pulses with suspense and shimmers with magic. . . . Ms. Willman lures the reader into a world both charmed and dangerous as skillfully as a mermaid singing her song on a polished rock in a mystical sea." —Nora Roberts

"From beginning to end, this love story, entwined with passion, intrigue, and mystical charms, held me in its spell." —Julie Garwood

"With a dash of fantasy and wonderful touches of mystery/suspense, Marianne Willman spins an enthralling tale of Gothic romance . . . will both chill and thrill readers." —*Romantic Times*

"Willman has an imaginative, poetic story." —*Publishers Weekly*

more . . .

"If you are a fan of King Arthur legends, or Jane Eyre-type novels, this one will be perfect. Marianne Willman's long-awaited new release is a perfect blend of fact with fiction."
                                        —*The Middlesex* (MA) *News*

"An interesting romantic intrigue that will thrill fans of the genre."   —*Affaire de Coeur*

PIECES OF SKY

"The wild, untamed West comes roaring to life in PIECES OF SKY . . . Willman writes a credible and exciting tale of love and violence."   —*Detroit Free Press*

"Phenomenal . . . The underlying power of PIECES OF SKY lies in Ms. Willman's sensitive portrayal of the Comanche culture combined with strongly drawn, highly passionate characters."   —*Rave Reviews*

COURT OF THREE SISTERS

"Rich and evocative as an ancient tapestry, spun in silver and gold. A tremendous book!"   —Nora Roberts

"Absolutely wonderful! A beautiful, compelling story . . . I loved every enchanting page of it."   —Jill Gregory

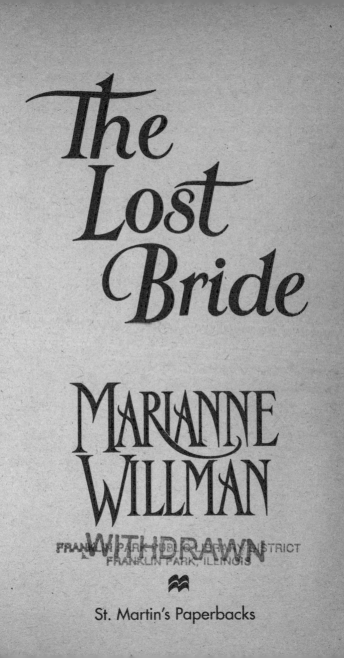

The Lost Bride

MARIANNE WILLMAN

FRANKLIN PARK ~~WITHDRAWN~~ DISTRICT
FRANKLIN PARK, ILLINOIS

St. Martin's Paperbacks

NOTE: If you purchased this book without a cover you should be aware that this book is stolen property. It was reported as "unsold and destroyed" to the publisher, and neither the author nor the publisher has received any payment for this "stripped book."

THE LOST BRIDE

Copyright © 1998 by Marianne Willman.

All rights reserved. No part of this book may be used or reproduced in any manner whatsoever without written permission except in the case of brief quotations embodied in critical articles or reviews. For information address St. Martin's Press, 175 Fifth Avenue, New York, NY 10010.

ISBN: 0-312-96624-5

Printed in the United States of America

St. Martin's Paperbacks edition / November 1998

St. Martin's Paperbacks are published by St. Martin's Press, 175 Fifth Avenue, New York, NY 10010.

10 9 8 7 6 5 4 3 2 1

For Fran Oldford and Katie Charlene Groce
For Leona Washington and Fran Lewis,
and
For John and Lowell
With Thanks and Love
and for my hero, Ky

WITHDRAWN
249-1986

PROLOGUE

§§

Tobias Lacey heard the rustling of unseen wings in the high, shadowy corners of his bechamber. Gnarled hands trembled on the soft linen sheets. The old man was dying, and he knew it. It was high summer, yet he was cold beneath his blankets and maroon brocade comforter. Not much time left. So much still to do. To explain.

Senses clouding again, he slipped back into his recurrent dream . . .

The years fell away like leaves. He was young again, and he stood in the highest turret of Lacey's Folly, watching the moon sift silver motes over the wooded crest of Pucca's Hill.

Biding his time until she came.

And at that exact moment when twilight gave way to night, she stepped out of the shadows at the foot of the slope, insubstantial as a ghost in her fluttering white gown. In the crystalline light, her fair skin was luminous as pearl, and her pale, unbound hair shimmered like beaten silver against the dark trunks of the trees. Her beauty was so remarkable it robbed him of breath.

As darkness gathered, he thought that she would surely turn and bolt back into the sheltering trees. Instead she hesitated. Then raising her head slowly, she looked up at the turret,

*where he stood framed in the arch of the open window. There
was such grief, such longing in her face, in every graceful line
of her body, that he trembled in despair.*

He had failed her again.

*"Forgive me!" he cried out, into the cool night air. "I have
tried! I swear it! I have done everything in my power . . ."*

*But she did not hear him. Slowly, slowly she became trans-
parent as the frosted moonlight. Now he could see the outlines
of the trees through her filmy garments.*

*But even as she faded, her grief remained, drifting like fog
in the gloaming. It smote him to the heart. . . .*

The strange dream that had haunted Tobias Lacey all his
adult life faded away—just as the woman in it had done.

The old man's anguish was so fierce, it broke through to
consciousness. His mind, hazed so long by illness and laudanum, suddenly cleared. He sighed with a sound like dried
leaves skittering across a wintry churchyard. He was not a
young man keeping watch from the turret of Lacey's Folly,
but a withered ancient in his own bedchamber in the dead of
night.

He was the last of the Laceys—and this hour would prove
the last of him.

"Look! He is awake."

Tobias Lacey turned toward the gentle voice. The room was
thick with shadows. For a moment he thought he would see
her again, the elusive woman of his dreams. But it was only
Chloe Hartsell, his companion and housekeeper, standing in
the light of a single branch of candles, with Dr. Marsh at her
side. Her mass of hair had come loose from its neat knot and
rioted around her head like a red-gold halo.

Ah, Chloe. Poor child. There was another tragic story. He
had tried to help her, or so he'd thought. But he saw now,
with the heightened clarity of approaching death, that he had
failed her, too.

He had been a very selfish man. He knew that now. Yet,

even if he could start over, he could not have done things any differently.

The doctor murmured to someone and Tobias realized that there were others in the room. Ah, yes. Martin Thorne, his greedy nephew, and his grasping sister, Olivia. His dear, solicitous relatives gathered like crows at a feast. What a shock they had in store, he thought, and a gleam of malice lit his eyes. There were quite a few surprises for all concerned.

His fingers scrabbled at the covers. Perhaps he should have told Chloe. He owed her that much. Tobias beckoned her forward with a feeble wave of his fingers. Her dress of plain navy bombazine rustled and the silver chatelaine of keys jingled softly at her side. Comforting, familiar sounds to the dying man.

She leaned close and took his hand in hers. Her hands were gentle and her silver-gray eyes were filled with concern. They were, he thought, much too old in so young a face. "Yes, Tobias, I am here. Do you wish another sip of water?"

He shook his head. What was it that he'd wanted to say? His thoughts were as fuzzy as the dark mist that seemed to fill the chamber now. "I need to . . . explain . . . tell you . . ."

The middle-aged couple at the foot of the bed almost elbowed Chloe aside in their eagerness. She caught the heavy bedside table to maintain her balance and held her ground.

Tobias struggled. It was growing too difficult to hold his eyes open. To take in yet another breath. Nothing seemed very important after all. He could just let go of his worn shell of a body and slip away, rising light and buoyant as a soap bubble drifting upward on a current of soft, warm air.

But there was something he must tell Chloe first. It was only fair.

"It will be difficult . . . for you . . ." He stopped to catch his breath. Tobias was mildly astonished to discover what great effort it took to speak, to hear how slurred and garbled the words came out. He licked his dry lips and Chloe held out a moist cloth to soothe them.

"Don't fret, Tobias," she whispered. "I will look after everything."

He took another wheezy breath. "Open the drawer."

Chloe pulled the tasseled knob of the night table and opened the drawer. Inside was a small box, like a miniature chest, of worn blue leather with tarnished brass fittings.

"Take it," Tobias gasped. "Don't let . . . *them* see. It holds . . . the key . . ."

She guessed immediately what he meant: the key to the locked room that was called the Bride's Chamber. Excitement made her hands shake. Leaning forward so that her body screened her actions from the others, Chloe palmed the box and slipped it into her pocket.

"The Bride's Room," Tobias murmured. "Go there . . . after I am gone. Look carefully."

She nodded and put her hand over his, shocked at how cold it was.

The others grew impatient. "What is he mumbling about?" Olivia said sharply.

"Is it the treasure?" his nephew demanded, moving in behind Chloe. She wrinkled her small, straight nose in distaste. Not even the brandy on Martin's breath could hide the cloying scent of his perfumed hair pomade.

"The treasure?" Tobias summoned a surge of strength. "Ah, yes. . . . You've been trying to find it . . . for years . . . when my back was turned. Every time you came to visit . . ." He gave a dry cough. "I always knew . . ."

Martin Thorne flushed darkly as sister poked him in the side. They'd both thought they'd been so clever and discreet in their late-night tapping on the paneling, looking for hidey-holes.

Chloe felt hot color flood her own cheeks and was glad her back was to the rest. Although her motives were quite different, she, too, had been looking for the lost Lacey treasure, vanished a hundred years ago: a jeweled casque filled with fabulous gems from the earth's four corners.

But Tobias was mumbling to himself again. Olivia insinuated herself between Chloe and the bed. She leaned down.

"What's that you say?"

The old man didn't hear her. His mind drifted back to the dream. His blessing and his curse. His father had been haunted by it, too. Tobias wondered who would inherit the dream after him.

Or—terrible thought—would it simply end with his death? No. *No!* It must not end. Panic made his heart flutter. He prayed he had done enough.

Then a peace came over him and suddenly, he understood: the dream, like the story behind the legend, was as real as these walls around him. It had endured for a hundred years and doubtless would endure a hundred more. Until someone solved the mystery and broke the spell.

Alas, that he was not the one!

"Uncle? Damn it, man, what of the treasure?"

The querulous voice roused Tobias once more. His heavy lids lifted. Pale blobs appeared out of the gathering mists to hover in the air over him. He realized his vision was dimming. But there was no mistaking the puffy outline of his nephew Martin's face, nor the long, thin one of his sister, Olivia. Oh, yes, they would be greatly surprised.

Tobias opened his eyes once more. Those clustered round the ancient tester bed stood as if turned to stone. The tension in the room grew until the atmosphere was thick with it.

He cleared his throat and began again, this time more clearly. "The Lacey treasure is . . ."

He stopped, heaved a sigh, and his eyelids flickered closed. *"Yes? Yes?"*

The clock on the mantelpiece suddenly whirred and clicked, then chimed three times. The old man smiled, as if he alone knew a very great joke, and breathed his last.

ONE

§§

THE SHADOWS WERE THICK AS CHLOE TIPTOED THROUGH
the silent house. Everyone else was long abed, except for Tobias's old butler. She paused in the doorway. Tobias lay at
rest beneath the sheets, cold as marble in the flickering candlelight.

Dawlish sat dozing in a chair in his master's bedchamber,
keeping his last silent vigil. The butler jerked awake and
glanced up at Chloe.

"Have you broken the sad tidings to Master Peregrine yet,
Miss Chloe?"

"No. My brother was sound asleep when I peeked in. I'll
be there when he awakens in the morning, and tell him then."

The butler nodded. "The lad needs his sleep. As do you,
Miss Chloe."

She smiled. Dawlish and Cook treated her as if she were
still the orphaned girl of sixteen that Tobias had taken in,
instead of a young woman of more than five and twenty years.
"I'll go to bed soon, I promise."

Chloe made her way down the corridor and went softly
down the staircase.

She moved quickly, purposefully toward the most ancient
wing of the house, by the light of a single, shielded taper.

There was no danger of her banging into anything and rousing the household: in her ten years at Lacey's Folly, she had
at one time or another swept every inch of the floors and stairs,

polished every stick of furniture and piece of silver plate, and dusted every bowl and candlestick and knickknack beneath its roofs.

And while she had cleaned and swept and polished, out of gratitude to Tobias and love of the house, she had kept her eyes peeled for any clues to the fabulous treasure supposedly hidden somewhere inside Lacey's Folly.

I could walk through blindfolded, or in pitch blackness, and not trip over so much as a string in the rug, she mused. *I know every squeaky floorboard, every low doorway and odd corner and angle like I know my own face.*

Except, of course, for the Bride's Chamber. Until his last bout of apoplexy, Tobias had gone there often. He had always kept it locked and had worn the key on his watch chain. She touched the small leather box in her pocket. Now the key was hers.

Her heart beat a little faster.

Tobias had been in pain for some months, and she was glad for his release. But she would miss him dreadfully! Chloe comforted herself with the knowledge that he had lived long past his allotted span of years. One door had closed and another opened, and her life would be forever changed. Just as it had ten years ago, when he'd first popped into her life like a djinni from a bottle. Indeed, he'd resembled one in a picture book.

He had been old even then, with yellow skin from his days in the East, a shiny bald pate and very odd clothing. The brocade weskit and long coat he wore with his old-fashioned knee-britches were a curious combination of garments that had been fashionable in England generations earlier and Oriental garb.

"*I knew your father well when he was a boy,*" he'd told her. "*His grandfather and mine were cousins. I didn't know of the tragedy until recently, for I've been living abroad. But now I am old, and I have come home to England to stay.*"

He had offered her a deal of sorts.

"*Come to Lacey's Folly and look after the house for me,*

oversee the servants. We live frugally but you will have good food, a warm bed, a well-stocked library—and you will be treated as befits a girl of gentle birth. And I shall set something aside so that, when I pass on, you will be taken care of properly.''

She had agreed, of course, and fallen in love with Lacey's Folly at first sight. It was a passionate, consuming love for the old house and its history, and she had been its proud chatelaine. It had been her task to keep the place in as good shape as possible, an ever-challenging job over the years, as expenses grew and the slim housekeeping funds diminished. She had made every sacrifice she could, to keep things in trim.

In the evenings she had read aloud to Tobias or played chess with him on the ivory and malachite board one of his ancestors had brought back from Persia. And like Martin and Olivia Thorne she had spent stolen hours searching for the treasure supposedly hidden somewhere within these walls.

Although, she was sure, her motives were more noble. Olivia wanted it for herself, but Chloe hoped to refurbish Lacey's Folly and see that Tobias spent his last days in pampered comfort. Alas, the treasure—if it existed—had never been found.

Perhaps she would find a clue to the treasure in the Bride's Chamber. Her heart galloped. She had always been both frightened and intrigued by the mysterious locked room—and she was about to learn its secret.

Chloe was in an older part of the house now. Ducking through a low arched door, she entered a series of dim rooms leading one from another in the old manner, and went out the far door. Closing it, she set the candlestick down on a table and relaxed. She was in the Old Hall, the most ancient section of the house, where floors and walls meandered, never once meeting at a right angle. This was the original part of the house still standing.

The hammerbeam ceiling was hidden in darkness. A small stairway led up from near the end of the dais to a railed landing with a single door: once the private lair of the masters of Lacey's Folly it was now the locked Bride's Chamber.

With shaking hands, she opened the leather box Tobias had instructed her to take, expecting to find the key. She groaned in disappointment. Inside were two darkish pebbles, like rough agates; a common roman coin, which she knew had been found on the estate; the colorful tip of a peacock feather, with its round teal-green eye; and a thin gold ring, with twin cabochon garnets flanking the oval mounting where the missing center stone should have been.

Chloe swallowed her chagrin. Perhaps there was something under the lining. Yes! She could feel the edge of something sharp and hard. Peeling back the interior lining, she found a small silver key. It had been a long time since she'd seen the key to the Bride's Chamber but . . . surely this wasn't the right key?

Closing the box, she slipped it back into her pocket, then lifted her candlestick and went cautiously up the stairs. The little key was far too small for the lock. She tried the handle anyway. The door remained firmly closed. Her disappointment was keen.

"I thought this is what you meant, Tobias," she whispered. "I thought you wanted me to come here. To look for the treasure before Martin and Olivia could find it."

Chloe put the candle in the wall niche and sat on the top step of the landing, her heart like lead. Whatever he'd been trying to tell her, she hadn't understood.

"I am sorry, Tobias," she murmured.

Suddenly the meaning of his death came home to her. He was truly gone. There would be no more chess games or reading Canterbury Tales nor the adventures of Arthur and his knights by the fire of a quiet winter's evening. Tobias Lacey was really gone.

She felt terribly alone. The tears she hadn't been able to let loose earlier welled up in her eyes. They ran down her cheeks as she buried her face in her hands and wept bitterly. Sorrow, loss, frustration, and loneliness were all a part of it.

When the storm of emotions was over, she was drained. At the same time she felt relieved, and yet terribly vulnerable. It had been years since she'd been able to give free rein to her passions. She had thought them long gone, efficiently dispatched to some remote attic of her being. Now here they were, fresh and raw and bursting with all the vigor of long repression.

There were so many enormous and conflicting feelings billowing out of her that she didn't know how to stuff them back in. Or even if she *could.* They seemed too large and overwhelming to fit inside her slender body, too heavy to carry in her heart any longer. Drying her eyes with her serviceable handkerchief, she rose shakily.

She heard a sharp *click*, followed by a faint creaking from the landing, behind her. It startled Chloe so badly she had to clutch the rail to keep from falling. She turned around. Her candle flickered in the wall niche and almost went out as a gleam of moving brass caught her eye.

The locked door to the Bride's Chamber was opening ever so slowly.

Her heart stumbled over a beat, then another. A feather brushed along her spine. She tried to reassure herself. The house was old, the jambs crooked. Doors at Lacey Manor sometimes swung shut without warning.

She had never seen one open on its own before.

Certainly not one that had been firmly locked only moments ago. Holding her breath, she waited. Nothing happened. Laughing at herself, she stepped toward the now open door, half expecting to see the ghost of Lost Lenore come gliding over the threshold. There was only a low, soft sound, like the sigh of the sea.

Then a cold draft passed by, touching her bare arms like wisps of gossamer. Her flame flickered, faltered, and then flared up anew. Chloe shivered but held her ground. There was a light burning in the Bride's Chamber. She had to investigate. Lacey's Folly was her responsibility.

Perhaps it is only Martin and Olivia, searching for the Lacey treasure, she told herself sternly. Another part of her brain answered, *If it is only the Thornes, then why does it feel like my hair is standing on end? I'm not afraid of them!*

Chloe forced herself to cross the landing to the threshold. She peered into the legend-haunted room. Inside, all was dark as death. Whatever light had caught her eye was extinguished now.

A branch of three candles stood on the heavy table inside the door. As she lit each wick from her taper, the shadows leapt back. There was no one in the square, walnut-paneled room but herself.

Chloe stood just inside the threshold in awe. For one hundred years this chamber had remained unchanged, unused, but kept ready. Waiting, according to legend, for the return of the Lost Bride.

From appearances, she could move right back in today. There was only the faintest film of dust in the room. Perhaps Tobias, until his last illness, had seen to it himself. Chloe stepped inside and let the aura of the room surround her. It smelled faintly of attar of roses and sandalwood.

The sapphire damask at the windows had faded to a soft, summer blue, the white silk hangings of the bed curtains had mellowed to ivory. The atmosphere felt rich with age and heavy with the residue of old emotions.

Chloe was deeply touched. The bride's chaplet of faded blue and pink ribbons and age-dried flowers still lay upon the coverlet, exactly where the bride of legend was said to have left it. It was protected now by a thin glass dome. Beneath it, the pink and white rosebuds had faded to lavender and antique ivory, their edges scarcely browned. The leaves were a dark, silvery green.

A fragile silk gown of palest green lay stretched across the bed. The neck and wrists of the long sleeves were exquisitely embroidered with roses and violets. Although Lenore Lacey had been eighteen at the time of her marriage, the dress looked like it would fit a girl of eleven or twelve years.

How very small, how slight she must have been, Chloe thought. *How frightened by it all.* It wrung her heart.

She felt the need to reach out to Lenore across the centuries.

As she touched the fragile silk gown on the bed, a flare of silvery light lit the room. Chloe jumped and looked around. It came from the gap in the draperies at the far window. The moon should be on the other side of the house, yet a stream of liquid silver poured through like a pathway leading from the bed to the sky.

She shivered and hurried to throw the draperies open. The rotted silk made faint sighing sounds as it tore. Chloe sighed, too, in relief. It was only the moonlight reflecting back from the bare, rocky peak of Pucca's Hill. Its great, pyramid-shaped summit glowed like a lantern carved from a hollow pearl.

It is no wonder so many legends surround the landmark, Chloe told herself. She could feel a touch of the magic herself, tonight. *Perhaps the villagers are right, and there is a fairy rath hidden beneath the hill.* A fantastic fairyland castle filled with music and glamour, and fairy revelers feasting in glittering splendor with their king and queen.

Not the dainty little winged creatures of popular art, but the human-sized fairies of ancient legend. The powerful Old Ones, who lived invisibly in the visible world and raced their coal-black fairy steeds on the wild night wind. Who feared nothing except the touch of iron, the sound of church bells, and the power of holy water.

Fairies who wove spells of glamour that turned hovels to palaces, who snatched babies from their cradles and left changelings in their place, and who carried off beautiful mortal women to bear their children.

Like Lenore Lacey, perhaps.

Chloe remembered the first time she had heard the legend. It was on the very day she'd arrived at Lacey's Folly . . .

Chloe sat on the small chair beside Tobias Lacey's desk in the library, almost pinching her self to make sure she wasn't asleep and dreaming all this: a fascinating house with lovely grounds yet to be explored; a snug room of her own with a marble fireplace and windows overlooking the rose garden; and Perry in the nursery with a nurse to look after him. And now this remarkable wonder: walls of books so high there was a brass-trimmed ladder to reach the upper shelves, and many paintings and all manner of curiosities displayed on stands or inside glass cases.

It was quite like a fairy tale, and she still couldn't believe their luck. To have a connection by blood to this kindly man, to this wonderful house, slight as that connection was. To be warm and well-fed. To be safe. To *belong!*

"You must put your past behind you and start fresh, with your first step inside this house," Tobias had told her when she had first set foot on Lacey land. "None of it matters."

She lifted her head defiantly. "It does to me, sir."

"Ah, but you are very young. When you have lived as long as I, you will see that individual tragedies fade with the years. What is painful now will grow less so in time. And now that you are here at Lacey's Folly, you will have a much better sense of time."

He took her on a tour of the house. Chloe stared with wonder. "The Laceys," Tobias said, as they reached one parlor, "have been travelers and collectors for many generations back. Some objects, like this jeweled dagger, are priceless. Others are worth little in themselves, but the stories they have to tell are rich beyond anything."

Although the spots of age were large upon his veined hands and balding dome, Tobias's eyes were bright with intelligence and vigor as he showed her one unusual item after another. He held up a visor from a knight's helm, curiously chased with mythical beasts.

"This is said to have been part of Sir Galahad's armor. It has been in my family for more years than anyone can remember." Chloe was enchanted.

"This scarab came from the tomb of a minor Egyptian noble," he said, pointing to a stylized beetle carved from lapis. He picked up a dainty damascened dagger with a translucent green stone in its hilt. "This belonged to Margot Lacey, who was maid-in-waiting to Queen Mary Tudor."

Tobias reached for a small, richly enameled case on his desk and handed it to Chloe. "But this is one of my most precious possessions."

She held it gingerly. The case was so beautiful she was almost afraid to touch it. She opened the hinged pieces to reveal a stunning miniature portrait inside, protected by a dome of rock crystal. The painted woman was exquisitely lovely, with light blue eyes and rippling silver-gilt hair.

Chloe examined the small soft mouth, the innocent features, untouched by life. "She is beautiful! And very young when this was done, I imagine. Is she an ancestor of yours, sir?"

"No, not directly—although her story is inextricably entwined with the history of the Laceys. The locals call her 'Lost Lenore.' She was scarce older than you are now, my dear, when the legend began.

"She came here as a young bride, and vanished on her wedding night, one hundred years ago. She went up the stairs in the Old Hall to prepare herself for her bridegroom. When the wedding party came up to witness the bedding, the room was empty. Lenore had vanished and was never seen again."

Chloe looked up from the lovely miniature to Tobias. "There must have been another way out, if that is true."

"What a practical girl you are," he said, somewhere between a laugh and a frown. "You have had a difficult time, but I hope the hammer and forge of life have not pounded *all* the whimsy and imagination out of you."

He rubbed his chin and chuckled. "There may be a secret passage, I suppose, but if so, no one ever found it. And as my family built the Old Hall, they should have known of any hidey-hole or secret passage."

Afraid she would drop the valuable miniature, Chloe handed it nervously back to her benefactor. "Then what do you suppose happened to her? People don't just vanish! And not on such a . . ." She paused and collected herself. "On such a happy occasion as her marriage day."

"Ah, you've put your finger on it: Lenore did not wed her husband willingly. Her father married her off to a man twice his own age—a man who was suspected of having murdered his first wife by throwing her down the stairs." He gestured to a wall of family portraits. "That would be Obadiah Lacey, on the end, the third row down from the left."

Chloe stared. Time and bad painter's varnish had darkened the portrait, but could not conceal the stern face, with its forbidding eyebrows and jutting jaw. "Did he, sir? Murder her, I mean?"

"I'm very much afraid there might be truth to that ugly tale," Tobias acknowledged. "Obadiah had a fearsome temper and once shot his horse in a fit of pique."

"How horrible! I think I do not like your legend, sir. She deserved a happier fate."

Tobias smiled. "There are two other versions, and I shall let you choose your own ending. Some believe Lenore ran off with a dashing young lover."

"Well, if I'm to have a choice of legends, I would prefer the one with the happy ending," she said with quiet intensity.

Her solemn pronouncements amused him. "I feared you had lost your romantic inclinations. I am glad to see that I was wrong."

Tobias clasped his hands over his waistcoat and smiled. He was right to bring the girl here. She would add life to the house. And order as well.

"Perhaps you will like this version even better: the third story, the one told in our village of Lesser Brampton, says that Lenore ran off to meet her lover at the foot of Pucca's Hill, but he was detained and she fell asleep waiting for him. Now, Pucca's Hill is said to be a fairy fort or *rath*. Do you know what happens to mortals who fall asleep on fairy hills?"

"No, sir."

"They are lured inside by music and fairy glamour, into a beautiful castle in an underground world, where all is feasting and revelry. If they refuse to eat or drink of the fairy food, they may return at daybreak; but once they taste the fairy food, they must stay for one hundred years, as young and fair during the passage of time as the day they entered the fairies' domain.

A beautiful mortal woman might become the bride of the fairy king.''

Chloe's forehead puckered. ''But what happens after that hundred years is past, sir?''

Tobias nodded his approval. ''You have an ear for the telling detail, child. After a hundred years, humans are given the choice whether to go or stay. Some, who have fallen in love with their fairy lovers, choose to stay. Others choose to return to the human world above ground.''

He stared at the little miniature of Lost Lenore, beneath its crystal dome. ''But unless their memories have been kept alive during that time, and unless they are rescued by a mortal's act of unselfish love, they will turn old as the first ray of sunshine touches them, and crumble to dust.''

Chloe paled. ''A horrible fate! I do not like that version at all, do you, sir?''

''Perhaps not. But, you see, it is the true one.''

''You cannot believe that!''

Tobias stared off into the distance, where the strange bulk of Pucca's Hill towered beyond the estate walls. ''I have my own reasons for believing so. And I will tell you this. My grandfather was a young lad at the time, you see, and he was there for the wedding feast. He followed Lenore out of the house.''

Tobias leaned forward and tapped Chloe's hand. ''And he swore a holy oath that he watched Lenore Lacey vanish—into the fairy rath beneath Pucca's Hill.''

Chloe returned to the present and let the fragile draperies of the Bride's Chamber fall back in place. The legend had been the driving force of Tobias Lacey's life. He'd spent it reading arcane books and searching for the secret door on Pucca's Hill. All because of a story his grandfather had told him, never guessing someone as romantically impressionable as Tobias would not only take it for gospel truth, but put his energies and resources into trying to prove the truth of it.

The villagers had thought him daft, but harmless. And now,

perhaps, wherever he was, he knew the answer to the mystery that had haunted him all his life.

Lifting the branch of candles, Chloe approached the fireplace and examined the painting she had only glimpsed from the doorway earlier. Here Lenore was in a three-quarters portrait that was life-sized. Lost Lenore, the woman who was at the center of the family legend. Chloe shook her head. The tiny miniature had not done her justice.

Or perhaps it was love that had caused Lenore to blossom into the fullness of her beauty. Even with the portrait in need of cleaning, the woman's fey, unearthly loveliness shone out. Hair spun from moonlight, dark-fringed eyes bluer than a summer sky. Translucent skin and features as dainty as a fairy child's.

There was a thin gold chain with a locket at her throat, and a tiny circle of twisted gold hung from her delicate earlobe, holding a garnet bead between two smaller gold ones. The dark red stone stood out like a drop of blood against her porcelain skin. Chloe looked up at the gentle, otherworldly features portrayed by an artist long dead.

"Was Tobias right, after all?" she asked the portrait. "Did you fall asleep on the fairy hill, and get taken to wife by the fairies' king? Or was it your delicate bones, your lovely portrait, that inspired the stories as the years went by?"

The candlelight shifted subtly and Lenore seemed to look directly down at Chloe for a moment. Then the shadows returned, and she was just a painted face on canvas in a shadowy, unused chamber.

And there, Chloe saw to her great surprise, was the heavy, ornate key to this room, propped up on the mantelpiece. She wondered then how it had gotten inside, and who had the other key—since *someone* had to have locked the key in here in the first place. She took it down from the mantelpiece and slipped it in her pocket.

She relit her taper, blew out the other candles, and tiptoed away, shutting the door behind her. Chloe locked the door of the Bride's Chamber securely. If Martin or Olivia came to investigate, they would not be able to get in without rousing the house.

Chloe went to the head of the landing, but as she was about to take the first step, she heard a sharp click. It was followed by a rush of cool air. She turned back in amazement, just in time to see the door swing fully open once again. The hair prickled at the nape of her neck and goose bumps rose along her arms.

She had the oddest sensation that she was not alone. That someone—no, that *Lenore*—was trying to tell her something. She went hesitantly back to the door. "Very well," she said, with far more courage than she felt, "leave the door open if you like. After all, it is your room!"

The light dimmed from silver to dull pewter. Chloe was tired and grieving, and on this strange night, in this strange place, her imagination was overwrought. Shadows loomed where none had been before. Old memories stirred the air like a rustle of wings. She looked up again at the portrait of the Lost Bride.

"I hope the sad versions are not true, Lenore. I hope, with all my heart, that you took the wedding jewels and ran from your cruel husband to your handsome young officer's arms. And I hope you lived a long and happy life together."

But the room seemed filled with unheard sighs and restless longings. Again, the strange metallic light shifted, and all sense of reality with it. The leaded cames of the diamond-shaped windows cast bars across the portrait of Lost Lenore.

A distant clock chimed the time. Half past four. Chloe didn't hear it. She was so caught up in the mood and the legend, it seemed as though she'd slipped back a hundred years in time.

At the moment anything seemed possible. Even that a human woman could be trapped beneath the fairy hill, pining for the green, sunlit world she'd left behind.

"If what the villagers claim is true," Chloe whispered fiercely, "if you are held spellbound by an enchantment in a fairy rath—then I pray that someone will come along to break the spell and set you free at last!''

A gentle breath caressed her cheek, and Chloe dropped her candle in fright, almost setting her skirt alight. It was far too much for her imagination to handle.

Hastily snatching at the candlestick, she managed to avoid a fire by a sheer miracle. Gathering up her skirts, Chloe darted down the staircase leading from the Bride's Chamber and fled to the safety of her own room.

LONDON

The clock struck four times. Almost dawn, yet the expensively dressed guests were eagerly alert in the crimson and gold parlor of London's newest and most notorious gaming hell.

All eyes were turned toward Lord Exton, sprawled at ease in a brocade chair, his latest victim sitting stiffly opposite. Gideon Stone, young rake-about-town and promising artist, was Exton's target tonight.

''There'll be blood before sunrise,'' a low voice prophesied. ''Exton will show no mercy.''

''I, for one, think it is a terrible shame,'' old Lady Brace announced in her harsh, carrying tones.

Her diamond necklace and ruby brooch glittered in the candlelit brilliance. Young Gideon Stone was a handsome fellow, with his startling blue eyes and glossy chestnut curls. ''There are few enough well set-up men of quality and good address as it is,'' the dowager said. ''I see no need for Exton to compel this good-looking young man to put a bullet through his head.''

Gideon overheard, of course. Her pity was like the lash of a whip, and her certainty that there was only one honorable way out of his predicament made his hot blood run cold.

Society had certain rules for young gentlemen unable to pay their gaming debts: death was the only honorable alternative.

His firm jaw tightened. He had no intention of dying young.

Not over a woman—and that was really what this charade was all about.

He'd met Mariah Lessington in Paris and he'd fallen violently in love with the glamorous young widow. She had borne her elderly husband a son and heir before the old man had cocked up his toes. Some said that, like Henry VIII's sister Mary Tudor, who was wedded to the old French king, Mariah had ridden her husband to death.

From the passionate days and nights they'd shared, Gideon could well imagine the story to be true. He'd been besotted with her. Unfortunate that it had taken him all these months to see her in her true light. He'd thought she was his angel, his muse, his adored one. Instead she was his succubus, sucking the life and the talent from him.

And he'd had no idea that she was Exton's mistress.

Gideon's throat was dry as dust. He forced himself to relax and leaned back in his chair as if he hadn't a care in the world.

"Your deal, my lord."

Exton smiled coldly. Tension rose like shimmering waves of heat to the sparkling crystal chandeliers.

The men were a contrast. Gideon Stone was not yet thirty. He was reckless, passionate and well-liked by his peers. Gifted with talent, good looks, and charm, he was, like all handsome young men, credited with far more virtues than his actions warranted.

But in the past months the drinking and gaming had increased, and his gaiety had become desperate and forced. His talent had withered from neglect, while he danced and drank and gambled the nights away in a desperate attempt to cover his losses. Like many an artist before him, he seemed to be walking the edge of the precipice, needing only the slightest misstep to send him onto the rocks of ruin below.

Exton was in his mid-forties, cold and controlled. While not handsome, with his dark, aristocratic looks and green eyes, most women found him intensely attractive. His wit was sharp, his wealth immense, and his many vices legend.

And he was determined to destroy Gideon Stone.

"Let us increase our wager," Exton said silkily.

The crowd gasped. "Ridiculous. Too high," someone murmured.

Jack Rathburn, Gideon's close friend, had been watching in despair. He leaned his blond head, put a restraining hand on Gideon's shoulder, and whispered his advice, "Don't let him goad you into something you'll regret."

Gideon shrugged off his friend's advice. "As you wish, my lord."

It was too late for caution. An increase in the stakes didn't matter. After all, he'd already wagered more than he could cover. They had started at easy stakes, but for the past hour they'd been playing deep.

Early on the cards had been on his side, and he could do no wrong. Hopes of paying off his creditors had spurred Gideon on. He had won every hand. And then the cards had turned against him. At first he'd thought that Exton was the superior player, and that he was definitely out of his league.

Slowly, as the candles burned down in their sockets, he'd come to the same conclusion reached earlier by the fashionable onlookers: Exton had cold-bloodedly set out to ruin him.

Gideon swirled the brandy around in its crystal bowl, savoring its bouquet, fighting the urge to dash it in Exton's face. For some time now he'd suspected that his opponent was not merely the masterful player his reputation made him out to be, but a cunning and skillful cheat.

His blood burned for revenge. To accuse Exton now would do no good. Gideon knew it would only make him look like a cowardly fool, trying to shift the blame for his losses. Unless he could prove the other man was cheating somehow, he was trapped.

Exton surveyed the younger man from beneath his dark brows and tapped his fingers on the tabletop. The moment of reckoning had come.

"Well, Mr. Stone?"

"Play your card, my lord!"

A murmur, a soft ripple of approval went through the room.

The gallant young artist would go down, but he would do so like a gentleman, with his colors flying. There was nothing but the tick of the clock as the marquis reached for the deck.

Damning his own pride and folly, Gideon smiled and sat back nonchalantly, although he was nearly blind with anger at the way he'd let himself be duped. Not just by Exton or Mariah, but by his own lust and stupidity. If he escaped this night unscathed, he'd never trust another woman again!

Exton fixed him with his cold, green stare. He had the sudden stillness of the cobra about to strike. Gideon had seen them during his sojourn in India, flared hoods and swaying bodies, hypnotizing their victims with fright, prolonging the terror. . . .

But all was not yet lost. Everything depended on this next— this last—turn of the cards.

Looking up, Gideon caught Mariah's limpid glance.

At the moment there was neither pity nor chagrin for her former lover on her classic features, only a faint smile of admiration for Exton's skill.

A shame that he took such a violent reaction to my little dalliance with Gideon. After all, Exton had been neglecting me, chasing that little blond opera dancer, and then taking the creature to Venice with him! It was only fair that she has served him back in kind.

It was too bad for poor Gideon, of course. He'd been married to his art when they'd met in Paris, and Mariah couldn't resist the challenge he offered. She'd known that he would give in eventually. He was too much of a man to deny his passions once they were roused. And she'd known exactly how to go about it.

Certainly, he had been an interesting and inventive lover. Gideon was several years Exton's junior, with an athlete's lean body and endurance. Perhaps that was what Exton could not forgive. Mariah certainly hadn't expected such violent jealousy from the jaded marquis. It was like balm to her injured vanity.

She heaved a tiny sigh for Exton's victim. Poor Gideon.

But la! she couldn't repine. She glanced at her reflection in the pier glass across the way. She had her wealthy protector back again, and a new emerald necklace at her swanlike throat, and matching brooch pinned at the cleavage of her perfect bosom, to console her. And there were always handsome would-be lovers waiting in the wings. In future she would just be more discreet.

Gideon's nerves were strained as he waited for the marquis. He forced his voice to be casual. "Do you play, my lord?"

Exton smiled and didn't reply, except to turn the card.

A gasp went round the room. The wicked marquis had won again. Only Gideon had glimpsed what seemed to be a bit of pasteboard tucked inside Exton's sleeve. By God, he'd expose the man for the cheat he was!

"Another game, Mr. Stone? One last chance to recoup your losses?"

Gideon eyed him coolly. "The hour is advanced. Perhaps we should call it a night."

"Come, come, man! Show some courage!" The marquis's dark eyes glinted as he ran his thumbnail along the edge of the deck of cards in his hand. "One last game. A simple cut of the pack. High card, double or nothing."

Gideon's jaw knotted. He could not ignore the insult, and the marquis knew it. He would wager everything on the chance that the cards would turn and Fortune would favor him. One single turn of the cards and he could walk away debt free. Or he could expose Exton for the cheat he was. It was a risk worth taking.

He took the cards that Exton held out to him, shuffled and cut the deck, then spread them out in a semicircle. Each man drew a card.

Gideon's queen of diamonds caused a ripple of amazement through the assembly; but it was Exton's ace of spades that drew their applause. Only the marquis knew that it had come from his sleeve and not the deck.

Or so he thought. But Gideon had glimpsed it clearly. The candlelight glittered in his blue irises. Rising from the table a ruined man, he bowed to his enemy. "I shall wait upon you in the morning to settle my vowels, my lord."

He leaned forward suddenly and lowered his voice so only Exton could hear. "*Unless you have some other card hidden in your coat sleeve that you'd care to play first?*"

Exton went white at the accusation and rose menacingly. His aristocratic face was twisted into an ugly mask of hatred.

"What are you saying, you impudent cur?"

Gideon reached out toward the marquis, intent on grasping the other man's sleeve and shaking loose the other ace he'd glimpsed tucked into the lining.

He waited a split second too long.

"Lord Exton!" A shout from the door and Exton whipped around, yanking his arm free. "My lord!" The marquis's secretary burst into the room, his face pasty and covered with sweat.

"My lord, you must hasten! Your son and heir has been stricken ill in Paris, and his wife bids you come with all desperate haste. I have the traveling carriage at the door. There is not a second to lose if you mean to sail with the tide."

Exton blanched. He pushed past Gideon, then paused on the threshold. "I'll send you word when I return to England, Stone. We will settle this then."

He was off in a flurry of retainers, leaving the room half empty.

Gideon was stunned and furious at the turn of events. Another second and he could have *proven* to all that his opponent had been cheating. Of course, that would have led to a duel. The marquis was a notable shot and Gideon was not. But on the whole, he'd rather face the man at twenty paces on a warm summer morning than lose his reputation to a damned ivory turner!

The others in the room moved away—all except Jack Rathburn, who stood firm. Their eyes avoided the young artist. In their minds, he was already a dead man.

"Good night," Gideon called out suavely, bowing to the crowd. "I wish you pleasant dreams!"

"I shall come with you," Rathburn said in concern.

"No!" Gideon was adamant. "I prefer to be alone."

A footman handed him his hat and cane, and he went out into a warm, star-sprinkled night. As he walked back to his rented room, he damned himself for not acting on his suspicions earlier, instead of waiting to see the proof of Exton's perfidy. Now, devil take it, it was too late to accuse the marquis of cheating. He had no proof, and no one would believe him. Who would take the world of a ruined man over that of one of the greatest lords in all the land?

Gideon turned the corner, cursing himself. Whether Exton returned in a week or a month, there was no way he could come up with the money to pay the debts. He had neither land nor possessions to sell, only his talent.

A talent he feared was gone. Killed by his own neglect and folly.

He unlocked the door of Mrs. Bigelow's neat little townhouse, took a night candle from the hall table, and made his way up to the top floor that also served as his studio. There were two bottles of claret left on the sideboard.

He opened the first and poured out a generous quantity. It went down like silk and then rose to his head like hot lead. The wine was finished before he knew it. Anything to blot out the memory of the night, and the disgrace that awaited him.

The second bottle was broached and emptied as easily. Drawing off his coat and cravat, he sprawled in the ramshackle armchair. Soon he was numb from his brain to his toes.

It was perfect, the state of heavenly oblivion he'd meant to achieve. He leaned his head back against the threadbare upholstery and closed his eyes . . .

Gideon knew he was dreaming.

It was like no dream landscape he'd ever seen. Incredibly beautiful, eerily compelling, and completely unknown. He felt almost as if he had stumbled into someone else's dream in error.

He stood at a high window, watching the rising moon sift

silver dust over a wooded hill. Waiting for something to happen. And at that exact moment when twilight gave way to night, she stepped out of the shadows at the foot of the slope, misty as a wraith in her floating white gown. He realized then that he'd been waiting all his life.

Waiting for her.

What a picture she made, airy and insubstantial against the dark mass of the hill. He must paint this scene exactly as it was now! Capture the moment on canvas. His wanted to reach for his charcoal and sketchpad, but he stood rooted to the spot, afraid the woman might vanish if he dared to even blink an eye.

For the span of a few heartbeats she hesitated, and he thought that she would surely turn and bolt back into the safety of the sheltering trees. Then she came forward and stopped full in the moon's silvery glow. In the crystalline light, he could see her with almost magical clarity.

Her skin was luminous as pearl and her pale, unbound hair shimmered like beaten silver against the dark trunks of the trees. Her beauty was so remarkable it robbed him of breath. His chest ached with it, and he despaired of ever capturing her likeness with his mere mortal talent.

Then raising her head slowly, the woman looked up at the turret, where he stood framed in the arch of the open window. There was such yearning in her face, in every graceful line of her body, that it hit him with the force of a physical blow. He gripped the cool stone of the sill to keep from staggering backward. He was certain she couldn't see him in the shadows of the turret window, yet the woman lifted her arms as if reaching out to him.

To him!

He knew then that this had happened before. And he knew that this time it would be different. This time she would wait for him to come to her.

But before he could move away toward the stairs that would take him down and outside to her, she turned suddenly—as she always did—and faded into the gloaming.

"No!" *The cry of grief, of remorse and anguished long-*
ing, was torn from his throat.

Too late! Too late again. . . .

A tremor ran through his body. Then another. He was
shaking as if caught in a violent windstorm. She was gone
without a trace.

This time perhaps forever.

"Mr. Stone? Wake up! Are you ill?"

Gideon jerked awake, out of the cool shadows of the dream
and into the reality of a stifling summer morning. His elbow
caught the half-full claret bottle on the table beside the chair
where he was sprawled. It fell against the empty bottle beside
it, and both crashed to the floor. The sound of their shattering
pierced his skull like a hundred daggers.

Blinking against the pain, he tried to open his eyes. Someone had filled them with hot cinders and then glued his eyelids
shut. Or so it seemed. Gideon took a deep breath and forced
them open. The brilliant, spearing light was even more agonizing than the sound had been.

Over a woman's shoulder he caught a glimpse of long windows and the shimmering glare of London's rooftops and
chimney pots, baking in the hot August sun.

His mind slowly cleared. Mrs. Bigelow, his landlady, stood
beside his chair, her bony face filled with concern. "Are you
ill, Mr. Stone?"

Gideon rubbed his face with his hand and tried not to exhale
wine fumes all over the landlady. "I'm quite all right, Mrs.
Bigelow."

She fisted her hands on her narrow hips. He'd been playing
deep at some fashionable gaming hell last night and lost again.
She could always tell.

Probably in the company of that flash Lady Lessington and
her crowd. Not that the woman acted like a real lady, for all
her high title and fine airs, her vulgar jewels and swishing silk
skirts. A female didn't frequent a bachelor's rooms unless she
was up to no good.

"You look like death in a shroud! And you gave out such a terrible groan it frightened Maisey clean out of her wits."

Gideon shook his head. A horrid mistake. He touched his throbbing temples gingerly. His head was still intact. It didn't seem possible.

"I was dreaming," he said thickly.

But all that remained of the dream were a few vague images, an unsettling impression of shifting identity, and a terrible, aching sense of loss.

"I've fetch you up another tray with a fresh cup of coffee, myself. Maisey was so upset she spilled the first one all over the floor. Thought you were dying, she did."

"No such luck!," he said, a little too loudly for the good of his aching head.

Mrs. Bigelow left, her light footsteps sounding like those of a marching band to his sensitive ears. Gideon leaned back in the chair and groaned. His head was whirling.

He might as well do something to clean up the mess he'd made. He picked up a rag smeared with Prussian Blue and smelling strongly of turpentine. Kicking the broken glass under the table, he dropped the paint cloth over the spreading puddle of wine and coffee seeping into the floor boards. Their scents were nauseating in his present condition.

Why had he ever tried to outmatch Exton at cards? And why had he ever taken up with Mariah—lovely, sensual, Mariah—in the first place? But he knew. She was every man's dream of a perfect woman: charming, witty, gay, and beautiful. Endlessly flattering and accommodating. Insatiable in bed.

He had hoped that she would be his muse, his inspiration. He'd envisioned a rosy future with Mariah at his side, the beautiful woman who would inspire his visions and enable him to produce the wonderful paintings he had dreamed of creating. Instead, she had mesmerized him with her ravishing face, her exquisite body, luring him deeper into sensual insanity, until she replaced art as his passion.

God, what a fool he had been!

Gideon moved past the chair where he'd drunk far too much

burgundy the night before, past the open windows with their
view of London rooftops frying in the unseasonably hot morning sun, past the tall painting on the easel. . . .

He paused and whirled about. There shouldn't have been a
canvas there at all. He hadn't attempted to painted in weeks
. . . months.

He looked down at his hands. They were streaked with Ultramarine Blue and odd dabs of red-violet. He vaguely remembered dreaming that he'd been painting. At least he'd thought
it was a dream. Perhaps it was the wine he'd imbibed. Coming
around to the front of the canvas, he stopped dead. *Impossible!*

But the painting was there for all that. Unfinished, but powerful, and despite his own familiar brushwork, not at all in his
usual style. He was a portraitist, and this was an empty landscape. Odd. Exciting. Unmistakably his work.

It was done in the silvery mauves and blues and violet hues
of twilight. A full moon rode to the left of a strange, pyramid-
shaped hill fading into the dark sky. Yet a thin arc of gold
indicated the last rays of sun gilding the hill's steep crest. The
rest was almost illusory: ruins, perhaps of a castle, vaguely
suggested; a single turret spearing into the sky.

And it wasn't empty after all. There was the suggestion of
a woman, her face blurred with distance, her white garments
flowing about her like mist, her fair hair silvered with the light
of the stars and rising moon. Excitement coursed through his
veins, making his head throb. Gideon scarcely noticed the
pain.

He focused on the painting. Or rather, tried to.

But if he looked too hard, both woman and tower became
invisible, just light and shadows. A sudden feeling of vertigo
overcame him. Gideon reeled and fought for balance.

Closing his eyes, he stepped away from the easel. He
opened them cautiously. *There, that was better.* He needed
some objective distance.

Arms folded across his chest, he inspected the painting. It
was . . . different. And it was good. Damned good!

He wasn't sure, however, if he liked it.

Gideon felt disturbed and unsettled by his creation. He had the uncanny feeling that if he stared at it much longer, he might be pulled deep inside it. Fall into the heart of the swirling, gauzy colors, become a part of its disturbingly beautiful, hauntingly mystical landscape.

Perhaps even vanish into it altogether.

Quickly, he shook off the sensation. Too much claret and too little sleep, no doubt. He tried to tear himself away, yet felt compelled to look at the painting. To stare at it unblinkingly.

The vertigo returned. The colors seemed to swirl and shift, to move and grow. The canvas itself seemed to give out light, like a mirror reflecting the moon's glow.

Gideon gave himself another hard shake and looked away. He'd been disoriented before, usually when he awakened suddenly, but he'd never felt anything like this.

Moving with the odd rhythms of a man awakening from a strange dream, he took the wet canvas down from the easel and turned its face to the wall.

The effects lingered for several long, breath-robbing moments. For just a moment, before his head cleared, Gideon didn't know where—or *who*—he was.

No. That wasn't quite right—he had the certainty that he knew exactly who he was.

But that person was *not* Gideon Stone.

TWO

§ §

GIDEON SAT WITH THE PISTOL IN HIS HAND. HE'D BEEN holding it curled up in his palm for hours now. He knew every line of the barrel and butt, every scroll and curve of it, as intimately as he might a lover.

It had been a very long night.

He had watched the cool blue shadows warm to lavender and rise as day broke over London. He had not moved except to breathe as the sunlight turned from silver to gold and crept, board by board, across his garret floor.

He imagined his friends and foes waking each morning, awaiting news of his death. For some reason—damned if he could see the logic of it—a gentleman facing ruin had only one recourse. He could only redeem himself with a bullet to the brain. It was insane! How could he ever be expected to pay his debts if he were dead?

No! He'd be damned if he did anything so final. He rose determinedly, removed the bullet, and put the pistol back in its case. It was far too sunny a day, and he was far too full of life to die just yet.

And I'll be damned if I put a period to my existence over a game of cards with a despicable cheat like Exton. God rot his ugly soul!

There must be some other way . . . if only he could find it.

He had gone over his options a hundred times. If he had any assets at all, he could go to a moneylender. He had none.

There was no use in applying to his remaining family for aid. Walden had made that very clear. When their father died of a sudden fever, Gideon's parsimonious half brother had inherited the title and sizeable estate. As a bonus, he had also acquired Gideon's lovely fiancée. Despite her proclamations of undying love, when push came to shove, Dorinda Spicer had decided she preferred marriage to the prosy Walden, whom she used to ridicule, with his cozy estate, to life with an artist struggling to make his name and fortune.

Their father had left it to his eldest son's goodwill to continue as he had done. Walden Stone, as it turned out, had not a drop of goodwill in him. The natural jealousy of the plodding, unattractive older son for the handsome favorite had come bursting forth like corruption from a lanced boil, while Gideon was still shattered and bereaved. Walden's first act had been to cut off Gideon's allowance entirely.

Their father was hardly in his grave when Gideon's half brother turned on him. The memory of that day came back with ugly force.

Walden picked a walnut from the crystal bowl before him and cracked it open. "I am under no legal obligation to you, Gideon," he said, letting the words sink in. "Nor do I see any reason to subsidize your erratic lifestyle. I am selling the Dower House to Mrs. Stowe. You have till next week to remove your things from there."

Gideon was stunned. "But . . . my studio! All my things . . ." He stared at Walden, appalled at the depth of envy and hatred the man had hidden until now. "You cannot mean it, Walden! How will I sustain myself while I establish my reputation?"

His half brother eyed his distress with feigned disinterest. "You're a well set-up fellow. Perhaps you might enlist in the army. Work your way up through the ranks. Or if you prefer to take Holy Orders, you might persuade your doting godmother, Lady Albinia, to give you the living of St. Mary in the Wold. It is not a wealthy parish, but I believe the vicarage is snug enough.''

''Good God, have you gone mad? I am not cut out to be a soldier or a priest. Damn it, Walden, I am an artist.''

His half brother's eyes narrowed. ''An artist who cannot sell his work is not an artist, but a mere dabbler!'' He smiled as the poisoned dart went home.

''There is a third choice. Perhaps I could let Stone Meadow Farm to you. It has not turned a profit these past five years, or the yearly rental would be much higher than it is. With hard work and good luck, you might be able to turn it into something worthwhile.''

''Stone Meadow Farm is aptly named, more stone than meadow!'' Gideon's anger rose. ''As to the 'farmhouse' it is a leaky, rat-ridden hut, no better than a cow byre. The only reason you are offering to hire it out to me, is that no one else will take it.''

Walden smiled, selected another walnut, and sat back. ''Let us be perfectly clear on my terms: turn down this generous offer, and I will never raise a hand to help you again.''

Gideon's lip curled. He picked up the crystal bowl, a gift he'd given their father, and hurled it at the fireplace. It exploded against the green marble, spraying shards of glass and walnuts all over the hearth. His half brother's face went white.

Striding to the door, Gideon grabbed the handle. ''You may take your meager charity, Walden, and choke on it! Gabriel's trump will blow on Judgement Day, and the dead rise up in their graves, before I ask you for a single farthing!''

He snapped back to the present, the familiar turpentine and oil smell of his garret studio. By God, he had been glad to see the last of Walden and to watch that infernal sneer vanish in surprise.

It had even seemed to work out well at first. He'd gotten several portrait commissions back to back, financing his career and his energetic bachelor-about-town existence. It had run through his fingers like water, though, thanks to Mariah.

Gideon pushed aside a lock of his tousled hair. Perhaps he should have taken Jack Rathburn's advice. "*Find yourself a wealthy heiress,*" his old friend had encouraged. "*With your looks and easy charm, you should surely snag one.*" But Gideon neither needed nor wanted a wife. There was no place for one in an artist's life.

From now on he must be married to his art. He had learned an invaluable lesson. His work was his identity, the very core of his soul. Without it, he was a feather in the wind, endlessly adrift.

He looked out the window, past the pigeons sunning themselves upon the outer sill, to where London lay glowing with promise in the morning sun. His salvation was out there, somewhere.

There had been a distinct hint—just the mere possibility, of course—that he was under consideration for a large commission. Lord Pulham was building a new ballroom addition to his country seat, and the architect had incorporated spaces for ten large paintings to go between the mirrors on the two long walls. The artist who got the commission would be set for life.

If Gideon got the nod, his reputation would be made and his fortune as well. He could easily pay off his debts to Exton by borrowing on his expectations. Hope pumped through him with every beat of his heart. He paced to the window and the pigeons eyed him suspiciously before flapping off.

Surely, he thought, such a grand commission would ignite his passion for his art once more. Surely the talent and techniques would rise from the ashes of the past.

If Exton didn't return from France and demand that he settle his debts first.

"*Mr. Stone?*"

He whirled around to find his landlady there. Evidently, Mrs. Bigelow had been talking to him for a minute or two.

"I beg your pardon?"

"The gentleman that has called to see you, Mr. Stone. He's been kicking his heels in the parlor for some time. Shall I send him up?"

Gideon's heart took a leap. He glanced at the visiting card she handed him, hoping to see Pulham's ducal crest, fearing to see the Marquis of Exton's name instead. The name was totally unknown to him: Albert Fortescue, Esquire.

His face went white. Exton must have sent him. The moment Gideon had dreaded had come. *So then. I have come to the end of the road.* He was glad his father hadn't lived to see this day.

Gideon ran the long fingers of one hand through his chestnut curls and crumpled the visitor's pasteboard card in the other. He left a smear of Cadmium Red along his temple, like a streak of blood.

"Damn Lord Exton to hell, and damn Mr. Fortescue with him!"

The landlady was shocked, but lowered her voice conspiratorially. "Shall I tell the gentleman that you're not receiving visitors this morning?"

"No. I must see him. Give me a few minutes, if you please, then send the fellow up."

Putting on a fresh shirt, Gideon shrugged himself into his best coat and cravat. As he brushed his hair before the bureau mirror, inadvertently spreading a thin line of red paint through it, his eyes caught something behind him. Two of his canvases were turned face out.

No wonder Mrs. Bigelow had made a hasty exit. One of them was the full-sized nude of Mariah Lessington. Turning slowly, he went to stand before it. Mariah in all her naked beauty, dark hair streaming over her shoulders, accenting her lush ripeness rather than enhancing modesty. Mariah as Eve. It had been Eve as temptress that he'd painted. And someone had changed it.

Where the woman's throat had been bare except for a few strands of drifting, dark brown hair, there was an exotic golden necklace. Her lovely fingers were ringed with jewels, her slender waist clasped by links of golden coins. And where a single glowing pomegranate had stood in the foreground, there was a massive bronze platter, bearing a man's severed head.

No longer Eve, but Salome.

He was stunned, although the symbolism was apt. Mariah had done everything but serve his head up on a platter.

The subject was not the only change. Where it had been romantically sensual before, now it was frankly, aggressively sexual. The kind of painting that might hang in certain clubs—or a gentleman's very private collection. Certainly not the kind of painting he could exhibit in the coming young artists' showing that had been arranged.

Gideon went forward and touched the paint. Fresh and wet. The brush strokes characteristically his and no other's.

Sweat broke out on his brow. He was losing his mind. He couldn't paint by day, yet in his sleep he had somehow roused himself and painted—this! A leap of fear made his heart contract. The other painting—had he changed that, also?

He went to the one of 'The Woman.' That was how he thought of her—simply, 'The Woman.'

His rapid heart rate slowed. Thank God! He hadn't altered it. She was still there, clothed in starlight at the foot of the hill. He looked a little closer. There was one addition. If he looked closely, he could make out a thin wedge of light among the trees, almost as if a door were half-opened in the distance, right in the center of the mysterious hill. What it represented was beyond him.

The sound of footsteps ascending the uncarpeted stairs was followed by a soft knock upon the open door. Frantically struggling to gather his shattered thoughts, Gideon squared his shoulders.

The newcomer cleared his throat politely. "Mr. Stone?"

Gideon turned to meet his fate. His visitor was an unprepossessing little man to be the messenger of Fate. He was a narrow bird of a man, stooped and slight of frame, and Gideon thought, irrelevantly, that his visitor should have been called Mr. Gray, for that color predominated in his hair and skin and garments.

The stranger bowed. "You are Gideon Stanfield Stone?"

"I am, and be damned to your formality, sir! There is no

sense in stringing this out,'' Gideon said harshly. ''Your journey is in vain, Fortescue. I cannot redeem my note of hand. That is all I have to say. You may go now.''

''Well, I, sir, have much to say!''

''I can only imagine. However I have no intention of listening to it!''

''But Mr. Stone! . . .''

''You have wasted your time in coming here,'' Gideon said with quiet menace. ''You need not waste your breath as well.''

The other man just stood there, blinking behind his thick eyeglasses. ''It would be to your distinct advantage to hear me out.''

''I'd rather throw you out!''

Gideon's tenuous hold on his temper broke. Cold determination turned to molten anger. ''Devil take it, man, be on your way with my message to Lord Exton before I hoist you by the collar and assist you down the stairs!''

The other gentleman blinked. ''Perhaps we should start over, sir. You seem to be suffering under a misapprehension.''

''And you seem to be suffering from an inability to understand plain English.'' Gideon advanced on the man. ''Go back to Exton and tell him I cannot redeem my notes.''

The newcomer spread his hands. ''I would be glad to convey your message if I knew the distinguished gentleman in question; however I have not had the pleasure of making Lord Exton's acquaintance.'' He paused and let Gideon digest his words.

''I am a solicitor, whom your several-times-removed cousin, the late Tobias Lacey, charged with overseeing the disposition of his estate. You, sir, have been named among his beneficiaries.''

He then smiled and gave a small bow. ''And now, if you still wish me to leave, I will be happy to do so. Although,'' he added, ''I strongly believe it would be in your interest to hear me out.''

Gideon was astonished. ''I think you must be mistaken. I never heard that I had any relations by the name of Lacey.''

"My late client researched your background extensively, sir. Your late mother *was* Amabelle Stanfield of Windrow Manor, and her paternal grandfather one Sir Eustace Stanfield Stone?"

"That is correct," Gideon said, frowning. "But I don't know your Mr. Lacey from Adam."

"Quite so," Fortescue said with a dry smile. "And that being the case, he had no time to form an ill opinion of you. Or so he told me when he had his will drawn up. I came to notify you of his bequest in person, since you didn't respond to my letters sent round to you."

A sheepish grin tugged Gideon's mouth at the corners. "Most likely I assumed you were a creditor, and fed it to the flames. What does this bequest entail?"

"Nothing onerous, I assure you." As he spoke, the man drew an envelope from inside his coat and held it out to Gideon. "I am not free to discuss the details until the official reading of the will, following the funeral. . . . I will say that the late Mr. Lacey was a man of property, with extensive collections acquired by generations of Laceys."

He looked around the sparsely furnished garret room. "I imagine you may find your portion of the bequests rather a pleasant surprise, although not without a few, er, . . . *encumbrances.*"

"Mortgaged to the rafters?"

"Oh, no. But I am not at liberty go into it, as I said. It is a substantial legacy, Mr. Stone."

Gideon was so astonished he could scarcely speak. It was too good to be true. He raised an eyebrow. "Is this some elaborate joke?"

"Not at all. But you will see for yourself, if you come. That is one of the requirements of the will: that all beneficiaries be present for the reading of the will, or forfeit their bequests. You will be put up at Lacey's Folly, of course. It's old, built in the Tudor manner. And although the furnishings are rather old-fashioned, you will find the place comfortable enough."

"As you can see, furnishings are not a priority with me,"

Gideon said wryly. "As long as there are no lice in the beds."

Mr. Fortescue was horrified. "Oh, no. Miss Hartsell, who acts as housekeeper, has kept everything in fine trim. Lacey's Folly is not fashionable, but I assure you it has its own charm. There is even a legend attached to the place, if you like such things. And it is rumored to be haunted."

"Haunted?" Gideon was caught now. "How intriguing! What manner of specter rattles its chains at Lacey's Folly?"

Mr. Fortescue was satisfied that he had hooked his fish. "That, Mr. Stone, you will have to discover for yourself. I don't think you will be disappointed."

Gideon watched his guest depart, then stood bemused. It seemed his luck had just changed for the better.

There was light, misty rain just before dawn the morning of Tobias Lacey's funeral, but by half past nine the sky was a rich, enameled blue. Chloe Hartsell pushed through the green baize door to the kitchens, wishing her spirits could lift as easily.

Her gray eyes showed the effects of lack of sleep. She'd been to bed late and up early again, juggling one crisis after another, with little time to mourn Tobias as she would have liked. Martin and Olivia Thorne had arrived two days before and set everything on end.

Although the Thornes were still abed, the kitchen was bright and bustling. It was a vast, stone-flagged chamber, with vaulted ceilings and cavernous hearths, a remnant of the days when Lacey's Folly had housed generations of family and a great number of servants.

"Good morning," Chloe said as she entered.

Cook looked up from the platters she was putting away and smiled wanly. It was a sad day, but Miss Chloe was looking after things, and soon the master would be safe away in the family vault, with all due honors and a fine homily by the Reverend Mr. Pickworthy. The house had done Mr. Lacey proud with a fine spread: the sliced ham, the cold beef, the simple jellies, and the variety of breads and cakes were prepared to be set out for the ritual cold collation. No one would say that the master had not been sent off in style.

"Is Mr. Fortescue's London gentleman arrived yet, Miss Chloe?"

"Not the slightest sign of him, I'm afraid. He probably took the wrong fork from the village." She eyed the empty milk jug and the telltale plate littered with bits of bread crusts and cake at the well-scrubbed table. "I see Perry has been and gone."

"Yes, Miss Chloe. Hungry as a bear cub, as always." Cook's round, red face split in a grin. "Master Perry ate two ham sandwiches, a wedge of cheese, three pickled eggs—and then polished off a slice of currant cake higher than he is!"

Chloe smiled and shook her head. "Do all ten-year-old boys eat so much and so often?"

"Ever since Adam and Eve, I vow. He's a growing lad, he is. Sprouting daily before our very eyes."

It was true. Perry had shot up two inches since spring, and Chloe had been forced to take him into Greater Brampton to buy suitable clothes for the funeral today.

"I'd hoped to find him here. I wonder where he's gone off to—he's not in his room." A sudden thought struck her. "*Good Heavens*! He hasn't gone off to tinker with one of his mechanical 'inventions,' has he?"

"No, miss," Cook shook her head. "He promised there'd be no explosions today. The lad knows as what's fitting toward the old master."

The old master. The woman's words echoed through the high-ceilinged room. No one spoke for a few long seconds.

Chloe turned and pretended to examine the funeral meats that were ready. *Oh, Tobias. I never wanted to see this day!* She remembered how different life had been before he'd succumbed to his last illness. *I wish we could have gone on forever, just as we were last summer, with nothing changing but the weather.*

She collected herself. This was no time to indulge her feelings.

Chloe roamed the long room, with its whitewashed stone walls and enormous open oven, no longer used. Everything was in order. Nothing to do but wait.

From the depths of the house, she heard Olivia's querulous voice raised in some agitated complaint. A moment later Agnes, the weary upstairs maid, came in, exhausted from the incessant demands of Martin and Olivia Thorne.

She put her hands on her ample hips and threatened to give her notice on the spot. "There's just the one of me, Miss Chloe, and the two of them, and I can't be in three places at once!"

Her long nose quivered with indignation. "Not with all the goodwill in the world, which I must say I don't have toward those two, with their sharp tongues and their la-di-dah airs. And twice they sent their breakfast trays back, saying how the food was all wrong, the eggs too hard or too soft, the coffee not hot enough or the scones half-raw or burnt."

"And that they are *not!*" Cook said, banging her heavy meat cleaver down on the hapless cutlets so that everything else on the work table jumped.

"Of course they are not," Chloe soothed. "I'll send to the village and hire Mrs. Wick and her daughter to come in as dailies, until things are more settled."

How she was going to eke any more wages out of the tight household budget was more than she could figure out at the moment. But she would cope. She always had.

"Lor' bless you, miss." Agnes curtsied and went off in a happier frame of mind. Chloe leaned against the larder door and rubbed her temples. She'd be glad when this long day was over.

Cook clucked her tongue. "No use wearing yourself out. What you need is to sit down in a quiet corner with a nice hot cup of tea."

Obediently, Chloe sat down at the scrubbed wooden work-table where she'd spent many a happy hour over the years. "Tea would be lovely."

"Not here!" Cook said, horrified. "You'll take your place

in the morning room like you did when the master was alive! Netty will bring it to you on a tray, all proper-like.'' She lowered her voice to a discretionary whisper. "Start as you mean to go on, so I always say.''

Chloe nodded. But for a moment she just wanted to put her head down, close her eyes, and pretend that everything was just as it used to be.

Perry would be out in the garden, digging holes at the roots of the old trees in search of buried treasure, while old Tobias told him stories and legends as old as time. But the boy was almost of an age to go away to school now—and, because of the unseasonable heat, Tobias's coffin was locked away in the ice house, packed in straw, awaiting burial. Tears glimmered in her gray eyes.

Cook wiped her hands on her clean apron. "Life changes, and we change with it, Miss Chloe. Now you go on into the morning room. I'll have that tea to you in no time.''

Biting her lower lip, Chloe nodded. Hard as it was, Cook was right.

In charge of her emotions once more, she went back through the servants' door that led into the great hall. Heaven knew there would be plenty of work on this side of the door keeping Martin and Olivia happy, and preparing for Mr. Fortescue and the gentleman from London. So much to do—but first that sorely-needed cup of tea!

The morning room, the only part of the Tudor structure regularly used, was past the library and down a connecting corridor toward the back of the house. It was Chloe's favorite place inside the manor. Twenty feet square, it was a cozy chamber, with deep window seats between the thick old walls.

The tall windows were made from dozens of wavy panes, some brightly colored, to let in the sun, and glimpses of the Old Hall on the far side of the gardens. The heavy stone fireplace, carved with the Lacey crest, kept the room warm even on the coldest days. No matter how strapped the budget was, Tobias was never stingy with a fire.

Chloe sighed. Of course, the carved plaster of the ceiling

wanted repair and the chairs were in urgent need of reupholstering. Dawlish, the old butler, said he was afraid the beetle had gotten into the woodwork. Something must be done, and soon.

Netty bustled in, a tray covered with a snowy napkin in her hands. She set it down on a small ebony table beside the sofa and whipped off the damask cloth to reveal a small china pot with matching teacup, and a dish of fancy biscuits.

"Just the thing to perk you up, Miss Chloe. Mr. Lacey's favorite jasmine tea and some of Cook's macaroons she put by for you."

Chloe was sorry when Netty hurried away. It made her feel quite melancholy to think that she would never sit here with old Tobias again, listening to him ramble about people long dead and events long past, while she busied herself with sewing. It made her restless to be alone here now.

She looked out the window and saw Perry perched on the terrace wall, like a statue in the morning sun. There was no book in his lap, no spyglass to his eye. He was normally only still when he lay asleep.

Newton, his puppy, trotted back and forth eagerly, hoping for a game of chase-the-stick. Perry took no note of him. Opening the door, she went out to join him. He heard her footsteps but didn't look up. "It's very hard, isn't it, Chloe?"

She sat beside him and tousled his white-blond hair. "Indeed it is. We will both miss Tobias. But you mustn't brood. He wanted us to go on as always."

Perry's face tightened. "I was remembering the day when Tobias first brought us to Lacey's Folly," he said solemnly. "With Cook and Dawlish and everyone waiting at the door to greet the poor orphans he'd rescued. Just like a fairytale."

Chloe hid a smile. "You were a babe in arms, Perry. You can't remember our arrival."

"N . . . no. But you and Tobias both told me the story so many times it *seems* as if I do."

She hugged him and he hugged her back, before remembering that he was ten years old and almost grown, and that now he was the man of the house, and must look after *her*.

They sat for awhile in the sun, neither speaking. Finally Newton rose, stretched, and gave an eager *woof!*

"He wants a good, hard run with you," Chloe said, patting the retriever. "Or a stick to chase. You really must take him and work off some of his excess energy before the funeral."

"Do you think it would be all right?" the boy asked doubtfully.

"It's what Tobias would have wanted."

Perry rose with alacrity and soon was off with his dog, across the green summer lawn toward the river.

Chloe went back inside. Through the window she glimpsed Perry down by the river. She stood awhile and watched his legs pound the turf as he ran off his grief. It was his first experience of death, and his bond with Tobias, like hers, had run deep.

Tears welled in her eyes. She missed him terribly. He had not always been an easy man to live with—an old bachelor, long set in his ways—but he had been very good to them. And now he was gone, and with him went her last slender link to her past. She felt as if she were perched, trembling, on the edge of a sheer cliff, with nothing but fog beneath her.

Tobias was the only living person, besides herself, who knew the truth: that Perry was not her younger brother, but her son.

She had been fifteen years old, orphaned when her parents died within days of one another, abandoned and disgraced. He had found her and taken her in, without question—although she had told him all there was to tell. Tobias had not been shocked to learn she was with child. He had seen much of the world in his time.

"*It will be good to have young people again at Lacey's Folly,*" he'd told her. "*And it is a fine place to raise a child. You will both like it there.*"

And so they had.

She smiled while Perry and his retriever pursued one another across the lawn, then she had to take a deep breath to keep her lip from quivering. Her heart broke with love: Perry was her child, but she could never claim him. Tobias had impressed that upon her from the start. *But oh, how hard it was!*

She watched him until he rounded the corner and vanished from view. He was completely unaware of his birth, and must remain so. If the world had knowledge of his bastardy, it would blight all his chances and ruin his every prospect for advancement in life.

She must not think of the past right now. She must think of the future.

Chloe drank the lukewarm tea and nibbled at the macaroons. The peace of the room surrounded her. She loved its faded velvets, its jewel-toned carpets from far-off lands, worn to soft, muted shades. The ancient wood paneling gave off a faint spicy scent, as if it held the incense of ancient candles and ghostly perfumes.

Ghosts. That made her think of the door to the Bride's Chamber mysteriously swinging open last night. The rush of air, and the sensation that she had not been alone. *All products of fatigue and imagination*, she told herself sternly. An imagination that was brought to vivid life by the tomes of myths and fairy tales in the library at Lacey's Folly. Hungry for adventure, pageantry, and romance, she had devoured their stories, absorbed them into her being.

Perhaps that was what had left her in such a fanciful mood. She could imagine Lenore sitting by the fire in a gown of emerald velvet. Meeting her lover. A tall, dark-haired man with a beard and a dazzling smile.

Yes, she could see them materializing before her eyes, scintillating bits of light gathering into whirling columns, coalescing into solid form. Chloe held her breath and watched.

There was Lenore in her glowing green dress, her fair hair plaited back with matching ribands. Earbobs of pearl and peridot swung from her dainty lobes and matched the necklace around her lovely throat.

And there was her lover, wide-shouldered in his dark cloak,

holding a gray hat with a long maroon plume. He had his back to Chloe as he leaned down to whisper something to Lenore. She was curious to see his face. Almost as if he felt her interest, he turned toward her and . . .

"*Miss Hartsell!*"

Chloe sat up with a jerk.

It had been just a dream. She'd fallen asleep in the chair. There was nothing in the room but dust motes dancing through two slanting sunbeams, and Olivia Thorne in the doorway, red with indignation.

"I have been looking for you this past half hour and more. Why are you sitting about when there is so much to be done?"

She advanced into the room angrily, as if it had been she who'd been up since dawn, and Chloe who had lain abed with a breakfast tray over her knees. "We have guests coming, and the linens must be aired out. I do not know how *anyone* could be expected to sleep well in that damp and lumpy feather bed in my chamber. I only hope that I may not have taken a severe chill because of it!"

Chloe colored at the unjust criticism. "You may be sure I have seen that all is in readiness for the guests."

The flush of anger did nothing to improve her in Olivia's eyes. The stark, black mourning gown the girl wore was obviously old, and its drabness ill-became her. Yet, if one looked closely, she was well enough in a quiet way, her red-gold curls pulled back in a simple knot at her nape, her eyes an odd silvery color that, in certain light, seemed to hold the palest touch of violet. Martin thought them pretty, but Olivia, pursing her mouth as if she'd sipped vinegar, thought Chloe's eyes were sly.

At the moment Chloe's gray irises were tarnished with annoyance. Since their arrival two weeks earlier, when Tobias had gone into his last decline, the Thornes had found fault with everything. The food was too plain, the windows too drafty, the butler too old, the maids too slow and slovenly. While the first two complaints had merit, the last two had none. No matter how hard Chloe and the other servants tried, there was no pleasing the old man's relatives.

Olivia's gaze fell to the teacup and dish, with the crumbled remains of the macaroons. Cook had told her the last of them had been finished yesterday. Her scowl deepened. "Before this day is much older, you and I must have a little talk. In fact, now would be a very good time."

Chloe resigned herself. "Yes, Miss Thorne? Is it something that cannot wait until after the funeral and the reading of the will?"

Olivia went rigid with anger. She was not used to servants—to *anyone*—speaking to her in such a manner. But that would be rectified soon. Once she was officially the lady of Lacey's Folly, there would be enormous changes made.

The first would be to replace Miss Hartsell with a *proper* housekeeper. An experienced woman, trained to oversee a house of this size and to keep the servants from stealing them blind. She had already sent an advertisement to the newspaper.

Olivia had never believed that story of a distant kinship between old Tobias and Chloe Hartsell. Hah! Olivia had her suspicions about *that!* Not that it mattered. *Miss Hartsell will soon find herself out the door. And that brat, Peregrine, with her.*

Her disapproving glance swept the chamber, fell on the outmoded carpets from the Indies and the dark, solid furniture trimmed in worn brown velvets and muted tapestries, the murky portraits of Laceys long gone. All would be banished. She would turn this house over from the attics to the cellars.

And she would make this parlor hers. Her own cozy little sitting room, where she would entertain all the fine, fashionable London friends she was *certain* to make, now that her brother had become a man of considerable substance.

Her jaundiced eye fell upon Chloe once more. "And another thing, Miss Hartsell."

Chloe stifled a sigh and resigned herself to more complaints. She made her face into a smooth, featureless mask, hiding her emotions. Her eyes were opaque as slate. "Yes, Miss Thorne?"

"I believe I will take some tea here while I go over my correspondence."

"Certainly. I'll ring for another cup." Chloe reached for the bell cord, but Olivia's next words sent hot color to stain her cheeks.

"Perhaps I have not made myself clear, Miss Hartsell. Whatever may have been allowed during the late Mr. Lacey's time, there will be many changes. Beginning immediately." Her bony fingers toyed with the mourning brooch at her throat.

"Despite your airs, your alleged . . . *connection* . . . with the family, you are merely the housekeeper here, when all is said and done. An upper servant, I suppose, but a servant nonetheless. It is not fitting that you should sit at ease among the family, sipping tea as if you were lady of the manor. From now on you will take your meals in your room, or in the kitchen with the rest of the staff. And that includes the *boy*, your . . . ah, *brother*, is he?" Her lips curled in a feral smile. "I am sure you understand."

Where Chloe's complexion had been flaming before, it was now as translucent and white as bone china. "Oh, yes! I understand well enough!"

She was shaking with fury, unable to speak. Chloe took a deep breath, picked up the tray with trembling hands, and left Olivia to gloat alone in the morning room. The teacup rattled dangerously against the saucer as she swept back along the corridor.

"*Damn her! Damn her to hell!*"

"Beg pardon, miss?" The startled parlor maid peered out of the drawing room. Poor Miss Chloe was white as rice powder! "Are you all right, miss?"

"Yes, quite fine, thank you. Go on about your business," Chloe said with a shaky smile. "I was merely talking to myself."

She hurried through the green baize door and into the kitchen and set the tray down. She was trembling with anger.

She snatched up her straw hat from its peg, took the flower
basket with her work gloves and a pair of shears, and let herself out into the garden.

Yanking a few weeds out by the roots always helped calm
her temper. Better pulling weeds than Olivia's hair, as her first
instinct had urged her to do. Following the moss-grown brick
path, she made her way past the formal beds and the herb
garden to the cutting garden beyond.

Safe among the tall stalks, Chloe blinked away a scald of
furious tears. A few deep breaths and she was in control of
her emotions again. *How dare Olivia Thorne! How dare she!
That spiteful bag of vinegar! And to say such things about
Perry, when he might walk in and overhear. Insufferable!*

But Chloe knew she was strong. She could tolerate a few
more hours of biting her tongue. Hadn't she had enough practice at putting up with Olivia Thorne's snubs and Martin's
innuendos the past ten years? She went along the garden path,
drawing strength from the smell of the fresh air, the rich soil
and the sun-warmed fragrance of the blossoms.

The garden was her solace from the early days. She inhaled
the sweet bouquet of the damask rose, more heady than the
finest French perfume. And the excitement beginning to dance
through her veins again was surely far more intoxicating than
the finest French wine.

*Let Olivia gloat for now. Her moment will be brief. But
after today she will be sorry. And serve her right!*

Chloe envisioned the reading of the will. The upper servants
would be there, sitting along the walls, alternately sniffling
with real sorrow and worrying if the master had remembered
them sufficiently for them to retire with dignity in their old
age.

Martin and Olivia, of course, would take the place of honor
on the brocade settee, in their role as chief mourners. If there
were tears in either's eyes, Chloe thought savagely, it would
only be those of glee as they anticipated their good fortune.

With everyone ready, Mr. Fortescue would take his place
at the big desk in the library, shuffle his papers, adjust his

pince-nez three or four times upon his bony nose, clear his throat loudly—

—and then the fun would begin! Hadn't Tobias promised her?

A cat-in-the-cream-pot expression suddenly illuminated Chloe's heart-shaped face. It would all come out in the reading of the will. *Oh! What joy then to see their reactions!* The servants would be surprised and the Thornes as mad as fire.

Chloe leaned down and whispered her secret into the glorious heart of an enormous pink rose. "Today is a very sad day, but it is also a wonderful day! For you see, I shall now truly be mistress here. After the reading of the Tobias's will, Lacey's Folly will be officially mine!"

She hugged the knowledge to herself. Tobias owed her nothing. He had rescued her and given her a home all these years. But he had told her many a time that when he passed on, he would leave Lacey's Folly to her entirely. Eventually it would pass to Perry, but for now their futures were secure.

The conflicting sorrow and happiness expanded in her heart, until it was almost too much to bear.

Oh, if only Mr. Fortescue's London gentleman would arrive soon! Then everything would be formally announced. The Thornes would be confounded, but she and Perry would have a home for life. Perhaps they would even find the Lost Bride's treasure.

Suddenly, the garden was cast in shadow. Chloe looked up, hoping that the day they said a final good-bye to Tobias wouldn't be marred by rain.

There was no sign of it: just a single cloud streaming directly overhead. Thin, filmy, pulling apart into patterns of delicate lace as she watched.

Looking, for all the world, like a gossamer bridal veil.

Perhaps, Chloe told herself, it was a message of reassurance from Tobias. "*A happy omen,*" she said aloud, and went back to gathering her bouquet.

THREE

GIDEON REINED IN. "DEVIL TAKE IT! WHAT AM I TO DO now?"

He was hot, dusty, and apparently lost. Sweat trickled beneath the curls matted on his brow. He'd left, secure in his directions, the neat Cotswolds villages nodding in the morning sun beneath roofs of thick reed thatch.

But the road he'd been following for the past hour had suddenly petered out into a rutted lane, scarcely fit for travel. He hadn't passed another rider or vehicle in that time. In fact, he hadn't even passed another village. Gideon wished he'd come down early yesterday and spent the night at Lacey's Folly, as Mr. Fortescue had suggested.

He scanned the roadside. He was not a countryman by nature, he decided, and the bucolic vistas had long ceased to entertain him. Nodding wildflowers embroidered the green velvet roadside, and beneath the hot sun, jeweled dragonflies wove ribbons of iridescent light among their fragrant petals.

Lovely in its own way, Gideon thought, *but not for me.*

He pondered whether to turn back. The groom at the Crown and Garter had given him directions: *"Take the road west, milord. Second fork past the church, and just keep following it to Lacey's Folly. You can't miss it."*

But, it seemed, he had.

Worse, he'd missed the funeral and his chance to pay his respects to his unknown benefactor; if he missed the reading of the will as well, the entire tedious journey would have been for nothing. The hopes of bringing his financial barque safely to port foundered on the shoals of despair.

Ah, well. The way his luck had been running lately, his unexpected legacy could be anything from a bound collection of dusty sermons to some monstrous Gothic piece of furniture too heavy to move and too ugly to sell.

Suddenly a dog yelped nearby, startling his mount. Gideon brought the horse under control and spied the waggly tail of a pup on the grassy verge. He caught a glimpse of a pair of small legs in worsted trousers near the ditch.

A tow-headed urchin lay in the tall summer grass, studying an anthill as if it were the most marvelous toy in all the world. He carefully poked a thin twig into the mound and watched the response.

"Hello there! You, by the roadside."

At the sound of Gideon's voice the boy scrambled up, face flaming. He wasn't one of the local farm lads, Gideon realized. Although the youngster's clothes were of decent quality, the boy was at the point where he was growing out of them—and they had, he was sure, started out the morning far cleaner than they were at present.

The lad brushed ineffectually at the bits of earth and leaf mold that clung to his clothes, adding more dirt than he removed. He grinned ruefully.

"Torturing the insects?" Gideon asked.

"No, sir," came the affronted reply. The lad pushed his mop of fair hair out of his eyes. "I am conducting a nature experiment."

"Ah, yes," Gideon smiled. "I vaguely recall performing much the same experiment when I was a lad. They certainly do scramble madly about when their nest is disturbed."

The boy grinned back in sheer delight. "*Don't* they, sir?" His face settled into more serious lines. "Although, it truly is an experiment, you know. I am writing everything down."

His freckled face turned wistful. "I was going to be a pirate, but Chloe says that's not a fit occupation for a gentleman, so

I have decided to become a naturalist instead.''

"A worthy vocation," Gideon said, suppressing a smile. "Do you know the road to Lacey's Folly?"

"You're on it, sir. Follow it round the curve and through the iron gates.''

Gideon thanked the boy and flipped him a coin for his troubles. "Don't go home so dirty your mother fails to recognize you, or she might box your ears."

"She wouldn't, sir!" the boy protested. "If I had one. I'm an orphan, so there's just Chloe. She understands that a scientist must get dirty at times.''

"Does she, indeed? A woman beyond rubies."

Gideon grinned and rode off, glancing back over his shoulder as he came to a bend in the lane. The boy and his pup were still there, happily worrying the ants. He could scarcely remember himself at that stage. Perhaps he'd skipped it entirely.

No, he did remember chasing Dorinda around the garden with a box full of beetles. And, now that he thought of it, he did vividly recall putting a toad in Walden's bed once. Or twice.

But ever since he'd first picked up a piece of charcoal, art had been his true and all consuming passion. He could not understand now how he had let Mariah come between himself and his work. *Addlepated male vanity, no doubt.* Exton was welcome to her.

Like Dorinda, she had been only a mirage, a romanticized ideal woman created whole cloth from his imagination, bearing no resemblance to reality. He seemed to have a rather disastrous penchant for them.

The lane went past a clump of beech and curved suddenly. Tall weeds poked up through the sparse gravel of the rutted drive. A sagging iron gate between stone pillars announced that he'd reached his destination. Both sections of the fancifully wrought iron stood open, no doubt permanently frozen that way. Even as he admired their intricate design, he was wishing himself elsewhere.

He patted the restive horse. ''I shudder to think what rustic joys await us at Lacey's Folly.''

Even the estate's name, which he'd thought intriguing before, had taken on somber overtones. The horse felt the same, evidently, and balked. Gideon patted the beast's neck and urged it through.

He entered an avenue of trees, giving vistas of lawns that had gone wild. Every now and then he caught a flash of a tower of warm, buff-colored stone, floating like a mirage above the leaves.

''Whoa! Easy there! Easy.'' His bay mare had stumbled into a deep rut, and only luck and good horsemanship kept Gideon from a nasty spill.

For a split second he was ready to say be-damned to it all and turn back toward town. From what he'd seen thus far, his legacy was sure to be a worm-eaten sideboard or a spavined horse. Common sense intervened. He'd come this far, he might as well see it through.

One thing was sure: nothing of value could await him at Lacey's Folly.

He changed his mind when he saw the house. Crossing over a packhorse bridge of lichened stone, where the water flowed dark gold and green below, he had his first sight of Lacey's Folly. It was charming. An ancient place cupped in the bend of the river, it had been added on to over several centuries to suit the various times.

The golden limestone of the Cotswolds, beneath a roof of dark coppery-colored flat tiles, gave the whole a unified dignity that was more than the sum of its parts: a half-moat that ran across the front gardens and formed a pond in the distance, past the sloping lawns. Lush gardens and climbing roses splashed color everywhere. A limestone causeway spanned the moat to a wide entry courtyard. There was a storybook air to Lacey's Folly, he thought, as if it lay drowsing under an old enchantment.

As he reached the other side and rode in closer, he could

see that the house needed repair. There was an older half tim-
bered section that needed pargeting, chimneys that needed
pointing—one with a bird's nest atop it—and an occasional
broken spout. But the grounds were trim and the windows
sparkled cleanly in the sunlight. His hopes rose. Perhaps his
overnight stay here would not be as uncomfortable as he'd
feared.

A flash of movement caught his eye. Through a screen of
willows, he spied a young girl carrying a basket of flowers on
her arm. Her somber black dress stood out against the riot of
colorful blooms, and Gideon immediately conceived it as a
painting in his mind. That surprised him so much he pulled
on the reins, and the horse stopped dead in its tracks.

He was used to thinking in pictures more than in words.
Yet it had been months since he'd done so. He wanted to
capture the mood in his mind before it was lost, but the horse
has smelled the stables and was getting fractious. Dismount-
ing, he looped the reins over a fence post and started down
the trodden path for a better view.

As he opened the wicket gate and passed through, his fingers itched to sketch the scene: the young girl, the brilliant
flowers, so bright and glowing against her drab mourning. As
she drew closer, he could see her face. Not a beauty, certainly,
but quite arresting. *Look at that graceful throat, those perfect
cheekbones!*

Then she passed the line of willows and disappeared from
view. He groaned in frustration. An idea had started to form,
to take on shape and color in his head. With the girl's disappearance, it slipped sideways, faded, and escaped completely.

The situation was nothing new: it had plagued him for the
past six months and more. *"Devil take it!"*

"Oh!" Chloe, unaware of his presence as she came through
a gap in the willows, was startled by his voice. Her cutting
basket tipped, spilling spikes of purple larkspur, blue delphinium, and a bounty of pale pink and ivory roses. Their spicy
aroma filled the air.

Gideon reached out to steady her and helped right the basket. Her eyes were wide with surprise as his hand closed round her arm. She jerked back. The jagged spine on one of the larger roses ripped the side of his hand, but he felt only a momentary sting.

"Forgive me, I didn't mean to frighten you."

Chloe, caught off guard by the sudden appearance of a handsome stranger in her garden, fought to recover her dignity.

"I thought you were Martin Thorne," she said, as if that explained everything.

His eyebrows lifted. "And what has this Mr. Thorne done to cause you such dismay?"

Chloe bit her lip. "Nothing. He is just the prosy sort of fellow one wishes to avoid."

An appreciative twinkle lit Gideon's eye. "I understand exactly," he said, "having met a few in my time. They are sure to disapprove of everything."

"I don't give a fig for Martin Thorne or his approval," she said straightly. "He is not the master here, no matter what he may think!"

Gideon flashed her his dazzling smile. "While I don't know Mr. Thorne, I applaud your attitude on general principles. I am very much opposed to prosy men and am inclined to think they should all be banished from the realm."

She smiled back at him. A handsome man, and witty, too. "Then we are kindred souls, sir."

Chloe stooped to pick up the fallen flowers.

Her straw hat fell back, held in place by the ribbon at her throat. Gideon knelt to help her gather them and saw her face clearly for the first time. *Those eyes. Like the reflection off a crystal clear stream, all silvery light and subtle depths.*

He stared at her, unaware that he was doing so, and caught a glimpse of creamy, rounded breasts as she leaned forward. He felt a reflex tightening in his loins and looked hastily away. She was not a girl, as he'd thought, but a young woman. And very likely one of gentle birth.

He wondered who she was. Her unpampered hands, out-moded garments, and untamed red curls had made him suppose that she was a servant in the house, although neither her speech nor her features belonged to that class.

Chloe wished that she'd gone around by the other path. When their eyes met, she felt giddy and breathless, as if her corset were laced too tightly around her ribs. *He must think me gauche and stupid as a simpering schoolgirl.*

Gideon realized she was appraising him as frankly as he'd been looking at her. Examining him and his perfectly tailored apparel from head to toe. And with the most singular pair of gray eyes he'd ever seen. Now they were liked clouded mirror, reflecting hints of color back at him.

"Are you with Mr. Fortescue?" she asked, rising. "He said there would be a gentleman arriving from London today."

"Yes. Gideon Stone is my name."

"I am Miss Hartsell, a distant relation to the late Mr. Lacey." She swallowed around the constriction in her throat: how difficult those last three words had been. How final. "I served as his companion and housekeeper. Mr. Fortescue has set back the reading of the will in anticipation of your arrival."

There was curiosity in her voice, which he couldn't satisfy. "Well, he'll be glad to know I'm here at last, I hope."

"Oh, dear. He has only now gone for a stroll along the river. We expected you much earlier."

"I was delayed by bad directions."

"Unfortunately, the cold collation served after the funeral was *not*. However I'll see that you have a tray sent up to your room immediately. Mr. Fortescue should be back shortly."

"Let me help you with your basket. It's quite heavy."

"Perhaps for dainty London ladies," Chloe said wryly. "I have carried much more than this on the walk here from the village."

"Perhaps London ladies are not so dainty either," he said with an edge. "However, no gentleman would allow a lady of his acquaintance to burden herself while he walked along empty-handed."

He took the basket right out of her hands without a by-your-leave.

"What passes for good manners in town might be considered a discourtesy in the country," she said coolly.

"Then I thank God I am a town creature," he told her and kept possession of the basket.

He looked just as handsome scowling as smiling, she thought, and was angry with herself for noticing. Looks were only skin deep. That's what she told herself every time she looked into a mirror. Physical beauty was no match for inner beauty. *And I have just shown myself deficient in both*, she thought, smarting a little.

She'd tried to show off a little to impress the London visitor and had instead come off like a country bumpkin. *I will have to be more gracious when I am mistress of Lacey's Folly*, she told herself. Although she didn't know why she'd even wanted to impress Mr. Stone in the first place. After today she would never see him again.

She felt even worse when she saw that he'd bloodied his hand. It had dripped and spattered across his starched cuffs as well. "Oh! You have injured yourself. Come inside and I'll attend to it."

Gideon was surprised to see the deep scratch and the bright crimson welling up. He gave her his handkerchief and let her bind up his hand. Now that he was aware of it, it was burning like fury. It didn't improve his mood any.

"We'll go in through the still room," she said. "It's much quicker."

Chloe led him toward an ancient door half-hidden by trailing ivy. She moved with unselfconscious ease. She had a lovely figure, Gideon saw. Womanly, but not substantial enough to suit the current mode.

Old habits died hard. As he followed her, Gideon wondered how she would look in more appropriate clothing. Then he wondered how she would look with none at all. His trained eye began stripping away the layers of garments, but he stopped himself before it went too far. There had been a funeral this morning at Lacey Manor. This was neither the time nor the place to indulge that line of thought.

"Watch your head," she warned.

He was so tall he had to duck to enter the arched door. Ivy brushed his head. They entered a cool room with worn flags and a stone, where rows of shelves held various vases and containers. A green baize door led into the main part of the house and a long, dim hallway led off toward the kitchens. She removed her hat and hung it on a peg.

"You may set the basket here, if you please. I'll be right back."

She was gone only a moment. By the time Gideon had set down the floral burden on the sink, he heard her soft footfalls on the flagged floor just behind him. He turned around and felt a prickle across the nape of his neck. In her dark dress with her hair coming loose from the ribbon at her nape, she looked old-fashioned and insubstantial, a ghostly image from another century.

Then she stepped past one of the small windows and the ivy-dappled sunlight pouring through the panes made her wild, red-gold curls blaze like tongues of flame. He took back the ghost analogy. There was nothing ethereal about her. She looked mysterious and mystical, yet vibrantly, radiantly, alive.

She was certainly the most unusual housekeeper he'd ever seen.

For a moment he felt almost giddy. His imagination, which had been blank as an unprimed canvas for so many months, was suddenly filling up, almost overwhelmed with a rich, visual tapestry. He wanted to paint her—by God, he had to paint her, exactly as she was now!

The black doubts came back then, crushing him with their terrible weight. Seeing the painting in his mind's eye was one thing: creating it on canvas quite another. Could he still do it? Or had his talents died of neglect? Lately it seemed that he could paint only in his dreams.

Chloe felt breathless and uncertain. Why was he staring at her so? It made her terribly conscious of herself, her unflattering dress, the way the humid air had made her hair escape from its chignon. Of the fact that she was a woman grown, and he was an attractive man. A *very* attractive man.

It had been a long time since she'd been in the company of a handsome man her own age. More years than she wanted to acknowledge. Up until now she had only thought of how things would be changed at Lacey's Folly when she was mistress of the manor. She had not thought beyond the garden gates. For the first time it occurred to Chloe that her position in the world would change, also. She would be a woman of property, able to meet and mingle with other people of similar station.

But not, of course, on the same plane as the Gideon Stones of the world. She had no illusions on that score. She was no fool.

Even as the inheritrix of Tobias Lacey's estate, she would be accepted only in a very limited way. There would be no carriage rides with the proper Miss Lincrofts, no invitations for her to dine with Lady Adderby at her country house, Sir Ralph Dunscote and his lady at the Hall. Her long isolation at Lacey's Folly and her lack of family made that impossible. She turned away.

Perhaps she might travel with Perry. Italy, Greece, Egypt. But always they would return to Lacey's Folly. Home! That must be joy enough.

"If you'll come with me, Mr. Stone?" she said, stepping into the room where she kept her household accounts.

It was a tiny chamber, holding two unmatched chairs, a narrow cupboard and table fitted with a row of cubbyholes across the back. He noticed that there were no personal touches, the only ornament being a simple porcelain vase bursting with peach and pink cabbage roses. Their scent filled the room.

Chloe moved aside the plain ink standish and a stack of ledgers. One was open and Gideon saw neat rows of writing, with dates and amounts of expenditures filling the columns. The spines of some journals were marked with the years in gold, but others bore handwritten titles: *Lancelot, Guinevere, Iseult, Elaine.* He wondered if they were romantic novels she read when she was supposedly doing her household accounts. The thought made him smile.

She was watching him again, he saw with a start. Her look was wary, intelligent, innocent of artifice. Completely at odds with the womanly curves of her body, and her tender, voluptuous mouth.

He felt a stirring of interest that had as much to do with his masculine urges as it did with his artistic ones. He brushed the first away. That was a path he wouldn't happily go down again. He'd learned there was nothing but disaster in store for an artist once he let himself be led by a particular part of his anatomy situated in the loins, rather than the eye, the brain.

From now on women would merely be potential subjects for his art. Shapes of light and shadow, objects to be captured by ink or paint, no more personal to him than a bowl of luscious fruit, or an enticing landscape.

If it were mere release he wanted, there were places a man could go if he were so inclined. There were always lightskirts, ready for a quick tumble and no regrets. Miss Hartsell, however, was a relative of his late benefactor and a gentlewoman, despite his first, erroneous impression. And after tomorrow he'd never see her again.

Chloe could hardly meet his glance without feeling dazzled. She felt herself blushing under his scrutiny and looked away.

A buxom housemaid came scurrying into the room with a tray containing a small pan of hot water, a squat milk glass jar labeled "Dr. Woodbine's Special Salve", and several strips of soft linen.

"Thank you, Biddy."

Chloe took a chair and waved Gideon to the other. "Your hand, if you please." He held it out and she dabbed at the jagged tear with clean linen dipped in water.

A dust-covered imp popped into the room. "Chloe, come quick! There's a horse loose in the garden, and Cook is chasing him with a frying pan. It's ever so droll!"

Gideon scarcely recognized the tow-haired boy he'd seen earlier by the roadside. He did recognize the fact that he'd completely forgotten the damned horse. Not to mention his bags.

"Good God! I can't believe it slipped my mind," he started to rise. "I'd better go see to it at once."

"Nonsense! Your hand must be attended to first." She looked up with a smile. "Although people don't usually go around misplacing their horses and then forgetting about them."

Gideon flushed with chagrin. Perry could hardly contain himself, and jiggled up and down with excitement. Normally he would be highly interested in the newcomer—visitors were few and far between at Lacey's Folly—but his main concern at the moment was the fuss in the garden. It was better than a Punch and Judy puppet show. "Do come, Chloe!"

She worked deftly, not raising her eyes from the task at hand. "Perry, are the groom or the gardener there?"

"Yes, both of them," Perry said with high glee. "It's a rare set-to! Rendulph is mad as fire that the horse ate the green tops of the vegetables and trampled the turnip rows, and old Henry's yelling at Cook for frightening the horse, and saying we must send for Dr. Higgins, as the horse is sure to be sick from everything he ate. You really must come and see."

"I have enough matters to tend to inside the house, without meddling between the gardener and the groom. Tell Henry the horse belongs to our guest, and to do whatever he thinks best. He knows how to treat the horse as well as any animal doctor."

Disappointed at her lack of interest in such a promising altercation, the boy skipped out the door. Gideon was abashed. "I really am terribly sorry about that damned . . . er, that horse, Miss Hartsell."

Chloe didn't answer. Gideon grunted as she probed the cut. *Devil take it, who would think such a little scratch could hurt so badly?*

He snatched his hand back. "Yeeow . . . er, young Perry didn't seem to take much note of me," he murmured, to cover up. Reaching out, Chloe continued to minister to his cut.

"No, he is quite nearsighted. And in more ways than one. I believe he does need spectacles, and I intend to purchase him a pair. Although he'll probably lose them hanging upside down from a tree, or playing knight errant in the woods. He has a marvelous imagination, you see, and at times that causes a problem. When something captures his interest, he becomes blind to everything else."

"Really?" Gideon looked amused. "Then I cannot fault the boy," he said with a very warm smile. "I am the same way myself, Miss Hartsell."

What does he mean by that? Chloe wondered. His intensity, the way he looked at her, unnerved her badly.

She wasn't used to handsome men noticing her at all, much less smiling at her. He might be making a simple comment, or attempting a mild flirtation. Chloe bit her lip. She knew so little of men and the way their minds worked. If only she had more experience of conversing socially.

She tried to keep her mind on her task, but it made her feel awkward to be holding a man's hand in hers. Such a strong, warm hand!

She concentrated on his injury. "This must be quite painful. It isn't a clean slash. The rose spur ripped the flesh quite raggedly. And, I'm afraid, quite deeply."

As she washed and dried his hand gently, Gideon couldn't remember the last time any woman had done him a kindness without expecting something in return. Not since the early days with Dorinda. The *very* early days.

"*Ouch!*" Gideon jerked back to the present as Chloe packed the salve directly into the slash in his palm. The sharp pain vanished instantly, replaced by a soothing coolness.

She wrapped the wound in soft linen and bound it in place with a neat knot. "It will heal cleanly now," she announced, "although a little jagged scar might form. I doubt there is any need to fear infection."

"Perhaps you should use a little of the ointment on your hands," he suggested. "They appear rather chapped."

Chloe flushed to the roots of her hair and hid her hands in

her skirts. Gideon cursed himself for a fool. He couldn't tell if she reacted from anger or embarrassment, but he felt an utter fool. Reaching out, he caught her small, rough hand in his own.

"Forgive me, Miss Hartsell! I spoke without thinking."

Like a gift from heaven, he had an inspiration then. It was her hands that made him realize what he must do. The way back to his art was not through trying to force it. He must go back to the beginning. He must learn anew, see through the eyes of a student, working with simple line and texture and form.

That was how he had first started drawing from life. Not with faces, covered by their many masks and veils, which an artist must strip away, but with hands that did not lie. They were as God, and the experiences of life had made them.

"You may not know, Miss Hartsell, but I am an artist. You have lovely hands. Fine-boned and shapely. They would make an excellent study. I hope you do not think me impertinent, but I should like to do a sketch of them. Will you permit me?"

She bitterly envisioned the sketch to show every nick and rough cuticle. "I doubt there will be time, Mr. Stone," she said brusquely. "Mr. Fortescue should be back at any moment."

A voice like a donkey's bray made them both jump: "*A man in here, alone with you, Miss Hartsell? What in heaven is the meaning of this!*"

They both jumped and looked up as Olivia Thorne let out her banshee cry from the doorway. The spinster quivered in her fashionable taffeta dress and jet beads, with all the middle-class outrage she could muster.

Rising, Gideon executed an elegant bow and held up his bandaged hand. "Miss Hartsell was kind enough to repair the damage I did to myself earlier. My name is Stone. Mr. Fortescue will have informed you that I would be here for the reading of the will."

Olivia saw her error. *So handsome and distinguished a gentleman!* If his flashing white smile weren't enough to recommend him, Gideon's fine clothing and polished address were. Immediately, Olivia was all gracious condescension. She assumed the manner of the grand lady of the house, and a flirtatious one at that.

"Welcome to Lacey's Folly, Mr. Stone. I will see that everything possible is done to make your stay comfortable." She flicked her hand in Chloe's direction. "Miss Hartsell, take Mr. Stone upstairs to the blue bedchamber where he may freshen up after his journey."

"I have put him in the burgundy chamber, instead." Chloe tried not to laugh at the ludicrous expression on Olivia's face. "I don't think Mr. Stone would care to share accommodations with me, Miss Thorne. I have had the blue bedchamber these past six months, in order to be closer to Mr. Lacey in his last illness."

Which you would have known, had you come down to spend any time with Tobias, except at the very last.

Olivia's eyes snapped with anger, but she tried to hide it. *How dare she make me look bad in front of a guest. And it was outrageous that a mere housekeeper usurp one of the main bedchambers! Why, what would she need with all that space?* She sent Chloe a look of malicious triumph. She would see to it that Miss Hartsell moved into the little room off the nursery that very evening, next to that loathsome child, Peregrine!

But she swallowed her bile and spoke graciously to Gideon, who, being a male, was only vaguely aware of the currents swirling around him. "Well, the burgundy room is one of the finest in the house, Mr. Stone. Are you feeling peckish, sir? You shall have a tray sent up to your room, immediately. Miss Hartsell will see to that also."

"Thank you, no." He gave her another brilliant smile. "I have delayed matters too long already. I shall be down as soon as I've shaken off the dust of the road."

"Very well. Have a servant escort you to the library when you are ready. There will be have some refreshments set out for you there. Miss Hartsell will see to it."

It seemed that Miss Hartsell saw to a good deal beneath this roof, Gideon observed.

Chloe rang for the maid to show Gideon up to his room. Agnes came at once to take the guest upstairs, and Chloe went off to round up the other parties.

As she walked away, Gideon caught a glimpse of her slender ankle. A nicely turned ankle, he noted appreciatively, even in black lisle stockings. Ankles like those begged to be clad in the finest silk. If she posed for him, he'd send her some from London.

No, Devil take it, I won't. She's a lady and would rightly be insulted. Gideon grinned. He could imagine the reaction, the outraged innocence and disdain on Miss Hartsell's face, if he dared to present her with something so intimate as a pair of silk stockings. *She'd box my ears!*

He followed the maid up to the second landing. They went down a long paneled corridor with hunting prints on the walls and stuffed pheasants and other game birds displayed in plaster alcoves. The carpeting was threadbare and the once-crimson wall covering faded to a soft terra-cotta, but everything was clean and polished to a fare-thee-well.

Agnes took him to a spotlessly clean bedchamber with a high tester bed, and latticed windows open to the breeze. They gave a view of treetops, the roofs of a nearby village beyond the crest of a hill, and a tantalizing glimpse of the tower he'd seen earlier, but much closer at hand.

"What is that stonework tower? A castle ruin?"

"Oh, no, sir. A part of Lacey's Folly, it is. It's what gave this house its name." She swept an imaginary bit of dust from the heavy walnut bureau. "One of the old Laceys married a beautiful foreigner. She pined for her homeland, so he built it for her. It was to be an entire house, but she died and he never completed the work."

Gideon looked pensive. "That's a very sad story."

"Yes, I'm sure," Agnes said, giving the room a last survey. "Chances are she wouldn't have liked England, being a foreigner and all. If that's everything, I'll send up some hot water, sir. You have just to ring if you require anything else."

Her off-handed dismissal of the old tragedy left Gideon bemused. Perhaps it was because she had grown up knowing the story. Or perhaps the people of other centuries were no more real to her than the characters in a fairy tale.

After washing and changing out of his travel clothes, he brushed his thick, curly hair back from his brow and deemed himself presentable.

Pausing at the foot of the stairs, he tried to get his bearings. He was sure he'd glimpsed the drawing room down the hall to the right somewhere, where the corridor took a turn. No, that turned out to be the music room. Miss Thorne sat at the pianoforte, her back to him, quickly leafing through the pages of an illustrated songbook. He retreated hastily. He was in no mood to be entertained by amateur musicians.

Olivia glimpsed movement in the mirror and dropped the book upon the pianoforte's keys, creating a discordant sound. She'd spent most of the morning turning the pages of Tobias's favorite songbooks, looking for some clue to the treasure hidden at Lacey's Folly. A sheer waste of time.

Martin had gotten the harebrained idea that Tobias had hinted at it once. But then Martin thought that everything Tobias had ever said to him was a clue. *Silly fool!*

She set the book down and tiptoed out in time to catch sight of Gideon vanishing into the center hall. *A very eligible bachelor, Mr. Fortescue had said.* Smoothing her hair and pinching her sallow cheeks to add some color, she went to hunt him down.

It seemed straightforward enough, but Gideon got lost twice trying to find his way back to the main hall. The deserted side parlor he stumbled on was chock-full of items, yet even they were meticulously dusted. Sunlight struck a rainbow from something on a window shelf, and he wandered over. It was a sharp-edged piece of quartz with hundreds of spiky crystals, each as clear as water.

There were others in the locked buhl cabinet beside it: mineral specimens large and small, clear and opaque, in all shades of green and blue and copper, red and purple, sun-bright yellows and black-striped rose. They were as brilliant and beautiful to his artist's eye as the pigments he mixed for his paints.

The room was an odd mélange of items. Shelves held stacks of yellowed maps in glassine envelopes. Stuffed birds in every hue were ranged upon the mantelpiece or wired to perches hung from the ceiling. He would have loved to see them flying free in their native habitats, glossy streaks of color, like smears of wet oil paint against the emerald green leaves.

A bow-front cabinet beside a window was filled with exotic seashells, some with intricate cameos carved into their surfaces. Gideon peered inside and was startled by a loud, harsh voice behind him: "Thief, thief. Get away from there. Aw-w-w-k!"

Spinning around, he laughed to see that one of the birds was real. A snow-white bird with an astounding crest edged along the top of a cabinet and laughed back. Then it hopped down to a white wicker cage with an open door, popped inside, and appeared to fall asleep on its perch. Gideon eyed the others suspiciously, but the white bird proved to be the one living exception.

A glass-topped table caught his eye and drew him by its collection of dark, iridescent jewels. A closer look proved them to be giant beetles fixed with pins to a velvet background. Gideon gave a shiver of disgust and wondered who had collected them. *And, for God's sake, why?*

There were delights as well as horrors: rows of exquisite jade items and Chinese snuff bottles carved from amethyst, rose quartz, milky agate, carnelian and shimmery opal. Gideon was struck by the possibility that his legacy would turn out to be one of these collections. If so, he hoped that it would be the lovely objets d' art—and *not* the insects. Although the way his luck was running . . .

A group of Egyptian artifacts caught his eye. A plaited rush slipper with bright blue faience beads. A gold wire bracelet. A glass bangle. A few nice scarabs and five ushebtis, little burial figures of servants weaving, baking, hunting, all meant to serve the departed in their afterlife.

Gideon lifted the lid of a glass box containing a small ebony wand and tried to make out the faint ink marking on the ancient cloth that wrapped it. To his dismay, the fabric was permeated with a gummy, resinous substance that made the thin wand cling to his fingers—and, he noticed with an oath, the front of his favorite jacket. *Devil take it!*

He tugged. He cursed. It held like boiled glue. The more he tried to disentangle himself the worse it got. He cursed again, long and fluently.

"Oh!"

He looked up to find Olivia Thorne in the doorway, a finger to prim lips, and her cheeks a fine shade of beet. "Here, Miss Thorne, come help me get rid of this . . . this . . . what the devil is it, anyway?"

Olivia stared dumbly. Now she was white. She seemed to have turned into a pillar of salt, like Lot's wife. "Um . . . uh . . . Egypt," she stammered.

"Yes, I construed that. But what is it exactly?"

"Mmmm . . . a mummy."

"Is it, by God?" He peered at it crossly. "What part of a mummy looks like this?"

He held it out to her, and it stuck to her sleeve before she could jump back. Wrenching herself free, Olivia turned and fled in horror, bumping into Chloe on her way out.

Gideon looked down and cursed beneath his breath. Now the damned stick was stuck to his shirtfront. "Miss Hartsell! Would you be so kind as to help me get this . . . this *thing* loose of me?"

In response, Chloe made a small choking sound. Her face was redder than her hair. Gideon glared at her a moment. "What in God's name has gotten into everyone?"

Then he looked from her flaming face back at the object in his hand. The length, the vaguely cylindrical shape of the blackened stick, and her great mortification suddenly gave him his answer: it was a mummified part of the male anatomy. A part which was not discussed in a gentleman's parlor with a young lady. He felt the heat rush into his own cheeks.

"Never mind," he said quickly and wrenched the offending remains loose with his handkerchief.

Dropping the item gingerly back on the display shelf, he turned to apologize to Chloe. Hell and damnation! She was gasping for air and grasping the back of one of the side chairs, on the verge of collapse.

Gideon hurried to her side. "My most profound apologies, Miss Hartsell. I had no idea . . . I couldn't have realized . . . come, sit down."

Taking her hands in his, Gideon began chafing them between his. The gummy resins made his fingers stick to hers. She was trembling violently. He pulled his hands back with a jerk. His fingertips looked like they'd been dipped in the inkwell. As did her hands where he'd grasped them.

"Forgive me, Miss Hartsell. No doubt this has been a terrible shock to your delicate sensibilities. Shall I ring for assistance?"

"N . . . no." She took a deep, shuddering breath and then broke out in another series of gasps.

Her eyes closed, and he thought she was about to swoon. Gideon delivered a smart, stinging slap to her cheek. Chloe put a hand to her face, now streaked with pitch, and glared at him indignantly. "How *dare* you!"

"Miss Hartsell, I had no choice. You weren't breathing! You were on the verge of hysteria."

"No," she protested. "I was on the verge of *laughter*!"

He dropped her hands and stood up. "I see nothing humorous in the situation!"

"Of course not," she said, fighting to keep from bursting into giggles. "You were the one stuck to the puh-puh . . ." And she was off again, in a gale of mirth.

Gideon was torn between astonishment and chagrin. He wanted to be angry, but it was no use. "A wonderful fool I must have looked," he muttered darkly.

"Oh, you did indeed!"

"That, my dear girl, was a rhetorical remark! Politeness required you to either ignore it or protest to the contrary."

Her eyes brimmed with laughter. "But if you could have seen yourself, dancing around with the . . . p-p-p . . . puh . . ."

"Enough of that!" he said briskly. But it took all his determination to keep from laughing aloud with her.

Chloe saw the sparkle in his eye. "It *was* quite comical, you know."

"You are a little wretch, Miss Hartsell! If you mean to leave this room alive, you must swear by all that is holy, that you won't tell another living soul. Otherwise, I will have to throttle you and hide your body in the moat."

"Oh, no," she laughed. "It is not the sort of thing one would bring up in ordinary conversation, is it? But I can't promise not to think about it. Indeed, I doubt I'll be able to!"

Gideon turned away to hide his silent laughter. What an original she was! He couldn't remember laughing so freely in months.

Pouring brandy from the crystal decanter on the side table onto his handkerchief for a solvent, he wiped his hands clean. Chloe had managed—barely—to gain control of herself. "At least you kept your bandage from getting soiled. I doubt that ancient resin would have done your wound much good."

"More likely give me a plague! Here, give me your hands, Miss Hartsell. It seems it's my turn to assist. You look like you've been playing in the coal skuttle."

She held them out like an obedient child. Gideon carefully cleaned the dark streaks from them. Her hands were small and dainty, but chapped, despite the unguent he'd applied earlier. "I'm afraid this will sting," he warned her.

"Not as much as lye soap," she said bravely.

But it did. It stung like a nest of hornets. Closing her eyes, she gritted her teeth, pressed her lips tight, and tried to prevent little hisses of dismay from leaking through her lips.

Gideon tried to be careful, and it was an ordeal for him to feel her fingers shake and to know he was causing her pain.

"Almost done," he said, holding her hands firmly as he rubbed at the last bit of resin. "There."

He looked up to find her staring down at him with such solemnity it startled him. "Are you all right?"

"Yes, thank you." Her eyes were overbright, but she blinked and he couldn't tell if he'd seen tears in them or not.

The butler tiptoed in behind them so quietly, he seemed to materialize like a ghost. "Mr. Fortescue has returned. He is in the library and is prepared to begin as soon as everyone is assembled."

"Thank you, Dawlish. If you'll collect the others, I'll escort Mr. Stone there." She smiled at Gideon, although her stomach was filled with the flutter of butterfly wings. "This way, if you please."

He followed her down a corridor paneled in ancient walnut, intricately carved. "The Laceys have been great collectors for generations, and there are all manner of interesting items displayed in the drawing room. I don't believe they have been inventoried in years. Some are going to the British Museum, while others are to be distributed to private parties. Perhaps that is why Mr. Fortescue asked you to join us today?"

Gideon sincerely hoped not.

She was still a little discomposed, and he suspected that those tears, if such they were, were not from pain, but because he had been kind to her. What kind of life had she led that such a simple act of compassion would unnerve her so?

His second thought as they reached the library was more selfish: Gideon prayed sincerely to heaven that his legacy was not one of the Lacey "collections."

Or that, if it were, it was *not* the one with the mummy parts.

The library had been little used of recent years. A bank of windows behind the enormous desk were half shrouded in dark, red-brown curtains, and the huge floor-to-ceiling bay at the far end of the room was smothered with the same fabric. It made the chamber dark and dim.

It could be a lovely place to sit in winter, Chloe had always thought. The removal of that hideous gargoyle cupboard would do wonders to improve the place. And she had always hated those heavy curtains. In the past her mind had played with new colors: a rich, amber silk to pick out the design in the carpet, or perhaps a soft, warm rose to bring out the tones in the paneling.

Gideon saw her staring fixedly at the window hangings. "Dreadful, aren't they?"

"Yes," she replied. "Exactly like dried blood, don't you think?"

He was a little startled. But she was right. It was the perfect description. "You have a good eye for color, Miss Hartsell."

Cook sat perched on a hard chair in the corner, apron fresh and back like a ramrod. Martin Thorne and his sister entered the library and took the seats of honor on the comfortable sofa near the desk. Dawlish tottered in behind them. His eyes were red-rimmed, but no one seemed to notice except Chloe.

Poor Dawlish. She hoped that Tobias Lacey had provided well for the old servant in his will. If not, she must reassure the butler that he needn't worry. She would look after him in his old age. There would always be a room with a fire and a place at the table for him as long as she was mistress of Lacey's Folly.

Chloe tried not to smile. She liked to think that she was a good person, neither prideful nor greedy. But oh! It would do her heart good to see the looks on Martin and Olivia Thorne's faces when they learned the place was left to her. The aftermath would be unpleasant, but she would survive it.

Gideon had been watching her from the corner of his eye. Emotions flickered over her mobile features, like reflected light from ripples on a stream. What an odd creature she was, half shy and half fierce. She was no beauty in the classic sense, but her face was interesting. Appealing. Her skin was creamy and flawless as a milkmaid's, with not even a smattering of the freckles seen so often in red-haired girls.

He remembered exactly how it had felt, as soft and dewy as a rose petal. The urge to check the accuracy of his recall was very strong. He gave himself a little shake. Immediately, she looked up at him.

He took in a quick breath. He was mesmerized by her eyes. If he could only describe them accurately to himself, put them into a category, he could loose their hold on his imagination. They looked darker now, like the clear but shadowed waters of a mountain stream. But there were sparkles and glints in their depths. Whether those depths hid mischief or temper, tears or passion, he couldn't tell. An interesting face, all in all. He wanted very much to sketch it.

As for the Thornes, brother and sister, he'd have sooner painted still lifes of the potatoes they so much resembled.

Mr. Fortescue entered, took his seat behind the desk, and cleared his throat loudly. A hush fell over the gathering.

"Thank you all for assembling. I believe everyone is present now . . ."

"All except young Master Peregrine," Dawlish said. "He was in that chair, reading, not twenty minutes ago, and . . ."

Martin Thorne interrupted. "And I told him to go outside. He was playing with a magnifying glass and nearly set the chair on fire."

"I did not," an indignant voice said from the doorway. "I was merely searching for clues."

Chloe patted the sofa beside her. "Come, Perry." The boy sat down. "No luck finding the lost treasure yet," he whispered loudly enough for all to hear. "But I found this." He pulled a tarnished brass button, heavy with verdigris, from his pocket. "We could put it in the button collection in the parlor."

Gideon smiled, then briefly examined the other occupants of the library. The servants looked anxious and ill-at-ease sitting among the family. As for Chloe Hartsell beside him, she seemed both eager and nervous, like a girl on the eve of her first assembly.

The thought struck him that she had most likely never attended one. Poor Miss Hartsell! He could not imagine what it had been like for her, immured within the walls of Lacey's

Folly like a nun in a convent, bound by blood and obligation
to a doddering old man. He hoped that Tobias Lacey had been
as generous as she obviously anticipated.

Mr. Fortescue looked around the room and counted heads.
He was reluctant to start on one hand, yet most eager to finish
and be on his way. This would not be easy. "*Ahem!*" Fum-
bling with his pince-nez, he affixed them to the bridge of his
patrician nose and took a deep breath.

"Now that we are all assembled, I will proceed with the
reading of the last will and testament of Tobias Henry Lacey,
of Lacey's Folly. The *new* will, which was drawn up two
weeks ago according to Mr. Lacey's instructions, and revokes
all previous wills."

A stir went round the room. Chloe remained at ease. That
had been after she and Tobias had talked about Perry's school-
ing. He had told her that he'd decided to make separate pro-
visions for the boy. She folded her hands in her lap and tried
not to glow with anticipation.

After the initial legal flourishes, the solicitor read a stipulation. "Before going into the bequests, I am charged to read
you this: 'It is my last wish that neither my household nor
beneficiaries follow the customs of prolonged mourning. I
hereby decree that the last day of official mourning shall be
the day of the reading of this will. Anyone who goes against
my wishes in this matter shall forfeit his bequest.' "

Dawlish and Cook looked distressed, the Thornes relieved.
Since Tobias had already made this very clear to Chloe, she
was the only one not surprised. Having gotten this out of the
way, the lawyer went on to the bequests.

" 'To Henry Dawlish, my loyal butler of many years, I
leave my ebony and silver walking stick, my collection of
German clocks, which he faithfully wound each week, the use
of Laurel Cottage for his lifetime, and the sum of one thousand
pounds outright.' "

Chloe smiled. Tobias must have been putting something
aside for many years, in order to provide for Dawlish in his
old age. The butler was overcome with emotion, dabbing at

his eyes with his handkerchief, so that he missed the angry astonishment the Thornes directed his way.

Mr. Fortescue continued with bequests to the steward, gamekeeper, and lesser servants, which also made the Thornes goggle. "He must have been insane," Martin protested. "He has given away more than the estate can bear."

The solicitor ignored him and turned the page. " 'To Master Peregrine Hartsell, whose enthusiasm and sense of adventure have helped to while away the tedium of my last years, I bequeath my gold pocket watch, and the jeweled Turkish scimitar and scabbard, with the proviso that he try and not slice off any parts of his anatomy playing with them.

" 'In particular, and because he shares my passion for them, I leave to Master Peregrine the complete collections of insect and archaeological specimens amassed by generations of Laceys, which I know he will appreciate and preserve.' "

"*Capital!*" the boy exclaimed, grinning like a jack-o'-lantern. He hadn't hoped for anything as fine as mummy parts and the cases of mounted insects! Chloe put her arm around his shoulders and gave him a quick hug. Gideon heaved a great sigh of relief.

The solicitor looked up briefly, smiled, and went back to the task at hand, naming the interest of several stocks "to be invested in funds, for his future education and establishment." Fortescue looked over at Chloe. "The amount realized will be sufficient to send him to the best schools, Miss Hartsell."

Chloe gave a gasp that was almost a sob, drowning out the legal details that followed. Olivia lifted her head like a hound sniffing blood and ignored them both. Her name came next.

" 'To my neice Olivia Thorne, I leave the small bust of Medusa. I also bequeath to her the collection of forty volumes of leather-bound sermons, in hopes of inspiring true piety. I also leave to her my mother's matched set of gray pearls, knowing she will value them far more.

" 'To my nephew Martin Thorne . . .' "

As the solicitor stopped to sip water from a heavy crystal

glass, both Martin and Olivia leaned forward. Mr. Fortescue took another sip and began again.

" 'To my nephew Martin Thorne, I leave the farm he currently occupies at Lesser Barnstable with the land, house, and all its furnishings. Also, the grandfather clock at the foot of the stairs, and the engraving of Wellington at the hunt, entitled 'The Meet at Melton,' so that he may see the proper use to which a gentleman puts his leisure time. I also leave to Martin Thorne my stuffed birds, of which he put me so much in mind, and my grandfather's sword, in hopes the ownership of forged steel will help to put some of the same substance into his backbone.

" 'To Chloe Hartsell . . . ' "

"But—that can't be all!" Martin exclaimed in indignant disbelief. "You've missed something, man! Look again."

Mr. Fortescue took off his pince-nez and polished them with his handkerchief. "Mr. Thorne, I have read your bequest in its entirety."

"Oooh, that hussy!" Olivia moaned loudly. "I knew she would poison his mind against us!" Martin shushed her as she put a bottle of smelling salts to her nose and sniffed.

A profound silence came over the room. Adjusting his papers, the solicitor continued. " 'To Chloe Hartsell . . . ' "

She leaned forward, heart hammering in her chest. Almost sick with excitement. Here it was, the moment when her life would change forever, in new and wondrous ways. She looked at Mr. Fortescue with lips parted and eyes shining.

He did not meet her gaze.

" 'To Chloe Hartsell,' " he began again, " '"my distant kinswoman, who has been companion and housekeeper to me, I leave my deep appreciation for her attention to my care and comfort. To that order, I bequeath her my dear mother's amber brooch and earrings, the collections of poetry, and the mineral specimens, and my grandmother's rosewood desk and chair in the morning parlor, which she dusted faithfully and with such care.

" ' "Also, I leave to Chloe Hartsell the Chinese jade and

ivory chess set with which she so often challenged my intellect, in the hopes that it will do the same for her.' "

Mr. Fortescue paused for breath. The room was as silent as a mausoleum. Even Perry had ceased his fidgeting. The only sound was Dawlish's hoarse wheezing. The old butler had fallen asleep in the heat, with his mouth open and his head back against the chair.

"And now for the final bequest," the solicitor intoned solemnly. " 'Excepting those items and holdings mentioned earlier, I leave the portrait of Lenore Lacey and all the rest of my worldly belongings, including Lacey's Folly, its contents, and its demesne, to Gideon Stanfield Stone, entirely and irrevocably.' "

This last bombshell left everyone stunned, as Mr. Fortescue had known it would. The effects would wear off soon enough.

He steeled his nerves and prepared himself for the aftermath. Any moment now the questions, the outrage, the threats and counterthreats, demands, and pleadings would break over him like a thunderstorm.

He squared the edges of the sheets of vellum, while observing the others' reactions. They demonstrated a veritable rainbow of emotions: Gideon Stone was red with astonishment, Martin Thorne and his waspish sister both almost purple with rage—and poor little Chloe Hartsell white with shock.

He glanced up at the portrait of the late Tobias Lacey that hung over the mantelpiece, then back at Chloe holding so tightly to the arms of her chair that her fingers were blanched. Her face and lips were bloodless, her gray eyes blank mirrors reflecting horror and disbelief.

Mr. Fortescue removed his pince-nez and polished them vigorously. Anything so as not to have to look at her now. He could not bear to witness her devastation as her hopes and dreams were destroyed.

Tobias, you old fool, he said to himself. *I only hope you knew what you were doing.*

FOUR

§ §

THE CLAMOR THAT FOLLOWED THE LAST PARAGRAPH OF Tobias Lacey's will was enough to waken the beagle pup. It sprang to its short legs and set to barking. He was almost drowned out by the others.

"No, this is impossible! There is some mistake," Martin Thorne sputtered.

"Absurd!" Olivia gasped. "The old dodderer was out of his mind. We shall certainly have this new will overturned."

"I assure you," Mr. Fortescue said, with quiet force, "that everything meets with the strict accordance of the law."

Olivia glared at him with a martial eye. "You are wrong. Tobias Lacey could not have been in his right mind, to take everything away from his family in favor of a complete stranger!"

"The will is valid, and two doctors have signed affidavits as to Mr. Lacey's competency." Fortescue was glad that he'd foreseen the objection and made the proper arrangements.

"Mr. Stone," he added, "while not personally known to Tobias Lacey, shared a common ancestor, several generations back."

Chloe didn't hear any of it. She was sick with hurt and disappointment. And fear. Her life, and Perry's, were in the hands of a total stranger. Her ears rang, her vision dimmed. Gripping the sides of the armchair tightly, she fought the horrid sensation that she might, for the first time in her life, fall into a dead faint.

Tobias, whom she had trusted implicitly, had lied to her! Over and over, he had lied, when he promised that he would see that her future was secure, that when he passed on, Lacey Manor would be hers. She was heartsick as she saw all the hopes she'd built for herself and her son crumble to dust. What would she do? Where would they go?

How, dear God, would they survive?

Gideon was equally astounded. He ran a hand through his thick hair, tumbling his curls into disorder. Lacey Manor— *his?* It was truly the answer to his prayers and seemed far too good to be true. If Dame Fortune had been turning her back to him lately, she had certainly made it up to him now. He could scarcely take it in.

"You are positive that I am the correct Gideon Stone?" he said at last.

"There is no doubt at all."

"And Lacey's Folly is mine?"

"Lock, stock, and barrel."

"And, should I wish to do so, I could sell the estate?"

Fortescue scrutinized him for several long seconds. "Not precisely. There is one further provision, Mr. Stone, upon which Mr. Lacey was totally set, and could not be dissuaded. The bequest to you is based on the stipulation that you provide a home for Miss Hartsell and Peregrine Hartsell, until such a time as she may marry. In such an event, you are charged with providing her with a suitable dowry, as well.

"If you do not agree with these stipulations, his bequest to you is null and void. In such an event, Lacey Manor and all its accouterments will be sold and all the proceeds given to the foundling hospital at St. John's."

The Thornes' outrage at this further insult was both bitter and brief. The solicitor raised his voice sharply.

"Except for Miss Hartsell, there is no reason for the other beneficiaries to remain." He looked at Gideon meaningfully.

"Perhaps you would like the others to retire to the drawing room while we discuss this business?"

Gideon, thrust suddenly into the unexpected role of host, took just a moment to adjust his thoughts to the strange new pattern. *He* was master of Lacey's Folly. "Uh, yes. Dawlish, will you see to it?"

The old butler rose with dignity. "Of course, sir."

Dawlish ushered Martin and Olivia to the door, like a border collie herding distracted sheep. The Thornes fell to quarreling in harsh whispers between themselves as they exited.

"This is your fault, Martin!" Olivia accused heatedly. "If you were any kind of man, you'd have kept a closer eye on what the old man was up to, and this would never have happened."

"And I say that this is all your fault," Martin rounded on his sister. "If you had seen to his creature comforts, made him calf's foot jelly and nourishing broth, and read to him every evening as Miss Hartsell did, he mightn't have taken such an aversion to you!"

Olivia's response floated down the corridor just before the door was shut. "Well, a lot of good it did *her*, for all I can see. A paltry necklace, a few odds and ends, and a piece of outmoded furniture. Hah!"

Gideon was so stunned, he hadn't heard a word of what the others had said. He came slowly out of his daze. His prayers had been answered in a most unorthodox way. He had the means to pay off his debts and restore himself in society.

"The estate is not encumbered by mortgages, you said. Does that mean I can put it up for sale? If so, I would prefer to do so as soon as possible."

The solicitor eyed the new heir obliquely. "I hope you are not too anxious to be rid of the property, sir. The stipulation is *not* that you provide *any* home for Miss Hartsell until she takes a husband to wed. It is that you provide a home for her *here*—at Lacey's Folly. You are also further instructed to provide an adequate dowry for her from the estate revenues. Then, and only then, would you be free to sell off the entire estate, should you choose.''

"The devil you say!'' Gideon was appalled. "I am in the position of having to maintain the property, for years if need be, in the hopes that Miss Hartsell will find herself a husband?''

"That is true. Of course, you may turn down the bequest, in which case the manor will be sold, and all the proceeds given to the foundling hospital. The choice is yours,'' the solicitor added dryly.

Another voice burst in upon them. "You're wrong, you're wrong, you're *all wrong*,'' an indignant voice, with all the fury a ten-year-old boy could muster.

They turned toward the voice. Peregrine's freckled face was ruddy with indignation. "It's supposed to go to *Chloe*! Mr. Lacey said that the house n' everything would be *hers*. He said it was in his will to go to her. He *promised*! Didn't he, Chloe?''

All eyes turned toward the corner chair where Chloe had perched for the reading of the will. Gideon frowned. The corner was empty, as if she had vanished into thin air.

Chloe cut through the drawing room and stumbled out the open doors, into the fragrant garden. She had no destination in mind, her only purpose being to get as far away as possible from the house and the scene of her crushing disappointment. She was utterly devastated.

Sobs of shock and despair caught in her throat, but she would not give way to them. Running blindly, she stumbled across the lawn, past the old-fashioned dovecote, cutting through the rose garden until she reached the pond. Brambles caught at her skirts, and she tore them free without slowing down.

Skirting the mossy bank, she paused beneath the screening canopy of an ancient weeping willow to catch her breath. She sat against the trunk of one at the water's edge, rigid as a ship's carved figurehead. Her reflection in the still waters mocked her inner turmoil. A swan glided by, breaking up her image—just as Mr. Fortescue's words had shattered her dream, leaving devastation in their wake.

She had worked like a servant for ten long years, without so much as wages to set by for the future. Nothing but room and board and occasional pin money. This morning she had awakened filled with hope and happiness. Secure in the knowledge that she was no longer the poor relation, but about to become the mistress of Lacey's Folly.

It had all been an illusion, a terrible, unthinkable jest. Everything she "owned," even this outmoded mourning dress found in a wardrobe, belonged to the house. To Gideon Stone. She had nothing to call her own except for a set of amber beads and the desk Tobias had left to her.

The delicate fronds parted and Perry ducked under. "Knew you'd be here." He plopped down beside her and bit his lower lip. His face was as woebegone as hers.

"Tobias lied."

"Yes. Yes, he did, Perry. And I don't know why." Her voice quivered and she tried to control it. "We must remember that it was his to dispose of as he pleased."

"It's not fair! But don't worry, Chlo. When I am a grown man, you will come and live with me. I'll look after you. I swear it, on my honor!"

She hugged him and held him fast a moment. She loved the little boy smell of him, the warmth of his body that had suddenly grown to be all arms and legs in the past few months.

"I know you will," she murmured against his bright hair. *Oh, but it is my responsibility to take care of you. That was my promise,* she thought plaintively. *And somehow I have failed you. Failed us both.*

Perry pulled out a blade of grass and made a whistle of it in his cupped hands. Chloe knew he was fighting against his own tears. He was growing up. After a moment he discarded the blade.

"Mr. Fortescue says for you to come back to the house,

Chloe, as there are 'portant matters to discuss. He says it's no
as bad as you think.''

''I can't. *I won't!*''

''Well, you'd better come back to the house anyway, 'caus
Miss Thorne is in the drawing room, stuffing those enamele
snuffboxes into her valise.''

''What?'' Chloe leapt to her feet. ''That odious woman!''
She charged off to defend Tobias's property, with Perr
running on ahead.

Halfway there, she realized it was Mr. Stone's property
now. For just an instant she wavered. Why should she care?

But old habits and a sense of fair play overruled her anger
Olivia had no right to take anything that was not hers. And
although she was not mistress of the manor, as she'd rightfully
expected, by God! she was still the housekeeper of Lacey'
Folly.

''Is it true, what the boy said?'' Gideon asked the solicito
when they were alone.

''Yes.'' Fortescue looked unhappy to be put on the spot
He tapped the papers in front of him with a thin finger.

''This was done only last month, just prior to his secone
stroke of apoplexy. In the previous will, which was drawn ur
five years ago, the bulk of the estate was to go to Miss Hartsell, who has never earned a penny for her services. That wa
to preserve her pride and her distinction as a relation, rathe
than a servant. Or so he told me. Make of it what you will.'

Gideon felt like an utter cad. His opinion of Tobias Lacey
rose and fell like waves on the sea of his emotions.

He looked out the window and saw Chloe approaching the
house in a most determined manner. ''The poor girl! Smal
wonder she is distraught. What do I do now?''

''The first thing I would suggest, Mr. Stone, is that you
draft your own will. You are now a man of considerable substance. Tobias Lacey lost a good deal of money years ago. I
made him very cautious, even while his investments pros-
pered.''

Gideon turned back to him. Mr. Fortescue watched the look of incredulity grow on the other man's face. "Yes, he let the place get very shabby. But I assure you, there is enough to refurbish the entire house and fill the stables. To command not just the necessities of life, Mr. Stone, but all its elegancies."

"In other words, the man was a miser!"

"I prefer to say he was prudent where money was concerned. He was, however, quite wealthy."

"For all the good it does me," Gideon said bitterly. "I have serious debts to pay and no means with which to discharge them, unless I set myself up as a matchmaker!"

The solicitor had heard of the fateful game of cards between Gideon and Lord Exton. Indeed, all of London had. He eyed the new heir gravely. "Mr. Lacey intended that the estate should remain intact, to be passed on to future generations."

Gideon paced the room. "Nevertheless, I will be free to do whatever I wish with the place, once Miss Hartsell is married off. Is that correct?"

"Yes, but you may be able to borrow against the estate. Perhaps not to the extent of your debts, if they are as heavy as you say," he added, quashing Gideon's suddenly blooming hopes.

"Meanwhile, I'm saddled with Miss Hartsell."

He glanced out again in time to see the hem of Chloe's black dress disappear around the wall into the rose garden. "It's a damnable coil. What am I to do with her?"

"I would suggest that that is something you should discuss with the lady in question," the older man said with a twinkle. "She may have some ideas of her own."

Gideon felt a surge of hope. "Do you mean there is already someone courting her?"

"I am not privy to Miss Hartsell's expectations. That is something you must discuss with her. But the way she danced attendance on Mr. Lacey, I sincerely doubt she had time for the normal social activities of a young woman her age. But one never knows."

The solicitor gathered up his papers. "I will be returning to

London in the morning. If there are no other questions at the moment, I would suggest you seek out Miss Hartsell and discover which way the wind blows.''

Gideon searched the garden in vain. He finally ran Chloe to earth in the drawing room, drawn there by the sound of an altercation coming through the open windows.

Reaching the terrace, he saw Olivia Thorne towering over Miss Hartsell menacingly. A wicker carrying case on the table beside her was tipped over, spilling several exquisitely made, little silver and gold boxes across the polished surface.

"Move aside, I tell you!"

Chloe stood her ground before Miss Thorne's wrath. "I will not unlock the display case. Furthermore, you will hand back the snuffboxes which you have removed from the table. At once!"

Olivia was purple with rage. "You are nothing but a glorified servant in this house! Give me the key, or I'll smash it open with—"

Olivia looked around wildly, then snatched up a hand-sized mineral specimen. ". . . with one of these stupid rocks! I always intended to have those snuffboxes. Tobias knew it!"

"I am the master here now," Gideon said smartly, stepping into the room. "Everything in this room is my property; however, if you are particularly attached to some ornament, I will gladly present it to you as a gift—when you leave, which I trust will be by early tomorrow!"

Olivia wavered a moment between greed and mortification that he'd witnessed the scene. The latter won out.

"While I hate to deprive you of acting the role of Lord Bountiful, I do not want your gift. If there were any justice, it would rightfully belong to my brother!" She shot him a vengeful glance and swept through the doorway with her head held high.

Chloe swept up the spilled snuffboxes and put them back in their proper places as gently as if she were settling flowers in a vase.

"Only one has suffered any harm," she told him, holding it out to Gideon. "I'm sorry to say that the rock-crystal top over this hand-painted scene is slightly scratched."

"Thank you, Miss Hartsell. I appreciate your defending my property," he said, looking the lovely little snuffbox over. "Quite frankly, I am amazed that you would notice such slight damage."

Chloe didn't look up. "It has been my responsibility for many years." She took it from him and put it safely away, then locked the glass case. "I should check the others."

"Leave them for now," he told her, touching her arm gently. She managed not to flinch, but it took an effort of will. Hearing him announce that he was master of Lacey's Folly, and Olivia's recognition of his authority, made it all seem too real.

He gestured to one of the long windows that let out into the garden. "Come stroll with me awhile. We must talk."

They went out into the sunshine and wandered in silence among the colorful flowers, until they reached the pond. He couldn't quite take in that all this belonged to him now. And not to this poor young woman who had expected to inherit it herself.

The pond was a man-made feature, where the small brook widened briefly into a deep, quiet pool, before spilling lazily over jumbled rocks on its way to the river beyond. Swans sailed majestically with the tranquil current. The water was dark amber, reflecting the willows and the white latticework of the small pergola. A peaceful spot to discuss the turbulent events of the day.

"This is as good a place as any," Gideon said. "We may be private here."

They entered, and Chloe perched on the edge of the cushioned seat opposite him, watching the swans glide away. She fixed him with her quicksilver gaze, and Gideon felt as if he were a butterfly and she a sharp pin.

"Olivia . . . Miss Thorne says that you will put Lacey's Folly up for sale. Is it true? Is that what you wish to do?"

He evaded the question. "More to the point, Miss Hartsell, is what you wish to do. Do you hope to marry and set up a house and family of your own? If so, I will do everything in my power to bring it about."

She bowed her head, and Gideon observed her closely. Life had not been kind to Chloe Hartsell. He guessed her to be perhaps twenty-three or twenty-four, not in her prime for marriage, but not exactly at her last prayers yet.

She was older than her years in some ways and younger in others. Something of the innocent girl about her still. Perhaps it was because she lacked the brittle mannerisms that passed for sophistication that had misled him. Or because she appeared so very fragile and vulnerable.

Until one looked at those capable hands, that is, and remembered the efficiency with which she had bandaged his injury, and the resolve with which she had faced Miss Thorne defending the snuffboxes.

"I am aware, Miss Hartsell, that today's events have been a great disappointment to you. I assure you, I knew nothing about either Tobias Lacey or his estate until Mr. Fortescue contacted me. Why he left Lacey's Folly to me is beyond my ken. I am most heartily sorry for the grievous effect it has had on you."

Chloe was silent while she gathered her thoughts. "You cannot know . . . cannot imagine . . . I expected to have a roof over my head for the rest of my life. To be secure. Now I am a virtual pauper. One whose future will be determined by the generosity—or lack thereof—of the new master of Lacey's Folly."

She swallowed her anger at him, at Tobias, at fate for the betrayal of her dreams. "When I was young, I harbored a few romantic dreams, as all girls do. But I am a woman grown. I must be realistic about my expectations, and they are not good."

"My dear girl, you speak as if you were ancient! You are still young."

She lifted her head and looked him in the eye. "I am not

your dear girl, Mr. Stone. I am more than five-and-twenty. I have no family, no fortune, and no beauty. I am far past the age when most women marry, and I have no acquaintance outside of servants and tradesman who deliver to our door.''

Her voice faltered and broke. ''Who would have me now?''

Her situation touched him, her frankness took him aback. ''Then there is no one . . . ?''

''No pining suitors,'' she said wryly. ''No secret lover waiting in the wings to carry me off.''

The finality of her voice convinced him it was true. Gloom settled over him. ''This is all very awkward,'' Gideon said, running his fingers through his hair. He would have to explain his predicament to her. ''I don't know quite what to say.''

Chloe's cheeks suffused with hot color. ''Do you not? You could say that you didn't want the inheritance and assign your interest in Lacey's Folly to me.''

His laugh was harsh. ''You forget, that would merely enrich a foundling hospital at my expense. I'm a charitable man, Miss Hartsell, but I am not a fool.''

''No.'' She sighed. ''I'd forgotten.''

The dappled shade threw a leafy veil across her features. He could not see her expression, but she was shivering despite the fine afternoon. Gideon could see she was in shock from the day's events. ''Here, take my coat before you catch a chill.''

She didn't protest, and he stripped off his jacket and settled it over her shoulders. She looked small and fragile inside its cocooning warmth. *Like a butterfly unable to break out of its chrysalis*, he thought. What had her life been like, with no companionship other than an elderly invalid, a small boy, and a handful of servants? Gideon was wrung with guilt and pity.

''The situation is not entirely hopeless, Miss Hartsell,'' he said hearteningly. ''You forget the conditions of the will: you shall have a dowry. I will undertake to make it a good one. That, in itself, makes you more eligible in the eyes of the world.''

She didn't reply. He eyed her garments, her glossy red curls escaping wildly from the unbecoming chignon. ''Come, cheer up! A more stylish way of dressing your hair, a few frocks and feminine furbelows, and I'm sure we can manage to snare you an eligible husband.''

She rose from the bench like an avenging fury, eyes blazing with passion. ''I don't *need* a husband. I don't *want* a husband! I want what was promised to me—Lacey's Folly!''

Chloe was shaking in a whirlwind of emotions. She clenched her fists and closed her eyes, willing herself to maintain some semblance of control. Oh! It was too bad of Tobias to have led her on so! *Far better to have had no expectations at all, than to have them snatched away!*

Gideon watched emotions flicker across her face with an artist's fascination. Her eyes could change from polished silver to dull steel in the span of a heartbeat. Now they were diamond bright, and he couldn't tell if the sudden sheen was due to suppressed tears, or merely a trick of the light.

Chloe found her voice again, startling him. He'd been totally absorbed by imagining how he would paint those everchangeable eyes. It couldn't be done. Not by him, not by anyone.

''It is very hard, Mr. Stone. Lacey's Folly is all I know. Tobias brought me here to live when I was a mere girl. My father's estate was in ruins. I . . . we were paupers. I can never express my gratitude for what he did. I worked very hard to make him comfortable, and to maintain the house despite increasing expenses and decreasing resources. I never aspired to be mistress here: if Tobias hadn't told me that he'd changed the will in my favor and that I was to inherit the estate, it would never have entered my mind! You can imagine my astonishment, my great gratitude.''

Her voice was filled with passion. ''I didn't care that there would be no monies to refurbish it, that the fees paid by the farmers to use the land were barely enough to put food on the table. I only cared that Perry and I would have a home that no one could ever take away from us.''

''But . . .''

"Please, Mr. Stone, let me finish. To have had my hopes raised so high and dashed so low . . . it is a bitter, *bitter* thing!" Tear-blind, Chloe bent her head so he would not see. "I had hoped to live out my life peacefully here."

"If we don't find you a husband, you'll get your wish," Gideon pointed out. "The will stipulates that you will remain at Lacey's Folly until you marry."

Her face brightened.

He hardened his tone. There was no use encouraging false hopes. "If you do not marry, then we shall both grow old inside these walls, with the roofs falling down upon our heads—because I can't sell off so much as a stick of furniture or a foot of land unless you take a husband first."

"Are you so anxious to do so?"

His brow knotted. This was no time for false pride. "I, my dear girl, am as penniless as you. More so, I dare say, as I'm savagely in debt."

Her head jerked up. Chloe stared at him in surprise. "I see."

She'd thought from his elegant air and fine clothes that Mr. Stone was well-to-do. "Have you no income at all, sir, or way of making your way in the world?"

"Egad, you don't balk at asking intimate questions of strangers, do you?"

"Since we're to grow old together beneath crumbling roofs, as you put it, I think I should know the truth of your circumstances."

She bit her lower lip and continued, "I don't suppose there is any work you could set yourself to doing? Tutoring, perhaps? Or . . . or we could make Lacey's Folly into a small school for boys. I could help you teach them.'"

"Good God, no! I am an artist," he reminded her hotly. "A painter."

"A good one?"

Gideon flushed and tossed a pebble into the pond. The ripples spread out in bright circles. "I was. Once upon a time."

"Can you not interest anyone in purchasing your work?"

He scowled at her. "You are the most impertinent young lady it has been my discomfort to meet. Very well. I will be frank. I gambled deep and lost. I am in dire need of funds. If I do not realize a certain sum within a very short time, my reputation is ruined. I might as well put a gun to my head. In fact, I will be expected to do so."

"Surely you wouldn't do anything so drastic!" she cried in dismay. "It will do me no good if the estate passes to the foundling home."

He sent her a dark look. "Your touching concern does you credit, Miss Hartsell."

She laughed. "I am not so coldhearted as that sounded. But I have Peregrine to consider, too." Chloe toyed with the bit of unraveling black ribbon at her sleeve, where she'd snagged it on a thorn. "He's very dear to me. He is all I have—and I am all he has."

An idea struck her, and she placed her hand impulsively on his sleeve. "I don't suppose that we could just keep on as before? *I*, for one, don't care if your reputation is ruined. You need never see anyone who might snub you. And I would stay on in the same position, and the house would run smoothly while you worked at your painting. But with payment for my services, of course."

Gideon shook his head. "I'm afraid that cannot be, Miss Hartsell."

"I see. You are thinking I am too young, that there would be scandal with us living under the same roof without an older female to chaperone, and that no man would ask for my hand because of it."

"Egad!" He rubbed his jaw. *The situation gets worse and worse.* "The thought had never occurred to me. No, I must sell the house and pay my debts. It is a matter of honor."

"If your debts are so enormous, I doubt the sale of Lacey's Folly would pay them off. It's in need of urgent repair."

He didn't know how to tell her gently. Instead, he blurted it out. "You are laboring under false information. Tobias Lacey, despite his habits, was a very wealthy man. In addition to his holdings, he left sums invested in funds. Unfortunately, I cannot draw upon them until you are married. Another little stipulation that Mr. Fortescue explained after you'd run off.''

All the color drained from Chloe's face. Her world tilted a bit more out of skew. *Lies and more lies.* Nothing Tobias had told her was true, it seemed. She felt ill and couldn't speak for a few moments.

"I imagine it is all tied up legally," she said at last.

"In a Gordian knot."

"Then," she said firmly, "you must find a way to cut through it."

"Impossible."

Bees hummed through the flowers. A soft breeze blew through the open latticework of the pergola. Chloe looked up and saw the pity in his handsome face, the worry clouding his blue eyes. A tear trembled on her eyelashes, then spilled down her cheek. She dashed it away, angry with herself for giving way to her emotions.

"Then I suppose you shall have to find me a husband," she said quietly.

"That I will, Miss Hartsell."

Gideon was wracked with guilt. He felt a sudden rush of responsibility and it shook him to the core. Until today he had answered to no one but himself. Now he had Miss Hartsell and her young brother to look after. Not to mention a houseful of servants. It was a sobering realization.

He took her hand in his. "I shall find you a husband—and a good one, at that. I give you my oath."

"Thank you." She pulled her hand free and rose. "Although how you will go about it is beyond me."

At the moment, it was beyond Gideon, too.

After Chloe was gone, Gideon sat in the pergola, trying to take it all in. The most pressing problem was finding a suitable husband for Miss Hartsell. *That would solve everyone's problems*, he told himself.

She was no beauty, that was true, but she had an interesting, attractive countenance. Surely she could be made presentable, with the right gowns and folderols. And there must be *something* that could be done about all that rioting red-gold hair. And then there was the matter of the chaperone. He'd ask Dawlish if there were any gentlewoman who might be willing to come to Lacey's Folly as a companion to Miss Hartsell until she could be taken off his hands..

How the devil I am going to pull that off is more than I can imagine.

Inspiration struck: he'd ask the advice and aid of his godmother. Lady Albinia Longsworth was a fashionable widow of middle years, still considered a famous beauty. She was not only up to snuff, she knew everyone and everything and was connected either through birth or marriage to England's elite. She would know exactly what to do to find Miss Hartsell a suitable husband.

At present she was visiting friends in the country, not far off the road back to London. The moment he got back to his room, he would pour his heart out in a letter and trust to her good nature to help him out of his quandary. Perhaps Mr. Fortescue would be good enough to take a short detour and hand deliver the letter on his way back to London this afternoon.

Gideon grinned. The opportunity to meet the fabulous Lady Albinia should prove a potent lure, even for such a dry old stick as Mr. Fortescue. Her beauty and charm were legend.

Suddenly, the situation no longer looked so bleak. If anyone could get Chloe Hartsell safely married and off his hands, it was his godmother. Once that was accomplished, he could pay off his debts and immerse himself in his painting.

A peace came over him. Perhaps a sojourn in the country was exactly what he needed. Far from the temptations of wine, women, and London's fast set. He could concentrate on his work once more, instead of frittering away his energies. It was as if a magic wand had been waved over him, lifting the weight of his cares.

His passion would surely come back. His talent was still

there, lying dormant within him. It would merely take time and effort to awaken it. He knew it.

Just as he knew that he would never make a fool of himself over a woman, ever again.

Gideon inhaled the mossy scent of the river, the faint fragrance of roses drifting on the air. Over the tops of the trees, he caught a glimpse of that intriguing tower he'd noticed earlier. He would have to ask Miss Hartsell about it.

Leaning back against the cushions, lulled by the soft breeze and the gentle sounds, he closed his eyes . . .

Gideon knew he was dreaming. He stood at a high window, watching the rising moon sift silver dust over a wooded hill. Waiting for something to happen. And at that exact moment when twilight gave way to night, she *stepped out of the shadows at the foot of the slope, misty as a wraith in her floating white gown. He realized then that he'd been waiting all his life.*

Waiting for her . . .

"I say, *wake up!*"

Gideon's eyes snapped open, and he blinked himself awake. The afternoon had faded while he dozed, and gray clouds billowed overhead.

Peregrine Hartsell peered down into his face intently. "I thought you were dead."

"You sound disappointed that I am not," Gideon replied wryly.

"I wasn't." The boy cocked his head. "But if you were, everything would go to Chloe, wouldn't it?"

Gideon stretched and stood up. "No, you young wretch. Not unless I made my own will and named her beneficiary."

Perry beamed. "*Will* you, sir? I say, that's capital of you!"

"Calm down, you obnoxious brat." His smile took the sting from his words. "I never said anything of the sort."

"It's the least you can do," the boy said, with an engaging

grin. "If it wasn't for you, Lacey's Folly would be hers. So it's only fair. Will you do it, sir?"

"Is that why you awakened me?" Gideon was getting seriously annoyed. "I'll have you know I was having a wonderful dream. Now it's gone."

"It's going to rain any minute, and that would have wakened you with a drenching."

He picked a ladybird off his sleeve and let it crawl over his hand, bright as a spot of crimson paint. "If you recall your dream, you should tell Chloe. She's very good at reading the meaning of them. If there is a meaning. But some dreams are just dreams, she says. Can you remember any of it?"

Gideon frowned up at the darkening sky. Trying to remember the dream was like trying to catch fog in a sieve. But there was something . . .

"A tower." He turned. There it was. "Just like that one."

Perry's face looked suddenly solemn. In the fuzzy gray light, every freckle stood out on his face. He started to say something, then thought better of it. "We'd best go inside before the clouds open. Oh, and Chloe says she needs you, sir. It's something important."

Gideon was surprised. No one had needed him in a long time. It was a rather pleasant feeling.

Before they reached the house, the clouds had scudded in, piling up like dark waves upon a shore. The wind freshened, bringing the deep, rich scent of the earth and the cool clean breath of rain.

As Gideon walked across the back terrace with the boy, someone lit a lantern inside. The warm glow fell through the tall panes, inviting them inside. Gideon stopped and looked up at Lacey's Folly, sturdy enough to weather any storm. Thinking of four centuries of Laceys growing up within its meandering walls. Imagining how it might have been to actually live here, surrounded by friends and family.

He felt a pang. It was a shame, a damned shame he'd have to sell it.

They entered through the glass doors to a cozy room where

the lantern now glowed brightly, joined by two others. Soft rain pattered at the windows. It seemed a scene of utter peace and tranquility, until Chloe spoke.

"Thank God you're here!"

Gideon was all concern. "What is wrong, Miss Hartsell?"

"It's the Lost Bride. She's been stolen!"

"*Who* has been stolen?"

"It's not a who, it's a what." She took up a small lamp and led him swiftly out of the room, explaining as she went. "A painting, connected with a Lacey family legend. Lenore Lacey vanished on her wedding night, a hundred years ago, and was never seen again. It's her portrait that is missing."

"Good Lord, who would take such a thing?"

"Certainly none of the servants. Nor can I imagine that Martin and Olivia would remove it from the wall. It has no value, except that of sentiment. I was looking through the other rooms, making sure that the Thornes hadn't taken anything, and when I got to the Bride's Chamber—it was gone."

"Vanished like the lost bride," Gideon said. "How romantic."

Chloe favored him with a look of disgust. "You wouldn't say that if you'd set eyes on the painting! She is the most exquisite creature! Like a princess from a fairy tale."

They entered the Old Hall, with Perry trailing silently behind, and went up the stairs to the Bride's Chamber. She unlocked the door, and he smelled polish and dust and attar of roses. As Gideon went inside, he felt a strange prickling over his skin.

"There's quite a strong draft in here."

"No," Chloe pointed out. "The draperies and bed hangings are not stirring."

Gideon looked around the room. She was right. But the sensation of cool air moving over his skin had created gooseflesh that was very real.

"An atmospheric place, as my godmother would say. She believes that certain places retain the impression of people who have lived there, or dramatic events that have transpired. Perhaps your lost bride was murdered.''

Light flared at the gap between the draperies, followed by an ominous roll of thunder. Chloe stared at Gideon. She set the lamp down on a table. ''Then you know the legend?''

''I know nothing about any portrait, or lost bride.''

Gideon noted the discarded bridal wreath upon the bed beneath its protecting glass dome. Then his gaze rose to the wall above the overmantel. A large, dark rectangle showed where the painting had hung. It added to the eerie feel of the room.

He wondered what Lady Albinia would make of it. She went to theosophist meetings, where they happily played at making tables tilt and waited for signs from Beyond the Veil, as she called it. One thing was for sure: if the thought of finding a husband for Chloe was not enough to lure Albinia away from her friends, hints of a haunted room and mysterious legend were sure to have her packed and on the road in a wink.

''Why do you think she was murdered?'' Chloe said anxiously, bringing his thoughts back to the missing portrait.

''People were not so civilized one hundred years ago. Inconvenient brides with large dowries often met bad ends. They fell down staircases, or wells, or wasted away with mysterious stomach pains caused by arsenic.''

Chloe was thoughtful. ''The pact between Lenore Dacre and Obadiah Lacey was an arranged marriage, to end a bloody feud, some say. Tobias said it was because of Obadiah's wealth. He was rich as Croesus. He was also elderly and cruel. And he was suspected of murdering his first wife in order to secure Lenore's hand.

''Lenore Dacre didn't want the marriage and fought against it vehemently. She had a lover, a handsome captain in the army, whom she wished to wed. Her father refused, and the marriage to Lacey went forth, despite the bride's tears and lamentations.''

''Tell him about the treasure,'' Perry urged. Chloe shot him a quick warning glance.

He shrugged. "Well, it might be that Martin took the portrait. It might hold clues to where the jewels are hidden."

"What treasure? Which jewels?" Gideon demanded.

Chloe gave in. "Obadiah Lacey's wedding gift to Lenore was a cask of fabulous jewels, which supposedly vanished the same night as his unwilling bride," she said dismissively. "I imagine he took it himself."

"Why would he marry her and murder her that same night?"

"She had a handsome young lover. One account says Obadiah killed her in a jealous rage. A second version claims she ran off with her lover before Obadiah found them out."

She went to the window and pulled back the draperies. The sharp summit of Pucca's Hill was illumined by a jagged spider web of light. It outlined the curve of her cheekbones, the elegant line of her throat, with pure silver.

"That is Pucca's Hill. It's said to be a fairy rath. People in the village claim that Lenore fell asleep there, on the fairy hill, waiting for her lover, who never came for her. She was taken inside the fairy rath and became the bride of the fairy king, and there she lives to this very day."

Gideon listened to her tale, but it was her face that fixed his attention. The contrast of her features as she stood there. Caught between the warm civilized lamplight and the cold blue, pagan splendor of the lightning, they were arresting. If only he could capture them on paper or canvas. She was like some elemental creature, half from the human world, half from the kingdom of fairy.

But she let the drapery drop, and the magic was gone. She was just Chloe Hartsell, the woman who stood between him and the settling of his debts. Another thunderclap shook the air.

"Well, there is no portrait here," Gideon said, looking behind the door and under the bed. "There's nothing to be done tonight."

She turned silently and went out to the staircase. Gideon followed. The room below smelled of damp stone and old wood, and he was grateful for the clean, lavender scent of his companion's hair. At the top of the landing, there was a curtain the same color as the stone. He hadn't noticed it before.

Chloe stopped and swept aside a worn velvet curtain to reveal the tiny Minstrel's Gallery, and the empty void of the old Great Hall below. "That is where the wedding supper took place. The men were quite drunk when Lenore vanished. No one saw her leave. Both sides cried treachery, and a bloody fight ensued. Half the guests were dead by morning."

Looking down into the shadows of the room, Gideon felt a tiny shiver. The shadows thickened and tried to take form. For a moment he could almost feel the rush of dark fear, hear the shouts of anger and betrayal, the clang of sword on sword. He blinked and stepped away from the gallery rail.

"You can feel it too," Chloe said softly.

He could almost have accused her of trying to frighten him. "Poppycock. It's just the gloomy weather that's put strange fancies in your head. He led the way down the stairs a little too quickly.

Neither spoke until they were back in the main section of the house, where Dawlish had lighted the lamps. "If this accursed place is haunted by evil deeds, why were you so set on inheriting Lacey's Folly? I would think you'd be glad to leave."

"You forget," she said simply. "I have nowhere else to go."

He looked at his surroundings. "At the moment, Miss Hartsell, neither do I."

She was silent for several minutes, and he could see that she was struggling with herself. Finally, she gave a little nod, as if she'd come to a decision.

"There is only one recourse then. We shall have to work together to find the treasure."

He eyed her as if she'd gone mad.

"Tobias said it was hidden somewhere in the house." She frowned. "Tobias was quite sure of it."

She looked up at him, her eyes aglow in the soft light.

Gideon was transfixed. "And you believed him?" he said quickly, to cover the moment.

"Oh, yes. He'd found a clue in the library, just before he had his last stroke. I am certain of it. He hinted broadly enough and was very excited. He wished to be alone, he said. But when he didn't come to dinner, I knew something was wrong. I found him gasping in his chair. That was the beginning of the end for him."

Tears shimmered in her eyes. Gideon offered his handkerchief. "I'm turning into a watering pot," she said. "Poor Tobias." She blew her nose, something no lady of Gideon's acquaintance would have done in front of him. He found her lack of pretense endearing.

"If we can find the treasure," she said, "it would solve both our problems. You could pay off your debts and still keep Lacey's Folly. And I could stay on and never have to take a husband at all."

She looked so serious, he was taken aback. Gideon tried to make a joke of it. "Miss Hartsell, I am beginning to suspect that your are one of those bluestockings who prefers a houseful of books and cats to a man. Why, you make marriage out to be a terrible thing."

Chloe lifted her head and looked him in the eye.

"It was, for Lenore Lacey."

She went out and left him standing in the empty drawing room.

FIVE

§ §

IT WAS NEAR MIDNIGHT WHEN GIDEON WENT UP TO BED to find his personal effects removed from his bedchamber. "What the devil!"

He rang the bell and Dawlish answered his call. "Your things have been placed in the master's bedchamber," he informed the new owner of Lacey's Folly.

"What? Who gave such an order. I am perfectly happy with this room."

Dawlish fixed him with a gimlet eye. "It is the way things are done here, sir. The master sleeps in the master's bedchamber."

Gideon didn't want to buck tradition. Upsetting the servants could make his life very uncomfortable indeed. "Very well, just show me where I may lay my weary head."

"Yes, Mr. Stone. If you will accompany me."

The butler led Gideon back along the corridor to the other wing and opened the double doors. The room beyond was beautifully proportioned, with carved paneling, a thick and colorful Chinese carpet, and a wonderful stone fireplace.

Gideon stepped inside a little gingerly. He really would have preferred not to spend his first night as master of Lacey's Folly in the same bed where the previous owner had breathed his last.

He felt a good deal better when he saw it. The tester bed was huge. It could have slept four across with ease. There were two steps leading up, and the heavy sapphire curtains could be drawn to make a cozy, private little room of it. It was a bed for deep sleeps on cold winter nights, a bed for making love. For making children. The thought startled him.

"When were my belongings moved?"

"Miss Hartsell directed the servants to do it while you were at supper."

"Thoughtful of her."

"Yes, Miss Hartsell thinks of everything."

Gideon was in no mood to hear Chloe's praises sung. "Thank you, Dawlish. You may go."

"Will you require any assistance in preparing for bed? I should be happy to wait upon you until such time as you can acquire a gentleman's gentleman."

"Devil take it, am I supposed to hire a damned valet, now? I have been dressing and undressing myself for years, Dawlish."

The butler tilted his head solemnly. "Things have changed, Mr. Stone. And we must all change with them."

"*Goodnight*, Dawlish!"

When the butler left, Gideon surveyed his new quarters with mixed emotions. It was a comfortable chamber, certainly, but at complete odds with the harum-scarum bachelor existence he'd led till now.

His set of silver-backed brushes with his monogram were laid out upon the bureau in military precision, his robe draped over the back of the wing-chair, and his slippers placed exactly in the center of a low footstool. He could not believe that he, Gideon Stanfield Stone, was now master here.

All well and good, he thought, *but I have no intention of setting down permanent roots in any one place. Least of all in a backwater manor like Lacey's Folly. With any luck, I shall marry off Miss Hartsell and be out of here in a winking.*

Stripping off his jacket, he intended to throw it over the nearest piece of furniture, as was his wont. Instead, he found himself arranging it neatly over the back of the chair beside the burlwood desk. It was as if he felt the spirit of Tobias Lacey watching over him.

A short time later Gideon climbed into the high bed, which was enormously comfortable, and prepared himself for a sleepless night. He wished his niggardly half brother could see him now. Walden would choke on his spleen.

Still, he was in a strange bed in a strange house. Even though it all belonged to him now, along with the disposition of the hand in marriage of one Miss Chloe Hartsell. He groaned aloud. There was far too much on his mind for sleep.

Gideon heard the clock chime three, but it was not the clock that had awakened him. He sat upright in the huge old bed where Tobias Lacey had died and listened. Someone was in the room with him. Tired and groggy as he was, he was sure of it.

"Who is there?"

No one answered. Then he realized the balcony windows were wide open, and the draperies were stirring in the cool night breeze. That was what he'd heard.

Feeling like a fool frightened by bogies, Gideon slipped into his robe and got up to close them. The view from the balcony was lovely. The temperature had dropped, and the world shimmered in moonlight.

To the left the distant river wound silver and black through the parkland, and to the right, blotting out the view of the village chimneys, was the dark rise of Pucca's Hill. It looked even more mysterious by night. Vaguely familiar, yet alien and un-English.

Taking in a deep breath, Gideon wondered how long it had been since he'd breathed clean, country air. He closed the doors, but left the curtains undrawn, and climbed back into bed. Just as he got into the bed, Gideon froze.

An old man stood smiling before the empty grate of the fireplace. Gideon could see him distinctly in the full moonlight. He wore a curious long brocade robe, like a Chinaman's tunic, and his round head was smooth as a gypsy's crystal ball.

Gideon threw back the covers. "Here, sir! What are you doing in my bedchamber at this hour?"

Forgetting how high the bed was, he launched himself off the mattress and went skidding to the floor. By the time he righted himself, the man was gone. Gideon checked, the door to his room was still locked. *How did he get in here, how did he get out—and more to the question, what was he doing in my bedchamber in the first place*?

Then he noticed the picture over the mantelpiece facing the bed. It hadn't been there at midnight. Gideon lit an oil lamp and went to examine it. It was a portrait of a woman. He held the lamp up higher and almost dropped it.

"Good God in Heaven!" The old man, the late hour, the day's events, all faded into oblivion.

This, he was sure, was the woman who haunted his dreams! Those wide-set sapphire eyes, that rippling silver-gilt hair! And that face, so angelic, so unearthly in its perfection, that he wondered if such a paragon had ever existed.

The artist who'd painted her had modest skills, yet the subject had transcended his lack: she was a woman to inspire a masterpiece.

He realized his hands were shaking. Gideon set the lamp down on a side table, then went around and lit all the lamps and candles in the room. The woman was even more beautiful now that he could see more clearly.

The classic nose, the soft mouth, the translucent skin, the delicate curve of cheek and throat, had his heart racing. She was the most beautiful creature he had ever seen. Perhaps the most beautiful woman who had ever walked God's green earth. Who was she?

Stepping closer, he noted the old-fashioned cut of her simple gown, the antique style of locket, and the simple gold twists with garnet beads at her earlobes. There were books, flowers, and various celestial globes in the background, but his eyes was drawn to a small brass plate on the bottom of the heavy gilt frame. He leaned in to read the single word engraved there, already knowing what he would find: *Lenore*.

His breath came out in a shudder. Lenore Lacey, the Lost Bride. *A woman dead these past hundred years.* It was like a blow to the heart. Gideon was filled with so deep a sorrow, so wild a yearning, it was sheer agony.

Lenore was delicate and lovely with the beauty of another time, almost of another world. There was fairy blood in the Lacey line, so Perry had told him. Looking at fair Lenore's portrait, with her silver hair and pearly skin, her obliquely slanted brows and oval eyes, Gideon could almost believe it. Here was a woman to inspire him.

His breath caught in his throat. If she existed today, she would be his model, his inspiration. If she were still alive, if he could see her in the flesh, his talent would come blazing back, kindled by her incredible beauty. Together they would create a sensation.

But she had been dust for a century, and he was filled with aching despair.

Lenore!

Chloe was busy early the next morning, seeing to the guests and making arrangements. The Thornes would be on her hands for another day or two and were keeping the servants hopping from morning till night.

She didn't see Gideon Stone, who had broken his fast early and was now closeted with Mr. Fortescue and the estate steward in the study. Martin and Olivia Thorne were sulking in the morning room, leaving Chloe with plenty of time to greet the next arrivals: her new companion, hired to give respectability to a house where a handsome young man was the new master, and the housekeeper who would take over most of Chloe's former duties. Chloe wasn't sure which she dreaded more.

First Mrs. Osler, the widowed sister of the village surgeon, was installed as Chloe's companion and chaperone. She was brown and weathered from being outdoors year round on her nature walks. Tall and thin and neat as wax, she had a bright smile, wiry brown hair, and an abstracted air.

She was also, she announced, "deaf as a post. You'll have to speak up, child." She put a hornlike device up to her ear. "Even with my ear trumpet, I'll be lucky to hear Gabriel's, come Judgement Day."

"I said that it is so good of you to come to us, and on such short notice!" Chloe shouted.

"No, no. A poultice will do no good, thank you. But I manage well, child, I manage well."

Mrs. Osler was pleased with the yellow bedchamber, which Chloe had prepared for her, and its small adjoining sitting room. She peered into the wardrobe and exclaimed over the view. "And all so spacious and cheerful. Much larger than Larkspur Cottage, I assure you."

After looking into the sitting room, she announced that she would settle in quite happily. "I am something of a poetess, you know, and I hope you will not mind if I retire to my room when the muse calls me."

"Not at all," Chloe said into the ear trumpet. "You must make yourself quite at home at Lacey's Folly. You have only to ask if you need anything."

"No, I'm not much for needlework. Never have been."

Chloe smiled and nodded and left her new chaperone with Agnes, distributing her belongings about the room. Agnes was in awe of Mrs. Osler, but the older woman soon put her at ease. Chloe thought that she and Mrs. Osler would also get along beautifully and was relieved that the older woman wouldn't be disturbed by Perry's scientific experiments. Some were extraordinarily loud—especially the ones that involved black powder or steam engines.

"I shall have to warn Mr. Stone about them," Chloe said aloud. Then she smiled wickedly.

Perhaps she'd let him find out for himself.

Mrs. Linley, the new housekeeper that Mr. Fortescue hired and sent down, arrived before noon. Chloe liked the woman at first sight. She was trim, nearing forty, with blond hair braided in a neat coronet, and her open manner and brisk air exuded efficiency and order.

But, oh! Chloe thought, *It is hard to give over the reins that I have held so long into a stranger's hands.*

The housekeeper sensed as much as they went over things together. "You need not fear that I will usurp your place here, Miss Hartsell. I understand my station. And Mr. Stone said you were to continue acting as the mistress here."

Chloe flushed with surprise. "That is very generous of him." *And of you.*

She didn't say it aloud, but her smile was understood. "I think we shall deal very well together. And you need not worry that I will interfere with your responsibilities. It is only," she added wistfully, "that it will take me a while to become used to it."

It was not as difficult, in some ways, as she'd anticipated: the following morning Chloe overslept for the first time in her life. She rose with the sun well up and started to ring for Agnes, then thought better of it, and rolled over on her pillow. With the new housekeeper in command, and the three village women hired earlier put on permanent duty, she had absolutely nothing to do. It was a very odd feeling. One that she might become used to far more quickly than she had imagined.

An hour later she awakened a second time to find her morning chocolate on the table, and Agnes smiling beside it. "You were sleeping like an angel," she said. "I didn't have the heart to rouse you, Miss Chloe." Her smile went sour. "Miss Thorne has been asking after those pearls she was promised. Wanted me to fetch them, she did, but I said I didn't know where you kept them."

"The sooner she has them, the sooner she'll leave. I'll see to it after breakfast, straight away."

After dressing in an ivory gown with lavender ribbons, Chloe hurried down to where Olivia and Martin Thorne sat in silence over the remains of their meal. They looked up when she entered.

"We will be setting out for Greater Barnstable shortly," Martin informed her.

"As soon as I have my pearls!" Olivia snapped.

He ignored his sister and dabbed at his loose lips with the damask napkin. "While I do not like to leave an unmarried woman alone with a man to whom she is not related, urgent business calls me home."

"I am not exactly alone, Mr. Thorne." Chloe slipped into a chair. "I have Mrs Osler and Perry, and a houseful of servants. My virtue is in no danger."

Olivia sat up straighter. "I, for one, would rather be dead than to sleep under the same roof as an *artist*!"

Chloe sugared her coffee. "I am sorry to hear you say so, Miss Thorne, for you have already spent two nights doing exactly that."

The other woman sent her a venomous glance. "If you had not poisoned Tobias's mind against us, this never would have happened."

"I did nothing of the kind," Chloe replied. *You did it all yourself.*

Martin gave a gusty sigh. "Lacey's Folly, in the hands of a complete stranger. It is not right."

"No, Mr. Thorne. But it is fact. The sooner we set our minds to it, the better."

Olivia set down her fork. "I have divined your evil scheme, Miss Hartsell. You have no intention of ever leaving Lacey's Folly." Her voice took on a horrid purr.

"So very *clever* of you to have hired a deaf woman for a companion. You mean to ingratiate yourself with Mr. Stone, do you not?" She leaned forward. "How far are you willing to go to accommodate him?"

"How dare you!" Chloe shook with outrage, spilling her coffee all over the breakfast table. "You are a wicked-minded, vicious woman! I have put up with your slights and innuendos for years, but thank God I will have to listen to you no longer. I shall be glad to see the back of you."

"Then you will see it now. Come, Martin!"

She stalked out of the room. Her brother paused, then rose to follow. "You must not mind my sister. She is overwrought." He lowered his voice. "I always imagined the three of us living here together at Lacey's Folly," he told Chloe. "Your position here would have been secure. We should have been so . . . cozy."

Chloe didn't need supernatural powers to understand his meaning. Martin's washed-out eyes ran over her figure with insulting familiarity. She glanced around for Dawlish, but the butler had left the room.

"If you do not find a congenial husband, you need not despair, my dear Miss Hartsell. You may always come to me for help. I could set you up in a little place of your own, where I could slip away to visit you. My sister need not know . . ."

It took great effort to maintain control. Chloe picked up the meat fork. Her voice shivered with ice. "*Good-bye*, Mr. Thorne. We shall *not* meet again."

Martin was about to reply, thought better of it after seeing the way she was gripping the long-tined meat fork, and took himself off.

There was a commotion in the hall, baggage thumping down the stairs, but Chloe ignored it. She was still sitting there, white-faced, when she heard a carriage drive away some time later.

Dawlish came in with a look of grim satisfaction. "They are gone."

"Thank God for that." Chloe stopped pushing around the cold eggs and ham on her plate. "Am I the last one down?"

"Yes, Miss Chloe. Master Peregrine has gone out with Mrs. Osler to show her the grounds, and Mr. Stone is in the library—*measuring*!"

"Good Heavens! Measuring what? You make it sound so ominous."

"We're to remove all the furniture and hangings from one side of the room, he says."

"Ridiculous!" Chloe started to rise, frowned, and sat down

abruptly. "Well, it is his house now. And it has not been used much of late."

"No, but it *could* be." Dawlish unbent even more. "You must do something, Miss Chloe, if you'll pardon me. But Mrs. Norwich and Cook are both quite upset. The smell of turpentine will permeate the drawing room and dining room, which *are* used, if Mr. Stone sets up in the library."

Light dawned. "He's making his studio there, is he?"

A sigh escaped Chloe. She couldn't have the servants declaring war on Mr. Stone or life at Lacey's Folly would be unbearable.

"Mr. Stone's wishes must be accommodated, Dawlish. You know that Mr. Lacey would have wanted it so."

"Yes, Miss Chloe."

He said it so haughtily that she had to laugh. "Don't worry. We must think of some way to accommodate him that suits us, as well. And I have an idea."

Chloe finished her breakfast and went to the library. Gideon had one side of the room half emptied. He was bursting with energy as he cleared out the last table from the ceiling-high bowed window. His hair was rumpled, and she noticed he'd torn a button from his shirt and scraped his knuckles. She stepped aside and let him by.

He'd rolled up his shirtsleeves and was carrying the heavy table to the far side of the room with ease. Chloe was impressed. He hadn't looked that strong or that muscular with his coat on.

"You are in a great hurry to make changes, Mr. Stone."

He flushed. "Only here, I promise you. I know better than to try and overset the running of a household to which I am a stranger."

Gideon set the side table down in a window embrasure, where it fitted perfectly and improved the look of the hall as well. He had a good eye, she had to admit. "I see you haven't changed the curtains yet."

He looked up, amused at her joke. "No, but now that the

Thornes have been gotten rid of, it is among the first things on my list.''

His brows drew together, and his face became serious. She looked so very vulnerable this morning. ''Miss Hartsell, I understand there was some unpleasantness this morning. If Martin Thorne ever comes within a hundred feet of you again, my girl, you have only to tell me. I'll thrash him from here to Dover and back!''

Chloe colored but didn't answer. So, he'd heard of Martin's outrageous proposition. She would have a word with Dawlish later!

Gideon saw her discomfort and didn't press the issue. ''I am anxious to get to work,'' he said, rolling down his sleeves. ''Mr. Fortescue has agreed to have my gear sent down to me as soon as may be.''

Then, if he won the commission from Lord Pulham, he would be ready to attack it with his former vigor and passion. ''The curtains and draperies *will* have to come down, of course, to let more light in. That should please you, Miss Hartsell.''

He started toward them as if he meant to tear them down from the wall there and then. Chloe forestalled him. ''Wait, if you please. I believe there is a place that will suit your needs far better than this. I have come to give you a tour of the house as we agreed last evening. You can see for yourself.''

''Very well.'' He'd moved all he could for now. ''I suppose this is as good a time as any. I have just a few more things to sort through here. And there is something addressed to you.''

He went to the desk, opened a drawer, and began rifling through a small stack of papers. Chloe had never seen anyone but Tobias do that. It gave her a start. As he leaned forward, sunlight from the open curtains illumined the wide set of his shoulders, tipped his hair with gold. Once again she was aware of her strong attraction to him.

It is only natural curiosity, she told herself. *How can I not find him interesting, when he is so handsome? So kind?* So very unlike Tobias and Dawlish, Henry and Rendulph and Perry, the only members of the opposite sex with whom she spoke on a regular basis.

Gideon pulled out an envelope and held it out to her. "This was among Mr. Lacey's papers. It is addressed to you."

Chloe took the envelope and stared at it numbly. "Thank you."

She turned away and went to the window, staring out, but blind to the rioting border of flowers. *Why did you do it, Tobias?*

Perhaps this would provide some answers. Looking down, she saw that she'd crumpled the envelope in her hand. After smoothing it out on her lap, she flicked the wax seal off with a fingernail and opened it.

My Dear Chloe,

By now I am dead, and you are left wondering what it is all about. I must tell you that I did not make the decision lightly. If I have wronged you, you must know that what I did was to right a far graver wrong. I had no other choice.

You will come about, child. I have faith in you. And you must keep faith, as well. I have lived long and learned that too often the humblest gifts are worth more than gold. Never doubt it. When you feel most alone, you must look to the Heavenly sphere for guidance in all that you seek. Mark these words of mine: faith and love are the true treasures in life. They may be misplaced, but they must not be forgotten. Mark these words well.

I wish you well in the future, dear girl, and know that you will raise young Peregrine to enjoy the manners and education of a gentleman.

Most sincerely,
Tobias Lacey

Chloe stared at his signature. How could she have anything to do with raising Perry now? He would be sent off to school soon and would likely have to spend all his summers there as a boarder. Oh! How lonely he would be, how restricted after the freedom of Lacey's Folly, and the woods, fields, and meadows he loved to explore.

Poor Perry. She was not the only one to be sent into exile from this house that had sheltered them so long. Thank God he didn't realize yet the changes Tobias's death had made— and would continue to make—in his young life.

Chloe wandered over to the window and looked out. Mr. Stone had promised to find her a good husband. If he found a veritable Prince Charming, it wouldn't make up for the loss of Lacey's Folly to her. She loved the house and grounds, the strange little alcoves and quaint stairways; the sense of generations growing up, growing old within its walls; the way the views changed with the seasons; and most of all, the gardens, which were her particular charge and joy.

Her heart ached. She had looked forward to spending the rest of her days here, with Peregrine coming home on school holidays, perhaps someday bringing his wife here. She had planned to leave it all to him one day.

On the heels of her thoughts, Peregrine went racing by with the beagle pup in hot pursuit. He stopped to unsnag his shirt-tails from a low-hanging branch. Oh, dear! She hoped he hadn't torn another shirt. They were already much mended.

He ran past the knotted herb garden and out through the low wooden gate in the wall. *What on earth is he up to?* she wondered. *And what has he done with Mrs. Osler?* Perhaps the pergola had inspired her, and she was communing with her muse.

Chloe stood with her hand on the window frame, waiting for him to come back. Instead, she saw him appear at the top of a rise, a few minutes later, carrying a shovel. *Treasure hunting again,* she smiled. Perry was certain he was the one to find the jewels that Lenore Lacey was said to have left behind. *Perhaps he really will find it and get us all out of this terrible coil.*

Perry had dreamed that he'd found it, she recalled. Tobias had always put much store in dreams.

"Come along, Newton. We have work to do."

The beagle pup barked once and ran beneath the trunk as Perry climbed over it. The dark, wooded slopes of Pucca's Hill rose up above them, blotting out a sky of cream-puff clouds.

His thoughts were sober. It was bad enough that he had to be sent away to school one day, but he could not bear to see Chloe leave the house she loved so well. He had tried and tried to find the treasure, so that Gideon Stone wouldn't have to sell the estate, and the three of them could stay on at Lacey's Folly together. He was sure Mr. Stone wouldn't mind: he was jolly good fun.

Unfortunately for Perry's hopes, he had thus far failed at every turn.

He had an idea, though. It was really quite simple, and he wondered that it hadn't occurred to Tobias himself. If he couldn't find the treasure itself, why there was another way. He would have to find Lost Lenore and set her free of the fairy spell that bound her. Surely she would be so grateful, she'd tell him where she'd hidden the treasure and share it with them.

Reinforced by Tobias and Henry, the old gardener, Perry had a profound belief in the truth of the legend—and in his ability to find the Lost Bride. This was different from pretending to rescue damsels in distress or playing St. George and the dragon. Those were only legends, but the Lost Bride was real. Tobias had told him so.

The beagle pup took off through the underbrush, digging at a burrow in the ground. "Newton, heel!" Perry called. The dog whined its disappointment, but came back.

The boy marked a tree with his pocketknife, then tried to sight up the hill with a small spyglass. He'd been studying old surveying books in the library and thought he understood a way to pinpoint just where Tobias said he had seen the light from the fairy rath on certain nights. Perry was almost sure he had seen it himself, last year at Lammas. By sighting along a line from different points at Lacey's Folly and plotting them on paper, he was fairly sure he knew where the door into the hill would be.

Chloe'd be mad as fire when she learned he'd disobeyed her and gone exploring on Pucca's Hill. *But she won't stay angry long, once she realizes I have found the treasure!* He started up the hill, but the dog barked and ran in circles and barked again. He was not eager to plunge into the heavier woods ahead.

"We have to go up the hill," the boy told him. The dog whined more loudly and lay down on the ground. "We *have* to go. That's where it happened."

Coaxing didn't work. Either Newton knew Perry had promised not to go up Pucca's Hill, or there was something about the dark wooded slope ahead that bothered him. It bothered Perry, too, but after a few minutes, he gave up and set out alone.

It was hard going through the thick brush and chill beneath the emerald weaving of thick branches. He wished he'd worn a jacket.

The hill was steep and strewn with rocky outcrops and ditches. It took most of an hour to reach the spot he'd fixed upon. It didn't look particularly special. An almost bare circle beneath the high arching branches, black against the thick leaves and sky. The fairy folk danced in the circles, and that was why the wild grasses couldn't grow. That was what Tobias had said. The "Old Ones," he'd called them, or the "Gentlefolk."

Perry had read all the books he could find on the fairies and taken steps to protect himself. Wearing a sprig of St. John's wort, a silver cross and iron ring for protection against fairy spells, he pushed aside the weeds and tall grass and made his way to the barren spot. It didn't look any different or feel any different from any other open spot he'd tramped through on Pucca's Hill.

But it's awfully still here, the boy thought suddenly.

Not a groan of tree limb or rustle of branches stirred the silence. No squirrels or woodland creatures scurried about on the ground or in the green canopy overhead. It unnerved him a little, and Perry wished that Newton had come with him. But he had a mission to complete.

His stomach rumbled. Pulling a packet of ham and cheese from his pocket, he looked for a place to sit and rest while he ate. There were outcrops of rock here and there, but the one dead ahead was a thin straight ledge of stone, almost like a doorstep. He climbed toward it. It was covered with three inches of dead leaves. As he brushed them off, he felt a sudden tingle shoot up his arm. It was like the time he'd been playing with the tinderbox and caught a spark.

Perry knelt and looked closer. A series of lines were carved into the stone. Worn by time and dripping water, ogham runes were still clearly visible. He wished he'd brought something with which to make a rubbing. There was a book that told of how to read them.

It didn't really matter. He knew it in his bones: this was the site of the door into the hill. He was as sure of it as he could be. Perry put his face close to the ledge, holding the iron he wore for protection more tightly. No light shone beneath the stone. But that could be part of the spell.

If only Tobias had not fallen ill so suddenly. He sighed. Tobias had discovered something and had been dropping hints all day. He'd promised to tell Perry everything but had been stricken with a fit of apoplexy only a little later that afternoon. And now he was dead. Perry fought to keep his mouth from trembling. Tobias had told him not to cry after he had passed on.

"It is very hard, Tobias," he whispered. "I hope I have done everything the way you would have wanted me to do." Wiping his eyes with the back of his hand, he sat down and pulled a piece of cheese and a hunk of bread wrapped in a handkerchief from his pocket.

He ate his fill and scattered a few crumbs for the forest folk. Stuffed with food and legends, he leaned back against the hill. The ground seemed unnaturally cold, and he sat up straight. This was a special place, Tobias had told him, where the edges of the real world merged with the invisible world. A doorway where the Celtic gods and fairy folk came out of a night to walk the land that they had once ruled.

Only three more Mondays, and it would be a hundred years since the Lost Bride had vanished into the fairy hill. That's what Tobias had told him. One hundred years to the day. And the door into the hill would open.

Perry wiped his mouth on his sleeve. If he did everything just right, Lenore Lacey could break free of the fairy glamour cast over her and be set free.

A bright-eyed bird flapped onto a branch, startling him. A breeze had sprung up, setting the leaves to whisper among themselves. Jumping up from his stony perch, Perry thrust the rest of his uneaten cheese in his pocket. He was about to run off to join Newton when he noticed something gleaming in the dirt at his feet. The light coming from the fairy door!

Kneeling down, he pulled out his pocketknife and scraped it under the ledge trying to see in the gap. There was none. Just a small bit of metal that had reflected a stray ray of sunlight, burning through the thick leaves above.

Perry pulled it out and cupped it in his hand. It was an earring, dainty and elegant, but dirty and slightly worse for wear. He rubbed it on his shirt. It was a small loop of twisted gold, with two gold beads flanking a slightly larger garnet.

His heart banged against his ribs like a water hammer. He knew who the earring belonged to—Lost Lenore. Hadn't he seen her wearing it hundreds of times, in the miniature Tobias kept in his bedchamber?

"Never give up, Lenore Lacey," he whispered fiercely. "I will be back at Ludsagnadh. I will set you free!"

The leaves shook and whispered like malevolent spirits, and Perry got the wind up. He took off downhill as fast as his legs could carry him. The bird watched him go, then opened its beak and rasped out a sound like a burst of harsh laughter.

Since Gideon had a few more papers to sort through, Chloe selected a small volume from one of the shelves and made herself comfortable in an armchair. He finished his task and looked up, surprised to find her there. He'd forgotten her presence for a moment. What a quiet girl she was.

She was framed by the bay window. He was intrigued by the way her hair had come loose around her face, the wild gypsy curls a lustrous contrast to the orderly pattern and texture of the brocade covering the high-backed chair. Her smooth curve of throat, the clean sculpted line of cheek and chin—stubborn little chin, that—added another dimension.

Chloe was suddenly aware that he was staring at her. She set the book down.

Gideon called to her. "Miss Hartsell, don't move, I beg of you!"

She froze instantly. "Is it a spider?" She was violently repulsed by them.

"No! Nothing. . . . Just . . . please, do not move until I give you leave."

She couldn't see what he was doing but suddenly heard the scratch of pen on paper. He was drawing her, she was sure of it. "I have not agreed to pose for you, Mr. Stone."

"Just a quick sketch. A little gift, if you will. My way of thanking you for all the trouble you have gone to to make me comfortable at Lacey's Folly."

She felt self-conscious. "Really, Mr. Stone, there is no need . . ."

"Don't move!" Gideon commanded. "I am losing the light!"

His tone so shocked her that she didn't move a muscle. Not because he'd been abrupt or loud, but because he'd sounded so passionate about it. So desperate.

Time passed and the room grew darker as the sun moved

past the end of the house. "Hold still," he said, as if sensing her restlessness.

"How much longer? Really, this is absurd. And I have a terrible crick in my neck!" Chloe protested.

She reached up to rub her neck, and Gideon stabbed the pen back into the standish in disgust. The drawing on the sketchpad was nothing compared to what he saw in his mind's eye. It was a good likeness of her, but it was not art.

"It's no use. It won't do."

The long windows behind the desk were open to the garden, and Perry came bounding in through one of them as Gideon was about to tear the sheet in half. He stopped in his tracks. "I say, that's Chloe!"

He ran to Gideon's side and took hold of the drawing. Chloe joined them. She had to bite her lip when she saw Gideon's disheveled appearance. His hair was tousled and he had an ink smear alongside his jaw. His shirtfront looked as if he'd been spattered by a rain of pitch.

Then she saw the sketch. It was a full-length, three-quarters view. Herself, yet not exactly. "Why, Mr. Stone, you are indeed an artist!"

Gideon took the sheet back from Perry and was about to rip it in two. "Please don't!" she begged. Her hand reached out. "It's quite good. Remember, you said it was mine. A gift."

He stopped. Not only was there surprise in her voice, there was awe. He looked down at the drawing again.

"I will do you a better one some other time."

She touched his sleeve. "Please."

"Oh, very well. But it should be far better."

Chloe took the sketch and examined it with a small frown between her brows. "Well, perhaps the face seems off a little. I can't quite put my finger on it."

Gideon was instantly nettled. What did she know about art? Impudent girl! *He* could criticize it because it was *his* creation.

"That is because no one sees themselves correctly when they look into a mirror," he said curtly. "Everything is turned around."

"It looks just like you, Chlo," Perry said. "Even the way the corner of your mouth turns up, when you're smiling to yourself."

She scrutinized her image. Mr. Stone had captured the play of light and shadow on her skirts and the draperies, and certainly that was the parlor with its long window and the table beside it. But—was her neck that long? Were her cheekbones that high? Her profile so elegant?

She looked up at Gideon, her eyes like diamonds.

"May I have it?"

"Yes. Yes, of course." He relinquished the drawing.

Perry listened in eagerly. "Will you draw me, too?"

"Yes, if you'll stay still for half a minute, you young rapscallion."

Perry immediately folded his hands and adopted a choirboy expression of innocence.

Gideon grinned and grabbed his sketchpad. "That's it. Look very solemn, as if you are praying, and lift your eyes to heaven. Excellent. Now extend your folded hands a bit. Yes, yes, you've got it. And raise your right foot slightly in back and hold it up, as if you are flying. Good. Now don't move an inch. Stay just as you are until I give you leave."

The pen whisked across the paper, making soft little sounds while Perry tried not to squirm. It was harder than he'd expected to stand so still and not even wriggle. Especially when his nose began itching, the very second Gideon commanded him not to move an inch. He wanted to twitch it desperately.

Chloe watched over Gideon's shoulder, amazed at the cleverness of those quick, sure hands. Strong hands, she thought, and was suddenly conscious of how close she stood to him. She moved a little bit away.

As the drawing formed, she tried not to laugh. "Why are you having him stand in that position?" she asked in low tones.

"To see if it's humanly possible for the boy not to be jigging up and down like a mechanical toy," Gideon murmured.

Perry heard them whispering. "Are you finished? Does it look like me?" he asked anxiously.

"Judge for yourself." Gideon sanded the sheet and held it up.

The boy examined the simple line drawing. Instead of the angelic pose he'd maintained, Gideon had sketched him hanging upside down from a tree limb, covered in fur and complete with monkey's ears, wide grin, and long, curling tail.

"Capital!" Perry exclaimed, grinning from ear to ear. "It looks exactly like me."

Chloe led Gideon up the stairs and turned left at the first landing. They passed Mrs. Osler on the way. "Have you decided to accompany us while I show the rest of the house to Mr. Stone?" Chloe asked.

"Oh, my dear, I've no time for scones now. The walk through your lovely garden has inspired me with rapture." She held up a notebook. "Sixteens stanzas already!" she thrilled, hurrying off to her sitting room.

Gideon watched her go. "I'm afraid you've made a poor choice of companion. Mrs. Osler looks to provide little company for you."

"Indeed?" Chloe smiled. "I find her *perfect* in every way."

That reminded Gideon of his strange waking-dream last night, and the portrait in his room. Lost Lenore.

He had dreamed of her again. In dreams, he could never quite make out her face, but now that he had seen it, he would never forget it.

He should tell Chloe that the portrait had been found. No, surely Dawlish would. For some reason he was reluctant to mention it to her. He felt more than a little foolish about his obsession with the painting of Lenore Lacey. It was his secret for now—if such a thing were possible in a house full of servants and guests.

Not to mention one small boy, who'd set off a rocket outside his balcony window at the crack of dawn! His brows drew together. He'd have to speak to young Master Peregrine Hartsell about that later. Incorrigible little demon!

The corridor meandered, then widened into an arch that broke through to an older wing of the house. Mrs. Linley's influence, and the addition of three housemaids, was already showing results. The paneling gleamed and the brass trim shone as it hadn't in years.

"I should show you the miniature of Lenore in the drawing room," Chloe said.

"I have seen it," Gideon said slowly. "Dawlish pointed it out to me. I have never seen such a face. Incredible, is it not?"

He'd had to tear himself away from it. Just as this morning he had to force himself to get out of bed and stop staring at the painting in his room. *Egad*, he wondered, half amused and half appalled. *Am I falling in love with the face of a woman dead and gone this century past?*

Chloe felt a pang of envy. No man would ever describe her in those terms. "We'll start with the gallery," she said, as if he hadn't spoken. "It will help you understand the history of the house if you have some faces to put to the names I'll be rattling off."

The gallery was a long chamber across the front of the old section, where generations of the family had taken their exercise on bitter winter days. A wall of windows spilled sun across the warm, honey-colored paneling on the opposite side. It was filled with all manner of paintings: generations of Laceys long gone were interspersed with mediocre English landscapes by artists who had since fallen out of fashion.

They went past an insipid rendering of Windsor Castle and an uninspired view of the Scottish Highlands before she stopped. A young man in gold brocade, with powdered hair pulled back in a queue, looked back at them from an ornate frame, His dreamy eyes were at odds with an eager, quizzical expression.

"Your benefactor," she announced. "The late master of Lacey's Folly."

Gideon regarded the portrait gravely. "So this is the man to whom I owe my good fortune."

And to whom I owe my lack of fortune, Chloe wanted to say.

She bit her tongue and went on. "And here is his great-grandfather, Obadiah Lacey."

While the painting was not particularly good, the artist had captured a certain ruthlessness in the stern visage. "He looks to be a villainous fellow. A veritable old pirate."

"Yes, he makes me shudder."

"Are there any here of Lenore Lacey?" he asked, as casually as possible. Chloe tilted her head. "I see the legend has caught your fancy."

More than the legend, he thought. *It is the woman behind it who intrigues me.*

"No," she replied quickly. "Only the one from the Bride's Chamber and the little miniature in the drawing room."

Mr. Stone seemed obsessed with the Lost Bride. She hoped he wouldn't get as bad as Tobias had become, totally absorbed in investigating the stories of Lenore Lacey's life and disappearance.

Chloe hurried him past some dreadful ancestral portraits, a few mediocre landscapes, and headed down to the far end. "These will be more to your liking."

Gideon was amazed. "Indeed they are!" There were several surprisingly good allegorical paintings in the Renaissance style. Anthony and Cleopatra, Bacchus and Ariadne, Adam and Eve. Aeneas and Dido.

He examined them closely. "Minor works of Correggio, Tintoretto, and the school of Veronese." And all with a similar theme of love and seduction.

"They were part of a bride's dower." Chloe hesitated. "There is one more."

She reached up to open the curtain at the far end of the gallery. Gideon had thought it masked a window. Instead it held an alcove, a wooden chair, and a large painting, done by a master's hand. Even in the dimness he could tell that.

"Mr. Lacey believed it to be an unknown Titian," Chloe said, pulling the curtain fully open.

Gideon stared in awe. "Indeed! Is that why it is closed off by itself?"

Chloe turned a fine shade of rose. "No, to spare the servants' blushes. They refused to come in here and clean with such a 'heathenish' painting hanging in full view, so Tobias told me. He said that his mother was not fond of it, either."

Gideon moved in closer to examine the painting. He could see why the simple country servants might find it disturbing: it was a masterpiece. Breathtakingly beautiful. Overwhelmingly sensual.

Venus, goddess of love, and Mars, god of war, captured in the very midst of their illicit passion. It was so real it seemed shocking. Gideon's own senses were stirred. He felt like a voyeur.

The scene drew him in. Impressions, sensations inundated him. A wooded glade, rich with light and shadow, deep with erotic mystery. He could almost smell the leafy greenness of it. A clear mountain stream, so liquidly rendered, it seemed it should flow right off the canvas and pool on the floor below.

Filmy white robes tossed in a heap on the near side of a mossy riverbank. The war god's burnished armor and sword on the opposite side. And in the very center of such dark lushness, haloed by a shaft of light, were the two lovers: golden Venus, her gleaming ivory body stretched back on a rock in the midst of the river. Dark Mars, with strong, naked legs braced against the rush of the waters. His scarred, muscular torso was arched over hers, their bodies already joined in love's most intimate embrace, caught in that moment of shattering rapture.

And when his eyes adjusted, Gideon saw that the forest around them was alive with the suggestion, the barest hint of an audience of nymphs and satyrs; yet if he looked too long they faded back into the shape of trees and leaves.

Gideon felt his heart pound, his breath come fast, and it was not merely the excitement of an artist worshipping at the altar of a master. The painting had the power of all great art to stir the human senses.

His were certainly roused.

He was suddenly aware of Chloe standing so close that he

could smell her hair. Like wild roses. Oh, God! Why didn't she go away! He couldn't look at her.

Chloe couldn't move an inch. She could hardly believe her eyes. It had been years since she'd seen the painting. So long ago that all she remembered was averting her eyes and turning away in embarrassment at all those naked limbs. Now it commanded her full attention.

Like Gideon, she was struck by the same elemental force of nature. There was an ache in the pit of her stomach and her breasts felt heavy. She knew she should blush and turn her face away and could not. All she could do was stare and try not to be overcome by the heat that rushed through her blood, the yearning to be swept up in such a fever of passion that nothing else mattered.

She was aware of Gideon, standing so close that she could hear his quickened breathing. They were mesmerized, ensnared in the artist's sensual net. Why, oh why, hadn't she sent him here alone?

Footsteps came pounding in behind them and they both jumped. "Chloe? Where are you?"

"Perry!" Chloe exclaimed, and fumbled to shut the curtains, colliding with Gideon who was trying to do the same thing. They stumbled against one another and might have fallen, if he hadn't caught her in his arms.

For just a moment their eyes locked, and they were caught once more under the powerful spell of the painting. A strong current passed between them, leaving Chloe feeling an ache in the area of her heart, and Gideon one in his loins. Then the boy burst in on them, with the curtains only half closed.

Perry stood with his arms akimbo, eyeing the naked figures. "Chloe, should you be looking at those paintings? I don't think it's at all the thing. Mr. Stone, you really shouldn't have brought her here."

"I didn't bring her here, you young scamp! Now what is it you want?"

"There's a messenger come for you from London. From Lord Pulham, Dawlish said."

"Good Lord!" Gideon started out of the gallery. "Miss Hartsell, we'll have to continue the tour later."

Chloe nodded, profoundly relieved.

After cutting some more roses and lilies, Chloe went into the stillroom to arrange them in vases. It was a task she always loved, but one for which she had frequently lacked the time. Now she could have decorated the tables and overmantels of Lacey's Folly from one end to the other and still had time to twiddle her thumbs. She would have to find something else to fill her days.

Gideon burst into the room. "There you are! I have been searching high and low for you this past hour!"

Her cheeks grew ruddy. "I wasn't aware that I was to give you my daily intinerary, Mr. Stone. I shall make a note of it for future reference. Would you, perhaps, prefer it in writing?"

"Sarcasm suits you ill, Miss Hartsell." He struggled with the urge to make a cutting put-down. After all, he needed to ask a favor of her. "I have received some news from town."

She noticed the thick sheet of vellum in his hand, and the ducal crest upon it. Chloe became aware of such tension and excitement in him that he could scarcely contain it. Whatever it was affected him profoundly. She went on with arranging the heady blooms.

Light fell through the thick old glass in brilliant ripples. Gideon noticed the pleasing curve of her arm in her short-sleeved gray frock. How fair and rosy her skin was against the scarlet and pink and golden-yellow blossoms. *What a charming picture it would make.* But that wasn't why he'd come looking for her.

She was impatient with his staring at her. "Well, sir? Is it good news, or bad?"

"Good, I think. Perhaps even excellent. The Duke of Pulham is adding a new ballroom to his county seat. He intends to commission eight life-sized allegorical paintings to decorate his walls. His secretary writes that I have been recommended to him for consideration."

"And he has selected you?"

"Nothing so definite." Gideon folded the letter and tucked it inside his coat. "The earl has empowered his secretary to commission each of us to do one full-sized life painting, and colored sketches of three more for the proposed series. He will choose the artist based on these."

If he could win the commission to complete the project, his reputation—nay, his very fortune, would be made. He frowned down at the letter. The inked lines faded away. He saw a fair face with wide blue eyes and silvery, moonlight hair. "If only I had a beauty like Lenore Lacey to inspire me!" he said without thinking.

Chloe felt as is she'd been slapped. She reached for a rose stem and felt a thorn go deep into the cushion of her thumb. She gave a little squeak and jumped. Gideon didn't even notice. He was too absorbed in his plans.

He had no acquaintance in the countryside, and he doubted the servants would take to his having some artist's model, likely no better than she should be, come down from London. He needed someone nearby. Someone readily available during the hours of good light and . . .

Looking up, he saw Chloe more clearly this time. Her figure was good, her face not unpleasing, and her hair was glorious red-gold in the sunlight. She would certainly do in a pinch. He favored her with a winning smile.

"All I need are a place with good light where I may set up my things and a model to pose for me. You have promised me the one, Miss Hartsell. Will you provide me with the second? Will you sit for a portrait?"

"I? Pose for you?" When he surveyed her with that white smile, that intense look, she felt suddenly breathless. She was already far too fond of his company. Being thrown together with him for long hours would surely make it even worse. *Danger. Danger there*! her heart warned.

"I am sorry, Mr. Stone, but duty compels me to decline." Her lips curved at the corners. "I have other matters of the first importance and can spare no time to pose for you."

His temper flared. "You are an impertinent chit! I have hired a housekeeper to relieve you of that responsibility, and there are three new maids in the house. Just what duty could you possibly have that would interfere with posing for me?"

She gave him an impudent smile. "Why, that of finding a husband, sir."

Gideon ground his teeth. "It will not be soon enough for me," he said.

"Nor for me!"

Chloe turned her back to him and began snipping the stems with unnecessary violence. Gideon muttered an oath, turned on his heel and left her to her task.

Although Gideon requested her presence to dine with him, Chloe pleaded a headache and took a tray in her room. She did not want to think of Gideon Stone, she did not want to pose for him, and she did not—*not*!—want a husband.

What she wanted was a good cry, followed by a good night's sleep. The first came readily enough, the second was more elusive. The episode in the gallery had awakened thoughts and emotions she was sure she had buried long ago.

She had started life out as an emotional, passionate child. Then circumstances had changed and forced her to change with them. She had locked that undisciplined child away and trained herself to be cheerful, brisk, and efficient.

The chief vestal virgin of Lacey's Folly, keeping the hearth and the home intact, she mocked herself. Then Gideon Stone had come, and she realized that the passionate child had grown up to be a passionate woman, in every meaning of the word.

Unable to sleep, she reached for a book and found the one she'd removed from the library earlier: an illustrated version of Ovid's Metamorphosis, which left very little to the imagination. Lusty gods and goddesses romped through the detailed engravings in a manner that would have had Olivia Thorne in a dead faint.

I shall have to keep these books in the locked case until Perry is a little older, she thought.

And then remembered that the books were not hers, nor was the decision of how and where to keep them. That belonged to Mr. Stone. She sighed. It was hard to relinquish her old responsibilities, and harder still to let go of her dreams.

Setting the book aside, she blew out the candle and watched moonlit patterns from the open window creep across the wall. After a while she kicked the sheet away. It was far too hot and her mind too agitated, for sleep.

Mr. Stone was intent on marrying her off as soon as possible. To be fair, it was in her own best interests as well. Life was cruel to impoverished spinsters. She only hoped she could find a kindly husband, not too old. One with children of his own, perhaps, who would not be averse to letting Perry spend the summer months and holidays with them.

Oh, if she only had beauty and charm, how different it might be! Then she might pick and choose among a selection of suitors. But the plain oval mirror on the wall opposite reflected her face and told her a hard truth.

It was not the only one she had to face. Since reaching adulthood she had spent her life with a young boy and an old man. A handsome and virile young artist as master of Lacey's Folly was a complication she hadn't anticipated. She had never spent time in the company of a sophisticated rake—and Gideon Stone was definitely a rake—with a ready wit and a manner honed by wide experience of the world. It was heady stuff.

For the past three days she found herself looking for Gideon Stone in every empty room, listening for the sound of his footsteps, his voice. When their hands brushed, she felt her thoughts roll into a snarled tangle. He filled her awareness waking and sleeping. She was drawn to him as if he'd cast a spell upon her.

Why, she didn't know. He was hot-tempered, spoiled, indulgent, impatient, singleminded, and selfish of his time and comfort, in the way she had learned most men to be—and he had taken Lacey's Folly from her.

No, that wasn't fair. He'd been as taken aback as she.

Chloe sighed again and turned on her side. She thought she

knew the problem. Because she'd missed so much of ordinary life that other girls went through, she was acting like a moonling. *Calf love*, she derided herself.

She was sure of one thing. She was *not* in falling in love with Gideon Stone.

The hour was late when Chloe finally fell asleep. Chaotic dreams invaded her mind, and she found herself fleeing some invisible danger, running down toward the river. She found herself in the pergola. Gideon Stone stepped inside.

"I've been waiting for you," he said, and her heart was full of joy.

It was hot, so hot. They took off their garments and discarded them on the riverbank. Holding out his hand, he helped her into the water. The river was warm and welcoming. She felt no shame in her nakedness. It seemed the most natural thing in all the world.

Then she recognized where they were: this was not the river beyond the gardens and lawns of Lacey's Folly, but the mysterious river depicted in the painting that hung in the gallery alcove. It simultaneously frightened her and filled her with eager anticipation. Her heart felt curiously light, as if it were filled with feathers.

Somehow she had stepped into the wooded glade in the painting and found herself in that emerald green paradise. What was it called? Ah, yes. *Venus and Mars with Attendant Nymphs*. But there were no nymphs to be seen.

Just Gideon Stone, a naked Mars, waist-deep in the clear, swift current. How masculinely beautiful he was!

She slipped into the water, and it slid over her limbs, caressed her skin like silk. Different, yet familiar. She was Venus, beautiful and erotic, sure of her welcome and wanton with need. Her breasts tingled with the kiss of the river. She cupped them in her hands, feeling the tips harden to her touch. She threw her head back, offering them to her lover.

And suddenly Gideon/Mars was there, his hands covering hers, pulling them roughly away. Now it was he who cupped her breasts, weighing them in his callused palms, lowering his mouth to cover them with kisses.

She arched against him with pleasure. She wanted to, needed to meld with him. Lifting his head, he sought her lips, crushing her against his wide, naked chest. How strong he was, as he wrapped his arms around her. She exulted in it, in his masculine hardness, his possessive embrace. She rested her head against his shoulder, secure in his clasp. Yearning, yearning . . . oh, dear God!

She felt his cool hands begin a slow exploration of her warm flesh. Oh, how her blood sang in time to the river's song! Flowing faster and faster, sweeping her away. She reached out to him for support and he pulled her hard against his loins.

His mouth came down upon hers again, not softly as she'd expected, but with a bruising ardor that equaled her own passion. Her hips moved against his in invitation. His hand caressed her thigh, moved higher along the silky inner surface, and slid gently up between her legs.

She felt a sudden heat, a pagan spark that burst outward from her loins, spreading along her veins with every beat of her heart. Igniting her blood into a river of fire, a sea of flame. She ached for him. How she ached for him! He touched her again, more deeply. She was liquid with desire, melting with fearful pleasure.

The heat that had spread through her limbs gathered back, coiled in the pit of her stomach. Moved lower. Her body shook and shuddered with surprise and wild, arching pleasure. Falling, falling . . . she plummeted backward into the warm embrace of the water, with a silent splash. It carried her along in her lover's arms. They floated away on currents of bliss.

She was suddenly caught in the swirling torrent, cut off from him. Unable to kick herself free of the entangling water plants that twined round her ankles, That pulled her down and down into the depths . . .

Struggling for air, her body still arching to the rhythms of the dream, Chloe awakened in a room misty with morning light. Her gown was rucked up to her hips and pulled down over one breast, and her feet were trapped in the twisted sheets. The hand that touched her so intimately was her own.

She heard footsteps in the corridor and was fully awake. Hastily straightening her garments, she freed her legs and pulled up the sheet. Her shift was damp with sweat. Chloe rolled over on her stomach. What on earth had she been doing? And what if Agnes had walked in with her morning coffee.

Her heart was still pounding. There was an ache, a hollowness inside her like nothing she had ever known.

She didn't know what it was, this heat and pain and deep confusion, with Gideon Stone at its center. It was nothing like the feelings of affection she'd once felt for someone she'd known briefly in the past. That had been a young girl's first infatuation—heady and all-consuming, but hopelessly foolish. Ultimately doomed. She was a million times removed from the person she had been then.

This was different. The sensation that filled her now seemed to have a presence, a life of its own. *Is it love?* If so, she didn't want it. What good was it to love a man who only wanted to be rid of her?

No, it must be a phantasm born of grief and loneliness. A fleeting infatuation roused by that moment in the gallery when they'd been under the painting's spell, and he'd held her to keep her from falling—an ordinary courtesy that her disordered mind was trying to build into something more.

In future she would have to be on guard. Not against Gideon Stone, but herself.

Rising, Chloe poured water from the pitcher into the basin and bathed her hot cheeks. The face in the oval mirror above the washstand was still hers, yet it was subtly different. Her dream of Gideon Stone had changed her. Shattered her. Arranged the pieces that made up the person called Chloe Hartsell into a completely different pattern. She felt as if she'd gone to sleep a girl and awakened this morning, a woman.

And she didn't know how she could ever face Gideon Stone again.

SIX

❧❧

CHLOE DAWDLED AS LONG AS POSSIBLE THE NEXT MORN-
ing, hoping that Gideon would have breakfasted before she
came down. She entered the breakfast room late, still disturbed
by memories of her erotic dream, to find Gideon lying in wait
for her at the table.

"Good morning, Miss Hartsell."

She took a seat with her back to the high windows. In the
bright morning sun, her hair looked the exact color of the
apricot marmalade in its cut crystal container, he realized. He
was intrigued by the way her hair changed with the light, from
copper to gold to deep molten flame, depending on the time
of day. He could paint it a hundred times and never once
would it be the same.

Chloe didn't look up. She mumbled something in return and
concentrated on her toast. He thought she looked heavy-eyed
and out of sorts from lack of sleep.

He'd lain awake, too, although for different reasons than
she had. Yesterday, when he'd sketched her spontaneously,
Gideon had felt freer than he had in months. There had been
no commission riding on the moment nor had his reputation
been on the line. Now everything was changed.

He noticed the hectic flush in her cheeks. "A hot morning,"
he said. "I was thinking of taking a cool walk down to the
river. I thought perhaps you might care to join me."

The river! She dropped her knife, smearing jam on her skirt.

Good Heavens, the river was the last place she wanted to go to with him. "There are many things I need to go over with Mrs. Linley, the new housekeeper, this morning."

"Nonsense!" He set down the empty coffee cup he'd been holding. "The very reason I hired Mrs. Linley was to free you from those burdens."

She looked mulish, and he changed his tactic. "Well then, perhaps somewhere closer. There's a tower I can see from my window, Miss Hartsell. I'd planned to do some sketches of it, but when I tried to get to it, I lost my way."

"Oh, yes. That is the place I thought would make you an ideal studio." *And keep you far away from me as well.*

"Will you take me there?" He gave her a winning smile. She was determined not to let his charm affect her.

"You can find it without difficulty. The way round the house from the outside is perhaps easiest. Go out the drawing room, through the rose garden, out the second gate in the wall, then down the lawn past the pond, turn left at the stump with the sundial and go about . . ."

He threw his hands up. "I am lost already. Is the other way less complicated?"

"That is through the end of the west corridor, past the billiard room."

His face brightened.

"Then you go through, cut over to the old wing, up a flight of stairs in the third room, then down the next set until you reach a door and . . ."

He looked completely blank. "Unless you wish future generations to stumble over my bones in a dead-end passage one day, I suggest you take me there yourself. Come, it's a lovely morning for a walk."

Chloe struggled with herself. Even with the windows opened, it was still and airless in the breakfast room. Her hair was sticking to her nape and springing up in tiny tendrils at her temples. It would be pleasant in the tower, which always seemed to catch a breeze off the water in summer, and any sunshine in winter.

Still she hesitated. She didn't want to be alone with Gideon Stone.

He seemed to read her mind. "Are you afraid to wander so far alone with me, Miss Hartsell? Do you think I will seduce you? I wonder who has been poisoning your mind with stories?"

Gideon frowned. He might have a reputation as a man-about-town, but it was nothing out of the ordinary. "You seem to have an ill opinion of my profession. Let me assure you that not all artists are as morally lax as popular speculation might lead you to believe. And even if I were such a rogue, it would be foolish of me to ruin your chances for an advantageous marriage."

Chloe set down her fork, nettled. She had spent the night dreaming that she was in his arms, and his every waking thought was directed toward getting rid of her.

"I have no such notions, sir," she snapped, "but it would be rude to Mrs. Osler, to leave her alone when she is just settling in at Lacey's Folly."

"Nonsense. She's quite used to looking after herself. In fact, she has already gone off with Perry. Looking for inspiration for her poetry, or for lost treasures beneath the courtyard cobbles, for all I know. They appear to be a matched pair."

"Yes, they've become staunch friends." Chloe smiled fondly. "She seems to enjoy his company, and he stayed at her heels yesterday like a well-trained puppy."

"Not in the least like that four-legged beggar of his, then!" Gideon said. "Newton chewed one of my bedroom slippers to ribbons."

Chloe apologized profusely, but he waved it away. "I should not have left my door open, as your brother cheerfully pointed out to me. Young scalawag! But he and Mrs. Osler spent hours in the drawing room last evening, examining the various collections. She seemed as fascinated by the peculiar souvenirs and grisly curios as he. I wonder if all poets are so very odd?"

"No odder than artists, surely!"

Gideon threw back his head and laughed. "Come, Miss Hartsell, you are determined to dislike me. Let us cry friends. We have to live together beneath this roof for God knows how many weeks, and we might as well do so in harmony. I will ask you again: will you show me the way to the tower?"

She gave in against her will. "Very well," she sighed. "Although it's not as complicated as it sounds."

He picked up his ever-present sketchbook from the sideboard. "I am ready if you are."

As they left the breakfast room they ran into Perry and Mrs. Osler, examining a glass case of heaven-knew-what, in the corridor outside the breakfast room. Gideon colored, hoping she hadn't overheard his comment. Then he recalled that she was hard of hearing and relaxed.

Mrs. Osler smiled at them, fresh and bright-eyed as Perry. "A lovely morning for a walk. We have already been out early."

"I had the best hunting this morning," Perry announced. "Mrs. Osler is a great gun! We tramped all over the fallow field searching for empty bird's nests and found this."

Reaching inside his homespun trousers, he dragged forth three acorn caps, a smooth stone for skipping across the river, and a mangled pewter button with something stamped upon it.

"I thought it might be a clue," he said, pointing to the crest.

"A clue to what?" Gideon asked. "The fabled Lacey treasure? I doubt it exists. And that, young friend, is from a common foot soldier's uniform of twenty years ago."

Perry's face fell, and Gideon felt badly for bursting his bubble. "Now that's a very nice find," he said more kindly, pointing to a rough gray pebble that was split into two pieces.

"I found it on Pucca's Hill, and Mrs. Osler showed me how to grind the end with one of the tools she gave me. Oh, Chlo, you should see: an ugly old brown stone, turned all tawny and striped when I ground off the outer rough bits."

"My late husband was very interested in the natural sciences," the widow told them. "Perry reminds me so much of dear Arthur, and I have given him a few of Arthur's things.''

"That is exceedingly kind of you.'' Chloe watched as Perry tilted a piece of pale rock from side to side, and a thin line of light moved across the vaguely rounded surface, giving it the look of a silvery cat's eye.

"Isn't it magical, Chlo?''

"It is indeed,'' Chloe replied.

Gideon tucked his sketchbook under his arm and reached out to examine it. "Moonstone,'' he said. "A very nice piece of it, too. You could have it made into a ring one day. Or a pair of cufflinks. There's surely enough for two.''

Perry rubbed the toe of his boot against the back of his other leg. He'd thought of giving the stone to Chloe, as a gift. But that was before he remembered. He mumbled something.

"Speak up, Perry,'' Chloe admonished.

He squirmed uncomfortably. "It's for Lenore.''

"For whom?''

"Uhmmm . . . I . . . uh, the Lost Bride. Henry said moonstone can protect you from fairy arrows and spells. If she's really held captive by fairy glamour under Pucca's Hill, it might help her escape.''

Chloe didn't know whether to smile or to cry. Perry was growing up. Lately he'd shown a new fascination with Lenore's story and her miniature portrait in the drawing room. *Like Tobias, he's fallen in love, just a little, with a pretty, painted face. He's developed his first case of romantic chivalry, and all for a woman who has been dead and gone this century past.*

With a little shiver, she remembered the night Tobias had died, and how she had fallen under the spell of the legend in the Bride's Chamber. However, daylight and eight hours of sound sleep had quickly dispelled such notions.

"Perry,'' she said, taking him aside, "You must not be listening to the gardener's tales. You know how Henry likes to tell a story after he's had his evening pint. And you are not to go tramping around Pucca's Hill. There are old pits and quarries there, and you might tumble in. You could break your leg, or worse!''

''Oh, Chloe!''

''Don't 'Oh, Chloe' me, young man.'' Another thought popped into her head. She eyed him sternly. ''Was it you who removed Lenore's portrait from the Bride's Chamber?''

Although he flushed, he met her gaze squarely. ''I didn't take it,'' he said indignantly. ''I couldn't carry it, if I had. It's much too heavy for me to lift.''

She remembered Dawlish said it took two men to hang the portrait properly when Tobias had the frame re-gilded. ''I'm sorry, Perry. I don't know what I was thinking. It must be the heat.''

Gideon was uncomfortable. ''It slipped my mind. As it turns out, someone hung the painting in my room. I found it there, over the mantelpiece.''

She looked up at him, astonished. ''Who would do such a thing?''

He regarded her levelly. ''I don't know. You must ask Mrs. Linley. But it is the most incredible portrait! Much better done than the miniature. Such beauty, such perfection!''

''High praise, indeed, from an artist.''

''I have never seen a woman to compare with your Lost Bride,'' he said simply. ''Helen of Troy could not hold a candle to her. Little wonder legends are spun about the mystique of Lost Lenore.''

Chloe felt a sharp pang of unexpected envy. His face, when he talked of Lenore's portrait, was transfigured. Tobias and Perry were not the only ones to fall for that lovely, painted face. Gideon Stone sounded half in love with her, himself. Chloe sighed wistfully. *I wish just once that someone would look at me like that.*

Then she laughed inside at her own absurdity. In the first place, she knew she was no beauty, but there were few women who would compare favorably with Lenore Lacey.

And Lenore would never grow old. She would stay eternally young, eternally beautiful, and for generations, men would continue to moon over her portrait, like youths with their first loves.

Mrs. Osler looked from one to the other. A change of topic seemed indicated. "May Perry accompany me on a walk to the village? I want to bring back some of my husband's scientific instruments and books that I left at the cottage. I think the boy might enjoy them."

"How kind of you. But please, take the gig and . . ." Chloe stopped, blushing furiously. The vehicle was not hers to lend.

"Ouch!" She turned in outrage. Gideon had pinched her arm.

"A wasp on your sleeve," he said, by way of explanation. "It must have come in the open window." But after the others left for the village, he turned to her sternly.

"You will go on at Lacey's Folly as you did before, Miss Hartsell. I will not have you turn yourself into a martyr—or me into an ogre—in front of the boy."

Her indignation was real. "If I act as I did when Tobias lived, you will accuse me of being free with your possessions."

Gideon wanted to shake her. "Have I done anything to make you think so?"

"When I said there was no need to hire a housekeeper, *you* told me that *you* were the master here, and that *I* had no say in such matters."

He laughed at that. "How you twist and turn things. Miss Hartsell, if I throttle you one day, it will be your own doing. Now come, show me the tower."

Instead of taking him through the house, she decided to show him the shorter way from the outside. It seemed safer. They went through the rose garden. With its paved paths and arched trellises, it was a lovely place to be on a summer's afternoon.

"I must compliment the gardener on his roses," Gideon commented.

"Then, sir, you must compliment me." She flushed becomingly. "Most of the shrubs were dead, the rest of it wild and neglected, when I first came to Lacey's Folly. It was a challenge. I grew many of the roses from old cuttings, which the gardener obtained by trading with his fellows, and Tobias had some sent over from an acquaintance.''

Her love for the garden was evident. She had tended it and nurtured it for years. It was, he realized with a pang of guilt, the only thing in the world that was truly hers. And now, officially, it was his.

"This dark red one is Lancelot," she said eagerly, "and this ivory one is Guinevere. The mauve and white, I call Lady of Shalott.''

He was amused. ''And do you name all your flowers individually?''

Chloe blushed. "Only the ones I have developed myself, by grafting stock and experimenting. These are my very own creations, you see. They exist nowhere else but at Lacey's Folly.''

Gideon didn't know what to say. Little wonder he'd never seen such glorious colors before. The garden was Miss Hartsell's canvas, and she had created something wondrous. A masterpiece!

He recalled the names he'd seen on the books in the account room while she bound up his gashed hand and understood now that the voluminous journals she kept were scientific records of her work. They walked in silence awhile as he searched for the right words.

"You have a prodigious talent, Miss Hartsell. I am amazed and more than a bit humbled.''

Chloe's color deepened. She made as if to brush his compliment away. Gideon stopped her. "I understand more than you think. Your work, your creations, are as important to you as mine are to me. I hope, Miss Hartsell—when you come to marry—that you will take what you want from this garden to establish your own.''

"That is kind of you," she said, after a long pause. "But I do not think I have the heart for it.''

Gideon felt even worse. He knew what she was saying: to

spend such love and effort, all for nothing—all for someone else—was more than she could bear to chance again. They went out the painted gate to the herb garden and down the open lawn.

"Tobias used the tower as his observatory and study at one time," Chloe said. "I believe it will make a perfect studio for you." *And keep the smell of turpentine out of the house, as well.* Which would make Mrs. Linley, Dawlish, and Cook very happy.

It was not far, but the sun was liquid fire in the open, and the heat made them languid. Being alone with him after her dream put Chloe's nerves on edge. She twirled her lilac parasol and chattered nervously.

"How kind of Mrs. Osler to take so much time with Perry," she said for the third time.

"Why are you so amazed? She takes great pleasure in his company. He has a keen mind." Gideon smiled down at her. "You and Perry are very close."

"Yes." He was watching her so intently that Chloe became even more nervous. "I . . . we . . . have no other family. To have lost both parents in the space of a few days . . ." She fought to keep a tremor from her voice. "It was devastating!"

For a moment she couldn't go on. Gideon wanted to take her hand and give it a comforting squeeze, but realized it would not be welcome at the moment.

"Forgive me for causing you pain. You need say no more."

She recovered herself. "Perry helped ease the pain," she said truthfully. "He was a wonderful distraction. And he has such an active mind and marvelous imagination!"

"I enjoy such children," Gideon said, amazed to realize it was true. "When first I came here, I was given the impression that he was your child."

"Mine?" That rattled Chloe badly. She almost stumbled and had to clutch his arm to avoid tripping on a tangled tree root. "Good God! Is that what people say?"

"Only Miss Thorne. Out of sheer spite, I imagine."

They continued on in silence some moments, while Chloe

assimilated his words. She selected her own carefully. "I would be *proud* to call Perry my own," she said when she recovered herself. "I hope someday that I can claim a son as fine as he for my own."

Gideon smiled. "As do I, Miss Hartsell. Therefore, the sooner we set about finding you a husband, the better."

Chloe refused to change the topic. She lifted her chin. "What else do they say about me, Mr. Stone?"

He hesitated briefly. "That you were no blood relation to the old man at all, but his mistress."

Chloe made a sound of distress and turned away. Gideon was instantly contrite. "I curse myself for a tactless fool, Miss Hartsell. If it makes it any better, no one else believes their lies."

So, Chloe thought, heart pounding, *he has been asking questions*. Mr. Stone was far too noticing a man. She must be careful with him. The secret of Perry's birth must remain just that.

A sudden fear struck her. She bit her lip. Could Tobias have left anything among his genealogy papers that would betray them?

He was meticulous in his research. In fact, he had been going through some papers rather excitedly only a few days before the fit of apoplexy that had laid him low. She would have to go through the library. Perhaps take his bound files up to her room to read, one at a time, so that no one noticed.

Chloe realized that Mr. Stone was scrutinizing her countenance. She schooled her features and angled her parasol a bit more.

The sun, filtered through her translucent parasol, cast intriguing shadows on her fair skin, making it glow like alabaster. *It might as well be from the rigid set of her jaw*, Gideon realized and cursed himself for a fool. He overstepped himself by speaking so frankly and lost their earlier camaraderie.

"The grounds are lovely. How far do the boundaries run?"

Chloe gestured to the horizon. "That is all Lacey land. Your land now, untouched since the Druids and the Romans, the

Angles and the Saxons passed by,'' she added. Turning, she indicated the strange pyramid hill to their right, on the far side of the rippling water.

"The estate encompasses both banks of the river and runs straight to the base of Pucca's Hill. There are thorny tangles and wide open areas between the ancient oaks. It is visited only by deer and wild boar. The locals avoid it, except for the poachers, and even they stay away unless they are hard pressed.''

"Are the poaching laws so strictly enforced?'' Gideon asked.

"Do you see the track on the far side of the pond? It is very ancient and leads straight as an arrow through the woods to Pucca's Hill. The villagers shun the place. They fear they might get drawn inside the fairy rath beneath it, like Lost Lenore.''

She glanced up at him through her lashes. "And those strange blocks of stone almost damming the stream?''

Gideon shaded his eyes and looked at the line of flat rocks gently lapped by the water, their sides flanked by flat stones leaning against them all higgledy-piggledy.

"They were placed there by the king of the fairies who live inside the fairy hill,'' Chloe said, "to lure foolish mortals across.''

"Nonsense.'' Gideon gave her a wry look. "If you are trying to frighten me, it won't work. The stones are the remains of an ancient clapper bridge, and you know it. I have seen several in my travels. But over generations the smooth top stones have been removed, most likely to local hearths.'' He laughed. "Such is the stuff from which legends are concocted.''

She laughed, too. "You have caught me out, sir. But do not tell Perry, I beg of you. It is all that keeps him from trying to go across. I'm afraid he might be swept away or injured.''

"Yes, it would be dangerous to cross there when the river is high.''

"That's what these two posts with the iron rings are for.

When the bridge was used regularly, a rope was placed across at either end, to warn people not to attempt it. Of course, Perry believes that the iron rings are to prevent the fairies from crossing from Pucca's Hill to Lacey's Folly.''

''Tobias certainly filled the boy's head with stories. He was telling a few at breakfast.'' Gideon looked up at the bald, pyramidal summit of Pucca's Hill above the tree line. ''And your so-called fairy hill, *is* a strange formation. I can see how stories were woven round it over time.''

''Tobias said it is actually a natural feature, a giant lime-stone outcropping, topped by ancient earthworks of the early Celts. But the villagers prefer the legend to reality.''

She turned away from the water at a sharp angle until they reached a high hedge. ''We are almost at our destination,'' Chloe said, leading him through a wicker gate in the hedge.

And there it was ahead, the single tower, just as he'd seen it from the distance. It was connected to the main house by an el-shaped wing and a small orangery, whose panes glittered in the sun. Gideon could understand now why it was quicker to go around from the outside. Lacey's Folly was not the snug rectangle he'd thought. The older wing meandered off, hither and yon, like a wayward stream.

The tower sat within a walled enclosure and was not as tall as he'd thought. It was only two stories high, with a high dome, and Gideon wondered what had thrown his eye off so.

He started forward eagerly, but a curious thing happened. The closer they got to the tower, the more his feet lagged, and he couldn't think why. His normal curiosity and urge to ex-plore were damped. A strange feeling, almost a sense of doom, grew more pronounced with every step.

The wooden door in the wall opened to a small, sunny gar-den filled with climbing roses and myriad other flowers. She cupped a bright poppy as tenderly as a mother caressing a child's face.

''More of your work, Miss Hartsell?''

''No, Mr. Stone. More of my delight.''

Chloe stopped at the wooden tower door, with a wonderful

old lion's head knocker in the center, and a handle of twisted brass. When she turned to Gideon, she was shocked by his sudden pallor.

"Are you ill, Mr. Stone? You've gone quite pale," she said, with concern.

"A touch of heat. I should have brought my hat."

She unlocked the door and let him into the base of the tower. It was cool, but had none of the chill he'd expected of a disused space. The thick-plastered walls were the color of honey, and the floor tiles a deeper shade, with a floral mosaic along the sides.

Gideon was astonished. "It is the most amazing place! One could imagine oneself somewhere in the Tuscan hills. I feel as if I'd stepped out of England and into Italy by the mere crossing of the threshold."

"The tiles and furnishings were brought over from Florence by Tobias's grandfather, for his first wife," Chloe explained. "A young Florentine lady, daughter of a famous patron of the arts."

She could almost feel the woman's spirit here. "Her name was Giovanna Tintori. She was only eighteen, and very beautiful. And she had a fine dowry. But she pined for her homeland so greatly that she wept and pleaded to return. Instead, he built her this little bit of Florence, bringing over workmen from her native Tuscany."

"The paintings in the alcove—they were part of her dower, then?"

Chloe blushed, remembering Titian's Venus and Mars, and her reaction to it. Remembering her dream of Gideon after.

She cleared her throat. "Yes."

Gideon examined the niches and ceilings with their ornate lamps, the gessoed panels with long Italian faces painted upon them, the rich tapestries hung on the walls, the small gilt table and chair, and the inviting chaise longue before the fireplace. "A lovely and intimate little apartment. Did the homesick bride decide to stay?"

"Yes, for one of the workmen was her former lover—or so

Tobias said. Giovanna lived here happily until succumbing to a summer fever. She is buried in the Lacey plot in the village churchyard with her husband—and his second and third wives, as well. One was only fifteen years of age when she died.''

''Egad! Either the times were hard on women or their husband were. I should think.''

Chloe cocked her head. ''Both, I should imagine. Things haven't changed that much in all the generations. Walk through the churchyard and read the newer stones: old Mr. Simmons, of Four Corners Farm, has three wives awaiting him there now. Two died in childbirth, and one of the milk leg, following childbirth. He is looking to take a fourth, but none of the village women will have him.''

''I can understand their reasoning!'' Gideon glanced over and saw Chloe watching him with a small worried frown between her brows. She looked as if she wanted to bite her tongue.

''Fear not, Miss Hartsell. Desperate I may be, but not so desperate that I'd try and foist an elderly husband with such bad luck upon you.''

She turned away in relief and started toward the steps leading up. Light fell from above, illuminating the double flight of stairs, and a tall window pierced the thick walls at the landing. A fresco of angels guided them up to the room above.

Gideon paused on the landing and looked out the window. On this side, the tower went down a steep drop to the rocks and rushing river below. No wonder the tower had seemed higher. From the approach to the house, it would look twice as high, rising above the flat meadows on the other side of the river.

For a moment he felt dizzy, and the feeling of doom rushed back. He clutched at the sill for support until it passed, then hurried up to the top floor. There were no curtains here, and light streamed in from four sides.

The room was simple, outfitted with a colorful, pillow-covered divan from the Orient, a long walnut table used as a desk and a high-backed armchair and a footstool upholstered in brown leather. A decanter of gold liquid stood on a side table, along with a tray and two glasses. Books filled a long shelf between the windows, and the niche beside the fireplace was stocked with wood against inclement weather.

"A cozy chamber," Gideon said approvingly.

Chloe's eyes misted. "Before Tobias fell ill, this was his favorite place on the estate. At one time he worked on his history of the Lacey family here, and later it became his observatory. You will see his star-gazing apparatus over in the corner. After he was no longer able to make the long walk . . . I continued to come here in my free hours."

Gideon walked over to the row of books. His long finger touched the works of the Brontës, Miss Austen, Mr. Thackeray and Mr. Dickens, Sir Walter Scott and George Sand. It slowed over Lord Byron, Lady Caroline Lamb's pseudonymous novel, and moved on to de Maupassant, Baudelaire, and some of the more ribald French writers, then stopped completely before several volumes of wildly adventurous Gothic romances.

"Old Tobias certainly had interesting tastes in reading," he said, turning to see Chloe's reaction. He enjoyed making the color rush to her fair skin.

She blushed hotly, as he'd expected. "Those are mine. They all are. Tobias gave them to me and I would sit and read and keep him company. I don't know why you appear to be so shocked! The ladies of your circle are surely acquainted with them all."

"Yes," he said, with his devastating smile. "That is exactly why I am so shocked. I imagined you had led a more sheltered life here. Now I have to rearrange my thinking."

He came across the floor to Chloe and stood looking down at her with a quizzical look. "Tell me, Miss Hartsell, are you really the innocent you seem?"

She felt a betraying rush of blood flood her cheeks. "I assure you, Mr. Stone, that I am neither uneducated nor a fool. I am not ignorant of what goes on in the world between men and women."

"That is not what I am asking."

Her color deepened. "Are you asking if I have ever lain with a man?"

"Good God, no!"

Now it was Gideon's turn to be flustered. There was a quality to her he hadn't seen in some time: not the gauche innocence of a girl straight from the schoolroom, nor the carefully rehearsed modesty of the debutante. *A purity of spirit*, Gideon decided. A quality that the more sophisticated ladies of the *haut monde* lacked. Not to mention an utter lack of guile.

"You must not blurt out everything that runs through your mind, Miss Hartsell. It's most unsettling." He rumpled his hair in agitation. "I was not casting aspersion on your character. I was wondering what type of man would make you a husband you might find tolerable."

Chloe looked away quickly. She was afraid she had already found her answer. One that wouldn't serve.

But Oh! How that would solve her problems. Every one, except that of keeping Perry's birth a secret until it died with her.

She laughed lightly. "More to the point sir, you must find a man who can tolerate *me*. Do you think my bookish tendencies will frighten off a potential spouse?"

Gideon cupped her chin in his hand and tipped her face up to his. The sunlight turned her brows and lashes to gold. "Only if he's a complete fool."

"I shouldn't care to marry a fool," she said quietly, trying to pull away.

He released her chin but placed his hands on her shoulders. "I hereby give you my solemn vow, Miss Hartsell: I refuse to let you marry an oaf or a boor." He gave her a tiny shake. "There, do you feel better?"

"Yes," she said, laughing a little. "But that cuts the selection by more than half."

"Well, you have a good opinion of the male sex!" Gideon folded his arms, irritated.

"I," she replied straightly, "am only judging by my limited experience. If Tobias Lacey was one side of the coin, his nephew Martin Thorne is the other. However, I sincerely hope that you may prove me wrong.''

Gideon hoped so, too.

"This room will make a perfect studio," he said, to change the subject. "Good lighting, especially from the north. Plenty of space to set up my easel and gear. A chair and couch for my model to pose.''

"Must you have a model?" She sounded doubtful.

"Of course I must! I paint from life, Miss Hartsell. Although I admit I did toy with the idea of trying to use Lenore Lacey as a subject. The paintings are to be personifications of either types of Love, or Virtues and Vices.''

"Then you must paint Love," she said decisively. "The servants would be scandalized enough if you bring a model down to Lacey's Folly, more so if you lock yourself away up here, portraying Vice. We'd have them packing their things and leaving.''

Chloe looked so daunted that he took her hand in his. "You must vouch for my respectability with the servants, Miss Hartsell. They hold you in high esteem.''

He touched her cheek, tilting her face so that the light gilded her bone structure. Chloe couldn't breathe. All she could do was look up at him, as if she were mesmerized.

Gideon was looking at her with an artist's intensity. Those dark blue eyes of his raked her face, noted the soft curve of her lips, the long, elegant line of her throat. She would certainly do.

"Fate led me to Lacey's Folly, Miss Hartsell, and to you. Your reputation is above board. If you were my model, surely the servants could not object. If I cannot have Lenore Lacey, then you must be my muse, my inspiration. Will you pose for me?''

How could she answer him, when the touch of his hand, the light in his eyes made her heart dance in double time, and her limbs grow weak? How could she agree, knowing the long hours they would spend together, when he already had such power over her?

How could she *not*, when she felt such jealousy every time he mentioned Lenore's portrait?

Chloe's fingers trembled in his, and his hand closed over hers protectively. "Say yes, Miss Hartsell, I beg of you."

"I must think . . ." She walked to the window and looked out at the river, rushing like her roiled emotions.

Gideon prayed, with a painter's single-mindedness, that she would agree. He had no inkling of what was going through her mind. The urge to create dominated everything. All he knew was that she was suitable and she was here, available to him. If he could not have Lenore Lacey resurrected to pose for him, he would make do with Miss Hartsell.

After several minutes' severe inner struggle, Chloe nodded. If he were busy painting her, he wouldn't have time to go looking for a suitable husband to marry her. And if he got the commission, he wouldn't have to sell Lacey's Folly.

"Very well. I will pose for you."

"Excellent." He picked her up right off her feet and whirled her around until they were both was giddy.

"You are mad, Gideon Stone!"

Laughing, he released her. "No, Miss Hartsell, I am inspired."

At his words her face took on a rosy glow. *Like pink alabaster lit from within*, he thought. It brought out marvelous violet tones in her eyes. He hadn't realized how pretty she could look under the right circumstances. She was a taking little thing, for all her brisk efficiency and needle-pointed wit.

He was glad he'd brought his field kit with him. Opening the box, he began taking out pencils and paper and his watercolor pigments and setting them out on the table. "We'll start today. Now!"

"So soon!" She paused in midstride.

How like a panicked deer she looks, all startled motion and angular grace. It wouldn't do to frighten her off.

"Make yourself comfortable with a book, Miss Hartsell. I'll set up my things and do a sketch of the river from the window to limber up."

''I thank you for the reprieve.''

Chloe selected a book but paused to watch him. Gideon was in profile to her, and she was struck anew by his handsome features, and his apparent disregard of them. Anyone seeing the careless knot to his cravat and the way he raked his fingers through his thick hair would know he didn't have an ounce of personal vanity.

It all went, she suspected, into his work.

Looking out the window, Gideon began drawing lines and squiggles and hatchmarks that quickly turned into a study of a toppled tree on the far side of the river. She was fascinated watching those quick, strong hands as they made sure strokes across the paper, creating something out of nothing.

She tried not to remember her dream, and how those hands had caressed her naked body. She concentrated on the sketch.

It intrigued her the way that adding a darker shadow here, leaving a bare spot there, could make a forest spring to life in its primeval splendor. He was so intent, she imagined he'd forgotten her presence completely.

Moving to the divan, she curled up against the pillows. From her vantage point, she could keep an eye on Gideon and his drawings, without interfering with his work, and watch the smooth flow of dappled water break into lacy scallops against the stepping stones beyond.

At first it seemed very curious for her to be doing absolutely nothing in the middle of the morning. Hard to imagine that this was how some people spent all their time, doing whatever pleased them at the moment.

I might as well enjoy it while I may, she told herself. *If he succeeds in finding me a husband, I shall not have many moments like this again.*

It was cool and peaceful in the tower room, with the laughter of the water and the piping of birds. After the excitement and worry of the past week, Chloe felt relaxed and completely safe with Gideon a few feet away. So safe, so contented that she fell asleep between one thought and the next.

Gideon smiled to himself. That was exactly what he'd

hoped for when he'd suggested that she read awhile. Now he could examine her more closely. It was considered poor manners to stare at a woman, but his work made it essential. This way he could spare her blushes.

His artist's eye began stripping away the unbecoming lilac round gown to reveal the womanly figure beneath. She had a trim waist, softly rounded hips, and a provocative curve to her shoulders—*wonderful shoulders, really*—and her slender neck. Her eyelids were delicate, her dark lashes dusted with gold at the tips.

She sighed and turned a little, and the low neckline of her gown pulled away. The top of her breast was half exposed, and he saw he hadn't done her justice. She was lovely. Why did she hide in such ill-fitting clothes? Then it occurred to him with a rush of shame that she hadn't the wherewithal to purchase anything better. *Damn Tobias Lacey. The miserable skinflint!*

Beneath his guilt, Gideon felt a stirring of tenderness for this poor young woman he had displaced, and he wondered again at his benefactor's sanity. He vowed that he would not set about getting Chloe a husband haphazardly. No, by God, he would handpick the man himself. She deserved no less.

There was something oddly intimate about drawing her while she slept. About tracing the soft curve of her arm, the swell of her breast, the line of her hip and thigh. The silky curl of her untamable hair, the satin texture of her skin.

Gideon stopped and examined his sketchpad. He realized, with a start, that he had rendered an exceptionally good drawing of Chloe Hartsell—except for the fact that he'd left off her clothes.

She was completely nude in the sketch, as if he had the power to see through the dimity. The elegant line of her torso, the gentle undercurve of her breast, the succulent, pebbled tip.

His blood was roused. It was almost as if he were making love to her. Making her, in a curious way, his own.

While he wrestled with the ethics of it, his pencil went skimming over the paper in rapid strokes, and he could no more stop himself from filling in the sketch than he could from breathing. It would be the basis for one of the life-sized drawings he would submit to Lord Pulham.

The title and the theme came to him: *Innocence Awakening.* Eve in the garden of Eden, awaiting the breath of life. Awaiting the first taste of love.

He looked up from the drawing to Chloe. Her face was flushed with sleep, her hair a damp tangle of lustrous curls. And her breasts . . . His hands curved as if to cup them. He threw down his pencil, shut his sketchbook, and went to the window to cool his fevered brow.

Careful, careful now!

Taking out his handkerchief, he mopped his brow. The breeze off the river cooled his face, but his blood still ran hot. He was a man used to carnal pleasures and he had abstained too long. He must rein himself in, hard.

She was not a lightskirt looking for a quick tumble or a few hours dalliance. She was a gentlewoman and a virgin, and she was under his protection. But as he stared out at the rushing water and green woods beyond, it was her naked body he was seeing before him. He turned back, thinking the sight of her fully clothed would push the other image away.

Chloe had turned on her side, and her bodice was down even farther, completely exposing one round, perfect breast with its soft rosy peak. Utterly luscious and delectable. His loins tightened with desire.

Gideon cursed and turned back to the river. She would be terribly embarrassed if he left her like that, more so if she awakened now. He would make a sound, knock something over, while his back was to her, and she'd wake and sit up, before she noticed anything amiss. Yes, that was it.

Ah, the shutters. They would do. Leaning out, he reached to pull the shutters . . . and was gripped by a sudden, dizzying sensation. Heat, followed by deadly cold. His body was so weak, he could hardly hold himself against the window ledge.

His hand clawed out, grasped the shutter, and it swung in with a loud creak.

Chloe awakened with a start. The book dropped from her lap to the floor. For a moment she was disoriented, then she realized that Gideon was at the open window, crumpling to his knees. She jumped up and hurried to his side. His face was like chalk.

"What is it?"

He was too ill to speak. Chloe fetched the brandy from the side table and poured out a generous tot. "Here, drink this."

Gideon found his head cradled against her breast, but at the moment he didn't care if she were naked or clothed. He was scarcely aware of her through the red mist that covered his vision. Gideon gulped in air, feeling his lungs expand with it. The mist cleared, and he was on the floor of the tower room, in danger of being as sick as the proverbial dog.

She pressed the glass to his lips and made him sip the brandy. "You feel feverish, Mr. Stone. Shall I fetch Henry and the stablelad to help you back to your room?"

"No . . . I thank you." He leaned his head back against the cool plastered walls and closed his eyes. "A touch of vertigo. Nothing more."

She held him in her arms, feeling the warmth of his body against hers. It was nothing like her dream. It was even more devastating.

She inhaled his masculine scent, the hint of rosemary and juniper of his cologne, and felt her heart turn over. Even in his sudden weakness, she was aware of the strength, the muscled hardness of his body. The yearning to have *his* arms around *her*.

His color was returning. "Are you afrai . . . mmmh, are you perhaps intimidated by heights, sir?"

"No. Devil take it, I've climbed mountains and never felt like this."

He opened his eyes. Hers were looking down at him with such a strange expression. "I don't know what caused it," he said, struggling to sit upright, "but it is passing."

He was definitely feeling better. Her soft shoulder supported him and he could smell the fresh lavender rinse she used on her hair. Glorious hair, really. He wondered what it would look like if she let it all down. He would ask her to unbind it when he painted her and . . .

A current passed between them, an awareness of something changed. Chloe sat back on her heels. "We must get you back to the main house. You need to be in your bed."

He thought of the featherbed waiting for him and imagined her there. Waiting for him. Her unbound hair spilling over the pillows, her limbs soft and rosy against the Irish linen sheets . . .

"No," he groaned, and pushed himself to his feet.

She misunderstood. "I don't think you should continue your sketching today, Mr. Stone. I think you have had quite enough."

Gideon shook his head ruefully. He had and he hadn't. That was the trouble.

"Chloe, Chloe, come quick!"

She heard Perry pounding down the corridor and rose from the desk where she was going over the week's menu. Her heart was in her throat. "Is it Mr. Stone? Is he ill?"

Perry popped into the parlor. "No, come see. It's like Cinderella!"

He whipped back out, and she was compelled to follow him out the main door.

An enormous traveling coach bearing a crest came bowling out of the woods and up the lane. Chloe felt a flutter of nervousness. True to Gideon's estimate of her character, his godmother had packed and set out posthaste, after receiving his letter. If Lady Albinia was as discerning as her godson, Chloe would have to guard herself well. Her interest in Gideon and her relationship to Perry would be in more danger of discovery now.

Gideon had spied the coach from his room and came down to join them. He didn't know if he felt dismayed or relieved. On the whole, he thought the latter.

"Your chaperone arrives, Miss Hartsell. Your reputation is saved. And your debut is about to begin."

There was no chance to talk further, as the traveling coach was almost at the front door. "I think you and Lady Albinia shall get along very well indeed. You must show her your roses. She is a notable gardener, too."

Yes, Chloe thought wistfully. Even in her isolation, she had heard of the gardens at Hetherton Hall. *Although I doubt she ever so much as pulled a nettle in her life! Lady Albinia has an entire platoon of gardeners to tend her properties. But this . . . this was mine!*

She waited inside the hall with Perry and smoothed his cowlick in place just as the steps were put down. A liveried footman handed Lady Albinia down from her fairy-tale coach. Gideon hurried out.

"As beautiful as ever," he said as he took his godmother's hand and kissed her cheek.

Lady Albinia was a regal brunette, trailing gauzy scarves, French lace, and clouds of expensive perfume. Sunshades and strawberry lotion had kept her skin smooth and fair, and more sonnets were written to her lovely violet eyes than to those of any acknowledged beauty half her age.

She brought with her an air of sophisticated excitement. Also, a coachman, two footmen, a most superior lady's maid with a face like ice, and more baggage than anyone at Lacey's Folly had ever seen in one place at one time.

"My dear Gideon, what a charming place you have here!" she exclaimed. "All that lovely half-timbering and ivy-covered stone!"

She whispered into his ear. "My dear, Walden will be fit to be tied when he learns you will not come crawling to him. He will be so very sorry that he can't spurn you again that I daresay he'll go into a sharp decline."

"The day is far too lovely to discuss my half-brother, Albinia, and so are you."

He approved of the Prussian Blue traveling outfit she wore, which brought out her dark coloring to perfection. "You are as fashionable as ever, I see. Everything of the first stare."

"And you are as silver-tongued as ever." Her famous violet eyes raked the facade of Lacey's Folly. "Which room is haunted? Can I see it from here? And where is this Miss Hartsell of yours?"

He kissed her scented cheek, tucked her dainty hand in his arm, and escorted her to the door. "The Bride's Chamber is the haunted room. No, it cannot be seen from here—and she is not *my* Miss Hartsell."

"Oh, dear. Is she very bad? Shall I ruin my reputation as a peerless matchmaker over her?" Albinia sighed. "I suppose she is gap-toothed, with spots, and no figure, lacks countenance, wears thick spectacles, keeps her nose in a book, and is so meek she can't say 'boo' to a goose!"

She fixed him with one of her roguish smiles. "Or is she perhaps loud and vulgar, with a voice like a corncrake, and bound and determined to make a great splash in society, which would be even worse. What have I gotten myself into? Oh, dear!"

Gideon laughed aloud. "You know from my letter that she is none of those things. The worst I can say of her—and I warned you of it—is that she has red hair."

"Most unfortunate! It is not at all the fashion." Lady Albinia clasped her hands. "If only she were dark. Dark is all the rage right now." She put that idea aside with another sigh. "Being a redhead, I suppose that she is covered with large freckles all over her body, as well?"

"Not as far as I have seen," Gideon replied cautiously.

She looked up at him from under her thick lashes. "*Not* a beauty, then."

Gideon didn't respond to her joke. He flushed, darkly. "If you are insinuating what you seem to be insinuating, I should be highly insulted. Miss Hartsell is a female under my protection. I would not take advantage of her."

Albinia rapped him with her fan. "Foolish creature! I only meant that you would have convinced her to pose for you by now, if she were. That is all."

Stepping out of the shadows, Chloe met them in the hall. From the bright color beneath her ivory skin, it was apparent that she'd overheard at least part of their conversation. She was dazzled by the older woman's beauty and fashionable air but didn't give herself away.

"Welcome to Lacey's Folly, Lady Albinia. If you will please come with me, I will show you to your room."

Albinia embraced Chloe lightly, startling her almost off her feet. A dulcet voice whispered in her ear. "That would be very kind in you, Miss Hartsell," she said softly, "but you must remember that you are no longer the housekeeper here. You are a young gentlewoman soon to be fired off into society. You may accompany me, but one of the maids should take us up."

"Yes, Lady Albinia. I'll . . ."

But the vision in Prussian Blue had already relinquished Chloe and turned back to Gideon. "You didn't tell me the half! She has an elegant figure and good carriage. And those eyes!"

She looked at Chloe again and nodded. "Yes. It will go very well. When I am finished, no man in his right mind will be able to escape the allure of those silver-gray eyes! I shall make you all the rage, my dear. Men will be throwing themselves at your feet!"

"Oh, no! I mean . . ."

Albinia reached out and took one of Chloe's hands between hers. "I know that I can be overwhelming at times—or so I have been told." She flashed a roguish look at her godson. "You must not be afraid, Miss Hartsell. I shall not force you to do anything you would not enjoy."

Gideon gave a bark of laughter. "Where have I heard that before? Just do as she says and everything will work out for the best. I warn you, she always has her way, once her mind is made up."

"Cruel," Lady Albinia said, but with a twinkle in her eye. She turned to Chloe, kindly but firm. "Although it *will* be best if you simply place yourself in my hands, Miss Hartsell."

From the corner of her eye, she saw the maid appear in answer to Chloe's summons. "Come along now, and we will get started before dinner."

Chloe thought it was rather like being taken up by a whirlwind. She was swept along by Lady Albinia, helpless as a leaf in a storm.

They followed Agnes up the stairs. "Wait until you see the things I have brought with me in my trunks," the older woman exclaimed. "Gideon described you quite well. His eye for color cannot be faulted. Although, what to do with your hair? Well, I shall let my dresser deal with that."

While Albinia talked sixteen to the dozen all the way up the staircase, Gideon stood at its foot, shaking his head. For his peace of mind, the sooner Miss Hartsell was safely married off, the better it would be. He didn't know what had come over him in the tower—not vertigo, but the sudden heat of unexpected arousal.

Yes, it would be better for all concerned, once Miss Hartsell was gone from Lacey's Folly.

He did feel sorry for her and tried to salve his conscience. *It is a woman's lot in life to marry and leave home*," he reminded himself. But no matter how worthy an individual she espoused, he was sure Miss Hartsell would deem marriage an inadequate replacement for ownership of Lacey's Folly.

There was another matter than stirred his sympathies: despite Albinia's vaunted record at matchmaking, he could almost find it in his heart to pity any young woman whom she decided to take under her wing. However, Albinia would keep Chloe Hartsell so busy, she wouldn't have time to repine.

He sat down and picked up the London papers, praying that he would not find news of Lord Exton's return there.

While her haughty maid unpacked, Lady Albinia bombarded Chloe with comments and questions over tea and cakes in the sitting room.

"We must face facts, Miss Hartsell. Young men who have money would look higher for a wife. Those with no money would hang out for a richer one. We must strike a happy medium to find you just the proper husband.''

Her eyes were bright with interest as she watched the expressions flit across Chloe's mobile face. ''You do not seem eager to wed.''

''Indeed, ma'am, I would rather not wed at all!''

''The life of a spinster can be harsh. I advise you to put a good face on it and let me help. I am a famous matchmaker, you know.''

''So Mr. Stone had told me.'' She sighed.

''Well, then. Do you know what manner of man would suit you best? Have you given the matter any thought?''

A wicked light danced in the silver depths of Chloe's irises. ''I can tell you exactly what would suit me best: an elderly man of some substance, with a kindly disposition, and no living relatives. Preferably with one foot in the grave, and the other on the slippery slope leading to it. And if he has no interest in bedding his wife, I shall be all the happier.''

And on that note, she horrified herself by suddenly bursting into tears.

So that's the way the wind blows, Lady Albinia realized, as Chloe fought to recover herself. *Miss Hartsell has developed a tendre for Gideon*. She sipped her tea thoughtfully. *This may be beyond even my fixing*.

''Are you ready, Gideon?''

Lady Albinia, resplendent in rose silk, hovered in the doorway of the parlor that had always been Chloe's favorite. It was cooler on this side of the house, and the parlor was a much more pleasant chamber than the collection-stuffed drawing room, with its often macabre treasures.

Gideon set down the paper he'd been perusing and glanced at the mantel clock. It was far too early even for a country dinner.

''Am I ready for what?''

His godmother stepped aside, and another woman entered softly. He leapt to his feet and swept his best bow.

She wore an evening dress of soft silk in a misty color that shimmered between pale green and silver, making Gideon think of spring and the underside of tender new leaves. Her only jewelry was a necklace of tiny pearls, with a teardrop of pale green jade. The pendant trembled enticingly at the cleft of ivory breasts half bared, and matching eardrops hung from perfect lobes.

Gideon stared. It took him a moment to realize it was Chloe.

The subtle color warmed her pale skin to ivory and made her thick-lashed eyes look enormous. And her hair! It looked less red and more copper, toned down by the color of her gown. The sides were rolled back and woven with narrow ribbons of the same shade, and the rest was caught at her nape in a silver net. She was not classically beautiful, no. But she was stunning!

"Turn around."

Chloe did as she was bid, slowly and with the awkward grace of a young colt. She was used to being in the background. To find herself the center of such attention was intimidating enough. To stand there, with her shoulders and half her bosom exposed was far worse. She felt a slow blush start at her breasts and sweep up her throat to her face.

He stood there gaping so long that Chloe got nervous. "It is far too grand for me," she said.

Gideon came to his senses. Stepping forward, he gave her his best bow. "No, no, Miss Hartsell. It suits you exquisitely. Albinia, where on earth did you come by that dress so quickly?"

His godmother laughed. "Ah, men! What wonderful creatures you are. I wore it to the opera with you last season. With a deep lace ruffle around the shoulders and hem, my emeralds, and a spangled shawl. Quite a different look altogether."

"Surely not!"

"I knew you wouldn't recognize it, Gideon, because my coloring is so different from Chloe's." She clapped her hands in glee. "It is not everyone who can trick an artist so well."

He saw that she was right. Not only that, the gown looked

much better on Chloe than it had on his godmother. He couldn't take his eyes off her. It was enough to get any healthy man's juices flowing. She looked elegant. And delectable. Two words he'd never have thought he would ever apply to her, a few days earlier.

"Well, what do you think?" Albinia said impatiently. "Does she pass muster?"

He didn't know what to say. "The transformation is amazing."

Instead of being pleased, both women looked piqued. "Thank goodness you never had an ambition to join the diplomatic corps!" Albinia exclaimed. "Your career would have ended dismally."

She gestured Chloe over to the sofa beside her. "Sit down, Gideon, and we will put our heads together. Now, let us make our plans."

Albinia began laying out her strategy like a general preparing for battle.

While she talked, Gideon listened in stunned silence, as fittings and routs and balls and cards of invitation were mentioned in rapid succession.

Chloe sat on the sofa and tried to listen, but she felt as if none of it concerned her. They were talking about some other person entirely. She glimpsed her own reflection in the mirror. It was like looking at a stranger. *If Perry were to walk in now, would he recognize me?*

Despite her fine feathers, she was still herself: an orphan who had lived out her life caring for a old man. Lady Albinia was so far removed from her, she was like a creature from another universe. *Or perhaps from the fairy rath beneath Pucca's Hill*, Chloe thought. It wouldn't surprise her in the least.

She realized, with an unwelcome twinge, that the world Gideon Stone lived in had far more to do with his godmother's than her own. They had their own customs and their own language, and none of it pertained to her. His raised voice brought her out of her reverie.

"But of course she must come up to London and stay with me," Lady Albinia was saying.

"London is out of the question, Albinia. Even with so few weeks left to the season." Gideon leaned against the mantelpiece. "I don't know where you came by such a ridiculous idea."

Lady Albinia's eyes went wide. "You wrote me that you needed my help in finding an eligible husband for Miss Hartsell. My dear Gideon, London is the place to be! The season is drawing to a close, true, but a new face may be just what society craves. Often a pretty young miss has made a splash by coming on the scene when everyone is jaded with familiarity."

Chloe regarded her with as much horror as was evidenced on Gideon's face. "I am neither pretty, nor young. And I cannot go to London! Indeed, there is no need."

"Or rather, no time." Gideon ran his fingers through his hair, the way he always did when he was dismayed. "I should have explained my financial plight. Well, I couldn't very well do so in a letter."

His face darkened with chagrin. "I cannot bear the expense of a London season, in any case. I haven't a feather to fly with. The devil is that I'm head over heels in debt and can't sell this damned . . . er, this place until Miss Hartsell is married. Terms of the will, you understand. So you see what a dreadful tangle I am in."

Lady Albinia glanced from him to Chloe and back again. "That *is* a problem." She closed her eyes a moment, marshaling her thoughts. "Really, Gideon, with all the goodwill in the world, it cannot be accomplished overnight! I am not a magician. I cannot simply conjure a husband for Miss Hartsell with a wave of my hand. I shall have to take a different tack." She tapped her fan on the arm of the sofa. "Tell me who is important in the neighborhood."

"I don't know a soul."

They both turned to Chloe. She blushed but lifted her chin. "Neither do I. Personally, that is. Tobias Lacey was reclusive by nature. He found all the company he could wish for beneath his own roof.''

''Unfortunate!''

''However there is old Mrs. Adderby at Sanford Hall, and Sir Ralph Dunscote and Lady Ralph. The Miss Combe and Miss Anne Combe, and their brother.''

''What about eligible men?'' Albinia asked. ''That is the crux of the matter.''

Chloe blushed. ''Mr. Combe is unmarried. And Sir Ralph has two sons, although they are a bit younger than I. Mrs. Adderby has a nephew.''

''Yes, I know her nephew, Joshua Breem, quite well.'' Albinia's eyes lit up. ''He would be an excellent catch.''

''Breem?'' Gideon was aghast. ''He is rather fond of his brandy, so they say. And he is a good deal older than Miss Hartsell.''

''A young woman often finds an older man a steadying influence. And perhaps he would be less inclined to drink so much if he had a wife.'' Albinia sighed with relief. One or two possibilities already. ''Well, that is a very good start.''

She snapped open her gilt fan. ''I will make sure Mr. Tobias Lacey's prohibition against a formal mourning period is set about. That will get us over the first hurdle. I will leave my card for Lady Adderby at Sanford Hall, while you, Gideon, will pay a call upon Sir Ralph Dunscote and his lady. Then we shall both leave our cards with the Combes. Or perhaps we might effect to run into them in the village.''

Gideon looked unhappy. ''Is this necessary?''

''Absolutely. I shall invite a few people down from London. The place is certainly large enough to have a small party down for a quiet weekend. And if we've no results by season's end in August, you can invite more down.''

As she rattled on, Gideon saw his chances of painting without distraction vanish like smoke up a chimney. ''Good Lord, am I to have no peace beneath this roof?''

''Not, my dear boy, if you intend to fire Miss Hartsell off properly. You will sponsor a few outings and picnics if the weather holds, perhaps even an informal country dance. Not that Miss Hartsell will dance, of course.''

Chloe listened in growing indignation while they discussed her future as if she were a mare for sale on market day. Disheartened, she went quietly out to the terrace and down to the rose garden for comfort.

She could not bear to marry Joshua Breem and live with Mrs. Adderby. Nor could she imagine herself living happily with such a dry stick as Mr. Combe. Neither would accept Perry. He would be packed off to boarding school posthaste.

No, a widower with young children would be the best bet, although she could think of none in the vicinity. All the others were too young to consider. Her spirits lifted.

Unless Lady Albinia can lure an eligible party in desperate need of a wife down from London, her chances of finding me a husband are remote. Which of course solves my *problem quite nicely, but not Mr. Stone's. Which is Mr. Stone's problem, entirely.*

Much cheered, she strolled through the gardens along one of the pleasant paths.

After walking all the way down to the foot of the garden, she rounded it and followed the path up the other side. It led her back to the far end of the terrace and she made her way across the flags to the open windows. Voices carried on the early evening air. As she got closer, the sounds became more clear, borne on the fresh breeze.

''Where has Miss Hartsell got to?'' Lady Albinia asked.

''I saw her down at the bottom of the garden a moment ago,'' came Gideon's reply.

''Good. Then I may speak frankly.''

''What do you think?''

'' I see two problems here that can both be solved easily and quickly. The first is settling Miss Hartsell. Her lineage is good, although not exceptional. She is unsophisticated perhaps, but her freshness and openness are an advantage. She is intelligent and well-read, and she has countenance. Her manners are easy and natural, and her breeding is apparent. All in all, a taking little thing. I find I like her very well.''

''Then there is no problem,'' Gideon said in relief. ''With your approval and contacts, she will surely find a husband quickly.''

Lady Albinia cocked her head. Really, her godson could be dense at times. ''Perhaps I shall find you a wife while I am at it. Goodness knows you need a wife to keep you from all the excesses to which you've already been exposed.''

''Save your breath, Albinia. I am not in the market for one.''

''Heaven only knows I have tried to set you up with first one pretty heiress and then another. There is nothing like a well-connected wife to help the fortunes of an aspiring young artist! But each time you have gone back to your painting before your interest could be fixed with the girl in question. Most annoying!''

''I thought this conversation was about Miss Hartsell,'' Gideon said irritably.

Lady Albinia snapped her fan open. ''It is. But I have a natural concern for you, Gideon. An artist's life is a most unsteady one. The wrong woman would be driven mad by your unwavering attention to your work. I have seen you 'in the throes of the muse.' ''

''Yes, and that's where I need to be. Miss Hartsell was foisted upon me, and now I have to foist her off on someone else in turn, so that I may get back to my work. I look to you for a quick solution.''

''If quick is what you want, the answer is right in front of you. Miss Hartsell could keep house on a shoestring and is used to entertaining herself. She is not the kind of cloying female to hang upon a man's sleeve, demanding constant attention and admiration.''

Lady Albinia fixed her godson with a beatific smile. ''The perfect wife for an up-and-coming artist! Miss Hartsell needs a home and a husband, and you desperately require the funds you can obtain once she is safely married. My dear Gideon, the solution is obvious: marry her yourself!''

"*What!?* Marry Miss Hartsell? Good God, Albinia, have you gone mad?" Gideon said savagely. "I am not *that* desperate!"

At that exact moment his godmother looked past his shoulder and stiffened. "Oh dear . . ."

Gideon glanced in the mirror above the fireplace and saw Chloe framed in the window behind him. "*Devil take it!*"

Chloe stood still as a statue. All the color had fled from her face, even her lips were blanched. Lady Albinia rose, and Gideon started toward her.

Their mouths were moving, but Chloe couldn't hear anything more over the roar of blood in her ears. She had already heard far too much.

Humiliated and blind with rage, she lifted her skirts and ran away from the house, into the sheltering twilight.

SEVEN

§§

CHLOE DIDN'T REALIZE HOW FAR OR HOW FAST SHE RAN in fleeing Gideon's words. Her only thought was to put as much distance between herself and the source of her humiliation as possible.

"*Hateful, hateful man!*"

Holding her skirts, she flew through a blur of twilit garden, beneath silhouettes of black lace trees, until she came out onto the pond's grassy slope.

"Miss Hartsell?"

Gideon's voice propelled her down to the water's edge and across the ancient footbridge, scarcely aware of the slippery stones beneath her feet. She could hear him mumbling and cursing as brambles caught at his clothes.

She slipped once, righted herself, and went on. Anything to avoid having to talk with *him*!

Chloe was shaking with fury. She raced breathlessly along a track that led straight and true, and the very brambles seemed to move aside to let her pass. Not so much as a twig caught her sleeve as she went deeper, ever deeper into the woods. They closed around her like a thick wool cloak, insulating her from everything outside.

Although she couldn't hear him any longer, she kept going. The way seemed straight and level, but when she glanced over her shoulder once, Chloe discovered she had moved to considerably higher ground. This was unfamiliar territory. She stopped to get her bearings.

It startled her to realize she had gone across the flat meadow and was on the steep slope of Pucca's Hill. Since first coming to Lacey's Folly, she had vowed that one day she would climb all the way to the summit. Somehow time was always too short . . . the ground too wet . . . the weather too changeable.

She realized now that she had avoided the hill as much as any of the villagers. And small wonder. There was a strange atmosphere here. *Not quite menace*, she told herself. More like *otherness*.

Although no wind danced through the treetops, they seemed to creak and whisper around her. She was afraid to listen. Afraid she might begin to understand what they were saying.

She cried out, ''I do not fear fairy raths or magic spells. I have lived in the shadow of Pucca's Hill for ten years. There is nothing here to frighten me.''

Nothing except those ancient pits which she had warned Perry about.

A hare bounded past, alarmed by all the noise she'd created. Chloe jumped, then laughed aloud. Suddenly everything seemed normal once more. Deciding to retrace her steps, she turned and stopped short. She could not make out the path that led down, only the ancient way winding to the summit. Everywhere she looked—except up, toward the summit—the path was hidden in masses of tangled twigs and branches. How had she ever gotten through them?

Perhaps if I climb a little higher, I can look out over the land and get my bearings.

Making her way along the hard, trodden track, she wondered who had first climbed up the rugged slope. Hunters following an animal? Worshipers climbing the hill to face the rising sun or to offer a sacrifice?

A tiny shiver ran through her. The eerie spell of the place was creeping back into her blood. The sheltering woods now seemed a treacherous maze designed to keep her in.

Chloe's heart pounded: there was only so much rational

thought could do against primeval instinct. *I must find the way back*, she thought, almost on the verge of panic.

She thought she saw a light ahead, down and to her right. She made her way toward it gratefully. It must be the drawing room windows of Lacey's Folly. Reassured, she went a little faster. The light would lead her back home.

And away from the strangeness of Pucca's Hill.

The outcrop that formed the landmark was so much larger, so much higher than she'd expected—and she was less than halfway up. So different from anything in the area that she almost could believe there was a fairy fort beneath it, where the Old Ones had gone to live their enchanted lives, safely away from the sound of the Christian church bells, the scald of holy water and cold burn of iron, forged by human hands.

How had she ever gotten so far from the house in so short a time? Surely only minutes had passed. It was so unnaturally cool beneath the trees, and the rapidly failing light had suddenly turned from misty lavenders to a shimmery, watery green. Chloe felt as if she were walking along the bottom of some ancient, magical sea. Half expecting a fish or mereman to swim by, she gasped when her foot caught a root and sent her sprawling.

"Oh!" The cry of pain was wrenched from her. She had twisted her ankle viciously on the exposed root. No, not a root, she saw when the tears of pain cleared from her eyes. It was a buried slab of stone carved with ancient runes.

They should have been difficult to see in the green twilight, except that moss had grown thicker in the grooves of the lines than along the flat planes of the slab. A series of whorls were carved beside them, the grooves as clear and clean as if made only yesterday.

Chloe touched them tentatively. A little spark seemed to jump from the stone to her fingertip. She recoiled instinctively, and the unease that had simmered in her mind bloomed into full-fledged panic. Despair wracked her soul. *O where shall I go? What shall I do? O who will take me in?*

She sat up in alarm. Those thoughts were not hers. They

were in her mind, but it seemed as if someone else had spoken them.

"Nonsense!" She said briskly. "Sheer imagination."

The panic, and the voice in her mind, vanished. Encouraged, she tried again to prove to herself it was all illusion. Her finger touched the whorls gingerly. Nothing happened.

She pressed more firmly. Moving her fingertip along the grooves, she followed the pattern again. Suddenly, Chloe felt the cold stone warm. It grew softer and seemed to melt beneath her hand. She was dizzy with surprise and something more.

Her head swam, but she seemed compelled to keep her finger tracing the grooves in their endless patterns, as they curved back into each other, over and over again.

The rhythm was hypnotic. Her vision blurred and her eyes closed. She was so sleepy. So very sleepy. And yet her fingers kept following the swirls as if they had a will of their own. Her hand was sinking, sinking into the stone. Up to the wrist . . . now the elbow. She could feel her shoulder pass into the stone effortlessly. Any moment the rest of her would follow.

Chloe's ears buzzed. Someone was singing nearby. A low, soft tune in a language she had never heard. So beautiful! So compelling that she wanted to follow it to its source. Gratefully, she leaned her head against the shifting rock, embraced by the sound. She was moving into it, through it, as though it were air.

"*Miss Hartsell!*

Chloe woke, suddenly and instantly. She was disoriented and bereft. And greatly annoyed. She couldn't feel the stone anymore, and the air was no longer rich and green. The lovely singing had ceased altogether, and someone stood over her, shining a blindingly bright lantern in her eyes. She turned her head away from it.

"Please, the light! It burns my eyes."

Instantly, the glare was muted, shuttered to a mild glow. Gideon Stone bent over her, chaffing her cold, pale hands between his strong, brown ones. His face was hard with concern.

Chloe pulled her hands free, near tears, although she couldn't say why. Except that she had been having the strangest, loveliest dream. She hadn't wanted it to end.

"Miss Hartsell, can you hear me?"

She struggled to sit up. "I can, and I assume half the village can as well. You needn't shout at me."

He rocked back on one knee, scowling. "Forgive me, but you gave me a bad fright. We have been searching for you for almost two hours. Then I saw you sprawled there against the stone. You looked . . . your color was so odd that . . . I thought for a moment that you were dead."

She brushed the hair from her face. "Yes, and then who would you get to pose for your precious paintings?"

He narrowed his eyes. "Give me credit for a little more human feeling than that, Miss Hartsell. You gave me quite a shock."

Pushing herself up to a sitting position, she looked down at the skirts of Lady Albinia's sage green gown. It was ruined.

Chloe burst into tears.

Gideon set down the lantern and fished in his pocket for his handkerchief. "There, there, my dear, you mustn't be upset. I dare say Lady Albinia has gowns by the dozens."

"*She* may, sir, but *I* have not."

He looked stricken.

A voice called out in the night. Gideon raised the lantern and swung it back and forth, hullowing down the hill. "Over here!"

Shouts came in reply. Another lantern moved toward them. Gideon took off his coat and wrapped it around Chloe. She was shaking with chill. Soon Henry, the old gardener, came through the undergrowth toward them. The dark clouds parted overhead, and the entire hillside was bathed in bright, silver light. It was almost light as day. Every stick and bramble stood out in high relief.

"Thank Heaven ye be safe, Miss Chloe. Pucca's Hill is no place to go a-wandering alone of an evening. Young Perry is fair sore we wouldn't let him come a-hunting ye. He said the

Old Ones would carry ye off and leave a changeling in yer place.''

"Perhaps that wouldn't have been a bad idea," Gideon muttered, so only she could hear.

"I am quite all right, Henry. If there are any fairies here, they did not want me.''

Either. Although she said it silently, Chloe's unspoken word echoed through Gideon's head. He was upset that his unthinking comment had caused her hurt. She looked so very vulnerable. He handed Henry the lantern.

"I don't need this now that the moon is out. Go signal to the others that she's been found. I will take Miss Hartsell back to the manor.''

The gardener nodded and set off briskly. Master Perry had been sent off to bed with some tale, but the servants had worked themselves into a state over Miss Chloe's disappearance.

Gideon blinked. Strange, but despite the bright moonlight, Henry had only gone a yard or two before he disappeared from sight. The silver trees stirred, murmured, and sighed against the backdrop of the polished moon. He could almost imagine they were leaning in, listening and watching his every movement.

"Let us get you back to a warm fire and some mulled wine, Miss Hartsell." Holding out his hand to her, Gideon tried to assist Chloe to her feet.

"Oh! My ankle!"

She almost fell. She had forgotten she'd injured it. There had been no pain until she tried to stand. Chloe discovered she couldn't put any weight upon it. Kneeling, Gideon took her foot in his hand, pulled off her slipper, and felt along the dainty bones.

"Nothing broken that I can tell. It's merely bruised. I shall have to carry you.''

He took out his handkerchief and bound her foot and ankle tightly. It immediately felt better. "I can walk," Chloe said. "It is only a little tender.''

"And have you stumble or fall into a rabbit hole? Here, lean on me." Gideon put her head against his shoulder, then scooped her up effortlessly. It was too late for her to protest, even if she'd wanted to. Chloe was forced to admit it was comforting to have someone look after her for a change.

The way was rough and jarring. She had to clutch at his jacket for balance. "Put your arm around my neck. I won't bite, I promise."

"Well, I will not."

Nevertheless, she did put her arm around his shoulder. They came to a break in the trees. There was the manor house far below. Lacey's Folly looked like a lighted doll house, the river no more than a trickle. Chloe could not believe she had climbed so high without knowing it. Something he'd said earlier struck her belatedly.

"You said you have been searching almost two hours?"

"Frantically, I assure you. Thank Heavens the night is so warm, or you might have been dead of cold."

"But . . . it seemed like mere minutes to me. No more than a quarter hour, I swear."

"You are suffering from shock, Miss Hartsell. You can tell by how high the moon has risen that considerable time has passed."

He was right. The moon was high overhead now, shedding plenty of light along their route. Chloe gave a little shiver. She would be glad once they left Pucca's Hill.

He carried her along a natural plateau carved into the side of the hill, where the going was easier. Chloe couldn't recall seeing it earlier. The house was lost to view. Not too far downslope from them, Henry's lantern bobbed along through the woods like a giant firefly.

Gideon slowed his pace until he was sure Henry was out of earshot. "Miss Hartsell, I recognize that this is my fault. I saw you run off. You evidently overheard my conversation with Lady Albinia."

"I was not eavesdropping, if that is what you mean," she said indignantly. "I had merely come round the garden in time to hear you . . . to hear you reject me in such terms of disgust!''

''I never meant . . .'' He stopped and glared down at her ''My comments were not directed against you personally What I was trying to say was that I have no intention of marrying anyone, and that I was not desperate enough to enter that state merely to thwart the terms of the will.''

''Save your breath! You needn't make polite excuses to me Mr. Stone. I know that I am plain, and I know that you do not find me desirable in the least.''

She gave a little hiccup that was supposed to be a wry laugh but came out more like a strangled sob. ''Perhaps you think yourself a prime catch, now that you are master of Lacey' Folly. Well, let me tell you, sir, that you are the last man on God's green earth I would ever consider marrying, if it mean the difference between a life of comfort or working as a taver wench for my keep! You are rude, self-centered, spoiled small-minded, egotistical and . . . and . . .''

It was his turn to be injured and angry. ''That will do, Miss Hartsell! I am quite aware of my numerous failings.''

She wouldn't let him know how handsome he looked scowling so in the lantern light. Satisfied now that the table were turned, Chloe pointed toward the distant lights.

''You are going the wrong way,'' she announced. ''The house is that way.''

''You are wrong, Miss Hartsell. You saw the moon reflecting off a rock. Lacey's Folly is straight ahead.''

''No, it is not. Put me down. I can walk now.''

''Obstinate woman!''

But he realized he had lost his bearings. There was something very odd about this place. He felt . . . different. Less civilized. As if a thin veneer were slowly melting off his body to reveal the elemental man beneath.

Chloe was aware of a charge in the air. Something tha frightened her even as it made her heart pound with anticipation. ''Put me down, Mr. Stone. At once!''

She struggled so hard he almost lost his balance. Gideon'

grip tightened. "Would you prefer I carry you over my shoulder, like a farmer with a sack of turnips?"

"You wouldn't dare!"

For answer, he set her on her feet, with her back against a tree trunk, and bent to swing her over his shoulder. Chloe felt panicked, unable to move or breathe. Mustering all her will power, she broke through the strange lethargy and pushed at him, hard. Gideon fell over backward, taking her with him.

Chloe landed atop him, with her face pressed against his. For a moment he didn't speak, and she was afraid she had winded him.

"Mr. Stone?" She lifted her head. "Are you all right?"

Instead of answering, he suddenly rolled over. Their positions were reversed. Now it was his body pinning hers down. He took her face between his hands, looking down at her, with a frown between his brows. The moonlight gleamed on her face and throat, her ripe mouth and her unusual eyes shining silver with reflected light.

"You are not plain, Chloe Hartsell," he said fiercely. "You are an incredible beauty, if only you knew it! One I find very desirable!"

"Don't mock me!" she said angrily, trying to wriggle free. "Don't you dare to mock me!"

"*Is that what you think?*"

His hands twined in the hair at her temples and his mouth came down on hers, hard and bruising.

From the moment he had set foot on Pucca's Hill, thinking her injured—or worse—she had filled his every thought, as she filled his arms now. From the moment he had lifted her into his arms in the dark wood, the small flame of attraction had flared into desire. Now it became a burning urgency.

He could feel her heart pounding beneath her bodice. His kiss changed, became softer. Infinitely tender, and all the more devastating for it.

Chloe was breathless. Dizzy. As if she were falling again, not deep into the rock, but into him. She was aware of the hard muscle beneath his fashionably cut coat, the breadth of chest and impressive width of shoulder, as her curves fitted against him. Of his eyes, wide and midnight dark.

"Chloe! Beautiful Chloe," he murmured against her mouth. Then his kiss altered once more, became hot and hard and conquering.

Gideon's hands moved from her face to her shoulders and slipped beneath her, arching her body up toward him. He groaned with desire and covered her mouth with kisses, felt her little gasps of pleasure burst against his lips like tiny sparks.

There was something about the night, the ancient mysteries surrounding them, that banished civilization and roused their most primal instincts. The wind set the boughs of the trees whispering in their ancient tongue. Memories of pagan rites rose like mist from the very earth beneath them. Ancient chants murmured through the voice of the woods. They stirred deep, sensual hungers in both Chloe and Gideon, called forth untamed cravings that cried out for satisfaction.

Gideon responded to the atmosphere more and more, with every drumbeat of his heart. She was as moved by it as he. She shifted, curving her body to his, welcoming his passion. That loosed his last hold on reason. Kisses were not enough. He wanted more.

She was like pure water, fresh and sweet and life-giving, and he had a powerful thirst for her. One that could not be sated so easily. His other hand slid along her side and up, to cup her breast. It filled his palm through the silky fabric, perfect and ripe. His long fingers brushed the tip and she shuddered beneath him. He kneaded it gently, and she made a soft sound, half protest and half surrender.

For an instant his conscience pricked him, and he lifted his face from hers. Chloe's arms wound around him, and her hands slid up his neck and tangled in his thick curls, pulling him back. They gave themselves up to the night. The moment. The utter, devastating need.

Chloe clung to him. It was like all her most ardent dreams

come true. They were falling, falling gently through the soft silver light. Together.

Heat poured through him and took her mouth in a passionate kiss. This time he caught her full lower lip between his teeth and nipped lightly. When her lips parted in surprise, his tongue slipped in, and he explored her mouth. He knew that he was the first to ever kiss her so thoroughly, and that made his blood heat even more.

The masculine urge to conquer and possess blotted out everything. Everything but Chloe—sweet, seductive Chloe— and the way she felt to his seeking hands, tasted to his questing mouth.

His finger darted beneath the low neckline of her gown, trailing between the warm cleft. Before she had time to react, he pressed kisses at the corners of her mouth, then followed the line of her throat, down and down to the top of her dress.

Chloe was lost in sensation. Submerged in a sensual dream. She felt the shock of his hand against her bare flesh, moaned in delight as his fingers sought the peak of her breast and caught it firmly. Waves of pleasure shot through her, and she wound her arms more tightly around him.

There was no past or present. Only now. Only Gideon.

Now she could feel his breath, warm against the silk bodice of her gown. His mouth covered the tip of her breast through the fabric, hot and moist and hungry. Her blood ran like a molten river through her veins, and she thought she would die from the bliss of it.

He was suddenly impatient with the barrier between them. His hands were at her neckline, pulling it lower, edging it down until her breast was free. He teased and tugged, then suckled deeply, once, twice, and suddenly her body was wracked with pleasure so intense, it jolted her from head to toe. He held her while she moaned and cried out. She bucked so sharply she twisted free.

"Oh, Gideon! For the love of God!" she cried out.

At her words, the universe suddenly shifted. Gideon came to his senses. He got to his knees, gasping for breath. Good

God in Heaven, what had gotten into him? Another few minutes and . . .

The moon shone down, clothing them in silver, and the stars burned holes in a sky of pure, ultramarine blue. Chloe lay on her side, one lovely breast exposed, while she panted for air and sanity.

Despite the cool wind, sweat stood out upon Gideon's brow. His need for her was a physical pain, and his loins throbbed with unspent passion.

He staggered to his feet, afraid to touch her, even to help her up. He knew he could have taken her—could still—and she would let him, willingly. They would become lovers. Passionate lovers.

And she would be utterly ruined.

He looked down at Chloe, wondering how he had ever thought her plain. She took his breath away. And she deserved far, far better than this.

She turned on her back, became suddenly conscious of her gown all awry, and straightened her bodice. The silk was still damp from his mouth. Heat pooled in her loins. ''Gideon . . .''

He averted his face and found his jacket, then held out his hand to her, helping her up. The moment she stood, he released her, as if she burned his flesh. He draped his jacket over her hastily and fastened the topmost button.

''We have to go back,'' he said. ''Now.''

She was still dazed and aching for him. She lifted her arms. ''Gideon!''

''No!'' His voice sounded harsh in his own ears. ''This is madness. We must leave this accursed place before . . .'' He didn't finish. He couldn't. It took every ounce of willpower not to turn and crush her against him, take her to the mossy ground, and finish what they'd started.

He broke off a dried branch violently and gave it to her as a walking stick. From the corner of his eye, he could see that she limped slightly, but he didn't dare carry her or even give her his arm. Not until they were at the pond, and he had no choice.

Gideon lifted her into his arms without a word and carried her across. Every atom in his body fought to make him turn back the other way. He made the crossing, then stood her on her feet again.

"I'm sorry. I cannot touch you. I dare not!"

She went with him mutely. The spell was still so strong upon her, she was afraid to speak. Chloe had never felt anything like the longings that had swept through her on Pucca's Hill. They had both been mad. She knew it now. Just as she knew that she wanted the madness to continue. The wild yearning that had shaken her and left her weak with longing had not been banished, only dulled. She ached to feel his body upon hers again.

They went in the side door, through the library, where no one would see them enter. The evening had grown cool, and a fire was lit in the grate. He sat her in a chair near the warmth of the fire and poured them each a glass of brandy in silence. He knelt beside her chair and handed her the glass.

"Drink it up. All at once."

She tipped her head back, coughed and sputtered, but got the brandy down.

It was like a warm fire inside her. Then the knowledge flowed through her. She realized it wasn't the brandy that had lit the flame, it was Gideon: she loved him. Deeply and irrevocably.

There. She had finally admitted it to herself. Almost from the first moment she'd seen him in her garden, before she even knew his name, she had known that he was someone who would become special in her life. She just hadn't known how. Chloe started shaking. No matter how she tried, she couldn't control the fine tremors.

Gideon looked at the cut crystal glass filled with amber liquid, then tossed the brandy back. He poured another, drank it down, and finally looked at her. How small and pitiful she looked engulfed in his big jacket. It was covered with dirt and bits of leaf mould. Shame burned through him.

Gideon's fingers curled around the glass, while he cursed

himself for a villain. She was young, alone, and he had almost done the unthinkable: taken her out of his own need, without a thought of the consequences to her.

In the leaping light, he could see the bramble snags, the earthy stains, and his own ravages to her dress. He snatched up a throw from the sofa and covered her with it.

"Your poor gown," he said softly. "It is quite ruined."

She smiled. Her eyes were silver stars. "I do not mind in the least."

Gideon set down his glass. He took her by the shoulders. "Chloe, Chloe! Do not look at me like that. This mustn't happen again. It was a wild aberration born of moonlight and emotion. I am attracted to you, yes! Very much so, I find. And it cannot be."

"*Why?*" The word was wrenched from her.

He swore beneath his breath. Why, indeed. He had been thinking of her all day, since he'd first captured her image on paper. In the act of doing so, she had captured his imagination in turn. "There is no future in it. You need a husband to protect and care for you. Give you children."

He gave her a hard little shake. "There is no room for such things in my life. Not now, perhaps not ever. Do you understand?"

"No!"

She clutched at his hands, and he held her away. "My dear girl, you are under my roof. Under my protection. I would be a cad to take advantage of you."

"But . . ."

He pressed a finger to her soft lips, swollen with his kisses. He tried not to think of her heart, beating so fast beneath her bodice, her breasts, so enticing to his hands and mouth.

His expression was severe. "An artist's life is a highly irregular one. I don't need the distraction of a wife and family, my dear, and you are not cut out to be a mistress. We must pretend tonight never happened. We must do everything to avoid such a situation again. If I thought that we could not withstand temptation, I would no longer ask you to sit for me," he said harshly.

"In fact," he said slowly, staring into the fire, "I think I would have to leave Lacey's Folly. Do you understand that?"

Her heart sank. She could not imagine Lacey's Folly without him now. It would be so empty! She would be so lost!

Chloe looked at him steadily, then lowered her eyes so he would not see her heart there.

"I understand, Gideon. I do."

"Very well."

He raised her hand, held it a moment, and kissed it. Then dropped it quickly, as he had before. "We have a pact then."

"We do."

Chloe waited just a few beats. "I sincerely hope that you may find someone else to sit for your painting, so that you may finish in time and win Lord Pulham's commission."

Gideon hadn't thought beyond the moment. He was stunned. The artist in him was appalled. All other considerations receded. "But . . . I need you! One has nothing to do with the other. You will still be my model, will you not?"

"How can I, under the circumstances? We should be alone for hours at a time."

He paced the room, avoiding her eyes. "That is true. But it would be completely different, I assure you! When I am painting, everything else goes by the wayside. It ceases to exist. I have no doubt that I would be able to look upon you objectively, as the central subject of the composition."

He was trying to convince himself as much as her. She could almost laugh, if she didn't feel so much like weeping. *Oh, Gideon!*

Chloe bit her bottom lip. "And if I agree to sit for you— you would give me your word you will not touch me, if I ask you for it?"

The fire hissed and crackled, dancing orange and yellow and blue. "Yes. Of course."

"Then," she said softly, "I will not ask it of you."

"Devil take it, Chloe, this is not a game!"

She didn't answer. In the distance, they could hear Lady Albinia's clear voice, and Mrs. Olser's deeper tones. They would not be alone much longer.

Gideon wrestled with himself. "If you are not averse to it," he said finally, "we'll begin the sittings tomorrow."

"Very well."

He glanced over at her. Saw how lovely she looked with the firelight turning her hair to gold and copper. What a picture that would make: woman as elemental fire!

A sigh of relief tore through him. That was better. Once he learned to think of her as part of the painting, he could stop thinking of her as a woman. Therein lay his salvation. And hers.

"Well, then. There is nothing more to be said." He rang the bell for the maid. "Shall I help Agnes get you upstairs?"

"No. She can tend to my foot here, by the fireside. I won't go up just yet."

Mrs. Osler came in the door with Agnes at her heels. "There you are! We thought you would come in through the drawing room."

She tucked the blanket more tightly around Chloe's shoulders. "Oh, you poor darling! I'll ring for the tea. Cook has had the kettle on the boil for you." She noticed Chloe's bandaged foot.

"Only a sprain," Chloe said quickly.

"I shall make you a poultice to draw out the inflammation."

As Lady Albinia came in, Gideon went out with barely a nod. Her lovely brow clouded as he brushed by. Her godson looked angry, Chloe as pleased as punch. Something had gone on between them, but what could produce such opposite effects?

While the other women hovered over her, Chloe lowered her head and watched Gideon leave the room through her thick lashes. A moment ago there was despair in her heart, but now everything had changed. She had changed.

A small smile curved her mouth, still tingling from his kisses.

She had seen how shaken he was earlier—still was—and
how his hand trembled when it touched her mouth. Tonight,
for the first time, she had felt her power as a woman. It was
a potent force, as wild and untamable as the tides.

He was not immune. Oh, no.

Her smile grew. The game was not yet over.

*He was dreaming again. Gideon knew it. Yes. The place was
familiar. Up in the tower, moving toward the window now.
Gliding across the moonlit floor as effortlessly as if he were
made of fog. Reaching the cool stone sill. Lifting a hand to
pull back the half-closed shutter.*

*Something was pulling him back. Away from the window.
Hands clutched at him cruelly, but he batted them away. Not
now! No!*

*Slowly, inexorably, he was losing the battle. He opened his
mouth to shout in protest, but no sound came out. Rage and despair filled him. He didn't want the dream to end: this time he
would see her face. This time he would know . . .*

The sound of the drapery rings sliding against the brass rods
brought him, cursing, out of a sound sleep. "What in the name
of hell . . ."

Dawlish stood at the window, dapper as always. "Good
morning, Mr. Stone. You said that you wished to be awakened
early."

"So I did. Curse your efficiency." A rueful grin took the
sting from his words. He and Dawlish had developed a comfortable relationship. He'd miss the old man when he retired
to his cottage.

Gideon threw back the covers and slipped on his dressing
gown. The sittings for the portrait were to begin today. Memories of last night on Pucca's Hill came rushing back, and he
pushed them away. No time for that.

He'd lain awake, alternately thinking of the narrow escape
he and Miss Hartsell had had, and of Lord Pulham's commis-

sion. He knew the other two artists in the running. The first he dismissed out of hand. It was not generally known that Warren Pettibone suffered from advanced lung disease and the ravages of alcohol. The task was beyond the poor fellow's capabilities. He could scarcely hold a brush.

The other man, Albert Hoving, would surely do traditional renderings of the Virtues and Vices. His technique was good, but Hoving hadn't had an original thought in ten years. *And,* Gideon thought, *Lord Pulham is more forward thinking. While he likes the romantic style, he prefers new ways of seeing them.*

If he could come up with the right theme, he could surely snare the commission. His reputation would be made. If only he had the right model! The painting must be perfect, the best he'd ever done.

He blinked in the strong light. Something flashed through his mind. Tantalizing, half-remembered images of a woman running through the twilight mist. As Dawlish left the room, Gideon's eye fell on the painting over the mantelpiece in his bedchamber.

Lenore Lacey. Now there was a face to inspire! If she were alive today, she would have all of London at her feet. And so would he, if he were the artist fortunate enough to have her for his model.

And then he wouldn't have to face the temptation of being alone with Chloe Hartsell for hours at a time. But, as he'd told her, once the painting started, she would cease to be a woman of flesh and blood and become pure light and color on canvas.

He could set last night's events aside, he assured himself. It was a dream, he told himself. An erotic fantasy.

But at the same instant he was remembering the taste of Chloe's mouth, the texture of her skin, and he knew that it had all been very real. Today would be awkward. But once they got past it . . .

Dawlish brought in the can of steaming water and filled his shave basin, then retired as discreetly as he had come. Gideon lathered his brush, whipped the foam all over his beard, and stood at the shaving stand in the golden morning light. In the mirror, he could see the portrait of Lenore over his shoulder. She seemed to be looking back at him. Now there was a beauty for the ages. A woman to inspire not only fantasy, but legend.

Sliding the sharp razor's edge through a layer of foam, he caught movement from the corner of his eyes. He nicked himself, cursed, and swung around, half expecting to see the shade of a bald old man in an oriental tunic.

It was only Perry, hopping impatiently on the threshold between the bedroom and dressing room. "It's about time you looked up, sir. I've been waiting ever so long!"

"You can wait till hell freezes over, you infernal imp. Look what you made me do." Gideon dabbed at the freely bleeding nick with a linen towel. "I'm liable to bleed to death."

"Not if you push against it with the towel. I read that in one of Dr. Osler's books. 'Press firmly over the wound until the blood flow ceases.' "

"I know that, curse it. What the devil are you doing in my room before breakfast?"

Perry's face lit up. "I have a marvelous surprise, sir. But you must come down to the breakfast parlor. Chloe is there," he added as an inducement.

An early face to face meeting, before I've had time to collect my wits. Just what I wanted to avoid, Gideon thought wryly. He'd been dawdling for that very reason, all, it seemed, to no purpose.

"I'll be down as soon as I'm shaved and dressed." He lifted the razor and scraped a smooth swath along his chin.

"Lady Albinia said you must have a valet. Then you could be ready in a twinkling."

"Artists don't have valets, young man, they have . . ." *mistresses.* Gideon almost cut his throat. A thin scarlet line marred his jawbone.

He turned on Perry in exasperation. "Out, you confounded pup, before I do something to myself that your reading can't correct. Or," he added when the boy lingered, "something to you!"

"Yes, sir. But hurry, sir. It's something wonderful!"

It was a good half hour before Gideon finished, shrugged into his shirt and coat, and went down to the breakfast parlor. Chloe gave a little start and colored when he walked in. Mrs. Osler looked up.

"Good morning, Mr. Stone." She eyed the bits of sticking plaster along his jaw and neck with raised eyebrows, but didn't venture a comment.

Chloe murmured a greeting and stirred her coffee. Gideon had meant every word he'd said last night. He hadn't looked her way directly. Not once. How she was ever going to sit for his painting under such ridiculous circumstances was beyond her comprehension. But something would come to her. She smiled into her cup.

Perry positively squirmed with excitement. "Do you think it is all right? Lady Albinia is still abed." He shot a disappointed look across the table. "Chloe says we're not to wake her."

"Ah, yes." Gideon heaped eggs and slices of thick country ham upon his plate. "My beloved godmother sees absolutely no reason to leave her chamber before noon, and finds it very odd that anyone would do so by choice—as, she says, nothing of interest ever happens before then."

"Well she is completely out!" Perry announced. "I have been up since dawn . . . and I have found the lost Lacey treasure!"

Even Mrs. Osler heard that. She set down her cup and stared at him. "Have you indeed?"

"Yes, and it's all thanks to the books you gave me," he said, grinning happily.

"Where is it?" Gideon asked.

"*What* is it?" Chloe demanded.

In answer, Perry darted out of the room, then returned a minute later with a humpbacked chest of inlaid wood. It was heavy and filled his arms. He set it on the table without the ceremony he had intended, rattling the cups in their saucers. "Here it is: the lost Lacey treasure."

Chloe sighed. Poor dear. "I'm afraid that is no treasure

chest, Perry. It's the Burmese box that holds the silver tea-spoons.''

He blushed. "I took them out. They're in the butler's pantry. I just wanted you to see the treasure at its best." He looked so gleeful, as if he were about to burst if he held it in much longer. "And the greatest thing is, it was under our noses the whole time!"

"Then what is it?" Gideon roared. "Confound it boy, open it up!"

Perry wrinkled his forehead. "Very well. But you must remember one thing. I found it," he said importantly, "in the *mineral* collection. So you see, it belongs to Chloe, not to you."

Chloe's heart turned over. "What is it?"

"You shall see! But first Gideon has to promise."

Gideon scowled. "Do you think me the kind of man to take something that is not legally mine? I am gratified to know it!"

"N . . . no, sir," Perry said hastily, flushing to the roots of his hair. "I didn't mean any offense, sir. I know you would never . . ."

"Enough. Let's see this fabulous find of yours then."

Chloe held her breath as Perry lifted the lid with a flourish. Like the reading of Tobias Lacey's will, this moment could change her life yet again.

"There it is," Perry said solemnly. "Lost Lenore's treasure."

An irregular lump, the size of a man's two fists, gleamed golden in the warm morning light. Perry's puckish face gleamed as brightly, the freckles across his nose like gold dust.

"Pirate's gold!" he announced proudly.

There was a stunned silence. Gideon and Mrs. Osler shook their heads simultaneously.

"Iron pyrites," the widow said.

Gideon was his usual tactful self. "Fool's gold," he said. "A common ore, worth nothing, I'm afraid."

Chloe let out the breath she'd been holding. Perry's head lowered a moment. He bit his lip, and her heart was wrung. He had wanted so much to help her.

"It's very nice fool's gold," she said, afraid he was fighting tears of bitter disappointment. After all, he was only ten years old. Gideon put his hand on the boy's shoulder by way of comfort.

But Perry was not discouraged. He closed the lid. "Don't worry, Chlo. I won't give up. I *will* find the lost Lacey treasure."

Or, failing that, he would find Lost Lenore. He had a plan.

After he freed her from the spell that kept her captive beneath Pucca's Hill, she would surely share her treasure with them. He went off to replace the chunk of iron pyrite and the silver storage chest, as optimistic as ever.

The plans to begin Chloe's sittings didn't materialize as early as planned. First Mr. Fortescue rode out with papers for Gideon to sign. That took up the best part of the morning, much to her relief.

Chloe passed the time feeding the ducks on the pond with Perry and Mrs. Osler. When the sun grew too warm for the older woman, Chloe took Perry around to the shady front lawn where they took turns throwing sticks for his puppy to fetch. Newton loved the game and yipped his loud approval.

Gideon was in a very good mood as he went over affairs in the library with the solicitor. "Then, with news of this possible commission and Lacey's Folly officially mine, there will be no trouble effecting a loan?"

"None at all, Mr. Stone. You may send a draft on your bank account to Lord Exton to discharge your debts." He polished his pince-nez against his sleeve and looked unhappy. "However, doing so will leave the estate strapped. While I would hate to see Lacey's Folly pass into the hands of strangers, I would advise you to find a husband for Miss Hartsell with all due speed."

"I expect to have accomplished that little task by summer's end." *But not before the portrait sitting is completed*, he added silently.

No, playing matchmaker would have to wait a bit longer.

Although Albinia had made up a list of potential mates for Miss Hartsell.

"*A young lady with a good settlement can always find a husband*," she had said yesterday. "*All it takes is winnowing out the wheat from the chaff.*" Easier said than done, Gideon thought, frowning. Chloe deserved a husband who would appreciate her for herself. And, by God, he was determined to find her one.

"And what of the other matter I asked you to undertake, Fortescue?"

"There is nothing in her background to cause you concern." The solicitor handed another paper to Gideon. "It is all in here. Miss Hartsell and her brother are distant relations of Tobias Lacey. They came of a well-to-do family. Unfortunately, their father speculated heavily, investing in a shipping line that failed. He lost everything, including their home, and died of a fever shortly after. The mother had died before him.

"Miss Hartsell and her brother were sent to cousins by marriage in Harrowgate. These generous souls put them out on the parish, when they learned the orphans hadn't a farthing to their names. Eventually, Tobias Lacey returned to England, heard of the tragedy, and was determined to bring them to live with him at Lacey's Folly. The rest you know."

Gideon was relieved. "Good. I want no skeletons dancing out of the closet to stop the girl from marrying quickly and well." He put the packet beneath the blotter. "And what of my supposed connection with the family?"

Mr. Fortescue shook his head. "Nothing has shown up thus far."

"Well," Gideon said, rising, "if Tobias was correct on the one, I will assume he was on the other."

"It makes no matter," the solicitor told him as they went out into the hall. "The will is valid, even if you were no blood relation at all. Martin Thorne, despite his angry letters of to me, full of appeals and threats, has no claim upon the estate, other than what he was granted in the will."

They went out to the drive where Fortescue's carriage was

waiting. Newton came bounding up, eager for a romp. Gideon rubbed the dog's head absentmindedly. Suddenly Newton's ears pricked. A moment later a horse and rider came over the packhorse bridge and up the long drive. It was a courier with a letter for Gideon.

His eyebrows rose when he saw the impressive seal upon it. Breaking it with his nail, he opened the letter. "More work for you, Fortescue. The local magistrate informs me that Olivia and Martin Thorne have lodged formal notice of their intent to contest Tobias Lacey's will."

The solicitor read it and shook his grizzled head. "The farm at Lesser Barnstable is a very nice property, yet they are determined to have Lacey's Folly."

Gideon scowled as they made their way out of the hall to the front door. "Determined to make trouble, you mean. It is not the house and land they're after, but some legendary treasure hidden on the grounds."

"If it has not been found in a hundred years, it will not be found now. If it ever existed." He mounted the carriage. The master of Lacey's Folly was still scowling.

"Do not be concerned, Mr. Stone," the solicitor said. "Believe me when I say that the will is right and tight. There is no one on the face of the earth who can overset your claim to the property."

Perry picked up the stick that Newton had dropped at Gideon's feet. "What if Lenore Lacey comes back? Would she own the treasure, or would it belong to the one who found it?"

For a moment Mr. Fortescue was nonplussed. "Ah," he said, trying to hide his smile. "Lenore. The 'Lost Bride.' "

He rubbed his chin and pretended to consider the question. "A very interesting situation that would prove, my lad. I'll tell you what I'll do. I will look into that—when and if the lady ever appears."

Perry took the stick and threw it with all his might. Mr. Fortescue was laughing at him. No one ever took him seriously.

Not even Chloe.

I'll show them! he vowed. *I'll show everyone. I'll find Lost Lenore and her treasure—and won't they all be surprised!*

The next week passed quickly. Lady Albinia set off for Greater Barnstable on a shopping expedition with her dresser, but promised to return early. In the morning she would return to London for two weeks.

"By the time I return, my dear Gideon, I hope your sittings are well advanced, for I mean to start taking Miss Hartsell about with me."

Gideon went out to hand her up into the carriage.

"Must you really go tomorrow?" he asked, holding her elegantly gloved hand in his. He wasn't sure he was ready to be so completely alone with Chloe Hartsell just yet. Lady Albinia's presence at the manor was a powerful deterrent.

His godmother adjusted her heavy silk shawl and offered her subtly rouged cheek for him to kiss. "If you expect me to produce miracles, I have no time to waste. Your task, meanwhile, is to do the paintings for Lord Pulham. Mrs. Osler will keep on eye on young Perry, so that Miss Hartsell is free to sit for you."

"I hope you know what you are doing."

She gave him a roguish smile. "You may be sure of it."

As Lady Albinia drove off in her carriage, the vehicle rounded a bend in the lane. An opening in the trees offered her a glimpse of Chloe down in her garden, and Gideon in pursuit.

Albinia smiled a secret little smile. Perry would keep Mrs. Osler too busy to interfere with matters, and she was sure that once her godson and Miss Hartsell spent enough time together, Gideon would see the light.

If I manage to stay away long enough, she thought happily, *nature will take its course and the matter will resolve itself.*

Gideon's thoughts were exactly opposite. He let himself in through the gate, thinking that he had already once passed over the bounds of what was proper. He was determined not to do so again.

Today he should make much progress with his work. With

Albinia gone, and Mrs. Osler and Perry off to visit her young nephews and nieces, they wouldn't have to break until the light failed. He'd already carried over a hamper of food that Cook had prepared in anticipation of a long session.

"Come, Miss Hartsell. It's time for our sitting. We've lost enough time as it is."

Chloe walked along the pathway with him, deep in thought. She picked the fading petals from a rose she had plucked and let them drift through her fingers. Since the night on Pucca's Hill, Gideon was so exceedingly formal and distant, it made an awkwardness between them.

"Miss Hartsell sounds so old-spinsterish," she told him. "I wish that you would call me Chloe. I have given you leave to use my Christian name."

"It isn't proper, and we both know it."

They went the rest of the way to the tower in silence.

It was the perfect studio. The light was extraordinary, there was always a breeze, and it was perfectly quiet and peaceful. He could work for hours undisturbed. Why then, Gideon wondered, did he dread going there a little more each day? As if he were waiting for something to happen.

Something decidedly unpleasant.

Gideon still felt uneasy outside the tower, near the edge of the low bluff, and inside, by the window overlooking the river. As long as he stayed away from those places, he was fine. The privacy and isolation were an artist's blessing and a hot-blooded man's curse.

"I have been thinking that perhaps I should move the sitting back to the main house," he said suddenly.

Chloe felt her heart roll over. She loved their hours together in Giovanna's little bower. "There is no time. You require every minute of good light to work upon the paintings. The deadline is growing near."

She went upstairs ahead of him, as always, to change into the fluid Grecian-style gown that Albinia had produced from one of her trunks. The fabric was so fine, it could be drawn through a ring, but there were quantities of it sufficient for modesty. It was slightly large on her smaller frame, but that only added to the cascading grace of the draping, Gideon said. He had refused to let Lady Albinia's maid alter a single seam.

As she hung up her dress and chemise and donned the flowing outfit, temptation whispered to her. There was the sketchbook on the table. And there, with its back to her, was the easel with the painting. He wouldn't let her see it until it was done. Gideon always smoked a cigar outside while she changed and got into position on the low couch. She had plenty of time.

No, she'd given her word. She'd wait until it was finished. Chloe sighed and draped herself along the couch and waited for Gideon.

"Don't move unless I give you leave," Gideon said irritably. "I warned you this would be a long session today."

"It feels like a hundred years," she retorted.

Chloe felt awkward. The sitting was going all wrong today. Gideon stared at her, paced a foot or so, stopped and stared again. He'd been doing it for hours and it was nerve-wracking. He would hold up his hand, as if measuring, step back a few feet, then shake his head.

He'd rooted around in the storage space and replaced the sofa with an upright wooden chair. Nothing would do for him but that they must use this chair he'd unearthed. Carved of dark wood, it resembled some ancient Gothic throne. Chloe loathed it. The seat was uncushioned, but at least he'd thrown down a thick velvet pillow, for which she thanked her lucky stars. But her posterior was growing numb, and her nose itched.

"No," he said suddenly, startling her. He made a sound of exasperation, crossed quickly over to her, and put his hands on her shoulders. They were stiff and tense, more so when the heat of his hands seemed to set her blood aglow. She tensed.

"You must relax, Chloe . . . er, Miss Hartsell. Sit at ease, as if you had nothing more urgent to do than contemplate your garden."

"It's impossible to do so with you glaring at me."

"I am not glaring! I am studying you."

"Well, it is most unnerving."

Gideon stepped back, frowning. Something was off. If he could just put his finger on it. It wasn't her hair, nor the folds of her gown. The white gauze layers that Albinia had unearthed from her trunk, and the lace snood that confined those masses of red hair, were the perfect symbolism for what he had in mind: innocent Love, waiting to be awakened by passion's first embrace.

Perhaps it was the pose itself, the way he had her looking away from him and out the window to the garden below. Yes, if he just moved her head and . . .

Suddenly, Chloe stood up. "I am sorry, but I cannot sit a moment longer. My legs are going numb."

"Miss Hartsell, I beg of you!"

"I have never sat down for so long in the middle of the afternoon, since I first set foot in Lacey's Folly," she said. "And," she added, a little forlornly, "summer will be gone before we know it. It is a penance to be cooped up by the window, looking outside on such a splendid day."

Gideon slapped a hand to his forehead, smearing burnt umber across his eyebrow. "Of course! Miss Hartsell, I could kiss you!"

"I would strongly caution against it, sir."

Especially after the events on Pucca's Hill. The words hung between them like a shimmering sword.

"Awkward phrasing on my part," Gideon said, and began packing up his gear. "The truth is, you have solved the dilemma. You are not a drawing room Miss, simpering at a window. You are freed from this prison, Miss Hartsell. I must paint you outside—in the little rose garden."

That is how he always thought of Chloe—in a garden, surrounded by her flowers. If the studio was his native environment, and the gilded society salon his godmother's, then the garden was surely Chloe's.

"Come. I'll take the chair outside."

She looked rather dubiously at the thronelike chair. "It will look very strange out in the garden."

"Hush!" An idea was forming, vague and illusive, in the back of his mind. If he could just wait until it solidified . . .

Chloe stood watching him, not moving a muscle. Gideon's head was thrown back, his eyes squeezed shut like a man in the throes of agony. She didn't dare to even breathe. Suddenly, his eyes opened, bluer than the sea and shining with light. His white smile flashed brilliantly. The transformation made her heart turn over.

"I've got it!" he said. "Go now. Hurry."

She went down the stairs, and he followed, carrying the heavy chair as if it were a tiny footstool. He walked a distance, and she expected him to put the chair down on the terrace. Instead, he went straight *into* the garden. He found a small gap in the colorful border, pushed aside the flowers and settled the chair in their midst.

"There," he announced. "Perfect!"

Chloe burst out laughing. "You've gone completely mad."

"You won't say so when you see the finished painting."

She gave him a saucy look that made her eyes flash silver and green. "What shall you call it, 'Madwoman Surrounded by Flowers?' "

"Sit, sit!" He settled her in the ancient chair. "And take that dratted thing off your hair."

Without waiting for her permission, he pulled the ribbon that held the snood in place. Her wild mane came rioting free, and the sun struck gold fire from the shining curls. Gideon stepped back, stunned by the effect.

"What is wrong?" she said quickly. He looked so strangely at her. She put her hands to her hair and tried to smooth it down.

"Don't move!" Gideon cried. "The pose—perfect! And you are utterly beautiful!"

He went inside to fetch his things, leaving her bemused. He had said it so unromantically, so simply—so unlike the wild way he had said it on Pucca's Hill—that Chloe knew he believed it to be true.

On this one particular day, in this one particular moment, for him, she *was* beautiful.

Her heart filled. The tower windows were open, and she could hear him whistling as he rummaged through the studio. How odd to think that a short time ago, she had never heard of Gideon Stone, and now her life—and that of everyone at Lacey's Folly—revolved around him.

At first she'd thought his arrival was a disaster, but now matters seemed to have taken a turn for the better. Chloe smiled to herself, utterly relaxed and content for the first time since Tobias's passing. As the bees droned through the blossoms, she closed her eyes and painted rosy pictures in her mind. They were as beautiful as anything that Gideon could produce: visions of a hazily golden future where one day faded into the next, exactly like this.

She heard him come out through the door and opened her eyes. Reality came back too soon. "You've moved your head," he said, frowning. "No, not like that!"

He set about arranging her head at the proper angle, her hands just so. His motions were brisk and firm, completely unloverlike. Chloe felt like a marionette as he moved her arm an inch, then tilted her head a little more to one side.

Stepping back, Gideon put his hand to his chin and considered her a moment, as if she were a problem to be solved.

"A rose!" he said at last. "You need a rose."

Taking his pocketknife, he cut one of the creamy-peach blooms for her hair, and a large crimson rose, with a two foot stem, to lie across her palm as a sceptre. A petal fell to her lap. He checked her as she made a move to brush it away.

"No! Leave it. It is the perfect touch."

"Will you tell me what the theme of the painting is to be?" she asked softly, when he approached the easel.

His eyes had that intense yet faraway gaze she was coming to know. "Hmmm? Oh, yes. I shall call it 'Innocence in the Garden of Love.'"

Chloe pinked with pleasure. Her face glowed with inner

light. "It seems very odd to think that perfect strangers will be looking at my portrait."

Gideon snapped back to the real world. "My God, I hadn't thought of it that way. Do you know, Miss Hartsell, this could make you all the rage."

"I doubt I should like that."

"Foolish girl! Why, if the painting is successful, who knows what may happen? You may look far higher for a husband than a mere country gentleman, then," he said lightly. "I should not be at all surprised if you snared a lord. Should you like to be Lady Chloe?"

A little of the light went out of her face. "Not in the least."

"What, you wouldn't give your heart and hand for a coronet?"

"No." *For, I believe, Gideon Stone, that I have already given my heart to you.*

An awkward silence ensued. He regarded her strangely, almost as if he had heard her silent cry.

Gideon stopped his teasing and went to work. The afternoon passed quickly. Gideon put aside his pencil and began to work rapidly in gouache. He dashed the color on, caught in a creative frenzy. The technique was uniquely his own, combining the Pre-Raphaelites' style and color, with the brushstrokes of the impressionist school. It was like painting with flower petals. *No*, he thought, as the scene in his mind took form on the easel, *it is like painting with jewels.*

Chloe watched him, fascinated. He was totally caught up in his artistic genius. She had never seen him more alive and vital. It made her heart beat all the faster.

She wanted to ask if she could get up and stretch a minute, but didn't dare: he looked as if he would murder anyone who tried to stop him.

"Devil take it," he exclaimed, looking around distractedly. The preliminary work was almost finished, but he needed his fan brush, which he'd left in the tower studio. His gaze was still unfocused. "Wait right here!" he demanded. "Stretch if you like, but don't go anywhere, I beg of you."

Chloe couldn't stand it any longer. The minute the door closed to the tower, she was out of the chair and halfway to the easel. What she found there stunned her. The work was dazzling. The glowing force of the colors struck her like the heat of the day. They were like stained glass, with the sun shining brilliantly through. The power and depth of Gideon's talent filled her with awe and breathless admiration. She was almost afraid to look at her likeness, to see how she looked through his eyes.

It was a shock. The figure of a seated woman dominated the composition, like a queen among her courtiers. Spiky purple and blue delphinium formed a phalanx of protective spears around her throne, while incredible roses bowed in homage. Roses so enormous, so sensually lush, had never been seen this side of paradise.

And in the center, virginal in white, Chloe sat at the very heart of the garden, with a rose in her hand for a scepter.

No. That wasn't true. It wasn't *her* at all. The attitude of a woman's head was sketched in, surrounded by shimmering cascades of hair. But the face was completely blank.

She stared in dismay. A few hours ago he had called her beautiful. She had read all sorts of meanings into his words. Now she realized they meant nothing to him. Her face was the same to his artist's eye as a cloud or a leaf or a curving branch against the sky. Just another anonymous rose in the garden. One so plain and undistinguished, he hadn't even tried to capture it.

Chloe was stricken. "He doesn't see me," she whispered. "He doesn't see *me* at all."

Whirling around, she ran back into the house.

EIGHT

§§

CHLOE SAT IN THE BRIDE'S CHAMBER, ALL ALONE. SHE wanted to be someplace where no one would think to look for her. It seemed to have worked. She'd heard Gideon calling her in the house and in the garden. He'd finally given up.

She wondered if he'd had the sense to figure out why she'd gone off.

Lenore's painting was back in its accustomed place over the mantel. Gideon must have had it moved back. Chloe wondered why, when he seemed so fascinated. There *was* something about the portrait. Something magical.

At the moment she could use a little magic herself.

She was still shocked by the blank face in Gideon's painting. It was almost as if he were waiting for another woman to come along, so that he might fill in *her* face instead.

Lifting the long-handled looking glass off the seat beside her, she examined her face in the silver frame. Was it her imagination, or did she look different? Older. Less innocent of life. Much more aware.

She laid it across her lap and looked out the window. From her place in the wide windowseat, Chloe had a view of the river meadows and the distant road. She tried to feel Lenore's spirit in the room. She felt a kindred spirit with the other woman who had risked her all for what she loved.

Is this where you waited that night for a first glimpse of our lover? she wondered. *Did he come and carry you away?*

Chloe sighed. There was nothing in the air but the scent of faded flowers and summers long gone. She had long ago given up her girlhood dreams of being carried off by a romantic lover. She had been perfectly content with her lot at Lacey's Folly, with Perry and Tobias. The promise of a secure, if unexciting, future.

And then Tobias had died, and everything had changed forever. And Gideon Stone had entered her life, like a bright comet streaking through a still, dark summer's eve.

"What a fool I have been," she whispered.

In his world, she barely existed. She was less than nothing, a shape, a blur of colors. As important to the greater scheme of things in his life as a ripe peach or cluster of grapes displayed on a plate in a still life painting. The focus of it all, yet totally replaceable. Interchangeable with a hundred other women.

Picking up the mirror once more, she stared at her calm, dry-eyed image and saw herself as she truly was. No longer a late-blooming girl, but a woman. A desperate woman who would do anything to get what she wanted.

Chloe knew exactly what that was: God help her, she wanted everything. Gideon Stone and Lacey's Folly, all wrapped together in a silver ribbon.

Right now that seemed as impossible as drawing down the moon. She glanced up at Lenore's portrait. *If I were truly beautiful, if I looked like Lenore, he would not ignore me. No man could.*

"Did you get your heart's desire, Lenore Lacey? Did it all work out?" Chloe whispered. She turned the looking glass face down. "I wish I knew how *your* story ended."

The light changed inside the room, took on a silvery quality. A soft, cool breeze blew through the room, although nothing stirred. The scent of lavender and lemon verbena grew suddenly stronger. Chloe sat very still. Her arms prickled with gooseflesh, but she was not afraid. She looked over at the bed and the dried floral wreath that had crowned Lenore's fair tresses, looking for a sign.

Something glittered and flared in the sunlight. She rose and went to it. The two halves of Perry's broken moonstone flanked an earring on the bed cover. A gold hoop with a round garnet and pearls. She looked quickly at the portrait.

Yes, it was the same earring that the artist had painted dangling from the Lost Bride's delicate earlobe. Slightly the worse for wear. The gold was scratched and dented, the garnet rubbed dull on one side, as if it had been dropped and stepped upon. A shiver ran through her.

Although someone had shined it up, the antique earring was cleaned imperfectly, and traces of earth were caught in the hollow center of the bead. Perry had obviously found it. But why hadn't he said anything about it? That was very unlike him. He'd been in and out lately, with his head somewhere in the clouds. She must have a talk with him.

As she held the piece of jewelry in her palm, her fingers closed gently over it. Suddenly, Chloe was filled with the strange sensation of being in two places at once. She was here, in the Bride's Chamber, yet she was somewhere else, dark and frightening and cold. Grief and despair washed over her in a heavy wave. Once again, thoughts that were not hers intruded into her own:

O where shall I go? What shall I do? O who will take me in?

Chloe dropped the earring as if it had turned molten in her hand.

She shivered and looked up at Lenore's portrait. "Poor thing. Oh, my dear! I do not think your story ended happily!"

There was only silence for answer.

Chloe was starting toward the door when she heard the sound of horses and carriage wheels quite clearly. Looking out the window, she almost feared to see a ghostly bridal party ride up in the late afternoon sun.

But the light had changed, become golden again. She laughed aloud at her ridiculous fancy: it was only Lady Albinia and her fine lady's maid returning from Greater Brampton.

And she'd brought guests as well, Chloe saw. Two elegant men on splendid hacks had accompanied her. And here she was, still in the flowing white costume she'd worn for her sitting with Gideon!

There was no way back through the house to her room without being seen. She had two choices. She could stay in the Bride's Chamber until they left and hope no one would come looking for her, or she could escape out the backstairs of the old wing and go through the shrubbery, around to the tower studio. Her dress and chemise were there, where she'd hung them on a peg. She could change out of the costume and come back through the garden.

She was tempted to stay there until the guests left. She'd be undisturbed. No one would *dare* look for her there. Gideon didn't permit anyone to enter. In fact, he thought he had the only key.

He was wrong. Chloe had found a duplicate in the desk Tobias had left her.

Going lightly down the dark and narrow staircase, she tiptoed through an ancient parlor with furnishings shrouded in holland covers, and out the back. It wasn't far to the tower. Not if she cut along the shrubbery and then darted across the herb garden. No one would see her from the house.

She was in error.

"Beauty in flight!" a deep voice announced, as she stepped into the herb garden. Chloe stopped in dismay.

A tall gentleman, dressed in the height of fashion, swept her a low bow. He was harsh-featured, and swarthy as a pirate, but decidedly attractive for all that. Perhaps it was his unusual green eyes.

"Do not be distressed, fair one," he said with amusement. "I am a mere mortal, treading in your garden. Only, tell me, are you Diana herself, or one of her nymphs?"

Chloe flushed to the roots of her hair. "More to the point, sir, who are you? And why are your lurking about Lacey's Folly in this manner?"

He laughed. "Very well, I will drop the flowery nonsense

and introduce myself. I am an old acquaintance of Mr. Stone. Lady Albinia met us by chance in the village and invited us to accompany her back to Lacey's Folly. Now, you must admit that Lady Albinia would not have done so if I were in the habit of, ah, *lurking*, as you put it.''

His clever speech made her realize how churlish she'd sounded. Since he was older, it would be very bad manners to demand his name again. ''I beg your pardon, sir. I was caught by surprise . . .''

''So I would imagine.'' The gentleman eyed her costume with interest. ''I take it this is not your normal attire? A pity.''

''Of course not. I was . . . I am sitting for a portrait that Mr. Stone is painting.''

''Ah, yes. Lord Pulham's commission. Mr. Stone is a very gifted artist.''

Chloe immediately warmed to the stranger. ''He is indeed,'' she answered. ''I do hope that Lord Pulham agrees.''

''With you as his model, I do not see how he can lose.''

He watched her blush deepen. Such lovely skin. A finely formed figure. The ankles of a goddess. But his scrutiny was making her nervous. He turned the talk.

''You are fond of Mr. Stone, I see, and have his best interests at heart. Have you known him long?''

There was something in his tone, or his wording, that Chloe felt carried a hidden meaning. ''Only since his coming to Lacey's Folly. But he has been most kind to me.''

She bit her underlip, wondering if she had said too much. She didn't want to have to explain her position in the household.

''So I would imagine,'' he murmured, and offered her his arm. Best not to alarm her further. ''Come. Let us stroll beneath the trees, where it is cooler.''

She found herself back in the shrubbery with him, without quite knowing how he'd managed it. There was something about him that was both attractive and repellent. He frightened her, just a little.

As they walked deeper into the shade she was made more

and more aware of her unconventional garb and the lack of anything beneath it. With Gideon it hadn't seemed so awkward. *Of course the situation was quite different*, she reminded herself.

The elegant stranger seemed to read her mind. "You are uncomfortable walking with me alone. Shall I take you up to the house?"

"They will be wondering where you are," she said in relief. "Indeed, why are you not with the others?"

"Mr. Stone is nowhere to be found. I thought perhaps he'd stepped out into the garden. We are about to take our leave, in any case."

His green eyes twinkled as he kissed her hand. "Please give my regards to our host, and tell him I shall have the pleasure of waiting upon him another day."

Chloe saw her chance to learn his identity. "And what name shall I give him, sir?"

"You may tell him Exton called." He executed a beautiful bow.

"I shall, Mr. Exton."

Amusement warred with chagrin. "You might more properly address me as Lord Exton, Miss Hartsell," he said mildly.

She was less startled to learn he was a lord than to discover he knew her identity. "How did you know my name, my lord?"

"My dear young lady," he said with a languid smile, "I know quiet a bit about you already—and I intend to make it my business to know everything else there is to know about you."

Her heart gave an uncomfortable lurch. "I should prefer to remain a bit mysterious, sir."

"A woman's prerogative."

He nodded and favored her with another of his languid smiles. "Until we meet again, Miss Hartsell. I hope it may be soon."

Chloe slipped inside, through the open parlor doors, and

hurried up to her room. A moment later she heard him ride off with his companion.

So that was the notorious Marquis of Exton. Even down here in the Cotswolds, his name and reputation were known. He was a very powerful man. ⋅

And, she sensed, a dangerous one. The way he looked at her, like a hawk surveying a field mouse, set her nerves jangling. She sincerely hoped their paths would not cross again.

Lord Exton and his companion rode down the winding lane from Lacey's Folly. "It is too bad that Stone was out," Mr. Maes said with a sneer. "He will be wondering if you came to call him out, or to make your peace."

"I believe I will put him out of his misery by sending him a note from town, saying that I wish him good fortune in the showing at the Royal Academy."

"Generous of you," Mr. Macs exclaimed. "I have never known you to show mercy to one of your victims before."

"I couldn't very well call him out with Lady Albinia present. She is not only his godmother, she is—how shall I put it? Ah, yes. One of my 'fonder memories' of youth."

"I see." The Lady Albinia had cut quite a swath through London in the early days of her widowhood.

They rode on in silence a while, enjoying the countryside. Exton thought of Chloe and smiled to himself. She was utterly delightful.

"Now," his colleague said, "I know you are up to something. You have that devilish look about you."

Lord Exton grinned wickedly. "You are a lover of riddles, Maes, and you have carried out several very nice seductions. But tell me, what is the most delicious seduction of all?"

His companion gave it some thought. "There is a trick to this, I am sure. Not a virgin, surely, nor that of a happily married young bride. Sisters, perhaps? Mother and daughter?"

"You bore me, Maes. The most delicious seduction is that of an enemy's lover. All the more delicious if the woman is

deeply in love with him, yet still innocent of the darker pleasures that love has to offer.''

"Can such a thing be done?''

"Oh, yes,'' Exton replied silkily. "Especially if one proceeds very, very carefully.''

"Exton! Here, in this house!'' Gideon was outraged. "While
I've been searching high and low for you, afraid you'd come
to some harm, you were in the shrubbery, dallying with Exton!'' *Damn his evil soul to hell.*

"I was not *dallying!*'' Chloe protested. "And Lord Exton
seemed to know you well. He was highly complimentary of
your skills as an artist.''

"The Marquis of Exton is no friend of mine.''

"Well, I didn't know.''

"You do now! I do not wish you to pursue his acquaintance!''

"You are being unreasonable.'' A white line of anger
formed around her mouth. "While you may rightfully decide
who is welcome and who is not beneath this roof, you have
no right to interfere with my private affairs.''

"Do I not?'' The realization infuriated Gideon. "By God,
we shall see about that later.''

Chloe watched him in amazement. "There is no reason for
you to act so possessively in regard to my acquaintanceship.
Nor, Mr. Stone, do you have my permission, or any authority,
to shout at me!''

Gideon eyed her filmy Grecian robes. "There is every reason. Go and clothe yourself.''

"Now you are being ridiculous.'' But she went.

Lady Albinia came in quietly after Chloe was gone. She
looked quite distressed. "That wasn't very well done of you,
Gideon.''

"That scoundrel, that *rake*, seeing her dressed in such a
fashion—?''

In answer, his godmother merely raised an eyebrow.

"It's different,'' he protested. "I am painting her portrait.

She is nothing but a subject posing for me. And you know Exton's reputation.''

He didn't mention rumors that the marquis presided over something called the 'Seduction Club.'

Lady Albinia widened her eyes. ''You are harsh, Gideon. Exton assures me he is a changed man. I believe that his son's narrow escape from death wrought a miraculous alteration in his character. Why, the very fact that he escorted me here today, in hopes of making his peace with you, shows evidence of it.''

''If he has anything to say, he can say it in London. I don't want him under my roof. Miss Hartsell is not used to the manners of the haut monde. I am sorry she was ever exposed to his influence.''

''Oh, and what of me?''

He had the good grace to laugh. ''Don't get your feathers in a ruffle. I would not like to see you in Exton's clutches either, my dear. However, I am very sure that you would know how to handle him, should he step out of line. Miss Hartsell,'' he said emphatically, ''would not.''

Lady Albinia left him to his paperwork and went upstairs to see how the packing was coming along. She wished now that she didn't have to go to London on the morrow. Just when things were getting interesting!

But at least Exton's arrival had served its purpose. He had flirted mildly with Chloe, and now Gideon was up in arms. A small smile curved her lips. All to the good. Jealousy was often a woman's best weapon.

She was surprised to find Chloe there in her chamber, helping Agnes and her dresser with the packing. ''My dear girl, whatever are you doing?''

Chloe smiled. ''I have little enough to fill my time these days, and you have been so very kind to me. I wish you did not have to go.''

''I'll be back so quickly, you'll hardly know I've been away.'' The older woman gave her a fond embrace. ''Mean-

while, you must take every opportunity to keep yourself *well*
occupied.'' She gave Chloe a slow smile, followed by a speaking glance.

''And Gideon, also.''

*Chloe was lost. She fought against the darkness that pushed
down upon her, the fear that turned her feet to lead. There
was nowhere to turn, nowhere to run. No hope at all. He was
dead . . .*

*Grief overwhelmed her. She had tried to save him. Tried to
warn him that it was a trap, that the men were hidden in the
tower, waiting for him. The memory tore jaggedly through her
mind, like lightning: she saw herself running, running across
the lawns toward the tower; his body falling, falling, falling
toward the river and the sharp rocks below.*

*A sob rose in her chest. She fled for her own life now. Her
feet were cold, and she realized that she was barefoot. The
ground grew soft, tugged at her feet. She found herself sinking
slowly. No! Fighting with all her might, she jerked herself free.
Floundering and stumbling through the black night, with her
hands extended. It was dark as the maw of hell. She could see
nothing at all and wondered if she'd been struck blind by fear.*

*Oh, God! She could hear the baying of the hounds. They
were closing in now. She slid and fell forward, knocking the
wind from her. She felt a sharp pain at her ear and realized
her earring had been torn away by a low tree branch. Her
earlobe burned with cold fire.*

*Curling up in a ball, she cradled her head upon a mossy
stone. It would be over soon, either way. She could no longer
feel her feet. Oh, if only she could lie down somewhere warm
and safe to sleep!*

*Suddenly, her fingers touched grooves in the stone. It grew
warm to her touch. The warmth seeped into her bones, comforting as a mother's embrace. Her fingertips caressed the
grooves, followed the spirals she could not see, tracing them
in their endless circles.*

Now the stone was pillow-soft. She sank into it. The cold ground was warm as a feather bed.

Someone was singing. A soft voice, in a language she had never heard before, lovely in its unearthliness. The soaring notes of the melody tugged at her heart, pulled her on, like a jeweled chain.

Without warning, a terrible claw reached out in the black-ness and clutched her shoulder. She cried out in alarm and whirled to see a fiery yellow eye . . .

"Miss Hartsell!"

Chloe's gaze slowly focused. She was not lost in Pucca's woods, but in the darkened corridor outside her bedroom. Still in the grip of her nightmare, waiting for the talons to sink into her flesh. She gaped in horror at the dark shape materializing before her, with its glowing, golden eye.

Gideon gave her arm a little shake. "Miss Hartsell, *wake up!*"

Her frantic movements told him she was still in the throes of a nightmare. He'd heard her cries and had only taken time to throw on his robe, expecting fire or robbers or some other menace—not a slender figure in a thin, white nightshift.

She tried to push him away, and Gideon almost dropped his lighted taper. He caught her to him with one arm, holding the candlestick away with the other. Her warm, trembling body was pressed against his. It seemed only natural to draw her closer for comfort. Her hair brushed his face and throat, send-ing a thrill of desire through him.

She clutched at his robe, pulling it open in her frenzy. There was nothing between them but the stuff of her gown. It might as well have been air. He could feel her nipples against his bare chest. The outline of her thighs, the sweet curve of her abdomen against his legs. His body reacted instinctively, and his grip tightened.

There was a creak behind him and he blew out the candle. Devil take it, they couldn't be caught like this! He propelled her down the corridor in the direction of her room, then shoved her through, shut the door, and fumbled to close his robe. The candlestick slipped from his hand and dropped with a thud.

"Oh!" Chloe was suddenly awake. One second she'd been fleeing for her life, the next she was in her dimly lit room with Gideon a foot away, in his robe. In the embers' glow she could see the heat in his eyes. He grabbed her roughly and held his hand over her mouth.

"Hush! I won't hurt you."

She was shaking with cold and nerves. Gideon drew her into his arms. Chloe leaned against him for strength. How warm and strong he was. She became aware of the texture of his robe through her gown, the soft whisper of brocade against her breasts. Aware of his body beneath the robe, and his breath stirring her hair. Desire pooled in the pit of her stomach, a deep pull of pleasure. An ache of terrible need. Perhaps she was still dreaming . . .

He tilted her chin up, ran the ball of his thumb along her lower lip. Her breathing quickened, as did his. She lifted her face to him, willing him to kiss her.

Gideon cursed beneath his breath. There was such invitation in her eyes, heavy-lidded with sleep, that he could hardly think. He took a deep breath. "You were walking in your sleep," he said. "I heard you in the corridor. You were having a nightmare . . . crying out softly."

Crying out for you, she thought. *Touch me, Gideon. Kiss me.*

He wrapped both arms around her, drew her tightly against him. Inhaled her woman-fragrance and knew he could take her here and now. Pick her up in his arms and carry her to the bed. Make love to her until she cried out again, this time in pleasure. Dear God, but he wanted her.

Taking a deep breath, he held her away. It was madness. He didn't dare give in to it, for Chloe's sake. His voice was rough. "Are you all right now? I must go."

She looked up at him, hungry for his kisses. Willing to follow him anywhere he led. Gideon cursed again. Her face was so transparent, her awakening passions so tempting . . . *Sweet Jesus!*

He stepped back and tied his robe tightly. "Go to bed, Miss Hartsell. You will be all right now."

The door closed behind him.

Chloe could have wept in need and anger and frustration. Her breasts ached, and her whole body was weak with longing. *Am I so invisible to you, Gideon Stone?* She prowled her bed-chamber, unable to think of anything but the way his hard body had felt against hers. The strong circle of his arms about her shoulders. The heat that had leaped between them. *Oh, yes, he felt it, too.*

She threw herself upon the bed and pounded the mattress in frustration.

Gideon went back to his room. No one else was about, thank God. Leaving her room was one of the most difficult things he had ever done. He was a man used to assuaging his needs and indulging his passions. Lately he'd been living like a monk. The temptation to take her, to make wild love to her, had almost overwhelmed him.

He knew that she had been as caught up in desire as he himself had been. For a few seconds there he had almost given it to it. She had wanted him to. *Willed* him to. There was no doubt about it.

But she had no idea of what she would be unleashing. Of what she would be giving—and giving up. He could not make her his mistress. What kind of cad would exploit a lonely young woman for a few hours of illicit love?

Thank God Mrs. Osler was deaf and the servants slept in another part of the house. If young Perry had awakened and come out into the corridor . . .

Gideon's jaw clenched. The sooner he finished the portrait and went up to London, the better. He could find some willing wench who knew the game, or some round-heeled, highborn lady looking for diversion. What he could not do was take an innocent virgin and ruin her life.

Good God, he thought wryly, *could it be I am developing a conscience?*

Stripping off his robe, he climbed into bed and pulled the sheet up. It had been another narrow escape for both of them. The danger was likely to continue.

He punched his pillow down. *The cure for me is a return to London's social life, and a member of the muslin company to warm my bed.* Perhaps that lively little blond opera dancer, who'd been throwing out lures his way.

And the cure for Miss Chloe Hartsell was just as simple: he must marry her off at the earliest possible moment. The next man who stirred her untried passions might not have the willpower to resist so easy a seduction.

She is too ripe and ready for the plucking.

Gideon rolled over and tried to sleep. It was near dawn before he succeeded.

Chloe tossed and turned until morning. *Oh, Gideon!*

She had convinced herself that the night on Pucca's Hill had meant something, even if he couldn't acknowledge it. He had blamed it on their heightened emotions and on the strange atmosphere of the place itself.

True, something had come over both of them, like a wild enchantment. But Chloe had been sure there was more to it. That beneath the surface, something was occurring, something that drew them together. And tonight, for a little while, she had been certain of it.

Then he had turned away.

I have been building castles in the clouds, she told herself sadly.

In her imaginings, she had felt safe, no longer in danger of being exiled from Lacey's Folly, trapped in a loveless marriage with a stranger for a husband. She had made a grievous error. Chloe swallowed her pride.

What she'd taken for attraction in Gideon's eyes was nothing but a healthy man's lust. She couldn't fault him for it.

They were thrown together by circumstance, and he was a man of strong passions.

Plumping her pillows, Chloe sat up in bed and tried to sort things out, while the fire burned down to glowing orange embers. They reminded her of those twin fires in Gideon's eyes tonight, just before he'd pulled her close. Raw heat and untamed passion.

Suddenly, she saw what must be done. It happened in a twinkling, as if blinders had been removed from her eyes. It was the same situation, but how different it looked when seen from a completely different angle.

There was a sudden, deep ache in her chest, and she realized immediately what it was—her new self separating from the old. The butterfly struggling free of its constricting cocoon. She was no longer a late-blooming girl, but a woman, fighting to free herself from a lifetime of convention. She must leap the gap between her world and that of Gideon Stone. She only hoped she had the courage to do so.

Gideon was an ardent man. He would be, she knew, a magnificent lover. That brief taste of his lovemaking had set free old longings and sensations she had boxed up inside her heart so long ago. He had loosed them all with his kisses, set them winging free, and she could not gather them up again and hide them away. Nor did she want to.

She thought of her father, for the first time in many years. He had been a dreamer, but one who had made his dreams come true. Until that last business scheme had gone awry.

Chloe made her decision. Like Lenore, she would risk everything she had, for everything she wanted.

If she lost, at least she would be the only one to suffer.

Chloe, Gideon, and Mrs. Osler joined Lady Albinia for early luncheon the following day, as she was setting out for London shortly. Their meal of fresh trout, which Gideon had brought in from the river, was removed with a fricassee of chicken, summer vegetables with savory in butter sauce, and an excellent molded jelly.

They had just finished, when Agnes announced that a messenger had delivered a small package for Chloe. It was elegantly wrapped in silver paper, with a large blue satin bow.

"What is it?" Lady Albinia asked, as Chloe took the parcel from the messenger.

"I don't know. It is from a rather exclusive establishment in Greater Brampton. I haven't purchased anything there in my life." She looked shyly at Gideon, but he shook his head.

"I cannot claim any credit," he said.

"Alter's Emporium!" Mrs. Osler exclaimed. "They carry only the finest gifts."

"Well, open it then!" Lady Albinia was as eager as a child to see the contents. She had a good idea as to who had sent it.

Chloe carefully removed the paper and ribbon, so as not to damage them, and opened the box. Inside was a satin box of the most expensive chocolates, and an exquisite folding fan of pale green silk and ivory lace, with pierced sticks of mother of pearl.

"Oh! How beautiful!" she exclaimed, taking it out. Her only fan was a rigid, square one of japanned paper on a lacquered stick, and rather the worse for wear.

"Read the card," Lady Albinia encouraged. She had seen the scowl form on Gideon's face and decided he had figured out the identity of the giver as well.

Taking out a thick white card, Chloe blushed as she read the printed name and the hastily scrawled initial. "From Lord Exton," she announced.

"What the devil is he doing, buying you gifts?" Gideon exclaimed. "Send it back! Better yet, give it to me. I shall send it back," he said darkly.

"It is not yours to dispose of," Chloe said hotly.

His godmother tapped his knuckles with her own folded fan. "It is unexceptional, Gideon. There is no need for you to get on your high horse. And since the gift is to Miss Hartsell, you cannot send it back yourself, you know."

"No indeed." Chloe snapped the fan open and closed, then

opened it again, and plied it at her burning cheeks. "And as Lady Albinia says it is quite proper, I shall keep it. I will send Lord Exton a note of thanks."

Pushing back his chair, Gideon rose. "If you will excuse me, ladies, I have letters to answer."

And, he thought wrathfully, *one in particular to write.*

Lady Albinia was off to London shortly after noon. "How we shall miss her delightful company," Mrs. Osler said, as they waved the carriage off. "So gracious, and always ready to add an intelligent comment or a witty anecdote. One wouldn't expect it in so great a lady."

"Yes, she is a person of quick understanding and infinite kindness," Chloe said thoughtfully. And wise in worldly ways. *If*, she thought, *I did not mistake her meaning, she instructed me to use this time to fix Gideon's interest upon me.*

Mrs. Osler looked around. "Now, where has that boy gotten himself to? I heard there is a fair in Lesser Brampton, and I thought I might take him in the gig—if you have no objections?"

Her cheeks were a little red as she spoke. Chloe wondered if Mrs. Osler and Lady Albinia had put their heads together and plotted to try their hands at matchmaking.

"Oh, he will enjoy a fair immensely. That is very good of you, Mrs. Osler."

"Not at all. He is a fine companion, and I enjoy his company very much indeed."

But the widow blushed even deeper, and although Chloe knew her fondness for Perry was real, she realized her surmise was right. They were trying to leave her alone with Gideon in hopes that something would develop.

Perry came skipping down the hall. "Are you coming with us, Chlo?"

"No, dear. I am sitting for Mr. Stone again today."

"All right," he said, and went out with Mrs. Osler without a backward glance. Chloe felt a tiny pang. Perry was growing up.

And now she and Gideon would be alone all day. The time had come to put her courage to the test.

"Is this for a celebration?" Gideon held up the bottle of wine that she had Dawlish put in their picnic hamper.

He was already drunk on sunshine and the first taste of success. His London friends had written to tell him that Pulham was impressed with his preliminary sketches. The betting in the clubs was short odds that Gideon would get the commission.

"I thought it was called for," Chloe said. There was a second bottle under the plate of ham and cold chicken. "We will drink to your inevitable victory."

He looked surprised. "Are you so sure of it, then?"

"I have not the slightest doubt."

Her words pleased him. "I will drink to your health. I could not have conceived of this picture without you for inspiration."

He meant it as polite flattery, but he realized it was true. There was no other woman who would have given him this particular vision. "If I am to be famous, then so shall you be. Like Rossetti and Elizabeth Siddal, or Millais and his wife, Effie."

"You forget the scandal that accompanied them," Chloe pointed out. "You will have a hard time marrying me off, if any attaches to my name."

Scowling, Gideon drew the cork. He hadn't the time or the inclination to think about matchmaking. He was still too busy trying to forget last night.

"At the moment only two things interest me: the painting, and my growing thirst." He held out a glass of straw-colored wine. "To our mutual success."

Chloe sipped at the wine for courage, while he drank his rather quickly. "A tolerable wine," he said affably and poured himself another.

He must get up the courage to look at her, to paint her without remembering the way her body had curved against his, the arch of her throat in the firelight as she almost dared him to kiss her. The hurt in her eyes when he had pushed himself away.

"And now, my dear Miss Hartsell, if you will take your position, the session can begin."

She settled into the chair. Her hands were trembling. He didn't really see her. Not even when she threw herself at his head, as she had last night. Embarrassment flooded through her, but she fought it valiantly.

Don't think about it. Don't think at all. Not until the moment is right.

But, oh! How lonely she had been, and for how very long! How wonderful it had been to be held, to be caressed. To be desired.

Gideon stood back and looked at her. There was something different about her today. He couldn't put his finger on it, but she had changed. Not just her expression, but her posture, the subtle tilt of her head, the thrust of her breasts. It came to him then, like a revelation. She was a woman aware of herself. Of her charms and feminine allure.

As was he, suddenly. But this time he would use it for his art.

Taking up his palette and paints, he began to work swiftly. *Yes, this is what had been lacking. The sensuality of a woman.* It altered the concept, but for the better. But try as he might, he could not seem to paint her face. He had blocked in the planes, the shadows beneath her cheekbones. The rest was blank.

It was hot. He had stripped down to his shirt and left the neck open. A bead of sweat rolled down his chest. It didn't seem to affect her, except to put more roses in her cheeks. A slight flush below her collarbone, perhaps. A pearly glow in her changeable gray eyes.

He noticed that one side of her gown had slipped over her shoulder. A lovely, rounded shoulder. And there was just a hint of her breast exposed. Gideon felt a tightening in his loins.

All the blood seemed to leave his brain and pool there, instead. *Damn it*, he was losing his focus.

"Miss Hartsell?"

"Yes."

"Your gown has slid down."

She looked at him steadily. "Yes."

Sweat stood out on his brow. He was finding it deuced hard to concentrate. "Please replace it."

Chloe licked her lips. "No."

"I beg your pardon?"

She lifted her chin and shrugged. "No. It is too hot." The shrug loosened the shoulder even more. The filmy fabric fell away, clinging to her breast by its tip. One good gust of breeze and it would be at her waist.

Wine and desire rose to his head. "Cover yourself," he said thickly.

She didn't answer, but her eyes dared him.

She looked at him through her lashes, and the blood pounded at his temples and in his groin. Her full lower lip curved mockingly, and he threw his brush down. "Then I will do it for you!"

She rose, and he thought she meant to run off again. Afterward he didn't know how it happened. As he reached out to pull her gown up, it slid from her shoulder, parted, and tumbled free on both sides. She was naked to the waist, and his hand was on her breast. His finger curled to cup it, his mouth ached to touch it. Sunlight gilded her torso.

"Dear God, you are beautiful!" he said. He stared at her, drinking in her loveliness.

She lifted her head with a proud defiance. "Yes. Look at me, Gideon. See me. Really see me."

He couldn't tear his eyes away. He was the first man to look upon her like this. The thought was incredibly erotic.

"Do you think a husband will find me pleasing?" she asked softly, touching her breast with one hand. "Will he desire me, do you think?"

"He would be a bloody fool if he did not!"

Gideon pulled her roughly into his arms and kissed her. His mouth came down ruthlessly on hers, his hands pressed into her skin, exploring her shape and texture with his sensitive finger tips. Her breast fit his palm exactly, as if it had been made for it. He flicked his thumb across the pebbled tip and felt her sway against him.

Chloe moaned when he touched her, and as she opened her mouth, his tongue darted in, hot and seeking. He took the kiss deeper, and she twined her arms around his neck. The world was spinning around them. They were at its very center, and nothing else mattered at all.

He gave a groan and released her lips, then trailed kisses down her throat, to the hollow and beyond. She arched toward him, offering herself to him freely. His lips skimmed over her, sending ripples of heat and cold through her veins until she was dizzy with desire, clinging to him for support.

Lowering her to the ground, he tangled his hands in her hair and kissed her mouth until her lips felt deliciously swollen. When he took the tip of her breast in his mouth, she cried out huskily. When he tugged at it with his teeth, she went mindless with need. If he stopped now, she would die of longing.

He didn't stop, couldn't stop. He wanted to devour her. All the days of tension, of fighting against instinct, were banished. She belonged to him. He would take her and make love to her and share her with no one, by God.

She gasped as his hands pulled at the frothy skirt of her gown, sliding it up her bare legs. He went mad when he felt her warm skin beneath his and realized there was no other barrier. He was all male hunger and instinct, no more able to turn back now than a river in flood.

"Chloe," he breathed against her warm, fragrant throat.

She was like a flower opening up to him, and he was wild for her. Her body jerked and arched when he touched her intimately. He was no novice. He knew when to retreat and when to advance again. He waited. The corner of his mouth teased her nipple, and she twisted toward him eagerly. He watched her face for the slightest sign. Her eyes were half open, and he kissed them closed.

Ever so gently, his mouth moved down to claim hers in a deep, searching kiss. The moment came when she was ready, and he knew it before she did. The second time, she lay quietly as he placed his hand over her, cupping her with his long fingers.

Lying beside her, with his mouth teasing her breast, he waited until she stirred beneath his hand. He stroked her lightly once, twice, and she trembled beneath him. He eased a fingertip in, feeling the enclosing warmth of her.

Slowly, gently, he probed more intimately, while his thumb kept up the easy strokes that sent tremors through her body. He paused, then slipped another in, and felt her stiffen in his arms. "Easy, love. Easy. I won't hurt you."

He knew it was a lie. There would be a little pain the first time, but he vowed that he would make her forget it, in the turmoil of sensation that followed.

Chloe had never imagined anything like his slow, sensual lovemaking. She wanted it to never end . . . She wanted more. She was mindless in the throes of passion, greedy with mounting desire. Her hips arched up to meet his thrusting hand, and she heard him groan.

Heat roared through him, but he fought to keep the fires banked until she was ready. She was lost, and so was he. There was no turning back this time, for either of them. He would take her to the edge, and over it.

He suckled her breasts, first one and then the other, while she murmured his name. She writhed with every stroke of his hand, every touch of his mouth upon her flesh. Each time she responded to a change in pace, in pressure, his urgency grew.

The heat was building now, in both of them. As he drove his fingers into her, a flush crept over her body. She was liquid, molten. He knew he couldn't hold off much longer. Her body spasmed with pleasure, which only doubled his. He rolled her nipple between his teeth, listened to her gasps of breath, and plunged his fingers deeper, harder, until she shuddered in ecstasy.

He halted, and she gave a moan of protest, moving against him. Her nails raked his shoulders, scraped down his chest. *"Gideon, Gideon!"*

Stripping off his clothes, he tore the remnants of the gauzy gown away from her. "So beautiful," he murmured, suckling her breast. "You are so beautiful. And you are mine!"

"Yes. Hurry, Gideon. Hurry." Something was building inside her, something fearful and wonderful, and at any moment, she would burst with the joy of it. He moved his knee between hers, urging her legs apart.

He slid into her a little way. She was silk and velvet, enfolding him. Welcoming him with an upward lift of her hips.

"I want to be gentle with you," he gasped against her ear. "I can't."

"Don't be!" she whispered fiercely. "Take me, Gideon. Now!"

He plunged into her, unable to rein himself in. She met him thrust for thrust. He lifted her hips to drive deeper, harder, until she bucked and shuddered and cried out. Desire roared through him, spilled over, as he took her with a wildness unlike anything he'd known before. He shuddered and arched back, then lowered his mouth to hers in a searing kiss that sealed their passion.

Afterward they lay still joined, tangled and sweaty in each other's arms. Neither spoke. There seemed no need for it, as they drowsed, satiated, in the dappled green shade.

His breathing grew deep and regular. His body was heavy against hers, but Chloe didn't care. She was replete with his lovemaking, entirely and completely happy.

She had gambled. And she had won.

Gideon didn't know how long he'd been dozing in utter contentment. Chloe was still asleep beside him, after he had made love to her again, slowly and lingeringly. She looked like Eve just born, naked in Eden. Beautiful in her innocence.

Yes, she is still innocent, he thought, *although the world would not consider her so.*

Guilt smote him. He'd known better, but he hadn't been able to resist the temptation. Now they would both pay the price. He rose and slipped quietly into the pond beneath the willows, so as not to wake her.

The water was a cool blessing, and he swam around, trying to clear the sleep from his head. Trying to clear his senses.

Trying not to think of the consequences of his seduction of Chloe.

No matter how eager, how willing she had been, he should never have let matters get so out of hand. She was under his care. She should have been sacrosanct. Forbidden. But as he looked across the silver sheet of water at her, he felt a fresh stirring in his loins.

Making love to her had been a beautiful experience. He'd never thought of the act of love that way before. It has always been a need to feed, like physical thirst or hunger. But this . . . this had been different. For himself, he couldn't regret it. Ah, but for *her* . . . !

Everything was changed. And it was his fault, all of it.

He damned himself for the fool he had been. Even now, though, if she awakened and held out her arms to him, he doubted he would have the courage to walk away. They were snared in a net of mutual desire, and he didn't know how to cut through its strands. Or if he truly wanted to.

She was so generous and giving, so passionate, yet so surprised by the depth of her ardor. So amazed by the pleasure she could take from him in return, the wild release that had her shuddering in his arms.

What would happen when she awakened, and the reality, the finality of what they had done sank in?

He swam back toward the bank and left the pond. It was so hot, the water evaporated from his skin, leaving him cool and refreshed in body. But not in spirit. He had lived his life for pleasure and taken it selfishly where he found it. Now there was someone else to consider.

Marriage was something he'd imagined as part of some nebulous future. Little as he wanted to, he'd have to consider it now. He couldn't abandon her. *Devil take it, what if there should be a child?*

He needed to get away from her to think. For some reason, he couldn't seem to think straight when he was near Chloe. Every good intention went out the window.

No, there must be no repetition of this episode until they'd sorted things out. But, Christ, he wanted her. Again. Now!

To hamper temptation, he dressed swiftly and left his shirt unbuttoned. As he went back toward the arbor, he frowned at the painting he'd taken off the easel earlier. It was beautiful. It was brilliantly composed and skillfully painted.

And it wasn't right.

Too rigid. Too ordinary. A bee buzzed through the lavender, catching his attention. Chloe was still asleep. She lay naked on the crushed grass, surrounded by vivid flowers, with her hair spread out like a swath of silk. Her mouth was still swollen from his kisses, her cheeks flushed with their lovemaking. His breath caught in his throat. How had he ever thought her plain?

She was heartbreakingly beautiful.

What a lovely picture she presented—one rounded arm arched gracefully over her head, the other lying against her hip, palm up, fingers slightly curled. A butterfly hovered overhead, then settled on her hand as lightly as a breath. She slept on.

A poppy dipped low as if to cup her breast, and another had shed its petals across her thigh like scarlet drops of blood. Sunlight fell through tender leaves, throwing a faint green tracery of airy lace over her abdomen. She was Eve in her bower, womanhood's first awakening.

He wanted to go to her, to cover her smooth flesh with his kisses, to twine with her in the shimmering air until they were one flesh, with her body arching against his in desire. To feel her heart pound in time with his, hear her soft moans mingle with his until the world fell dizzyingly away and they clung, gasping, to each other. Dear God, how he ached to touch her!

Gideon didn't dare. It hit him like a bolt of lightning. *This* was how he should paint her. Not an idealized portrait of innocence untouched, but this beguiling vision of perfect trust.

Undeserved trust, his conscience pointed out sharply.

Again, he felt the pain of his betrayal of her. There she lay, as natural as a child in sleep, sure that he would protect her from discovery or intrusion. And the one thing he hadn't protected her from was his own selfish desire. It didn't matter that she had been a willing partner. She had been swept away on the wings of his ardor, and her own inexperience.

Gideon brooded. At the moment he didn't like himself much.

Would she come to hate him?

While part of him wrestled with the aftermath of their love-making, the artist in him had no such qualms and took over. He went to the easel. The blank, primed canvas replaced the painting on it without conscious thought on his part. The palette was in his hand, and colors were swirled and blended one into another, while he saw the painting take form in his mind's eye.

The song of the birds faded away, the hum of the bees was silenced. Gideon was in that cocoon of concentration where everything vanished but himself, the canvas, and his subject.

He painted like a madman, slashing on color, capturing the shape and texture, the play of light and shadow, until Chloe came achingly alive on the canvas. He captured the velvet sheen of skin, the silken skeins of hair, the soft violet shadows. It was urgent that he get down what he could before she awakened.

The background didn't matter. He blocked it in with swabs of color. He could fill it in later. But there would only be this one time when she slept like this: Innocence, satiated with the first, heady taste of the forbidden fruit.

His loins tightened as he outlined her breasts, daubed in the tender nipples, as if he still felt their taste, their texture, on his tongue. A fresh breeze had sprung up, hinting at rain to come by evening, but his forehead beaded with sweat as he worked.

Quickly, he worked in the leafy pattern across her thighs and abdomen, fighting the heat of desire that roared through his veins. Now the hint of soft curls, the shadowy vee of her legs, the sensual curve of hip and thigh.

The brush seemed to leap and dart of its own accord, making love to the painting of Chloe, just as he had made love to her with his own body. By the time she stirred, he was on fire with passion, almost panting with need. His hand shook with the effort to restrain himself. He could do no more.

He took the painting down, turned it around with its top edge resting against the tree so it wouldn't smear. Somehow, he knew he mustn't show it to her. Not yet.

Her eyes flickered open, unfocused at first. Then she saw him and memory bloomed in her eyes. The fire that burned within him couldn't be quenched. He drew off his shirt and watched the way her face changed as his muscles rippled. Watched the sudden awareness of her body, her nakedness, as he came toward her. He knew he'd been right to paint her then and there.

God help them both, she would never be that innocent again.

Gideon knelt at her feet without speaking, then lifted her foot in his hand. His strong fingers caressed the instep, stroked the delicate arch. His lips followed, moving slowly up her ankle, her calf, the satin skin inside her thigh. And all the time he watched her face. Her eyes. They grew heavy with desire, heated with passion. Her mouth parted, and she sighed. It was both invitation and surrender.

Chloe closed her eyes. Her body quivered as his lips moved up to the cleft between her breasts. His warm breath was agonizing pleasure. She had never known . . . never guessed . . .

Then his mouth closed on her nipple, taking it gently, firmly, and she was lost. His hands worked their magic again, skimming trails of delight along her curves and hollows, sending ripples of sweet madness through her until she was half mad with desire.

Chloe abandoned herself to the moment. To him. *Gideon, my love!*

Her earlier shyness was submerged beneath waves of incredible need. To reach that pitch of fevered pleasure, to give it back to him tenfold, and then to share the shattering fulfillment. She murmured his name low in her throat. Oh, how she wanted him! Only him.

Gideon seemed to sense her change in mood. He took her with infinite tenderness. He slid inside her so effortlessly, so easily, she was caught by surprise. He filled her, and the ache of emptiness she'd carried for so long was filled, too. Nothing that felt this right could be wrong, she told herself. She belonged in his arms. Even if he didn't know it, yet.

She wrapped her arms around him, clinging to his hard-muscled strength. Joy washed through her. She wanted this moment to go on forever. Because when it was over, she would have to face the truth. He didn't love her.

Not yet.

She knew that. But he wanted her. Needed her.

She prayed with all her heart that it would be enough.

His lovemaking this time was slow and easy, giving her time to sort out the multitude of sensations. He was an exquisitely skilled lover, as if he could read meaning in the slightest movement of her body, guess her desires by the softest alteration of her breathing. As he began to move more quickly, she found herself matching his pace. The heat of the day poured over them, melted through them like liquid gold, until they dissolved in the white hot blaze.

As she clung to him, shaking with sensation, wracked with emotion, one thought rang through Chloe's head.

I will make you love me, Gideon Stone. *I will make you love me!*

NINE

§ §

THE TEA TRAY WAS BROUGHT IN AS THE CLOCK CHIMED
ten. The household kept country hours and would be retiring
soon. Lady Albinia looked across the room to her godson.
She'd returned from London eager to see how her matchmaking had fared. So far, she couldn't tell if her little plan had
progressed as well as she'd hoped.

Mrs. Osler winked across her own teacup. "What do you
think, my lady. Will there be wedding bells?"

Albinia looked up where Chloe was playing a romantic air
on the pianoforte, while Gideon turned the music pages for
her. She'd never seen him act like this before. Attentive, yet
wary. "Too early to say," she replied briskly. It would not
do to discuss Gideon's private affairs with Chloe's companion.

Mrs. Osler looked anxious. "I do not mean to presume, but
. . . you would not object if a match were in the offing?"

"My goodness, my godson is a grown man, and Miss Hartsell a grown woman," Albinia said lightly. "Who am I to
interfere in their business?"

Secretly, she wavered between optimism and concern. Since
her return this afternoon, she had watched them carefully, trying to decide. Although she had looked higher for him, it
would be a good match: Miss Hartsell would be a steadying
influence on Gideon, and Lady Albinia would be very happy
for them to make a match of it. But she saw no signs that it
would happen.

The fact was that neither Gideon nor Chloe had said anything at all to her. Perhaps it was all just friendship. Gideon
had never been hard to read before. His emotions were too
volatile. Certainly, his actions toward the girl did not seem
very loverlike.

Lady Albinia's fair brow was marred by a slight frown.
Perhaps she had made a serious error. She was fairly certain
that Chloe was falling in love with him. A one-sided regard
could prove disastrous for the girl.

"They are talking about us," Chloe whispered to Gideon.

"How can you tell?"

"Woman's intuition," she smiled. "And the looking glass
over the mantelpiece."

"We have to talk, also," he said.

In the past week they had snatched stolen embraces, but
there had been no opportunity to be alone for long. Even when
they were in the midst of a sitting, there was too much chance
of being interrupted. Especially by Perry. Only this afternoon
the little rapscallion had almost caught Gideon trying to kiss
her in the garden.

And once, thinking they were alone outside, he had been
about to yank the Grecian gown down off her shoulders, mad
with the need to see her, touch her, only to hear the clip of
shears and discover the gardener pruning the branches of the
trees overhanging the spot.

Henry, damn his eyes, seemed to have appointed himself
unofficial watchdog. If he wasn't trimming the hedges, he was
rattling about the climbing vines or digging up things. Gideon
was growing impatient.

There was always the tower room, yet he found himself
increasingly reluctant to go there. The vertigo that had at-
tacked him only at the upper window, now seemed to affect
him in the lower chamber as well. He was thinking of moving
his things back to the house. When he wasn't thinking about
Chloe.

She was a drug in his blood. He could think of nothing else
but making love to her. He had to have her again. Heat curled

in the pit of his stomach and spread out through his body like flame. Since that day in the garden, he had only made love to her again in his dreams. He knew he could not wait much longer.

Under cover of turning the page, he whispered in her ear, "I am going mad, Chloe. I cannot bear to lie alone another night, tortured by your image and torn by longing."

A sharp thrill went through her. She stumbled over a chord, trying to read the notes and not look at Gideon. She had been so afraid that it was over. That it had ended with Lady Albinia's return.

"Chloe," he murmured, leaning to turn the page before she was anywhere near the end. "I am a desperate man. Will you come to me tonight?"

Her fingers faltered and stopped. She took a deep breath and closed her eyes. "Lady Albinia would hear us."

"Then we must meet in a place where no one will find us." Inspiration struck. He leaned down to speak in her ear, and his hand brushed her breast. Desire sparked across the gap between them.

"The Bride's Chamber," he whispered. "At midnight."

Her hands trembled on the mute keys. *The Bride's Chamber.*

His voice seemed weighted with significance. Did he mean to propose marriage? The possibility was overwhelming, the sudden flood of joy almost more than she could bear.

This was more sudden that she'd expected. But he was a gentleman, she a young lady, and they had lain together. If a kiss in private could be considered almost an engagement in this day and age, surely he meant to make it right between them. Her insides quivered in anticipation.

"What is it?" he said huskily, when she hesitated. "Do you mean to turn me down?"

His words vanquished her doubts. "Oh, no! I mean . . . yes." She looked up shyly, her face radiant. "But do we . . . do we dare risk it?"

"The servants will not go near that haunted room at night."

He smiled at her hesitation. "Or," he said, "are you afraid of Lost Lenore? Don't worry, my dear, I shall protect you from 'things that go bump in the night.' "

Chloe laughed. Her heart felt light and free for the first time since the reading of the will. It would be all right.

"At midnight, then." *In the Bride's Chamber.*

She rose from the piano bench and joined the others at the tea table.

Gideon closed the piano and joined them, and the talk turned to the latest news from London. Chloe sat back and sipped her tea in a state of bliss. Everything had worked out. The gamble had payed off, and she had won.

She was loved. Even if he hadn't said the words, yet.

It was such a perfect moment, she was almost afraid.

Lady Albinia lifted an eyebrow. "You look flushed, Miss Hartsell."

Chloe smiled politely and took the teacup she offered. Her silvery eyes were dreamy and opaque. "Too much sun today, I fear. The shade moved away before I did."

"You must put crushed strawberries on your face," Mrs. Osler announced. "It will draw out the redness and preserve your complexion."

"I shall have Perry pick some in the morning."

"He seemed quite put out that you wouldn't let him stay up past his usual hour," Lady Albinia said, swirling the last of the tea in her eggshell-thin cup.

"I believe there is a meteor shower this week," Mrs. Osler exclaimed. "Perhaps he was going to try out his spyglass."

Gideon laughed. "Last night it was something else. If he had permission to stay up until midnight tonight, he'd do it tomorrow and every night after that."

Chloe was sorry she hadn't relented. It didn't seem fair when she was so happy tonight. "Actually, it was something to do with Lost Lenore, and I didn't want him to go wandering about in the darkness. Perhaps I was a little short with him earlier."

But how could she not be, when she was in the library with

Gideon, hoping to steal a kiss, when he'd interrupted them? Soon, though, there would be no need to hide in corners for a quick embrace.

She set her cup down. "I'll peek in on him on my way up to bed. He still lets me tuck him in. I suppose I should take advantage of it while I may." A wistful little smile played over her mouth. "It won't be much longer, and he'll consider himself far too old for such coddling."

After tea, they all said their goodnights and went up to bed. At the top of the stairs, Chloe took the hall leading to the old nursery, where Perry still had his room. He'd bristled when Gideon had asked if he'd like a larger room of his own. Chloe smiled, remembering.

"I wouldn't move for anything, sir. The old nursery is perfect for a scientist. The bedroom is all I need for sleep," Perry exclaimed. His freckles stood out in indignation. "The nursery shelves can hold all my books and experiments, and I keep my menagerie in the governess's chamber."

"Menagerie? Good God, what have you got in there?" Gideon said in mock alarm. "Ponies and goats, or griffins and unicorns, no doubt."

"Just my rabbit and fish, and the bird that Tobias left to me," the boy said, ticking them off on his fingers. "Two turtles from the pond, and a sort of crab creature I haven't found in my books yet."

"Egad! Anything more?"

"Oh, just some yellow and brown striped caterpillars in glass jars. By Jove, I almost forgot. They're spinning wonderful cocoons! You must come and see them, sir. That's all, except for the dog. But he sleeps in my room, of course."

"Of course," Gideon said, and grinned.

Thinking of the conversation made Chloe smile to herself, as she left the drawing room and went up the stairs. She was relieved that Gideon seemed to be amused by Perry and glad that Perry liked Gideon.

"He's a capital fellow, Chlo. The best."

The lamp at the top of the staircase had gone out, and she

had to go back for a taper. It was not like Agnes or Mrs. Linley to let such things go unnoticed. The candle cast a yellow haze around her, which made it difficult to see up to the landing. It gave Chloe the strange illusion that she was floating upward through nothingness. For a moment she almost turned and went back down.

It is only Perry with his earlier talk of ghosts and goblins, of the approaching Lammas night, and of the Old Ones that has me feeling on edge, she told herself sternly.

She hadn't realized how much of the old legends Tobias had instilled in the boy. A tiny sigh escaped her. She didn't want him to go away to school so soon, but perhaps it was selfish to keep him here. He needed the company of other children, a boisterous pack of boys, perhaps, to draw him out.

A smile touched her lips. There were other alternatives . . .

The flame of her candle flickered yellow and blue as she took the last few steps. There was quite a draft coming down staircase. She'd fetch a shawl after she tucked Perry in for the night.

When Chloe reached the upper floor she saw that the lamp in its niche was full of oil, but the wick was unlit. Removing the chimney, she wound the wick up a bit higher. It was charred on the end, as if it had been blown out by the draft. She lit it from her candle. Warm light bloomed, chasing the shadows away. She hadn't realized till then that she'd been holding her breath.

Perry's room was on the left, two doors down. She knocked softly, then turned the knob. Starlight and moonlight flooded in the open window, and a cool breeze stirred the curtains. Beyond, Pucca's Hill rose in the distance.

"Is that you, Chlo?" he mumbled.

"Yes. I've come to tuck you in." She looked for his dog, who usually curled up at his feet. "Where's is your boon companion?"

"Under the bed."

"No wonder. It's quite cool. You shouldn't sleep with the

window open on such a night," she said softly. "You'll catch your death."

"I have to watch the hill," he murmured sleepily. "Watch for Lenore."

"You're dreaming, darling." She sat on the edge of the bed and smoothed the hair back from his forehead. "I'm sorry if I was short with you earlier."

"S'all right," he said, and turned over.

Leaning down, she kissed his temple and tucked the covers in. "Sleep well."

Her only answer was his slow, even breathing. She closed his window, but left the curtain open, then hurried to her room.

Agnes was waiting to brush out her hair. The maid had placed Chloe's night rail out on the bed, with her robe beside it. Agnes was very pleased to have been elevated to the role of lady's maid, even if she wasn't quite sure of her duties just yet. She'd told her young man all about it when they had walked out together last evening, on her half-day off, and he had been properly impressed.

"*Maybe they'll hire me on at the Folly, too, Agnes. If the new master stays on, he'll need to take on another groom or two. Or,*" he'd said, dreaming of grander things, "*maybe even a footman.*"

The maid's eyes grew misty at the thought of her Sam becoming a footman at Lacey's Folly. Chloe noticed.

"You look tired, Agnes. Go on to bed. I've undressed myself all these years, one more night won't matter."

"Thank you, Miss Chloe, but it wouldn't be fitting. I wouldn't want Lady Albinia's fine dresser looking down her nose at me."

"Just this once, Agnes."

The maid bobbed an awkward curtsey and left.

Chloe waited until she was gone, then lay across the bed, counting the minutes until she could meet Gideon in the Bride's Chamber.

Yes, she thought, with a slow smile, there was significance

to that. Tonight, Gideon would make everything official. She wondered if he had a ring.

He was waiting in the shadows of the Old Hall.

"Do you think she will mind?" Gideon joked as they slipped into the Bride's Chamber.

Chloe looked up at the painting of Lost Lenore. In the wavering candlelight, her eyes seemed to follow them. "I hope not."

It seemed deliciously wicked to be here alone with him, while the rest of the house was abed. Chloe lifted the glass dome with the bridal wreath and placed it on a table. Gideon pulled back the covers, where she'd already placed fresh sheets. Chloe bit her lip. If that was bold and wanton of her, so be it. But he didn't even notice.

"I thought you wanted to talk," she said.

"We must." He lifted her chin and kissed her. "But first things first. I cannot even think of the right words when you're standing here alone with me at last." He dropped another kiss on her mouth. "I should have thought of this sooner."

A light might be seen from the other wing of the house he thought. Blowing out the candles, he went to the window facing Pucca's Hill and opened the curtains. The moon was almost full, and the room came alive with silvery light. Chloe looked as if she were carved of precious metal. But when he touched her, she was warm. So warm in his arms.

Gideon kissed her until they were both breathless. "I cannot wait another moment," he said, nipping her earlobe.

He undressed her slowly, by the light of the moon. Chloe felt as if they were suspended in time. Nothing mattered, except the two of them. Here, together. Now and for always.

He took off the lace collar of her dress and slowly unfastened the row of tiny buttons. If this was how he meant to start, she was willing enough. No, she was eager! Her body burned for his touch.

He sensed her growing excitement. "Do you want me to

make love to you, beautiful Chloe? Tell me that you want me.''

"I do! Oh, I do Gideon. More than you can know!"

Her words were like a spur to his ardor. He reined it in. Tonight he would take her slowly. Introduce her to sensations and pleasures she had never imagined. The thought of what he meant to do went to his head like champagne. He was drunk with passion for her.

As the garment parted inch by inch, he pressed his mouth against her skin, inhaling her fragrance. Touching the tip of his tongue to her tender flesh until she swayed against him. He slid off the dress, and she stood in her chemise, with the moonlight outlining her figure and turning her hair to silver gilt. Gently, he reached up and pulled the pins from her curls. They tumbled to her waist like a shimmering veil.

"You look like a bride," he said, catching up handfuls of her hair and running his fingers through it. *Like silk floss*, he thought, already anticipating how it would look when she lay naked on the bed beneath him. A shiver ran through him.

Chloe felt as if her heart would burst with joy. Gideon stripped off his shirt. The wide muscles of his chest and shoulders rippled, and she ran her hands over his skin, memorizing every contour. He was beautiful and strong, and he was hers. She couldn't believe how fortune had blessed her.

She pressed her mouth against his chest, and he groaned softly. When she nipped him with her teeth, he was startled. Delighted. Incredibly aroused. Her mouth skimmed over him, and her tongue darted out, just once, to taste his skin.

Gideon grabbed her and kissed her passionately. "Chloe, Chloe, you are driving me insane."

"Here." He sat on the edge of a chair in her chemise and untied the ribbons that held it closed. He pushed the hem up over her thighs and trailed his hand along them, while he kissed the cleft between her breasts.

"I love the way you taste," he said. "And the scent of you. Like wildflowers and honey."

She waited for the declaration of loving *her* to follow. It didn't.

Instead, he slid her hem higher, moved his mouth lower. It was all right. He desired her. Her needed her. And even if he didn't know it yet, she knew he loved her. Knew it with every breath in her body, every beat of her heart.

Then she forgot everything as he brushed her inner thighs with his lips. She gasped and clutched his hair. When he grasped her hips to pull her closer and dipped his head, she was startled. Her first instinct was to push him back. Then he kissed her, intimately, and she no longer cared what he said or didn't say. From the first touch of his mouth, she was lost.

She shivered with pleasure. Her fingers tangled in his thick hair, urging him closer still. The caress of his tongue was so unexpected, so darkly arousing, she was dizzy with it. Heat rose from her loins to her head, and she felt herself go liquid for him. His breath added to the heat between her legs. His tongue probed softly, insistently, and she clung to him, shivering with need and pleasure.

Gideon filled his mouth with the taste and texture of her. He would give her the same delight she gave to him, set her blood roaring to match his. When she writhed and bucked, he pushed her back against the chair. His hands cupped her buttocks and angled her closer, and he plundered her with his tongue while she moaned and arched with pleasure.

He loves me, she exulted. Yes. And this most intimate act was the final proof of it.

Deeper and deeper. With every stroke, she was in a frenzy of passion. Just when she thought there was nothing more he could do, he suckled the hard, hidden bud, and all conscious thought was banished. Pleasure shot through her like sparks, like flames, like a wall of wildfire. Her body jerked and convulsed in passion.

She cried out while he held her tightly and brought her to the crest again. She didn't think she could endure any more. Then he brought her there again and swept her over the edge. She fell headlong into a storm of sensation that was so violently exquisite, she thought she might die of it.

When she was done, he rose and pulled her into his arms. "Ah, sweet Chloe. I have dreamed of that all week," he said huskily. "I have made love to you a hundred times in my mind. In a hundred different ways."

Now she was here in the flesh. He picked her up and placed her on the feather bed, then stripped off the rest of his clothes, lay down beside her, and began again. She clawed at his shoulders, pulling him down to her. The rasp of the hair on his chest against her breasts was a remembered pleasure. The touch of his mouth on their tips was sheer glory.

This time when he entered her, she was more than ready, rising to meet him boldly. Their bodies were slick with sweat as he drove into her, urging her on. She wanted to take him so deeply that she would merge with him, body and heart and soul. And when they did, it was so unbearably beautiful that afterward, her cheeks were wet with tears.

"Did I hurt you, darling?" He kissed the tears. "Forgive me."

"No," she whispered holding his face so their lips touched. "It was so wonderful. So beautiful. I never knew it could be like this, Gideon. And I know you would never, ever hurt me."

He kissed her to silence, then lay holding her until they both fell asleep.

It was nearly dawn when Chloe opened her eyes. She smelled the earthy scent of fresh rain. The room was mysterious, all lavender in the early light. It was not her room. Perhaps she was dreaming . . .

Through the open curtains, she glimpsed a limestone sill still damp with dew, but beyond, the sky was clear, streaked with gold and rose. The dawn of a perfect new day.

It took her a moment to realize that she was naked. And where she was. And who she was with. Gideon was still beside her, his head heavy against her breast. She shifted a little. He mumbled something, and his hands reached out to her before he was even awake, touching and stroking.

"No," she whispered. "Wake up, Gideon. We must get back to our rooms!"

His eyes opened sleepily. He leaned forward and nipped her on the breast lightly. "Wicked vixen. I think you've cast a spell upon me."

"Do you? I believe you lured me here under pretense of needing to talk," she joked, twining her fingers through his thick hair. "Now we have no time. The servants will be stirring shortly."

He rolled over and pinned her down. "We have to talk. About the future."

Her heart skipped a beat.

Gideon looked down at her, remembering how quiet and shy she had been at their first meeting. Now she was a temptress, and she reveled in it.

His fingertip circled her nipple. "Things have progressed too far and fast between us, Chloe. We have to—"

A rooster crowed loudly, startling them both.

"Good God, the servants will be below stairs at any moment." It wouldn't do to create a scandal beneath his roof. Especially with Albinia present.

"Hurry, put on your things." He tossed Chloe her garments without ceremony, and pulled on his own. "If you take the back stairs, you can be in your room before they know you're missing. If I'm caught, I'll say I was up for an early stroll."

It was an unromantic ending to their passionate night, but Chloe was consumed with giggles as he helped her dress. "I feel like a naughty child."

He grabbed her by the shoulders and kissed her soundly. "You are a naughty child. Now go to your room."

As she reached the door, he stopped her. "Will you meet me again tonight? Here, in this room?"

"I will."

She ran lightly down the stairs, turned at a door in the Old Hall, and hastened back to her room. *He loves me*, she thought in wild joy. *There is no doubt! He does love me.*

Washing in cold water from her pitcher, she shoved her clothes into the wardrobe, put on her nightshift, and climbed beneath the sheets. How lonely her narrow bed felt without the warm length of his body beside her. She could not wait until they no longer had to creep about and meet in secret.

Until she had the right, as his wife, to fall asleep every night in his arms.

Chloe fell into a pleasant doze, where she and Gideon wandered through some hazy, golden future. Less than an hour passed before she heard a tap on her door. Chloe sat up groggily. It was too early for her morning chocolate. And Agnes never knocked. "Yes? Come in?"

Mrs. Osler entered, still in her robe and nightcap. "Oh, Miss Hartsell, I don't know how to tell you!"

Chloe's heart froze. She flung back the covers. "What is it? Is it Dawlish? Has something happened to him?"

"No." Mrs. Osler wrung her hands. "It's young Perry. Henry was up early. He found a rope dangling from your brother's window. I went to check. Oh, Miss Hartsell, I've looked everywhere. He's gone missing. And his bed has not been slept in!"

Chloe threw back the covers and put on her robe, tying it as she flew to the door. Hurrying down the corridor, she turned toward the old nursery. It was just as it had been last night when she tucked him in: the curtains were closed, the covers still plumped up—but Perry was not beneath them. He'd rolled up his pillows to mimic his sleeping form.

Chloe checked the other rooms quickly. He was not in the nursery or menagerie, and neither was his puppy, Newton. She went to the window, now open, and looked out. A rope ran from the shutter pins sunk into the limestone, down to the ground.

Angry and frightened, she peered over the rail for the sign of a sprawled body on the ground, afraid of what she might see. The lawn was clear. *At least he made it safely down*, she comforted herself. *And when I get my hands on him . . .*

Chloe pulled the windows shut, then blew out the lamp and hurried toward the stairs. As she passed Lady Albinia's room, she became aware of a strange tableau.

Gideon knelt beside his godmother, chaffing her hands in his. Lady Albinia appeared to be in a near faint, propped up against the pillows with a tray across her lap. A china cup lay broken on the floor beside the bed.

Chloe stopped. "Dear God, what has happened here?"

Her maid stood beside them, wringing her hands. "My lady had a restless night . . . bad dreams, she said. She asked for tea with herbal drops to settle her nerves. I turned my back and heard a crash."

Lady Albinia struggled to sit up with Gideon's help. Her face was paper white. "Your . . . Perry—is he all right?" she demanded weakly.

Chloe's blood ran cold. "Perry is not in his bed," she said quietly. "It has not been slept in."

Gideon looked sternly at his godmother. "Do not frighten her with your nonsense, Albinia."

Lady Albinia's lips were blanched. "I must. I dreamed of Perry all night. Of a voice as sweet as a siren's call luring sailors onto the rocks. Black, cold . . ." She shivered, and her voice grew faint. She struggled against it.

"Then it was there again, in the tea leaves." Her eyes were like sapphires in a stark white face. "A warning," she whispered. "A boy . . . a cold, dark place . . . death."

Chloe ran across the lichened packhorse bridge to where Henry and Rendulph were searching the tall grasses of the meadow. The ground was lush and damp from last night's rainfall. She had dressed in the first thing that came to hand, and her slippers were already soaked.

"You'll not find him here," she called out. "I know where he has gone: to Pucca's Hill."

Henry's weathered face grew pale. "Not in the night, he didn't."

"I am sure of it. You men go up the side from here. I'll fetch Mr. Stone, and we'll go across by the old clapper bridge. He might have gone that way."

She ran back toward the house, skirting the pond. It had overflowed its banks and lapped at the pergola.

Gideon appeared on the path at the foot of the garden. "He's not in the tower," he called.

"No! I *know* how he thinks. And I know where he is. He's somewhere in the woods on the hill. Oh, please hurry! We must find him."

"What the devil would he be doing there?"

Chloe headed for the clapper bridge. "Searching for the fairy rath, and Lost Lenore! Oh, Gideon . . . It is a hundred years to the day that she vanished."

"The water is too high," Gideon shouted. "We'll have to go around."

"No! He's near. I can can feel it!"

She clutched at one of the posts with the iron rings for balance and kicked off her slippers.

"Chloe, damn it! Wait!"

There was no time to lose. She started across before he could catch her.

As her stocking feet touched the remains of the clapper bridge, her heart was hammering so loudly, she couldn't hear the deep rush of the water. The water flowed over the ragged stones, tugging coldly at her feet. Slapping at her ankles.

If the bridge were still intact, she would be several inches above it, on a smooth and fairly level surface. Instead, she had to try and pick her way over the foundation, avoiding the sharp edges of the tilted rocks that braced it. She slipped, bobbled, and caught herself in time. Behind her she could hear Gideon cursing.

The current was so swift, it impeded her way. Then Gideon was on the bridge, reaching for her.

"Damn you, Chloe, turn back. The river is rising. You'll be swept away."

A sob caught in her throat. "I have to find him!"

She felt Gideon's fingers brush her sleeve and tried to run. The water was past her ankles now. The river was rising fast. She lunged for the opposite bank, just as Gideon caught her round the waist.

"No, no!" She was wild with fear. The closer she got to the opposite bank, the stronger the feeling of doom. Chloe tugged at Gideon's hands. They almost tumbled off the rough stones together. He held her fast.

In that one sharp moment, when he almost lost her to the river, he was terror-struck. Not for himself, but for Chloe. One false step and he might lose her to the angry river. *God help me*, he thought, stunned by the knowledge, *I love her!*

There was no time to think of it further. As he wrestled with her and with the onslaught of emotion, he heard something. *There!*

An animal whimpering nearby. Or perhaps a small boy, grievously injured. He glimpsed something in the grass beyond and felt sick at heart.

By sheer strength of will, he picked Chloe up off her feet and carried her to safety on the near side of the river. "I see him. On the other side."

He dumped her on her feet and gave her shoulders a violent shake. "Stay here, or I will throttle you on the spot! I will bring him to you. We will do the boy no good if we're swept away ourselves."

She nodded, unable to speak around the fear in her throat.

Without looking back, Gideon forded the rising water over the ruins of the ancient bridge and made it to the far bank. His search didn't take long. Perry was lying in a waterlogged hollow on the other side. His skin was a strange blue-white, like milk that had been skimmed, and his left leg was bent awkwardly. There was a bend in the shinbone where none should be.

"God in Heaven!"

Gideon knelt beside him. His eyes stung. The boy was barely conscious. His clothes were sopped, and his left foot was still wedged between two upright stones of the clapper bridge.

"Easy, young fellow. You're found. I'll take you home. To Chloe."

Freeing the boy's foot from his shoe, he looked around for something to splint his leg. A walking stick lay near Perry, and Gideon took off his cravat and used both to immobilize the leg. The boy had to be safe and warm before they could even think of setting it properly.

He lifted Perry in his arms as gently as possible; but the boy cried out sharply. Then his head lolled back, and he fell into a faint. Gideon was relieved. It would make the crossing easier. The poor lad was in shock, and there was no time to waste in going the long way round.

As he struggled across the bridge to Chloe with Perry in his arms, Gideon realized how he had changed since he came to Lacey's Folly. And he realized he cared not only for Chloe, but for this small, enthusiastic, and sometimes irritating young scalawag, as well. They had insinuated themselves into his life and wrapped around his heart.

And he thanked God for it!

Chloe waited mutely on the other side. The moment she first saw Gideon rise, with Perry lying limply in his arms, her heart had stopped. Her body was leaden with fear.

The water was above Gideon's ankles, and she realized he still had his boots on. Whether they would help or hinder, she didn't know, she could only watch and pray.

A fresh surge of current pulled at him, but Gideon kept his balance. Despite the cool morning, sweat beaded on his brow. He must save Perry. He must get him to the house and packed in blankets and hot water bottles, before the shock carried him off. The thought was unbearable.

When Gideon stepped off onto the solid ground, he heaved a great sigh.

She looked at them both with such fear, such love in her eyes, that Gideon felt as if his heart would break with it.

What a fool he had been to think of finding a husband for

her. He would cast himself in that role, with a joyous heart. There was no other woman for him than generous, loving, guileless Chloe.

He thanked Heaven that he had realized it before it was too late.

She clutched at his sleeve, trembling. "Is he . . . ?"

"Don't fear, my little love. He's only in a faint. His leg needs setting, but he's young and strong and will be fit in no time!"

Chloe wasn't fooled by his hearty tone. She knew him too well. Gideon was afraid. She touched Perry's face, kissed his chill lips, and saw the rapid pulse beating in his throat. She couldn't move. Couldn't speak. Couldn't think.

Gideon took command. "Run back to the house and have them prepare a warm bed. Go!"

Chloe ran across the lawn, oblivious to her wet stockings and lack of shoes. Mrs. Osler and Lady Albinia saw her coming and hurried out to meet her. Her usual sense of purpose was back and focused on saving Perry.

"Gideon's found him," she said breathlessly when she reached the house. "Lady Albinia, tell Dawlish to send a groom for Dr. Marsh. Have the servants fetch hot water and blankets to his room. Gather up anything you think we might need, Mrs. Osler. And hurry!"

"You're exhausted, my dear."

Gideon's hand rested gently on Chloe's shoulder. It was late afternoon, but the drapes were closed at his window, and a screen placed to keep the room dim. "Go and lie down."

"He is so still," she whispered.

"He's been given laudanum. His leg is set. Dr. Marsh says he is young and will recover. In a few days he'll be up on crutches, hunting for fairies and lost treasures."

"He had better not!" she said vehemently.

"Let Mrs. Osler take over, or my godmother. They are both itching to play nurse." Gideon's hand stroked her hair. "And I must talk with you."

"I have no time for that," she said, not looking up.

He laughed. "Little fool, that is not what I mean. This time I really mean to talk."

Chloe looked up at him. "I will stay until he stirs. When he awakens, I must be at his side."

He saw there was no arguing with her. Empires might rise and fall, but Chloe would not leave the boy's side until he came to his senses.

There was no place for him right now. He understood. "Very well. And you may tell him we'll begin our drawing lessons while he's laid up. It will be the perfect opportunity for me to teach him."

"Will you have the time for it?"

"I can spare it for him." Gideon touched Perry's cheek. "He's a brave lad. I've grown quite fond of him."

Chloe gave a little sob of relief. Everything was so unreal, like a waking dream. But it would all work out. Perry would be fine. And the three of them would live happily ever after at Lacey's Folly, just like in a fairy tale. It *must* be so!

Gideon lit a single taper in a shielded lantern and left it on the nightstand. It would soon be dark. Leaving reluctantly, he paused in the doorway, amazed at his change of fortune in the past few weeks.

Albinia had been right all along. Chloe was the woman— the only woman—for him. The revelation was still new and wonderful to Gideon.

How beautiful she looked, leaning over the sleeping boy. The candlelight framed them in a golden halo. It made a lovely picture. *Like a Renaissance Madonna and child*, he thought. *My Chloe!*

Gideon watched them a moment, smiling. Then he went down to the drawing room to report to the others.

Gideon had forced Chloe to come down for a while, concerned for her nerves. She sat in the parlor beside Lady Albinia, white with worry and exhaustion. She'd eaten nothing of her dinner.

It would soon be evening, and Perry had still not awakened.

"Perhaps Dr. Marsh gave him too much laudanum," she said for the third time.

Lady Albinia put her hand over Chloe's. "Dr. Marsh impressed me as a man of good sense. And he has Mrs. Osler's complete confidence. Remember that sleep is often nature's best medicine."

A short time later Mrs. Osler came down. Chloe looked up in fear.

"It's all right," the widow said. "Agnes is with him. He is starting to stir, and I wanted you to be there when he opens his eyes."

Chloe left without another word and hurried up to Perry's room. He made a small sound of distress, then opened his eyes. "Chloe? Oh, I hurt so."

Agnes withdrew. "I'll tell Cook to fix a tray of broth for him," she said.

Chloe took Perry's hand in hers. "Your leg is broken, but Dr. Marsh is certain it will heal perfectly."

"Will I get to use a cane and crutch?" he said sleepily. The idea seemed to please the boy. She smiled radiantly down at him. "You may use a dozen, for all I care."

Perry grinned weakly. "You are a great gun, Chlo." He looked around, more awake by the minute. And more in pain. "Ohhh! It hurts when I try to move."

"Yes." She held a glass to his lips. "Drink half of this now. It is laudanum and willow bark extract. I will give you the rest after you've taken some broth." She watched him swallow the bitter concoction and sighed.

"Why did you do it, darling?"

"I was trying to rescue Lenore," he answered in a woebegone voice. "I went to the place where I found her earring. I knew it was the entrance to the fairy fort. But I waited and waited all night long . . . till sunrise. I was on my way back, when . . . I slipped on the rocks and caught my foot. Oh, Chloe, it hurt so!"

"Yes, my darling. You were very brave."

"I heard your voice. And Gideon's. I was never so glad in all my life."

"Nor was I!" She kissed his forehead. "Your adventure had a happy ending, but Perry, it could have ended terribly. You must promise you will never disobey me like that again."

He saw the shadows beneath her eyes, heard the strain in her voice. "I'm sorry, Chlo. I . . . I had to do it."

He shifted again, and his face rumpled with pain and disappointment. "And now it's too late. Last night . . ." He tried to suppress a sob. "Last night was a hundred years since she disappeared. Tobias told me so. I thought I could find her . . . bring her here. And she would share her treasure with us. And we should all go on happily together . . ."

"Oh, Perry!" Chloe stared at him in dismay. "You should never have risked your life for an imaginary treasure."

"It's real," he said, wincing with pain. "Tobias told me before he fell ill. He'd found a clue. In the Bride's Chamber. I looked and looked, but I couldn't find it. So I thought I would find Lenore when she came out of the fairy hill." He turned to Chloe solemnly. "I knew she would be afraid. Everything has changed so."

She leaned down and kissed him. "That was gallant of you to want to help her." *And incredibly foolish.* But Chloe held her tongue.

"It wasn't just for her, Chlo. I thought . . ." He squirmed, trying to get comfortable, and winced again. "It was a secret, but . . . I know . . . I heard you weeping that night when they read the will. I couldn't bear it, Chlo! The thought of you leaving. Having to marry someone you don't even know and go away with him."

His small hand squeezed her tightly. "I thought . . . if I found the treasure, then Gideon wouldn't have to sell off everything. And you would never, ever, have to leave Lacey's Folly."

She smiled tenderly and smoothed his hair back from his brow. "What a dear, dear boy you are. I couldn't bear it either, Perry." She leaned down. "But I have a secret, too. Don't worry, love. Lacey's Folly is not lost to us after all. We shall be staying right here, with Gideon, quite cozily. Nothing will change. We will go on exactly as before.''

"Do you mean it?''

"Yes, my darling.'' Chloe reassured him as his eyes fluttered closed. "I admit I was very worried for a time. But . . . I had a plan. It was very difficult. But it all worked out for the best, exactly as I had hoped. We are safe now. Never fear, dear heart. No one will separate us. We shall not have to leave Lacey's Folly, ever. I have made sure of it.''

She heard a sharp sound from the doorway and looked up. Gideon stood there, rigid and pale. His features were harshly shadowed, as if he were carved from his namesake's rock.

"What an enlightening conversation,'' he said bitterly.

"Gideon!'' She rose quickly.

He clenched and unclenched his hands at his side, as if he wanted to strike out at something. "There is a saying that people who eavesdrop hear no good. Well, that proverb has proven itself true tonight.''

"You misunderstood . . .''

"No. Now I finally *do* understand. Everything begins to make sense.''

Agnes bustled in behind him, with a tray and bowl of broth, unaware of the problem. "I'll sit with Master Perry, Miss Chloe. Such a nice broth as Cook has made up for him!''

"Thank you, Agnes. I'll be back shortly. I . . . I believe that Mr. Stone wishes to speak privately with me.''

"Yes, by God,'' he said ominously. "That I do!''

Gideon took Chloe by the arm and propelled her out of the room without a by-your-leave. Agnes gaped after them.

"Gideon,'' Chloe whispered fiercely at the head of the stairs, "you are hurting my arm.''

He was in such a white heat of fury, he didn't even hear her protests. He had been fooled again by a woman's schemes. And this time the pain, the anguish of the betrayal, went deep.

He marched her down the stairs ruthlessly. She could barely keep up with his pace. When they reached the hall, he steered her to the library, opened the door and thrust her in. He locked the door behind them.

"So," he said, his voice like the crack of a whip. "Is that what it was all about? To lure me into becoming your lover, so that you might get what you really wanted?"

"No! Gideon . . ."

"Make me no protests of your innocence. You have condemned yourself with your own admissions. I heard it all." Standing there, thinking again that she looked like a Madonna in the candlelight. Hearing that it had all been a ploy, that once again he had been wax in the hands of a calculating woman.

"You missed your calling," he told her. "You should have had a great career upon the stage! That night, with your play-acting the sleepwalker's role—I see it was your first plan, hastily thrown together. You hoped to rouse the entire household and have them catch us in a compromising position, *didn't you?*"

"That isn't true . . ."

"And then," he went on, still in a blind fury, "when that didn't work, you laid your little trap in the garden." He pounded his fist on the wall. "So clever a trap, that I thought *I* was the seducer. All so you could have exactly what you wanted: Lacey's Folly!"

"You are twisting everything about," Chloe cried. "It wasn't like that! It was you, always you, I wanted."

He turned her own words against her. "So, you don't deny it! You contrived it all. But I was not the true object of your desire. I was only the means to an end."

"Gideon, let me explain!"

He strode toward her, and she shrunk back before the coldness in his face. "What can you hope to say that I will believe?" His lip curled. "That you were a virgin when I took you? I know better now. I should have realized it then."

She was stricken mute. There was no way to explain that he would understand. Not now.

He loomed over her like an avenging god. "Some women

are whores for pleasure, others for money or gain. And you—
you hoped we would marry and solve all your problems: you
traded yourself, like a common whore, for Lacey's Folly!''

''How dare you!'' Her hand moved so fast, he almost didn't
see it. Gideon caught her wrist before she could connect the
flat of her palm with his cheek.

He held her wrists in his iron grip. ''Spare me your little
scenes of false virtue. Your plan has failed, Madam!''

He forced her hands down to her side. There was anguish
beneath the anger in his voice, but she was too distraught to
hear it.

''You are a clever schemer, Chloe. You had me worried
earlier, with your defense of Exton. I wondered why you
would encourage a man like him to dangle after you. I thought
that, in your innocence, you did not recognize him for the
libertine he is.''

A knot in his jaw worked as he scrutinized her. ''Now I
see: he was insurance, in case I did not come up to scratch.
You would trade Lacey's Folly in a moment, to become the
wife of a marquis, debauched though he may be. I wish you
joy of him and only hope you don't fall low enough to be his
discarded mistress one day!''

''How can you say such things of me!'' Chloe was torn
between indignation and despair, shaking so badly she
couldn't think. ''How can you even look at me, if that is what
you believe?''

Gideon rounded on her with a snarl. ''Circumstance might
compel us to share this roof a few weeks longer, but I'll tell
you this: I want you out of my sight from this moment until
I leave for London next week. *Is that clear?*''

She was frozen, unable to move. Releasing her with a look of
cold contempt, he whirled on his heel and started for the door.

Chloe was desperate. She had to try to clear this up before
matters got even worse. She went after him, holding out her
hands. ''Gideon, please. Hear me out. For the love of God!''

He turned to face her. ''Love? A strange word for you to use.''

She swallowed her pride. ''I love you, Gideon.''

"There is no love in you," he said wrathfully. "Only greed!"

"What I was saying to Perry . . ."

"Ah, yes. Perry!" He paused with his hand on the knob. "Tell me, Chloe. Does he know that your only brother died and was buried within weeks of your parents' demise?" His face set in granite. "*Does Perry know he is your son?*"

Chloe's face contorted. She recoiled, then clutched a table for support, faint with shock.

He knew! There was no use denying it, or trying to explain. "For his sake, swear to me Gideon, that you won't tell Perry!"

He shrugged off a flash of pity. "Don't worry," he said in a hard voice. "He will not learn of it from me."

He went out, slamming the door behind him.

Chloe sank to the sofa, weeping silently. Her terrible secret was out, and her world lay smashed in pieces at her feet.

Gideon left the house. Large and sprawling though it might be, it was too large to contain his anger. Chloe had made a fool out of him.

A willing fool, he thought savagely.

He should have realized it the first time, although he'd never made love to a virgin. His former companions had been women of wide amorous experience. With Chloe, he'd been too consumed with passion at the time. And later, with guilt.

And all the time, her blushes were a sham. He had not been the first. Nor, he thought angrily, was he sure he was the second. She might have had other lovers in the past. He ground his teeth in chagrin.

Small wonder she had been so eager for his touch. No shyness, no protests. And the way her arms had twined about him, the thrusting of her hips. Oh, she had known what to expect, well enough. And she had led him a merry dance.

The worst of it, the part he couldn't forgive, was that she had made him care for her. Or, at least, for the innocent girl he had thought she was. Not the conniving schemer she had proved to be.

He stumbled over the burrow of a small animal. "Devil take it!" And take Chloe Hartsell, too. God, what an idiot he been to fall for her lures.

She wasn't the first, nor probably the last. What fatal flaw was there in him that the three women he'd cared for, had all betrayed him?

Dorinda had been his boyhood love, but in the end, it was his status she loved more. His relationship with Mariah had been totally different: infatuation on his part, and mere lust on hers. She had not cared for him, only for his body.

But Chloe . . . *Ah, Chloe!* He had been so long in realizing his feelings for her, but when he knew—when he *thought* he knew—he had found the perfect woman for him. It had been like finding the most wonderful treasure on earth. Someone who would be his partner in every way and return his love with every particle of her being: heart and mind and soul!

He laughed at the bitter jest. She hadn't wanted anything of *him* at all. She had only wanted slate and stone and wood. It was Lacey's Folly that she loved.

Gideon wished night were not approaching, so he could take a horse and go careering madly over the countryside, racing away from his hurt pride and bitter betrayal. Instead, he cut out across the lawn and down beyond the pond, toward the river.

On the horizon to the west, there were only a few streaks of fading red along the treetops. Closer at hand, the rising moon was reflected in the dark water, making a false image.

Like Chloe, he thought, viciously. *A vision of purity and loveliness—but all lies and illusion!*

Chloe went up to Perry's room. Mrs. Osler sat by the bedside, reading. The draperies were drawn against the last bit of sunset, and Agnes had moved the screen so that it shielded the boy from the lamplight.

Mrs. Osler looked up. "He has been peacefully asleep this past half hour. Why don't you get some rest, my dear? I'll spend the first watch with him."

"That is very good of you, but I don't believe I shall sleep at all."

"Nonsense. You will do him no good tomorrow if you are exhausted. Even if you can't sleep, rest awhile."

Leaning down, Chloe kissed Perry's brow. "He is feverish."

"Dr. Marsh said he would be. I have already given him a fever powder. He'll be better by morning."

The widow touched Chloe's hand. There was sympathy in her eyes. Although she didn't know what words had been exchanged, she'd heard the loud voices and slamming doors. "Go, now. I'll call you if he awakens."

Chloe was reluctantly persuaded. "I'll be back at midnight."

She went to her room, heartsick. This morning the world had been a bright and shining place. How quickly everything had changed.

Standing at the window, she saw Gideon strike out across the lawn in growing twilight. Her heart was breaking. She still couldn't believe that she had lost him between one heartbeat and the next. A careless word, a badly turned phrase, and she had ruined everything.

Dashing the tears from her eyes, she stared into the silver light. He vanished among the trees. What could she say or do to convince him that he was wrong? To force him to realize that she did love him?

Nothing.

She took a deep breath and calmed herself. It is not too late. I can win him back. *I will think of something. Dear God, I must!*

Her heart lifted a little. After all, there were ten days before he left for London.

In ten days, surely something would happen.

Gideon felt a prickle of unease. He looked around in surprise. While he was wrestling with his anger, he'd walked all the way around to the tower. How the devil had he done that?

He felt compelled to go inside, although his skin prickled. Unlocking the door, he entered. It was dim inside. The light was failing fast. He found the tin box of matches and lit an oil lamp. As he climbed the stairs, the hairs prickled at the nape of his neck. Someone—some*thing* was breathing heavily at the top of the stairs.

"Who is there? Show yourself!"

Perry's pup came scrabbling out of the corner, yipping and whining with joy. Gideon laughed in relief. Bending down, he patted it. "Hallo, Newton. So this is where that young scoundrel locked you away so you wouldn't follow him. Come along, you can keep me company."

He mounted the steps. The pup sat at the bottom and looked up at him, wagging his tail. "I will not carry you, if that's what you're thinking."

Lifting the lamp, Gideon went up to the second story. It seemed curiously darker here, despite the tall windows. His lamp made a small circle of golden light, leaving the rest of the room in deep shadow. It fell upon Chloe's portrait, the one of her in the high-backed throne, where everything but her face was finished.

"That is why I could never capture you," he said harshly. "Because it was all a mask. Nothing more."

Like Mariah, she was false to the core. Christ, but she had played him for a fool!

Turning away, he realized that the inside shutters were closed on the window overlooking the river. He might as well close them all. He didn't know if he would ever use this room again. There were too many memories of happier times associated with it. Newton scrambled up the stairs behind him and barked, as if to call him back.

Gideon set the lamp down on a table and reached for the shutters. Outside, the last faint light was fading away, the world dissolving into shades of lavender and violet and blue. A memory stirred.

He knew this scene. This moment. It was as if he'd been waiting for it all his life.

Every sense was heightened. There was movement in the distance, through the trees. Gideon stared. He recognized it now. This was the scene in the painting he'd done in his sleep, the night he'd lost his wager to Exton. The setting of his recurring dream, that sprang now from cobwebby fantasy into vivid reality. The beagle began to whine.

"Silence, Newton!" The dog whimpered at his command but lay down with his head on his paws. Gideon held his breath.

At that exact moment when twilight gave way to night, she stepped out of the shadows at the foot of the slope, insubstantial as a ghost in her fluttering white gown. The moon shone down on her, making it seem as bright as day. In the crystalline light, her fair skin was luminous as pearl, and her pale, unbound hair shimmered like beaten silver against the dark trunks of the trees. Her beauty was so remarkable it robbed him of breath.

As darkness gathered, he thought that she would surely turn and bolt back into the sheltering trees. Instead, she hesitated. Then, raising her head slowly, she looked up at the tower, where he stood framed in the arch of the open window. There was such grief, such longing in her face, in every graceful line of her body, that he trembled in despair.

He waited, heart beating wildly. This was the moment he dreaded. This was where the woman became transparent and vanished into the night.

Instead, she came across the remains of the ancient clapper bridge, fleet and frightened as a doe pursued by hunters. Her gown streamed out behind her like gossamer wings, and her hair floated on the night air like a wedding veil. She flew across the bridge as if she knew every inch of it.

When her bare feet touched the grass on the near side of the bridge, she stopped and looked hurriedly around, as if trying to get her bearings.

She looked up to the window in the tower, illuminated by Gideon's lamp. Her face was transfixed with joy. She started toward him, lifting her arms imploringly, then fell in a crumpled heap.

TEN

§§

JUST AS CHLOE WAS ABOUT TO LEAVE HER ROOM TO CHECK on Perry, Agnes burst in, all in a dither. "Oh, Miss Chloe! Do come!"

"Perry . . . ?"

"Master Perry is sleeping comfortably. Mrs. Osler is with him. It is Mr. Stone, miss. He is asking for you to come with all due haste. It is most urgent."

Taking up her shawl, Chloe hurried out. "Where is he?"

"In the library, miss."

Running lightly down the stairs, Chloe could not imagine why Gideon had sent for her. Especially at this hour. If he had calmed down enough to listen to her story, he would have come to her room.

A horrible thought struck: unless he planned to force her out of the house in the morning? No, he would not, he *could* not be so cruel. He was hasty and hot tempered, but he was not cruel.

Then it must be something else. Something he'd found in Tobias's papers? A clue to the treasure? But why send for her? It made no sense at all. There was no way to satisfy her curiosity but to go to him and discover what he wanted.

She opened the library door in some trepidation, expecting to find him alone. Instead, there was a scene of bustling activity. Chloe took in the tableau by the sofa, where a figure in white lay stretched out beneath a red woolen blanket. Mrs.

Linley was pouring out a tot of brandy, while Gideon knelt beside the sofa, chaffing the victim's hands.

"Lady Albinia!" Chloe exclaimed, hurrying to the sofa. But the woman's long hair was not brunette, it was silvery blond and fine as silk floss. Chloe stopped short when Gideon tenderly brushed the hair back from the woman's fair brow. She knew that face as well as she did her own.

The words were startled out of her: "*Lost Lenore!*"

"Hush," Gideon said urgently. "Say nothing you'll regret, or we'll have the household in a superstitious uproar. Except for Perry and Dawlish, the servants have only seen the miniature in the drawing room. They do not know her face as well as you and I."

Chloe sank down on the rug beside him. She didn't share his view. Anyone who had ever dusted the miniature would recognize this woman's face. Still, she couldn't take in the evidence of her own eyes. "But . . . it cannot be! Do you really think . . . ?"

Gideon turned to face Chloe for the first time, reluctantly tearing his gaze away from the woman's face. "Don't you? Look at her! That unique, uncannily·beautiful face . . ."

Instead of answering, Chloe lifted the woman's hair to bare her earlobe. Nothing hung from it. She reached over and moved a lock of hair on the other side.

"My God!" The earring she sought was there, bright and fresh as the day it had been made: a twisted circle of gold, with a round garnet flanked by two smaller beads.

"I see you recognize it, too."

"Yes. I don't know what to say."

"Say nothing! We must keep this between ourselves for now."

"But it can't be Lenore!" Chloe whispered. "Not after a hundred years. Lost Lenore is a fairytale creature. This is some imposter hired by Martin and Olivia Throne to stir up trouble. The plan went awry, and she came to grief somehow."

Gideon didn't seem to hear her. He smiled down at the woman wonderingly. "One hundred years—and a day. That

is how the old stories go, you know. And that is where your
. . . where Perry made his miscalculations.''

"Then you truly believe she is Lenore Lacey?''

"I have no doubt of it.'' His voice was low but intense.
"This seems like utter madness, I know. But I tell you, I have
seen her face in my dreams almost nightly! It began well before I ever set eyes on Lacey's Folly. I dreamed I stood in the
tower and saw her appear as she did tonight, misted with
moonbeams, at the foot of Pucca's Hill.''

A fist of fear struck at Chloe's midsection. Tobias had
dreamed of Lenore almost every night from youth to death.
She had been his obsession.

Now she would be Gideon's.

She stared down at the young woman. No, almost a girl.
*Why she was only eighteen when she vanished. And I am al-
most five and twenty.*

Chloe reached out and touched the stranger's cheek. It was
chill and clammy. Instantly, Chloe became brisk and efficient.
"She is in deep shock. We must get her into a proper bed.''

Mrs. Linley joined them. "The yellow bedchamber is being
prepared. It's a snug little room, and I was sure you wouldn't
mind, Miss Hartsell. It is close to the servants' stairs, to save
them work fetching and carrying.''

"Yes, the very room I would have chosen.'' *Not the Bride's
Chamber,* Chloe thought with a shiver. "Mr. Stone will carry
her up.''

"Biddy has already laid a fire, and I have sent Annie up to
warm the sheets with a warming pan.'' The housekeeper
folded her hands. "Who do you suppose she is? She looks to
be a gentlewoman. But why she was wandering around the
grounds in such a flimsy garment at this time of night is beyond me.''

Chloe tried for a plausible story. "I can only surmise that
she is from the village. Mrs. Osler might know. Perhaps . .
perhaps she has been ill and awakened in the night in her
delirium.''

Gideon looked sharply at Chloe. *How easily the lies drip*

from your tongue, his eyes said more clearly than any words.

She rose, unable to face his disdain. "In the morning we shall have to make inquiries."

"Ah, yes," Mrs. Linley exclaimed. "I believe you must be correct. How her family must feel! They are surely insane with worry if they have noticed she is gone."

As Gideon lifted the woman, she moaned once, softly. Her head rested against his shoulder as if it belonged there. Chloe could scarcely bear to watch. "I'll lead the way."

The lamps on the stairway had already been lit. Chloe took up an oil lamp at the head of the steps and went briskly down the corridor to the yellow bedchamber. A new fire crackled in the hearth, and the room was already warm, but the woman shivered in Gideon's arms as he carried her to the bed.

As he placed her gently on the mattress, her eyes flew open, and she mumbled incoherently. Gideon brushed the hair back from her forehead. "You will be all right," he said gently. Chloe's heart sank when she saw the tenderness, the concern in his face: once he had looked at her that way.

The woman said something more in a slurred voice, then gave a shiver, and closed her eyes, slipping back into unconsciousness.

Mrs. Linley pulled the covers up to the woman's shoulders. "She is chilled to the bone, poor dear. We must get her out of these clothes."

Chloe turned to the maid. "Biddy, fetch one of the flannel nightshirts from my bureau. And my heavy woolen shawl, as well."

Gideon started to remove his jacket. "It's devilish hot in here already."

"You, sir, may keep your jacket on. You will not be staying."

"But . . ."

"You may come back when we are finished," Chloe said firmly. "I . . . Mrs. Linley will call you."

He shot her a frustrated look, but went out, closing the door behind him.

The housekeeper helped Chloe strip the damp gown from the unconscious woman. It was hard going, since they undressed her beneath the bedclothes to keep her warm. She was a dead weight, and the wet garment clung to her skin. By the time Biddy returned with the flannel gown, Chloe's hair was clinging to her temples in damp ringlets.

Once they had her dressed, Chloe brushed the leaves and tangles from the woman's hair as best she could. "Oh! She has a knot on the back of her head. She must have struck it when she fell."

Mrs. Linley touched the lump. "Quite a large one! That would explain why it is taking her so long to rouse, and why she hasn't spoken."

She *tsked* and shook her head. "A similar thing happened to a young sister of mine. She fell from an apple tree and broke her head. It was three months before she spoke again— and that was to ask for a coddled egg, one morning. My mother was so surprised, she dropped the entire bowl of raw eggs upon the floor, and we all ate porridge instead. And a happy meal it was!"

Chloe was astonished. "And did she recall everything that had happened?"

"Not a thing, until she saw our mother standing there laughing and crying amid the broken eggshells. Of course, that was different, for we knew who she was. I hope this poor creature will have all her wits and be able to tell us her name and direction when she awakens."

So did Chloe. It seemed that the woman might regain consciousness soon. She was restless when anyone touched her, but always calmed down at the sound of Chloe's voice. They quickly had her warm and dry and presentable.

"You may tell Mr. Stone he may return."

Gideon was there in seconds. "Has she come round yet?"

"No, but she did try to push us away as we got the wet things off."

"Perhaps you might get some tea or broth down her," the

housekeeper suggested. "I tried brandy downstairs, but she refused to take it. I feared she might choke."

"Water to start, then perhaps tea to warm her."

Taking the glass Mrs. Linley handed her, Chloe eased a few drops of water through the pale lips. The woman swallowed. Encouraged, Chloe tipped the cup once more. The woman drank a little, then suddenly choked and spluttered, and opened her eyes.

Chloe found herself staring back into the sky blue irises she knew so well from Lenore Lacey's portrait. She forced herself to smile, although she was so startled, she almost dropped the glass.

"Hello," she said gently. "Can you tell me your name?"

The woman stared mutely. Then she saw Gideon standing at the foot of the bed, and her eyes opened wide in alarm. She tried to struggle up, and Chloe supported her with her arm.

"Do not be afraid. You are safe among friends. You are at Lacey's Folly."

The woman gave a little cry of dismay, her eyes rolled up, and she fell back against the pillows in a dead faint.

Mrs. Linley looked concerned. "Oh, dear. What if she is not ill, but mad?"

"Nonsense. She is just frightened," Gideon snapped. "If you fear she will harm you, you have only to look at her. She has the face of a gentlewoman and the strength of a kitten. I doubt she could kill an ant."

You would say that if you'd found her with an axe dripping blood and a body at her feet, Chloe thought bitterly. *You think that her physical beauty makes her perfect.*

This time it was Gideon who seemed to read her thoughts. He flushed in the candlelight. Then he turned his gaze back to the woman on the bed and forgot everything else. This was the face that had haunted his dreams.

This was the face that he must paint.

Mrs. Linley retreated. "Would you like me to check on Master Perry, Miss Hartsell?"

"If you will be so good. Tell Mrs. Osler I'll be there shortly."

When the door closed and they were alone, Gideon went to the head of the bed. "I still find it hard to credit. How could a woman vanish and then reappear a century later?"

"I am sure it is coincidence." Chloe had convinced herself that her explanation was true. "This has been Lacey country for four hundred years. There are bound to be descendants scattered throughout the area, and some of them could very well resemble the portrait of Lost Lenore."

"You forget," Gideon said sharply. "She was a Lacey for less than a day. I do not even know her maiden name."

"Dacre. Lenore Dacre," Chloe said slowly.

"The Dacres are not from this part of the country," Gideon told her. "I know the family, and I know their ancestry. Your theory will not hold water."

Chloe was exasperated. "You are being foolish beyond permission. There is some logical explanation." She eyed the woman's earring. "More and more, I am beginning to suspect the hand of the Thornes behind this 'amazing' event. It will prove a plot gone awry. We shall hear the truth from her when she rouses!"

As if on cue, the woman in the bed moaned and tried to speak. The words came out in a slurred mumble. Waving Gideon away, Chloe lowered her voice.

"Stay back in the shadows, since the sight of a man seemed to alarm her. I will ask her name again."

She pulled up a chair and sat beside the bed. Once again those remarkable blue eyes opened and stared at Chloe. This time she seemed more alert—and markedly less frightened now that Gideon was out of sight.

"I am Chloe Hartsell. You need not fear me. You are snug and safe."

The woman's lips trembled. She looked around the room anxiously, then relaxed. Chloe gave her more water. "Are you hungry? Would you care for some bread and broth?"

The woman listened intently, as if trying to translate from

a foreign language. After a pause, she nodded.

"Good," Chloe said. "An excellent sign for your recuperation. I will not ask you anything that you do not wish to answer. But if you are so inclined, I hope you will at least tell me your name?"

The woman's eyes closed, and her forehead puckered with concentration. The clock ticked away the minutes. Then her forehead smoothed, her eyes opened, and she licked her dry lips.

She whispered something so softly Chloe couldn't hear. She leaned closer to the woman. "I beg your pardon?"

The sounds were lilting and liquid. *Perhaps they aren't even words at all,* Chloe thought. Certainly, if they were words, they were like no language that she had ever heard.

The clock struck three.

"You are mad," Chloe told Gideon as he paced the library floor. She was longing for bed and weary of arguing with him. "She cannot be Lenore Lacey."

"If I belong in a lunatic asylum, Miss Hartsell, you belong there also. I see it in your face. You don't want to believe it—but you do."

My name is Chloe! She cried inside. *You used to call me Chloe.*

Aloud, she said, "You are wrong, *Mr.* Stone. I do not believe she came out of a fairy rath after a hundred years."

"Then why are you wide-eyed and shivering like a leaf in the wind?"

"It has been a long and terrible day." Chloe put a hand to her forehead. Her temples throbbed. "I am exhausted. I want my bed, Mr. Stone, and you insist on keeping me here, trying to convince me that the poor creature you found is the Lost Bride of Lacey's Folly—a woman who exists only in legend!"

"Do you think so? I wonder what Perry will say when he sees her?"

"You must not encourage his fancies," she said angrily. "I am glad that he will be confined to his own bed the next few days. By the time he is up and about on crutches, her family will have turned up to claim her and take her home.''

''What?''

The shock on his face stunned her.

''Well, you dismissed out of hand the idea that she is an imposter, hired by Martin and Olivia Throne, to work some mischief,'' she added.

''What could they hope to obtain by such a ruse?''

Chloe shrugged. ''I cannot guess their intentions. But if she is not their creature, you must examine the alternatives. She did not materialize out of thin air! Either she lives in the vicinity, or she is visiting nearby. Henry and Rendulph will ride around and make inquiries in the morning. There may be a mother and father—even a husband—who are distraught over her disappearance.''

Gideon went to the fire and stood warming his hands, not speaking, and unwilling to hear what she had to say.

Chloe was relentless. ''If no one claims her, we shall have to send out a notice to the inns and the churches round about. There is a third possibility to consider: that she is one of those relatives of whom no one speaks, the kind who is locked away in an attic, with a discreet servant for a keeper.''

Gideon whirled around. ''That is what you would like to think, isn't it? That she is an escaped madwoman. You have taken an acute dislike to her.''

''That I have not,'' she snapped indignantly. ''I feel only pity for the poor, lost creature. It is you, *Mr. Stone,* laboring under strong feelings about the woman.''

He advanced on her slowly, his eyes filled with sudden confusion. ''Would you care to explain to me exactly what you mean by that?''

She stepped nimbly around a table and went to the door. ''No, I should not. I am going to bed.''

Chloe closed the door and ran down the hall toward the back stairs, knowing he wouldn't think to follow. Gideon stared after her, then poured himself a glass of brandy and stared into the amber liquid, trying to scry meaning in its depths.

She went up to Perry's room in the old nursery, where Lady Albinia was taking a turn at his bedside, still looking bandbox fresh in her rose silk dinner gown. The boy was sound asleep.

"I hear we have another guest at Lacey's Folly," she said, setting aside her book when Chloe entered.

"Yes. Her identity is unknown, but perhaps in the morning, when she recovers from her shock, she will be able to tell us her name and direction. I don't wish Perry to know of it, if you please. He is such a curious child, he might try to crawl out of bed to go visit her and take another tumble."

Lady Albinia laughed. "Yes, I can see him hobbling down the corridor to show her his latest pebble or the fine fat spider he has trapped in a jam jar." She gave an elegant little shiver. "He thinks me a very poor creature. I told him he may show me anything he finds—as long as it does not have more than four legs!"

Chloe laughed. "You must be very careful what you say to him. Perry is quite literal minded. He might decide to find you a lovely snake or two."

"God forbid!"

"I'll stay with him now, Lady Albinia, and bid you a good night. Thank you for your kindness."

"You will do me more of a kindness if you go to bed yourself." She eyed Chloe sharply. "If you fall ill, the house will be at six and sevens, despite Mrs. Linley's good offices. You must take care of yourself, child."

"Indeed, I could not sleep a wink."

"Very well." Albinia lingered. She knew something was not right between Gideon and Chloe, and she had been so hopeful before. She started to say something about the matter, but decided against it. Leaning down, she kissed Chloe's cheek.

"If you ever need a friend, Miss Hartsell, I want you to know you will always have one in me. You may confide in me or not, as you wish, but you may always turn to me for advice or assistance. Be sure that I will do everything in my power to forward your best interests, whatever they may be.''

To both their surprise, Chloe burst into tears. Lady Albinia was horrified. ''My dear, if I have said anything to distress you . . .''

''No, no!'' Chloe fumbled for her handkerchief. How could she explain her profound loneliness? ''It is just that . . . outside of Tobias and Perry . . . I have never had a friend. Someone I could talk to, as one woman to another.'' She dabbed at her cheeks. ''Until now, I had not realized what I lacked.''

Lady Albinia gathered her into a scented embrace. ''Oh, poor child.'' After a moment she held Chloe away and looked at her straightly. ''You need not fear, Miss Hartsell. I will stand your friend, without reservation. Do you understand me?''

''Yes.'' Even if Gideon abandoned her, Lady Albinia would not. It comforted her, a little.

''Good. Shall I stay with Perry tonight, after all?''

''Agnes has set up the truckle bed here for me, in case he should waken and be frightened. She will take a cot in Len . . . in the room with our . . . with Mr. Stone's new guest.''

''Very well. I will see you at breakfast. Sooner if you need me.''

After she was gone, Chloe lay down on the truckle bed, listening to Perry's soft breathing. He would sleep well tonight. She could not.

Every time she closed her eyes she could see Gideon's face, the way it had lit up every time he gazed at the beautiful creature occupying the yellow bedchamber.

She wondered what Tobias would have done. Would he be as convinced that the woman was truly ''Lost Lenore?''

Chloe stared up at the ceiling. The puzzle pieces fell neatly into place. Of course. She had been right all along: the woman was no creature of myth, she was as real as Chloe was herself. This was a plot of some sort, concocted by Martin and Olivia Thorne.

The more she thought of it, the surer she was. If Lenore

Lacey were actually alive, she would have first claim to Tobias's legacy. Mr. Fortescue would know. But how the Thorne's expected to prove such a ridiculous story in a court of law, or what good it would do them, was beyond even Chloe's fertile imagination.

As she fell asleep she was still trying to figure it out.

She was standing in the shadows of the tower room. Gideon stood before her in candlelight, yet his gaze went through her to someone beyond. Chloe turned slowly, Lenore stood there, in a gown of azure, with the tiny sparks winking from her gold and garnet earrings. In the gauzy candlelight, she looked like an angel incarnate, too beautiful to be a mere mortal woman.

Gideon stepped forward to meet her. Chloe realized she was invisible to them.

Lenore flung herself into his arms. "I fear he saw me leave. You must flee, Robert."

On the heels of her words came the clank of weaponry. He looked from the window. "We are discovered!"

Taking her arm, he hastened her toward the stairs. "The horses are hidden in the clearing on Pucca's Hill. Go now! Out the back door. I will fend them off and meet you on the hill." He kissed her once, quickly. Fiercely. And drew his sword . . .

From her invisible vantage point, Chloe watched Lenore hurry down the stairs in a flutter of silk. Watched him follow her and bolt the garden door. Felt the shudder of the breaking wood, heard it splinter beneath the hammering of fist and axe . . .

Chloe sat up abruptly, heart pounding. He was hopelessly outnumbered!

Slowly she realized her surroundings. *Only a dream,* she reassured herself. It had seemed so real, she almost expected to hear the rush of booted feet, the deadly sound of steel on steel.

She lay back against her pillow and listened to the clock strike three. It was going to be a very long night.

Perry was restive in the morning, already chaffing at being confined to bed for the day. "Tomorrow you may come downstairs, if Dr. Marsh gives his approval," Chloe told him.

It upset her that she must look after their unexpected guest, when Perry needed her attention. Once again, it was Mrs. Osler to the rescue. When she wasn't unofficially tutoring him in the natural sciences, she was giving him wonderful treats.

"Today, young Master Peregrine, I have something special." She brought out a box of tin soldiers and began to set them up on the squares of his counterpane.

Perry's boredom vanished. "Oh, by Jove, they are capital, Mrs. Osler!"

Chloe went off with a smile to tend to her other patient. Gideon had promised to come by later and give the boy another drawing lesson. Between the three of them, they could keep him well occupied.

She set off for the yellow bedchamber. At least she wouldn't have to explain to Perry about "Lost Lenore" for another day. Hopefully, the woman would regain her senses and tell them her identity—and that would be that!

The new guest was propped up on the daybed by the window, overlooking the summer garden. She was even more ethereally beautiful by day. Her skin was as translucent as porcelain, with faint blue veins beneath the skin. She was very thin. Perhaps she had been ill recently. With her fair hair spread out on the curved back of the daybed, Chloe thought she looked like a storybook princess.

Sleeping Beauty. It is no wonder Gideon is so taken with her.

The housekeeper took Chloe aside when she entered. "She has not spoken yet," Mrs. Linley announced. "Nor will she take in ought but sips of water. She has refused tea and toast and Cook's wonderful chicken broth. I didn't know how to tell Cook!"

Chloe hid a smile. It was Cook's pride and joy and almost as clear as spring water. "I believe she thought it was warm water, but when I brought the spoon to her mouth, she suddenly closed her mouth and turned her head away."

"I will have Dr. Marsh look in on her when he comes to check on Perry."

"Perhaps she is mute, although I thought . . . perhaps I was mistaken," Chloe said in low tones. "Or she may be frightened to find herself alone among strangers. I shall try to ease her mind."

She approached the bed. "Good morning. I am Chloe Hartsell. We met last evening when you were brought here."

The woman smiled tremulously but didn't reply. "You took quite a shock out in the cool night air. I hope you are feeling better today?"

The woman only frowned and concentrated, as if she were trying to understand by sheer will, but made no reply.

"She hears you well enough," Mrs. Linley said.

Chloe pulled up a chair. "Can you speak at all? Can you tell me your name?"

The woman just smiled, shook her head, and gave a tiny shrug. Chloe had a brainstorm. "Perhaps she is a foreigner." Chloe tried the French she had learned from Tobias, and a smattering of Italian, without result. In desperation, she uttered a few halting words of Gaelic from a poem she had learned.

The woman's brows rose in surprise, and her face lit up with puzzled recognition. But still she didn't speak.

"Send Biddy up from the kitchen," Chloe told the housekeeper with relief. "Her mother was from Limerick, and she speaks the Gaelic tongue."

Biddy bustled up to serve as interpreter, smoothing her immaculate apron.

"Please tell her that she is safe with us," Chloe instructed, "and that we are trying to help her."

When Biddy spoke, the woman had some difficulty following, as if she were used to a different dialect. But when the maid finished, the woman nodded.

"Excellent, Biddy," Chloe exclaimed. "She understands. Please inquire if she is staying somewhere in the district and who we can notify of her whereabouts."

The woman shook her head in the negative. She indicated the room about her, the garden beyond the window, and waited.

"Tell her she is at Lacey's Folly," Chloe began, when the woman gave a great cry of fear and shrank back among the linens.

There was someone at the door. A moment later Gideon was admitted. "How is our guest?" he asked in low tones.

"She hasn't spoken and doesn't seem to know her name or where she is from."

"She is still in shock. Things have changed since she lived here," he said slowly. "It is only natural, if she is Lenore Lacey."

Chloe shot him a look of dismay. "Good Heavens, the events of the past day have addled your brains!"

"I know what I saw, Miss Hartsell. I know what I *dreamed*!"

"Ridiculous. There is proof that she is not Lost Lenore," Chloe said firmly. "Lenore was an Englishwoman, born and bred. Yet this woman does not understand us when we speak. She does, however, recognize Gaelic."

Gideon made a wry face. "I suppose you must be right," he said at last. "But that face! That hair! You must admit the resemblance is uncanny." He sighed. "But Lenore Lacey would understand English, not Gaelic."

Biddy overheard. "Not if she be Lost Lenore, sir, and lived with the Old Ones beneath the hill," she piped up. Her eyes were round with wonder. "'Tis said they speak the ancient Gaelic when they speak among themselves. 'Tis their native tongue, my mother told me."

"Thank you, Biddy, you may return to your duties," Mrs. Linley said sharply. "And you will say nothing to the other servants of this."

"Yes, ma'am. I mean, no, ma'am." The maid bobbed a

curtsey and left, with one swift glance back over her shoulder at the mysterious woman in the bed.

Gideon waited until she was gone. "You mustn't be hard on Biddy, Mrs. Linley. She was trying to be helpful."

"I only hope she may hold her tongue," the housekeeper responded. "Servants' gossip spreads like wildfire. It would be all over the village before the day is out."

"What happens at Lacey's Folly should be of no interest to the inhabitants of Greater Brampton," Gideon said firmly, as he stepped further into the room.

Mrs. Linley and Chloe looked at once another. *He doesn't understand much of country life,* their exchange of gazes said.

The woman looked over when she heard his raised voice. She stared at Gideon as if she were seeing a ghost. Although her skin got paler still, this time she didn't swoon away. Her color came rushing back, illuminating her features from within. With a radiant smile, she held her hands out to Gideon.

He went to her, too stunned to speak. She clutched his hands and held them to her lips.

"She seems to know you," Chloe said wryly. It was difficult to get the words out, for her throat had gone dry as cake flour.

"It is because Gideon rescued her," Lady Albinia said, coming into the room.

Gideon didn't hear either one of them. "Lenore!" he whispered. He said the name so reverently, as if it were a prayer. His face shone like the woman's, with a rare, internal light.

Lady Albinia bit her lip. *Oh, dear! This complicates everything!*

It was extremely painful for Chloe to see. She crossed her arms protectively across her chest, as if shielding herself from further hurt. *That glow! It must be the mirror of my face when I see him,* she thought. A profound grief welled up inside her.

I have lost him forever, she said silently.

No. I am fooling myself still. I never truly had Gideon's regard. Never once, even in the throes of passion, has he looked at me that way.

*   *   *

Perry had a slight fever and was confined to his rooms for two more days, but was allowed to be up, with his leg solidly splinted. A few hours of hobbling about the nursery soon palled. He waited until Mrs. Osler went to fetch a book and put his plan into action.

It was tedious but not difficult to make his way down the corridor to the staircase, which he went down by the simple means of sliding down the banister. Of course, trying to hold on to his crutches at the same time made a dreadful racket.

Gideon burst out of the parlor. "You young miscreant! What are you doing, trying to kill yourself?"

Perry suffered the indignity of having Gideon haul him off the banister and set him down on the steps. "I've come to see the woman everyone is whispering about," he said firmly, none the worse for well. "Henry said you found her by Pucca's Hill. Oh, Gideon—is it *her?* Is it *Lenore?*"

As if in response, Chloe came out of the parlor with the woman behind her. She was wearing one of Chloe's summer dresses, and her hair was pulled back to suit the current fashion, which made her look quite different; but the resemblance to the portrait was still there.

The boy leaned one arm on the newel post, the other on his crutch, and stared at her. He didn't seem at all surprised to see her. The look he shot Chloe was victorious. "Told you so," he said.

"Although the resemblance is uncanny, she is not who you think," Chloe said quietly.

"I found her earring on a slab of stone on the hill," Perry answered. His eyes shone. "I knew then it was the door to the fairy fort. I knew she would come!"

He tried to bow to the woman, but the crutches hindered him. "Tobias told me all about you. And what to do. I left you the moonstone and the St. John's wort and the iron ring on the rune stone."

Aha, Chloe thought, *that explains the missing rings by the clapper bridge.*

"I heard you weeping," Perry whispered to the woman. " '*O who will help me? O who will take me in?*' "

The woman stared at him. Chloe stared, too. She had heard those words ringing through her own head on Pucca's Hill. She had seen the rune stone. Traced her finger around and around on the swirls of the design above the runes, until she felt as if she were falling into the hillside.

The woman gave the Perry a gentle smile, but looked puzzled.

Chloe put her arm around the boy. "She can't speak, darling. It appears that she is mute."

"She doesn't remember how, is all. She doesn't remember anything," he said in disappointment. His shoulders slumped, but only for a moment. He realized what the problem was.

"She's still under the enchantment, and she can't tell us about the treasure yet. But she will. Just as soon as I find some way to break the spell."

Chloe walked to the village on Wednesday. It was her usual day for errands, and she wanted to take fresh flowers to the churchyard for Tobias. The weather was fine, and she was too nervous and restless to use the gig. What she needed was exercise to calm herself, and time alone to think. *There is nothing like a brisk walk to clear one's head.*

That was what she needed most of all.

When she left Lacey's Folly, the mute woman—they had taken to calling her Lenore, for want of a better name—was ensconced on the sofa in the parlor, looking out at the garden. Lady Albinia was with her, doing her correspondence at the rosewood desk that Tobias had left to Chloe.

And Gideon had been sketching earlier. Pages and pages of his latest inspiration, filling the sheets of drawing paper with detailed renderings of her lovely cheekbones, her perfectly bowed mouth, those beautiful sapphire eyes. Although she didn't speak, the woman seemed content as long as Gideon was near to hand.

Chloe couldn't bear to be near them. To see Gideon so

absorbed. *Besotted* was the word that came to mind. He worked like a madman, and Chloe had seen the lamps burning in Giovanna's tower late at night. She had wondered if the woman was with Gideon then. Were they painting, or . . .

No! she pushed the images from her mind. A hundred times a day, she prayed that Lenore's family would come to claim her and take her away. They had put up notices far and wide, informed all the proper authorities, but her background, like her true name, remained a mystery.

"Are you putting advertisements out for husbands for me?" Chloe had asked earlier, seeing the pile of letters beside Gideon's godmother.

"Good heavens, no."

Lady Albinia set her pen in the standish. "These are invitations for a select shooting party, which Gideon will hold after the season ends."

Chloe shot a look at Gideon and his model, sitting on the far side of the room. "Do you really think he will stop painting long enough to entertain them?"

"If need be, I'll send for my own gameskeepers to arrange the shooting. That is not the real reason for the party, in any event. I am inviting several likely bachelors for your approval, Miss Hartsell. One is a barrister, likely to rise in his field, another a clergyman, with a snug living near Minster Lovell. And then there is a very handsome lieutenant." She cocked her head teasingly. "Do you think you should like to follow the drum?"

Chloe was not amused. "I would take a one-eyed fisherman in the Outer Hebrides, for all it matters to me. All I need is a home for Perry, where he is welcome between school terms."

Lady Albinia smiled. "I do not think Perry would like the northern islands, and I know that you would not be happy there. You couldn't grow your roses. They would not survive the salt winds and winter gales."

Chloe looked out at the garden. Her face was void of expression. "I have done with roses," she said quietly.

Gideon hadn't appeared to be paying attention, but he'd

heard every word. He looked down at the sheet of paper before him. Instead of Lenore's pose, he'd done caricatures of a prosy clergyman, a sharp-nosed barrister, and a lecherous lieutenant. The charcoal snapped in his hand.

He threw it down in disgust and left the room.

Lenore hadn't seemed to notice his departure, and Chloe ignored it. Only Lady Albinia had watched him leave the room, with a glint in her lovely eyes. Shortly after, Chloe had set out for the village of Lesser Brampton. A brisk walk always cleared her head.

Instead of the long way around by the packhorse bridge, Chloe took the old footpath that cut across the meadow and over a stile. It was rougher country, but less than half-an-hour's fast walk. The sun was pleasantly warm, the breeze refreshingly cool.

But as Chloe left the estate, with a basket of flowers, her feet felt leaden. Despite her defiant words, she knew that she would miss having an ornamental garden quite desperately.

Suddenly, she hoped that Lady Albinia would live up to her matchmaking reputation. Chloe knew that she had to get away from Lacey's Folly as soon as possible. To stay and watch Gideon fall more in love with 'Lenore' each day was tearing her heart out.

It would be easier for Perry if she married the barrister or clergyman; but after having Gideon for a lover, she didn't think she would be happy with a chaste kiss or two. And the barrister might prove embarrassingly inquisitive about her past. Perhaps the dashing officer would be a better choice.

Providing, of course, that any of them offer for me.

She was glad to be alone and away from the house at this time of day. The time when she and Gideon had usually been together. *Now my place has been taken by another. The sooner I become used to it, the better.*

By the time she reached Lesser Brampton, her mood was very low indeed. Her first stop was the apothecary's shop. ''I need some of Dr. Totten's fortifying drops for Perry, a packet of headache powders, and a vial of laudanum,'' she told the clerk. "I'll pick them up after I run my other errands."

"An hour or less, Miss Hartsell, and it will be all ready for you," the clerk promised. "I hear you have an unexpected visitor at the Folly."

Chloe was startled, until she remembered that Henry and Rendulph had taken notes to the local doctors and surgeons and clergymen. "Yes. We hope to locate her family soon."

The apothecary's apprentice looked up from his bench, where he was pounding herbs with mortar and pestle and gave her a conspiratorial wink. "If what they're saying is true, you'll have to look for them in the churchyard."

"I do not understand your meaning," Chloe said frostily.

The apprentice shrugged. "They say she is the lady of legend came back from the fairies. The Lost Bride."

Chloe gave a little laugh. "Do they, really? Then I'm afraid they are doomed to disappointment. She is a visitor from Scotland and speaks the Gaelic tongue. She wandered away while exploring the neighborhood and became lost. We expect her family to claim her today and take her away with them."

This time the apothecary himself came out from the back of the shop, fixed his apprentice with a gimlet eye, and then tried to placate Chloe.

"You are a fool, Ham Shepley, and had best get back to what you do know, instead of stirring up trouble with your betters. Miss Hartsell, I shall fill your order, personally."

"Thank you, Mr. Nutting."

Chloe strolled down the village main street, past the green, aware of people watching her strangely. Speculation of the mysterious woman's identity seemed to be the main topic of conversation in the village.

Chloe turned toward the church with its square Norman tower and alternating bands of honey and white limestone, stacked like a layer cake. Until today, it had been the most noteworthy thing about Lesser Barnstable. It appeared the legend of Lost Lenore was about to take its place.

The basket on her arm was filled with Tobias's favorite flowers. She went through the gate into the old churchyard.

with its leaning headstones, all mossy and worn. The Lacey family mausoleum stood in the very center, surrounded by its own wrought iron fence.

"Well, Tobias, Perry is searching, but we have not found our missing treasure," she said, as she knelt on the green sod and sat back on her heels. "Instead, we have found a woman who looks like your beloved Lenore, and she has set the household on its ear. I wonder what you would have made of it all."

She took the flowers from her basket and began arranging them carefully in a stone vase. "I don't know what your plan was when you changed your will. I wish I could understand."

Chloe shook her head. "I am grateful for everything you've done for me and for Perry. But oh! I am so lonely. Lacey's Folly is filled with people now, but I miss our talks and our chess games. Most of all, Tobias, I miss you. Dreadfully."

Suddenly, it was overwhelming. She sat back on her heels and closed her eyes, fighting the sting of tears. She had lost so much in the past few weeks: her friend, her inheritance, her home. And now, her lover and her future.

Her hands fisted in her lap. "Unless you are looking down from heaven, you will never know how I rue the day that Gideon Stone first entered my life!"

"My sentiments exactly," interrupted a bored masculine voice. "Good afternoon, Miss Hartsell."

Chloe recovered from her startlement and looked up, as a shadow fell across Tobias's grave. Lord Exton stood a few feet away, looking stylish, handsome, and decidedly out of place in a country churchyard. Noting her tears, he offered his monogrammed handkerchief. "Dreary duty on such a sunny day," he said, cocking his head.

"It is not duty, sir." She took the handkerchief, wiped her eyes and blew her nose. "I do it out of love."

"Most commendable. You may keep the handkerchief," he said, when she tried to give it back. He smiled and held out his hand and helped her to her feet. "You are a person with a great deal of love to offer, one would imagine."

"Do not waste your imagination on me," she said briskly. "I am sure you have more weighty matters to consider."

"At the moment, my dear Miss Hartsell, there is nothing on my mind but you. Will you show me about the church-yard?"

"There is nothing much to see."

His dark eyes regarded her. Exton's smile widened. "Ah, there I disagree with you completely."

"Are you always so flirtatious, my lord?"

He looked taken aback. Then he laughed. "Are you always so refreshing?"

"Is that the London word for plain speaking?"

He laughed and took the empty basket from her. "Come, Miss Hartsell. Let us cry friends. Perhaps you will let me buy you a glass of lemonade."

Chloe looked doubtful. He couldn't resist teasing her. "Are you reading something nefarious into my offer? I give you my solemn oath, Miss Hartsell, that if I had seduction in mind, it would be in a place far more suitable than a well-frequented inn next to a church in your home village. Also," he said thoughtfully, "somewhere infinitely more comfortable."

She burst out laughing. "Now you are being absurd. No my lord, I do not think you are offering me anything more than a glass of lemonade."

"Good," he said, taking her arm and leading her out of the churchyard.

Because the weather was fine, the landlord had placed two tables beneath the trees beside the inn. Exton led her there. I was cool and peaceful in the shade. The same river that flowed through the Lacey estate wound nearby, splashing down in a series of small steps, before spreading out between leafy banks.

The landlord bustled out immediately with a pitcher of lemonade for Chloe, a tankard of his best ale for my lord, and a few dainties prepared by his wife. "Why, Simons," she exclaimed, eyes twinkling silver in the dappled light. "One would think you knew of our arrival in advance."

"Uh . . . ah . . ."

"Spare the man his blushes," Exton told her, dismissing he man. "I see you have found me out."

"You were very sure of yourself, my lord."

"No," Exton replied suavely. "Only hopeful."

"Poor Simons. If he had bowed any lower, he would have craped the skin off his nose."

Exton sent her an admiring glance. "Do you always say vhat is in your mind?"

"No, sir." She bent her head. "I did at one time, but am ast learning the error of my ways."

"A pity," he leaned over, lifting her chin with one finger. "It is your openness that enchants me."

Chloe stiffened, and he realized his error. He removed his and and made easy conversation. She wasn't used to light irtations. While she concentrated on watching a ladybird nake its way across the table, Exton sat back, aware he had noved in too quickly. He chose his next words purposely.

"You see how careful I am not to cast the slightest shadow n your reputation, Miss Hartsell. I would not want your Mr. tone calling me out. Albinia Longworth told me he was ex-emely angry that I spoke to you without a proper introduc-on."

Her face clouded. "He is not 'my' Mr. Stone. He may be aaster of Lacey's Folly, but he has absolutely no say over here I go or what I do." She lifted her glass. "In any event, e is quite preoccupied at the present. I doubt he would notice f you carried me off across your saddle bow."

Exton was amused. She was delightful. "You tempt me. hall I try it, Miss Hartsell?"

"Only if you wish to have my hatpin stuck between your bs," she replied. "I prefer more elegant means of travel."

"Excellent. You are a woman of sense. When you and Lady lbinia come up to London for Lord Pulham's reception and xhibit, I shall send my coach-and-four to fetch you."

Chloe sipped the cool lemonade. "I have no plans for Lon-on, sir."

"Then you had best talk to Lady Albinia." He grinned down at her. "I think she has made more than a few plans for you. In fact, you are both to be my guests at Exton House."

Her eyes flew wide in alarm.

The marquis was chagrined. Most women of his acquaintance would be delighted to be his guest in London. He gave her a look of irony.

"Do you fear drafts and leaking roofs?" he teased. "I assure you that Exton House has every comfort."

"Lady Albinia has sung its praises. She says it is the most elegant place imaginable."

"Ah, then it is the owner of the house who has alarmed you. Tell me, do I seem such an ogre to you? Your scruples are groundless. There will be many guests, so you need not fear you'll be held captive, alone and at my mercy, like some Gothic heroine."

A blush rose to cover her cheeks. "Now you are being absurd. No doubt you think me ungracious. Forgive me. It is just that I had no notion of going to London at all. I was a young girl the last time I set foot there."

"And you are such a doddering old creature now, I suppose."

He laughed again and realized that he found himself doing it quite often in her company. Chloe Hartsell was a tonic to his weary soul.

"Well, now the secret is out. I hope Albinia will not be angry with me," he said. "She intended it as a surprise for Mr. Stone. I was told he had no plans to bring a party to London with him, and I extended my invitation to her while she was in town. Naturally, you were to accompany her and be my guest, as well, at Exton House."

If his invitation surprised her, she gave no sign of it. She traced a finger down the sweating glass, making a damp spot on the finger of her glove. Gideon had not said a word of her going to London to see the exhibit. Not even *before*. That should have told her something.

How blind I have been. I was never more than a diversion

to him, while he—he was my life! Fool that I am.

She had completely forgotten Exton's presence. The marquis watched her thoughtfully. She had gone away, as surely as if she'd left the inn. He regarded her keenly.

Exton was a man of the world. He'd known from the beginning that she had a tendre for the dashing young artist. Given her sheltered life, and Stone's vigor and handsome face, it would be little wonder if a stronger attachment had formed. If so, there was trouble in Paradise. Miss Hartsell gave every sign of someone who had been banished from Eden. And then there was the matter of Stone inheriting the estate out from under the poor girl's feet.

Something has happened to distress Miss Hartsell. I sincerely hope the cause of it is Gideon Stone. If they've had a falling out, all to the better. That will advance my own plans considerably.

A breeze loosed a curl from her bonnet. He remembered it as it was when he'd first met her, tumbling about her shoulders, and wished he could see it that way now. Since his earlier visit to Lacey's Folly, Miss Hartsell had been very much on his mind.

At first he had only thought of her as a means of revenge upon Stone. He'd spent a good deal of time thinking of the ways and means. But it was true that he'd changed since his son's near fatal illness. Not enough to give up all his carnal pleasures, it was true, but enough that he had examined his life and found it lacking.

His friends had begun to bore him long ago, with their incessant sensation-seeking. Exton had already explored every vice. *Perhaps,* he thought with mild surprise, *it is time I turned to virtue for relief.*

Chloe Hartsell intrigued him. She was a combination of intelligence and naivete, of common sense and girlish fantasy. Of innocence and passion. Yes, there was passion and intensity in everything she did. He wondered how far it had taken her.

It didn't matter. While he was unsure of her relationship with Gideon Stone, he had no doubt at all of Chloe Hartsell's character. Upright, honorable. Refreshing as a glass of clear water on a dusty summer noon.

Whether she was still a virgin was of no moment to him. If she erred, it would always be on the side of love. She was still untainted, unsullied by the true evils of the world. Just the kind of woman he'd dreamed of in his youth, when he was still a dashing romantic, before time and disillusionment had turned him bitter.

I am tired of sordid games, he thought suddenly. *Weary of sophisticated society and its frenzied gaiety, its falseness and labyrinthine intrigues.*

He couldn't remember when a woman had captured his fancy so quickly, or so deeply.

A revelation hit Exton like a lightning bolt. He realized that he no longer wanted to spoil Chloe's innocence. Ah, no. He wanted it for himself!

Her purity of heart would be his salvation. With her at his side, he would be like a man reborn. His hand shook a little as he reached for his glass of ale.

Somehow, without his being aware of it, little Miss Hartsell of Lacey's Folly had done what none of society's famous beauties had done: she had taken his rogue heart and made it her own.

And she, the little wretch, was off in a brown study, thinking of something else. *Or,* he brooded, *more likely, of* someone *else.*

She seemed to have forgotten his very presence. His pride was piqued. No other female had ever treated him so. It made him all the more determined to have her. He reached across the table and took her hand.

"Miss Hartsell? Is my company exhausting you?"

She came back to the present with a start. Exton was watching her with a curious glow in his eyes. It made her self-conscious. "Forgive me. My mind wandered."

"Egad, you know how to put a fellow in his place!"

Chloe laughed. "That was not my intention, sir. What brings you to Lesser Brampton, my lord?"

"I could say it is on my route from place X to place Y. That, of course, would be a lie. And you do not approve of prevarication, I'm sure. So, my dear Miss Hartsell, I shall tell you the truth." He stretched his long legs out beneath the table.

"Lady Albinia spoke extensively of you when we were in London. She once mentioned that it was your habit to come into the village on a Wednesday afternoon. Wanting to meet you again, I plotted like a general, just so that I should run into you today, seemingly by accident, and invite you to join me for a glass of lemonade here beneath the trees."

Chloe suspected he was pulling her leg, but couldn't be sure. "You did say you intended to know everything about me, Lord Exton. I suppose by now you even know which tea I prefer and how I like my eggs cooked."

He laughed. "No, you little rogue. But I will make sure to find out before I leave."

His gloved hand suddenly covered hers. "Must you return to Lacey's Folly once your errands are complete, Miss Hartsell? I should like you to drive out with me a while. The day is fine, the countryside beautiful, and I would like to hear your thoughts on a matter of great importance to me."

She hesitated. Gideon would be furious.

It wasn't difficult for a man of his experience to read her thoughts. He smiled at his own cunning. "Or perhaps I overstep my bounds. Mr. Stone might not care for you to be seen jaunting about the neighborhood in the company of such a scoundrel as myself."

Her face flamed. "Mr. Stone may go straight to . . ."

Chloe took a big swallow of lemonade and choked on it. When she finally got her voice back, she had made up her mind. She gave the marquis a dazzling smile.

"Mr. Stone has nothing to say as to how I spend my time, or with whom. I should love to go for a drive with you, Lord Exton."

"Excellent, Miss Hartsell." His voice became almost a purr. "There is something I wish, very much, to say to you."

*   *   *

The afternoon was advanced when Exton set Chloe down at Lacey's Folly. The groom ran out to stand at the horses' heads. *A spanking fine carriage*, Rendulph thought approvingly.

"My regards to Lady Albinia and, or course, to Mr. Stone," Exton said, handing Chloe down from his carriage. He kept her gloved hand in his long after he should have relinquished it.

"Shall I see you at Exton House, Miss Hartsell?"

She didn't hesitate. "You shall indeed, my lord. And I thank you for your kindness in inviting me."

He lifted her hand and kissed it. "The kindness, my dear, is yours. Until then."

Mounting to the driver's seat, he nodded to the groom to release the horses, tossed him a coin, and drove off in fine style. "There's a man who can drive to the inch," Rendulph said admiringly. "I doubt there's a team he can't handle."

"No," Chloe said slowly, her mind in a whirl. "I don't think there is much of anything he can't manage, once he sets his mind to it."

She wasn't even halfway to the door when Gideon came charging out, red with anger. "What the devil were you doing with Exton?"

"He kindly offered me a ride home from the village."

Taking her by the arm, he led her inside the manor. "You've been gone the best part of the day. Are you aware of that?"

She flushed and felt a little guilty at leaving Perry for so long. "The time flew by so pleasantly, that I lost track of it."

Gideon was furious. Especially when he saw the bit of fine white linen protruding from her pocket and recognized Exton's crest. *What the devil is she doing with his handkerchief? A lover's keepsake, to tuck beneath her pillow?* His eyes narrowed

"I don't know what you think you're doing, Miss Hartsell, but it won't fly."

Her chin jutted up. "I was doing exactly what you told me

to do, sir; keeping out of your way as much as possible until the day I leave Lacey's Folly to take a husband.''

He wanted to shake her. ''If you go jaunting about the country with a rake like Exton, your reputation will be in tatters. Not a man in England would offer for you!''

Chloe's anger equaled his. She smiled with icy hauteur and lifted her chin. ''Well, sir, you are out there!'' Her eyes were like polished silver, hard and bright.

''The problem solves itself, for the Marquis of Exton has asked me to be his wife!''

ELEVEN

§§

GIDEON COULDN'T BELIEVE HIS EARS. HE SCOWLED AT THE departing carriage, and the sudden pounding of blood through his veins drowned out everything else. Chloe to marry *Exton?* Impossible!

He was deaf to everything but his own thoughts, and the angry pounding of his heart. Sound returned gradually: Newton's eager barks, the clip of Henry's shears, the fluting song of birds.

He became aware of Chloe staring at him. Gideon shook his head. No, it couldn't be true.

"I misheard you," he said, his brow clearing. "I thought . . . I imagined you said that Exton has made you an offer of marriage."

Chloe drew herself up. "I assure you that your hearing is intact. The marquis did in fact ask me to be his wife."

The seconds spun out while the earth seemed to tilt beneath Gideon's feet.

"*What?* Are you mad, or is he?"

"Thank you for your wishes for my happiness, Mr. Stone!"

"You won't be happy married to a rogue like Exton. I'll wager my life on it!"

"Lady Albinia has told me there is no better husband than a reformed rake."

The fierce scowl was back. "Balderdash! Nor, let me tell you, can I understand why one of the greatest noblemen in the land should would wish to marry you. Exton may look as high as he likes."

"Oh!" Her indignation overflowed. "You are insufferable!"

"And you are not of his world!"

Gideon's mind whirled. Chloe in the clutches of that rogue, exposed to the careless morals of the haut monde and the vices of Exton's particular friends. His hands curled into fists of impotent rage.

She was too naive. Blinded by the glitter of wealth and position and ease. What charms did Lacey's Folly have to compare with Exton's country seat, his London town house, or his many other properties? And to Chloe, who had nothing of her own, how great, how overwhelming the temptation must be.

But try as he might to be rational, Gideon's strongest emotion was fury.

"Listen to me, Chloe! You have no notion of what you are getting into, do you? Have you given any thought to the differences in your upbringing and your stations in life? Or has the thought of a crest and coronet, a presentation at Court, robbed you off all good common sense?"

She was too angry to argue with him. "You have made your views abundantly clear, Mr. Stone. I have my own on the subject!"

Ignoring his questions, she brushed past him and ran lightly up the stairs.

"Devil take it, Chloe!"

His voice followed her up the stairs. She hurried to the room and locked her door when she reached it, expecting him to come pounding up after her. She leaned against the door. Gideon hadn't followed her.

So, then. It was truly over. For just a moment she'd thought his rage had held the kernel of jealousy. It seemed she was mistaken. It was his dislike for Exton that had caused his fury.

Newton whined outside her door, but she ignored him. After a moment she heard him pattering down the corridor toward the nursery. Putting her parcels on her bed, Chloe unwrapped her purchases and went directly to check on Perry.

He was sitting in the windowseat with a book on his lap and Newton curled up beside him. The puppy yapped a welcome. Mrs. Osler looked up vaguely. The widow had a lapdesk and was scribbling verse as fast as her muse dictated it. Evidently, her muse was a rapid one. The pen fairly flew across the paper.

Chloe smiled. The widow heard perfectly well when she was caught unawares, such as when a boy stirred in pain, or a small dog yipped.

"Hello, Chlo," Perry said, putting aside his book.

The puppy stood up and yawned, and Chloe eyed him more closely. "Newton is getting very fat. Are you feeding him extra scraps?"

"It's Lenore. She's always feeding him choice morsels. I say, who was that who drove you home? I saw from my window. He looked to be a splendid fellow, and his carriage is bang-up to the knockers!"

She didn't even comment on his use of slang. "Do you think so? That was the Marquis of Exton." She set a package on his bed. "He sends you this wooden puzzle he purchased in the village. The building pieces may be taken out and set up for your toy soldiers."

The boy unwrapped his gift eagerly. "Oh, I say! This is very clever. Lord Exton is a capital fellow." He glanced at Chloe under his lashes. "Even if Gideon says he is an arrogant bounder and an unmitigated rake." Whatever a rake was. He didn't want to show his ignorance.

"Mr. Stone," Chloe said icily, "is entitled to his own opinion."

"But—do you like Lord Exton?"

Chloe thought a minute. "Yes. I believe I do. He is . . . different from what we are used to, Perry. He is a very great lord, and it is natural that he should have a sort of arrogance about him. But he has been most kind to me."

"Capital!" Perry reached down and tousled Newton's ear.

"Chloe, have you and Gideon quarreled?" he asked anxiously. "About me?"

"Whatever do you mean?" she asked sharply. Her heart was banging away like one of Perry's rackety steam engines.

"About me going off to school? We had a talk about it while you were gone. Gideon thinks I should stay here with a tutor, until I am brought up to speed."

Relief left Chloe weak-kneed. She bit her lip. "You are not Gideon's ward, Perry, you are mine. If I marry, and you do not go away to school, you shall live with me."

His relief was greater than hers. "I won't like to leave Lacey's Folly anymore than you, Chlo. And Gideon is a fine fellow. There's none better." He gazed at her solemnly. "But home will be wherever you are."

She knelt down, wrapped her arms around him, and put her head against his narrow shoulder. "Oh! I do love you so, Perry. More than you can ever imagine."

"I love you, too." His face went from grave to mischievous in a twinkling. "And if you don't marry Gideon, then I hope you marry someone like Lord Exton. By Jove, I've never seen such fine horses in my life! Do you suppose he'd take me for a drive?"

Chloe laughed through a mist of tears. "I think I may be able to arrange it." She glanced at his book. "What are you reading today?"

"I've been going through some of Tobias's books." His eyes shone, and he lowered his voice. "This time I *really* know about the treasure! I believe it has been misplaced. It might take a while to put my hand to it, Chlo, but you won't believe me when I show you."

She smoothed back his hair. "Of course I shall."

Perry would say no more on the subject, and after she dosed him with his tonic, she went off. Mrs. Osler was still writing away, sixteen to the dozen. She smiled vaguely, then frowned down at the lines of her new poem. Chloe took the hint and went downstairs in search of Lady Albinia.

She ran her to earth in the sitting room. Gideon's godmother was reclining on the sofa, a vision of expensive elegance in white silk and lace. She looked up from her book as Chloe entered.

"You're home late, my dear. I was sure you'd be back hours ago. Gideon asked after you several times."

Chloe's eyes were shuttered. "I met Lord Exton in the village churchyard, and he was kind enough to drive me home."

Lady Albinia closed her book. "What on earth was Exton doing in Lesser Brampton? There is nothing there to interest him."

"He said he has taken a liking to the countryside since his past visit." Chloe looked down at her hands. "Lord Exton told me of his invitation to London."

Albinia set aside her book. "I'd meant to discuss it with you later today. It could be most advantageous, in terms of launching you successfully. I hope you did not turn him down?"

"No. Although our worlds do not mesh—as Gideon told me quite pointedly."

Turning away, Chloe pretended to select a volume from the closed shelves. As she swung them open, the glass doors reflected the outside world of lawn and garden and cloud-flecked sky. She could hide her own face and watch Lady Albinia's expression at the same time.

"Exton makes his own rules. If he wished, child, he could raise you up to the highest circles in the land." Lady Albinia gazed at Chloe shrewdly. "Could Exton be courting you?"

"It is more than possible, ma'am." Chloe stood very still and straight. "He has offered for me."

"Good Heavens!"

It was all Albinia could do to contain her wonder. "Little Chloe, to be a marchioness! Mariah Lessington and half a dozen other beauties will be wailing and gnashing their teeth in envy."

Then she thought of Exton's wayward reputation, and the way that Chloe's heart was in her eyes when she looked at Gideon, and restrained her raptures. She wanted to go to

Chloe, to read her face and know what was in her mind, but the younger woman's stiff posture kept her at bay. She felt her way cautiously.

"A fantastic success for you, my dear! An unequal match from a worldly standpoint, of course, but a brilliant one. Am I to wish you happy?"

"I have not given my reply." Chloe selected a volume and started to close the glass door of the bookcase. "It is very daunting. I find I like him well enough as a companion, but to marry him! There is so much to think about. So many things to take into consideration and . . ."

Her voice cut off abruptly and she froze in mid-gesture.

Lady Albinia realized that her companion had been looking at the reflected garden in the glass door. She turned to look outside.

The tall windows framed an interesting tableau. Her godson had dragged an old high-back chair—almost a throne—from somewhere, and set it up outside. Lenore sat there, posed like the Queen of Summer, while Gideon plied his paints like a madman. He was rapt in concentration, every atom of his being focused on the woman they called Lenore, as if his very life depended upon it.

Upon *her.*

"Oh, my dear!" Lady Albinia breathed. She rose and started to go to Chloe. But she was alone in the room.

Exton drove away from Lacey's Folly in a brown study. The little wretch was teaching him a needed lesson in humility. She hadn't leapt to his lure, as he'd expected.

He smiled ruefully. He'd been too hasty. He should have waited until Chloe Hartsell came up to London with Albinia, before he dangled his coronet before her not-so-very-dazzled eyes. He had botched it badly, yet he was sure there had been a moment when she'd wavered. Oddly enough, it had been when he'd mentioned Gideon Stone.

The marquis replayed the entire scene in his mind.

*   *   *

Chloe had looked around to where the rows of neat cottages gave way to flourishing hedgerows and glimpses of verdant fields. "This is not the most direct route back to Lacey's Folly, my lord."

Exton laughed. "Do you imagine it is an abduction, my dear? I could easily arrange one, if you wish."

"No, my lord. And I am not your 'dear.' "

"Very well, sweet scold. I merely wish to take the more scenic way, since the afternoon is so fine. And so we might have a long time to converse."

He returned to their former conversation. He'd been talking about his travels in Italy, and she hung on every word. The history, the art, the city itself, fascinated her.

"I should love to see Florence one day," she sighed dreamily. "Rome, Venice . . ."

Her eyes were like stars. Exton decided to make his move. "You have a lively mind and great curiosity about the world. Are you quite content with your life in this peaceful little backwater, Miss Hartsell?"

"My garden is my chief joy. I enjoy the peace and the pace, and it is a wonderful place for Perry to grow up."

She sighed and looked down at her gloved hands, clasped in her lap. All that would change now. Perhaps it was time.

"Since Tobias died, I realize how cut off I have been from real life. From stimulating conversation and pleasing company. I have never had a friend like Lady Albinia before. I wish that her home was nearby. I shall be very lonely once she returns to town."

Exton stepped through the door she'd opened—exactly as he'd planned. "If you lived in town, you might see her as often as you pleased. Her town house is not far from mine. I believe you will enjoy London enormously, even though the season is winding to a close."

She nodded. "There are times when I think of the wide world that I have never seen and ache to discover it." A little smile played about her lips. "I have read as much as I can. My way of traveling from my armchair. I believe you might set me down in St. Mark's Square, or in the heart of Paris, and I could find my way around.''

"Should you like me to do so? I could whisk you there aboard my yacht.''

"Now you are being absurd! I doubt Lady Albinia would wish to leave London now.''

Exton reined in, beneath a canopy of trees by the roadside, and took her hand in his. "I was not thinking of her coming with us.'' He saw her startlement plunge in. "What I had in mind was more of a honeymoon trip.''

Chloe's eyes widened. "I do not understand, my lord.''

"Do you not? Miss Hartsell . . . sweet Chloe, I am asking you to be my wife.''

Her reaction was not at all what he expected. She pulled her hand back and examined his face. "Are you jesting?''

There was a glow in his green eyes unlike anything she had ever seen there before. "My dear, I have never been more serious.''

After a moment she shook her head. "You do me honor, my lord. However, I do not see why on earth you should wish to marry me. Nor, indeed, any reason that I should marry you.''

He stared at her a moment. "Refreshing! In hopes of not sounding conceited,'' he said with an odd smile, "I can think of a dozen women who would accept my suit with alacrity. Dare I ask what it is about me that you find so repellent? My title, my person, or perhaps my character?''

Chloe flushed to the roots of her hair. "I find you quite well, but do not know you enough to have formed any judgement of your character. And only a fool, penniless as I am, would sneeze at marriage to so great a lord.''

"Then marry me!''

She was so distressed, she couldn't answer. Exton already knew the reason. She was enamored of Gideon Stone. His mouth firmed in stern lines.

"Forgive me if I overstep, but I have your concerns at heart. You have been locked away at Lacey's Folly like a nun, my dear. It would only be natural if you have developed a tendre for Mr. Stone. No, no,'' he said, when she murmured an unconvincing protest.

''I will say only this on the subject,'' he continued. ''You are aware enough of the world, through your reading, to know that artists make poor husbands. They are constitutionally selfish and often unfaithful. They may make a woman the object of their attentions, yet turn away from her as if she never existed when their muse—or another woman—absorbs them. Inconstancy is their very nature, scandal their close companion. They blow hot and cold, like the wind. And,'' he added softly, ''are as likely to settle in one place.''

Chloe shivered. Lord Exton was right. Everyone had heard the stories of artists and their models. The wild lives, the violent loves, the dark scandals. Passions that lasted till the paints were dried upon the canvases, then vanished when a new face, a new inspiration, came along.

Would the same thing have happened between herself and Gideon, if he hadn't unearthed her secret? Would the rupture of their relationship have been so irreparable, if Lenore had not appeared on the scene?

Doubt and insecurity perched on her shoulders like harpies, whispered in her ear: The only time Gideon had mentioned love in her presence was the very moment when he'd repudiated her. *If he loved me, he could not have willed himself out of love so easily.*

She had to face the questions that had been hiding in the back of her mind: *Did he make love to me because I was a woman worth making love to, or was it because I am a woman worth painting?* she thought forlornly. *Or simply because I was there?*

Exton watched the emotions flicker across her mobile features and felt a pang of pity. The urge to pull her into his arms was strong, but one he resisted. He had given her quite enough to think of for one day.

''Forgive me if I have overstepped, Miss Hartsell. I have only your best interests at heart. I will take you home now.''

"I have no home," she said softly, speaking only to herself. "Only a place to lay my head."

She had been silent for the rest of the ride back to Lacey's Folly.

Not a bad afternoon's work, Exton decided, as he left Lacey's Folly behind him. He had rushed his fences with Chloe Hartsell and frightened her off a bit, initially; but all in all, he was happy with the results. He had planted the seeds, and even now, he knew, the possibilities were blooming in her mind. Soon, he would reap the harvest.

She deserved a better hand than what fate—and Tobias Lacey—had dealt her. But he, the Marquis of Exton, would make it all up to her.

Exton threw back his head and laughed. Chloe Hartsell was a pearl beyond price. And Gideon Stone was a damned fool.

Chloe managed to avoid Gideon as much as possible over the next few days, even taking most of her meals upstairs with Perry. On the fourth day, Gideon came up and carried the boy down for luncheon, himself.

"And afterward, you will go out into the fresh air. I have set up a chaise longue for you in the pergola, and a comfortable chair for Mrs. Osler, so you may read or watch the swans along the river."

Perry was delighted. "Excellent, sir. I have been fretting about being indoors. Thank you!"

Chloe merely sipped her lemonade and ignored them both.

That night Gideon paced his room by moonlight. The deadline for Lord Pulham's contest drew near. He was glad the picture of Lenore was back in the Bride's Chamber. He couldn't bear to see that beautiful face. Not when he had failed to capture it himself.

It was eating him alive. He could not sleep, could scarcely eat. He wanted to be painting every moment of the day and night. Only the failure of light and Lenore's frailty kept him from working from first light to last. False starts had him frantic, and he had scrapped four promising beginnings already. In the morning he would start as soon as she was able.

He had to paint Lenore's portrait, and this time, it must be perfect.

Lenore! He wished that she would speak. He wanted so much to hear her voice. To know her story. Notices had been placed with the authorities, broadsides sent round the neighborhood. No one had come to claim her. Yet.

Try as he might, Gideon could only think of two reasons for that. Either she was indeed a poor, mute madwoman escaped from a locked attic, or she was the Lost Bride of legend. Neither seemed possible.

Or totally *impossible.*

She was lovely and docile and sat posing for hours without a murmur or wiggle. Unlike Chloe, who . . .

. . . who was jaunting about the countryside with Exton, damn his rotten soul to hell! Four times this week. He was furious every time he thought of it. Exton was so sly and crafty, he'd even taken Perry and Mrs. Osler along, for propriety. He'd sent the boy puzzles and games, and there had been candy and fruit from his succession houses for Chloe, and flowers, as well. *Impertinent blackguard!*

Chloe had all the flowers she needed right here at Lacey's Folly.

"*They are not my flowers, they are yours,*" she had shouted at him. Oh, she was deep in Exton's toils, no doubt picturing herself in a marchioness's robes and coronet. He curled his hands into fists. Well, Exton was welcome to her!

And if he harmed Chloe in any way, he'd kill him! *Tear the miserable cur to pieces with my two strong hands, by God!*

Gideon's ambivalence about Chloe was torturing him. He was torn between anger at the way she'd coldly manipulated him, and at himself for being taken in. He was haunted by memories of their halcyon days together, the passion they'd shared, and he was shaken with such physical longing for her, it heaped fuel on his wrath. Gideon clenched his jaw.

He would be glad when she was out of his sight for good

and all. She was another Mariah Lessington, using him for what she could get. And he, fool that he was, had been on the verge of imagining himself in love with her. Thank God it had been no more than mutual lust. He must think of it that way. It was the only way he could keep his sanity.

Albinia had reminded him that if Chloe married Exton, he would be free to sell Lacey's Folly. Gideon had realized then that he had no intention of doing so. The place had gotten into his blood. It was, he realized with a shock, his home.

Just as it had been Chloe's. When he thought like that, he could almost forgive her for pretending to love him.

And she didn't know what she was getting into with a man like the wicked marquis. As a gentleman talking to a lady, he couldn't mention the so-called Seduction Club, or the rumors of other vices.

"*Exton is a notorious libertine and a cheat at cards!*" He had finally warned her in desperation.

"*Yes, he told me you'd say that, in an effort to besmirch his name,*" she had answered. "*It is your word against his.*"

Gideon went back to pacing the floor and cursing beneath his breath. Between Chloe Hartsell and Lenore, and the weight of Lord Pulham's competition on his shoulders, he had no peace at all.

Chloe met with Mrs. Linley in the housekeeper's neat little office. "I am having a problem with the staff," Mrs. Linley said frankly. She poured out two cups of steaming tea.

"Some, like Biddy, are afraid to wait upon our mysterious guest. Others are uneasy at the very idea of being beneath the same roof with her. Something must be done to convince them that she is *not* a fairy bride released from Pucca's Hill. The way things are, I doubt we can get replacements from the village, should they decide to leave."

Chloe took the teacup the housekeeper offered her. "Yes, the village is rife with gossip and superstitious speculation. I have invited the vicar to dine with us this evening. That should help. Unless during the fish course, she turns him into a squealing pig before our very eyes.''

Mrs. Linley's eyes boggled. Chloe realized that even the level-headed housekeeper was not immune. ''I was making a joke of it,'' she said. ''I hope I didn't offend you.''

''Oh. No. *Of course* I realized you were not serious.''

''Thank you for taking the time to tell me this. I think we shall have to take our visitor on a long drive around the village. Once they see her with their own eyes, they will realize she is merely a woman. It should help nip the speculation in the bud.''

Chloe's plan was put into effect over Gideon's protests. ''How the devil am I to finish the portrait? It's due in London in four days time.''

''We must show the villagers that your unknown guest is flesh and blood, a woman who belongs to the present time and lives in this world, and not the one of faerie.''

''Are you so sure of that?'' he asked.

''There is little one can be sure of in this life.'' Chloe said pointedly. ''But I am sure she is a woman, exactly the same as I.''

She looked so vehement, so passionate, it gave Gideon a pang. He shook his head with a little smile that had her heart stumbling in her chest. ''I doubt there could be two such as you in the entire world.''

''I wish I knew the meaning of that, sir!'' she snapped.

Gideon turned away abruptly. ''So do I, Miss Hartsell. So do I.''

Chloe went back up to the yellow bedchamber to see if all was ready for their outing.

''Stunning,'' Lady Albinia said, as her dresser added the final touch to the stranger, by pinning on a flat hat of white and navy straw, swathed in tulle. ''But then, anything would look marvelous on such a beauty!''

The woman they called Lenore blushed and stared at her altered image in the dressing table mirror. For the past few days Chloe had the increasing suspicion that the woman was beginning to understand what they were saying, perhaps even remembering bits and pieces of her past. The telltale flush in her cheeks made the suspicion definite. What was the woman hiding?

"There," Lady Albinia's maid said with satisfaction. "She is ready."

At Chloe's behest, Lenore was decked out in one of Lady Albinia's stylish London outfits, with her long hair braided into a demure coil at her nape. She looked like a wealthy and stylish visitor to Lacey's Folly. She did not seem to look forward to their proposed outing.

"A carriage ride on such a lovely day will do you enormous good," Chloe told her, and Lenore's eyes showed that she understood. She licked her lips and gave a little nod.

"Now for some jewelry." Albinia looked into her jewel chest, frowning. "Pearls are always unexceptionable," she murmured.

"Wait," Chloe exclaimed. "I know the very thing."

She removed her own gold chain with the gold and silver cross Tobias had given her on her eighteenth birthday. She placed it around the woman's throat.

"There. Everyone knows that fairies can't tolerate man-made iron, or holy water and others symbols of the Christian faith. This little cross will go far toward stopping the stories that are making the rounds."

The woman touched it gingerly, then smiled. "I . . . thank you . . . for . . . for the loan of it."

Her voice startled everyone. It was soft, melodious, and slightly foreign in intonation. A little strained, from disuse.

Biddy, who had just come in with a message for Chloe, almost fainted on the spot. She plopped down on the footstool without a by-your-leave. "God bless us all! Why she speaks the language as well as anyone."

The woman's brow puckered. "Yes . . . it has been coming back to me. I . . . I am starting to remember now. Little things."

Chloe headed Biddy off. "How fortunate that you've regained the power of speech. You must have taken a tumble and hit your head the night that Gideon . . . that Mr. Stone found you. Biddy, be so good as to ask Mrs. Linley to come up to us.''

She waited until the door closed, then sat on the bench beside the woman and took her hand. ''You look dazed. Do you recall anything of what brought you here?''

The woman shook her head. Her thoughts were so fuzzy, like the inside of a milkweed pod. ''Truth to tell, mistress, I recall nothing until a few moments ago. I believe that I have been in a dream. I do not recall how I came to be in this very room. Yet I do recall your face.''

''I see.'' Chloe was thoughtful. ''You seemed to be awake, yet like a sleepwalker. I realize that you were still suffering the effects of your misadventures. You have been here at Lacey's Folly seven days,'' she explained gently. ''You were found wandering in the woods at the foot of Pucca's Hill in your shift.''

The woman's eyes grew larger, the irises darkened with fear. Lady Albinia made a sign, and her dresser disappeared discreetly. ''You are among friends,'' she said quickly.

The woman bit her lip and looked around in sudden fear. ''Your garments . . . your hair. This gown I am wearing. So odd . . .''

A cold hand clutched at Chloe's heart. She was afraid to ask the questions she knew must be answered. Second by second she could see bits of awareness creeping back into the woman's face. ''What is your name?''

The woman seemed to reach back into her memory and pull it out with effort. ''Lenore. Lenore . . . Dacre.'' She gave a little shriek and put her hand to her mouth. ''No, 'tis a *Lacey* now I am. *God help me!*''

Her despair was real. Chloe took the woman's hands in hers. ''Hush, hush. You are safe with us.'' She felt their joined fingers tremble and didn't know which of them was shivering. Perhaps both.

She looked into those beautiful, sky blue eyes that she knew so well from the portrait. "Lenore . . . can you tell me what year it is? And who sits upon England's throne?"

"Why, 'tis the year of Our Lord, 1780. George III is king, God save him."

Chloe felt as though the bottom of her stomach had dropped out.

She was holding the hands of a woman who should be dead and gone, yet she was as fair as the day she vanished. Unless it was some sort of terrible hoax.

The door opened suddenly, and Gideon walked in, all unprepared for what he found. The woman tore her hands from Chloe's and pressed them to her heart.

"Robert! Oh, my love! I thought you were dead."

Chloe's blood froze. *Lenore is looking at Gideon as if he is all her hope and salvation. All her world!*

The woman went to Gideon with a dazzling smile and reached out her hand to his. "My heart is full to bursting. I cannot believe it is you, my darling, alive and well. I . . . I saw them throw you from Giovanna's tower, onto the rocks below! I should have known you would escape!"

Gideon stopped in his tracks. As his fingers closed around hers, a sudden dizziness assailed him. His ear roared, and he felt a rushing in his head, a swiftness, as if he were pulled abruptly back through time and space.

He was in the yellow bedchamber in golden sunshine, and in Giovanna's tower at the same time, facing out the window to the frothing, moonlit river below. It was both daylight and dark of night. He was Gideon Stone, and he was someone else entirely. And then he was hurled out into blackness.

Falling, falling, until he exploded in agony against the rocks' jagged teeth. The cold black water swirled over him, tugging, tugging madly until it suddenly tore him free and carried his broken body away.

Gideon pitched forward on the floor and lay senseless at Chloe's feet.

*　　*　　*

Gideon came to in his room, where Dawlish and Henry had managed to carry him. "Take the cursed smelling salts away, for the love of God!"

"Well, he is himself again," Albinia said calmly.

His godmother stood at the door, ushering the servants out, while Chloe applied a damp towel to the cut over his eyes. He touched the side of his forehead, where a lump the size of a hen's egg was forming.

"Do you still say it is impossible?" he asked.

"It is not proof that she is Lenore Lacey," Chloe answered. She applied a sticking plaster to the cut with a little more force than was necessary.

"I remember a time when your hands were more gentle," he snapped, referring to his arrival at Lacey's Folly.

She colored, thinking of other times. Gideon cursed inwardly. The awkwardness came rushing back. He didn't know what to say to her.

Perry came hobbling into the room on his crutches. Newton padded in behind him. The pup was putting on a good deal of weight. "I say, Gideon, are you all right? What happened?"

"He caught his boot in a worn place in the rug," Chloe answered quickly.

The boy considered her answer. "Oh. I thought it might have been part of a fairy curse. First my leg, then Lenore, and now Gideon, all struck down."

Chloe eyed him sternly. "Perry, have you been talking to the servants about the legend? Biddy and Agnes in particular?"

"Just a little." He hung his head. "You never said not to."

"He has you there," Gideon told her.

"No," Chloe responded, "he has you." She placed her arms akimbo. "And did you perhaps mention that her lover was named Robert, and that George III was on the throne when Lenore Lacey vanished?"

"Uh . . . em . . ." Perry flushed to the roots of his hair.

"The mystery is solved. If Perry has been talking to the maids, you may be sure they have been gossiping in Lenore's

. . . in your new guest's room, thinking she did not understand them. They have put the whole story into her head. I have no doubt of it.''

Gideon sat up and instantly regretted it. He put a hand to his head. The room spun, but he knew exactly where he was and who he was.

He wanted to talk to someone about what had happened just now, when he'd seemed to be in two places at once. It had happened before the night of his wager with Exton, when he'd awakened from his dream and discovered the painting of Lenore and Pucca's Hill. He wanted to talk to Chloe. Alone.

''Off with you, Perry. Go bedevil Cook for some of her shortbread.''

''But Gideon . . .''

''Go away, you young scamp.'' The boy's face fell. Gideon softened. ''If you stay out of mischief, I'll give you some sketching lessons this evening.''

''Will you, sir?'' Perry's countenance brightened. A scientist needed to record his findings in drawings as well as in words. ''That would be capital!''

Still grinning, he went off to pester Cook and Agnes.

''And close the door!'' Gideon shouted after him.

Chloe waited until they were alone. She eyed Gideon wrathfully. ''You needn't take it out on Perry. You must not blame him for my mistakes.''

''I don't, curse it!'' He winced at the sound of his own voice. ''I need to speak to you. To clear up something in my mind.''

''Let *me* speak, if you please. This needs to be said.'' Chloe's gray eyes darkened with memory.

''I was fifteen, newly orphaned, and had just lost my younger brother to the same fever that carried off my mother and father. And I was head over heels in love with a young man who had ambitious parents. Those ambitions did not include a penniless orphan as a daughter-in-law.''

Her voice trembled. ''My father's estate was entailed and passed to a complete stranger. My mother's dowry was gone, squandered on heaven knows what. Not yet out of the school-room, I learned I was to be taken away from the only home I had ever known and apprenticed to a seamstress. Instead, I ran away.''

"Good God, I cannot wonder at that," Gideon exclaimed.

She put out her hand to stop him. "I went to Gretna Greens with my lover. His name isn't important. Only that he was also young and foolish, and that he loved me dearly."

Gideon was appalled. "You needn't . . ."

"Let me finish, I beg of you!" Chloe closed her eyes and fought for courage.

"We were underage and had insufficient funds. His father caught up with us before we reached Scotland's border. By that time we had been gone three weeks. You will understand my meaning."

He nodded. She was so pale, her lips almost white, that Gideon could hardly bear to look at her now, much less speak. Chloe took a shuddering breath and continued.

"While I was at the market, my lover's father arrived and whisked his son away by force. I was stranded near the border, with neither funds nor protector." Her eyes were like a silver mirror, clouded with remembrance. "I took a job at the inn. I was sure he would find a way to come back and rescue me."

She twisted her hands, remembering. The pain of it was etched on her features, and Gideon's soul writhed with pity.

"Soon I was four months gone with child, and there had been no word," she said quietly. "I was brokenhearted. I did not know until much later that he was already dead, killed in an accident two days after he was taken home. He had taken a horse and was on his way to find me, when he was struck by a runaway mail coach. That is all I know. I . . . I can only hope it was instantaneous."

"My dear . . ."

"Do not say it!" she warned. "I do not want your sympathy."

She couldn't bear to hear him use the same endearments he

had used before. Not now. Her throat worked as she swallowed her tears.

"When the innkeeper's wife learned I was with child, she turned me away. Tobias found me weeping by the roadside. My gown was torn and muddy, my hair snagged with burrs, yet that kindly old man stopped to see what assistance he could render.

"He was amazed to hear my voice and realize I was a gentlewoman by birth. When he heard my name was Hartsell, he determined that he was related to my father, distantly. I told him everything. He didn't care one whit. Tobias arranged for me to have my baby comfortably, under an assumed identity. Then he brought us to Lacey's Folly, where Perry was passed off as my late brother, for whom I named him." She turned and faced him resolutely. "The rest of my tale you know."

Gideon was rendered speechless again. Chloe, seeing the horror in his eyes, mistook it for disgust. Her own burned with anger.

"That, sir, is my sordid history. You see, I have limited my 'whoring,' as you called it, to two men only. I hope you are not disappointed in me for it."

Squaring her shoulders, she turned her back on him, heading for the door.

"Chloe! For God's sake!"

He was off the bed in two strides and caught her by the arm. "That wasn't necessary."

She jerked her arm out of his grasp. Gideon felt so ashamed of himself he didn't know where to start. "I didn't mean . . . I wasn't prying into your background. I wanted to tell you . . . to talk to you." *Dear God, think of a neutral subject!* He cast around in his mind. "About . . . about *Lenore*."

All the color drained from her face. Her skin had the luminous whiteness of fresh snow. Her voice was ice.

"There is nothing you can say that I wish to hear. What was between us once is gone. After we go up to London, I doubt our paths will cross again."

His head was a little muzzy, and he was distracted by her change of subject. "What is this talk of you going to London? I made no such arrangements."

Chloe gave him a tight little smile. "No, that is true. But Lord Exton has. I shall be his guest, at Exton House."

"You will do no such thing!" he exclaimed. "Your reputation will be ruined."

"Not with Lady Albinia as my companion and chaperone. She will be his guest as well."

Shaking off his grasp, she went out the door, with Gideon's curses echoing behind her.

It was a perfect afternoon for Gideon to work outdoors. Lenore took her pose as uncomplainingly as always. *She never fidgeted or said she was tired, as Chloe . . . as Miss Hartsell had.*

He cursed beneath his breath and concentrated on Lenore. The sun was filtered through the leaves, and a light breeze skipped over the river and across the lawn. A butterfly landed on one of his discarded watercolor sketches, as if expecting the flowers to be real.

The artist ignored the insect and examined his latest attempt. Crumpling it in despair, he threw it down beside the others. *His muse had abandoned him since he and Chloe . . . Miss Hartsell . . .*

He threw down his brush. Nothing worked. "Damn the woman, she is driving me mad!"

Gideon glanced at his subject again, but Lenore hadn't heard him. She sat with her back to a willow, with swans in the background. He was trying to do a rendering of her as Ophelia. Try as he may, he could not capture what he wanted: the passion of a heartsick young woman, transformed by a gentle madness.

Suddenly, he realized why—Lenore's face was too beautiful. Too composed.

Too blank. So very different from Chloe.

Like Lenore's past, there was nothing behind her eyes. It was all on the surface. He wondered what she thought of, what interests might spark some light of curiosity in her. She had little concern, seemingly, even in discovering her true identity. She was like a placid child, seeing only what attracted her immediate attention. A lovely flower, turning her face this way and that to catch the sun. Ah, *there* was a potential topic of conversation.

"Are you fond of flowers?" he asked.

"Flowers?" She looked surprised, as if she had never considered flowers before. She smiled, as if a thought had just occurred to her. "Oh, yes. They are pretty."

Well. No passion there. "Animals?" he said desperately. "Do you care for them? Dogs and cats, puppies and kittens?"

"Yes, they are very nice, also."

Gideon was ready to tear his heart out. She looked like a fairytale princess in real life, but on the paper she was as flat and dull as her replies. Something edged sideways into his mind. An idea, taking nebulous shape, growing out of the deepest shadows of his psyche. Terrified he might lose it before he had even glimpsed the idea, he held his breath and waited for it to form. He knew he couldn't force it, or it would slip away again, become a blank white canvas filled with nothing but his own despair.

Color and light flooded his mind like music, but the inspiration had nothing to do with Lenore. Chloe's mobile face and quicksilver eyes intruded, shocking him profoundly. With an oath, he brushed the picture from his mind and tried to concentrate on Lenore once more.

He needed to make simple conversation with Lenore, draw her out of her daydreams. Spark some interest in her, somehow.

His gaze fell on Pucca's Hill. "There are many legends in this part of the countryside. Tell me, do you believe in fairies?"

Her face altered in the blink of an eye. It was like a ripple had gone through her, as if she were a reflection in a stream. Then it was gone.

"I do not wish to talk of fairies," she said softly, and went back to her own thoughts.

Gideon recognized defeat. He spent the rest of the hour sketching swans and willows. When he went back to his studio later, he saw that he had also done several vignettes of Chloe's face. Startled and angry, although he couldn't really say with whom, he closed the cover and put the sketchbook aside. There was work to be done.

Henry and the estate carpenter had made up some crates to protect his paintings. The oils would be wet for weeks to come and must be protected from smears. Especially the newer ones. He ranged the finished paintings along the wall, with the latest of Lenore in the center.

They were good. No, damn it, they were exceptional! He wouldn't sell his talent short. These paintings done in his weeks at Lacey's Folly were a huge leap forward for him. The best work he'd ever done. Now he just had to chose which of the three was best to enter in the showing.

By God, he intended to win Lord Pulham's commission and take London by storm!

"You *must* remember something more," Gideon said. They stood in the drawing room, surrounded by the ubiquitous Lacey collections. Some of the furniture dated back two hundred years.

He was desperate to instill more life in Lenore's portraits, and to that end, he was determined to force her memory to return. She merely looked blank. "Come, Lenore. Which way was it to your chamber from here?"

"She wouldn't know," Chloe said in exasperation.

Martin and Olivia Thorne had written to say they were coming to pay their respects to Tobias in the churchyard, and that they would stop at Lacey's Folly on their way. To Chloe, this was just one more sign that they were somehow involved in the mysterious appearance of 'Lost Lenore.' If she could smell a plot, why couldn't Gideon?

What is it about Lenore that has turned his brain to porridge?

"Let us go out on past the library," he said, as if she hadn't spoken.

Chloe led the way, back rigid. She was angry that Gideon insisted she come along with them. It was painful to see him so besotted with the other woman.

"This part of the house didn't exist a hundred years ago. We'll go out to the maze, and in through the door of the Old Hall. If she is indeed Lost Lenore, it should strike a chord."

Gideon's experiment was a failure. If Lenore should have gone left, she went right, if west, she went east. In the Old Hall she stood and gazed silently around, not even seeming to notice the stairway that led to the Bride's Chamber.

"Nothing is familiar," she said disconsolately.

"But you must remember *something!*"

She turned to him, almost weeping with frustration. "Only you, Robert. Only *you.*"

"My name is Gideon," he said, shaking his head. "I am not Robert."

Chloe went past them and up the stairs to the Bride's Chamber and unlocked the door. "Try this room," she said sharply. Why Gideon had insisted on her accompanying them was beyond her. Every minute was sheer torture.

Lenore entered. There was no gasp of recognition. She moved through the room, puzzled, and shook her head.

"She doesn't seem to know this room, either," Gideon said in disappointment, as Lenore looked around.

Ah, but I do! Chloe thought. *This is where we last made love.*

He was aware of it, too. The chair, the bed, the very scent of the room overpowered him with memories. He almost wished that they could go back in time to that night, with Chloe lying naked in his arms in the moonlight. Turn back the clock. Take back the hateful, hurtful words.

But it was no use. It had all been a lie.

And now here was the very image of Lenore Lacey, in the

living, breathing flesh. He reminded himself how exquisite Lenore was. A beauty beyond compare. An inspiration any artist would envy. The woman whose face would make him famous.

And there was no way that the things he'd said to Chloe could ever be erased. If they were etched in his mind in acid, he was sure they were burned into her heart. The memory shamed him. She rarely looked at him directly and avoided him at all costs. He couldn't blame her. He deserved all the scorn she could heap upon him.

He ached when he thought of her, alone and abandoned by the side of the road, waiting for her dead lover to return. Fifteen, orphaned, and with child. It wrung his heart. And he had taken her few happy memories of that time and besmirched them with his foul accusations. He was not proud of it.

Gideon could forgive her for being desperate enough to do anything to hold onto Lacey's Folly. He couldn't forgive the betrayal of his trust. *Never again,* he told himself, steeling his heart.

He had almost convinced himself that he loved her. Or, rather, the woman he had thought her to be. Once again, he had taken a woman of clay and tried to fashion her into something she was not. The fault was as much his as hers, he knew. But it was too late to go back.

While Lenore roved the chamber, he went to her portrait hanging in its accustomed place over the hearth. Something caught his eye. He had dreamed that he'd begun to clean the portrait, but it had not been a dream after all. The lower-right corner had been stripped of years of yellowed varnish. The translucent green of the fluted column behind Lenore and the iridescent blue globe beside her painted hand glowed like stained glass. And there was something more. Reaching up, he took down the heavy painting without difficulty. Yes, there it was, in the lower corner. A signature cleverly worked into the design of the small chest the woman held on her lap.

"Come see this." He pointed to it.

Chloe blinked. "Robert Stanfield."

A shiver ran up Gideon's spine. "My middle name is Stanfield. It is an old family name. Stanfields lived in the area a century ago. I saw their names in the churchyard when I paid my respects to Tobias Lacey.''

He looked over to where Lenore stood at the window, frowning out at Pucca's Hill. "Perhaps he was an ancestor of mine. I found Lenore that night, and for some reason, she has confused me with him.''

"That would explain it," Chloe said firmly. "Perry must have seen it, too. Perhaps Tobias brought him here or told him the name of the painter. And somehow, the Thornes found out, as well.''

Her brow furrowed. "At some time Tobias might even have brought Martin to this room. After all, he was the nominal heir for decades. I am more and more sure that they are behind this. If 'Lenore' had not fallen and struck her head, we could see their plot more clearly!''

Gideon sighed. He hadn't heard a word she'd said. He only had eyes for Lenore. "I was sure she would know *this* room, at least.''

Chloe wanted to shake him. "You must admit that she knows nothing more about her supposed background than any of the servants. She cannot name an important event from the reign of George III, or even describe the fashions and personalities of the age. She is parroting what she has heard the servants say, and that is all.''

"I am beginning to think you may be right," he conceded. "Everything you say is true, and yet . . .''

And yet, Gideon thought, *it does not explain my dizziness at the tower window, the sensation of falling. The odd sense of being two men at once, in two very different places.* Nor Lenore's 'recognition' of him.

Chloe might be right, but he didn't want to think about it. Not now.

"Lenore, is there nothing that stirs the faintest memory?" he begged.

She didn't answer him for a moment. Her face was abstracted. Blank as unsculpted stone. Finally, a light came into her eye. "That hill. I remember seeing it before.''

"Of course," Chloe told her. "That is where you came

from the night Gideon found you. Perhaps we should take a walk through the meadow, where you can have a closer look.''

Lenore shook her head. "No. I can't go there. I am forbidden.''

Although they pressed her, she wouldn't give them anything more.

They went out of the house and around to the tower. Lenore balked. "Please, it is so very hot, and I am tired. If you wish me to sit for you later, I would like to rest. And Chloe has arranged a picnic luncheon for us by the pond.''

Gideon's disappointment changed to excitement. "Excellent. I'll fetch my things and sketch you after, while you rest.'' He turned to Chloe. "When you go back to the house, would you ask Dawlish to send us out a bottle of that nice Rhenish wine?''

His unthinking exclusion of her was like a slap. Fury warred with hurt in Chloe's breast. After taking charge of Lenore, keeping her company, and seeing to her every comfort, he had dismissed her like a serving wench in a taproom.

"But Chloe must come with us," Lenore exclaimed. "It was all her plan. She must come.''

"Oh, no," Chloe said brightly. "I have packing to do." *A set of hairbrushes and a nightshift to throw in a valise, while the two of you drink wine by the pond.* She set off for the house and delivered the message. Dawlish sighed. "Very well, Miss Chloe.''

He knew her too well and had guessed at too much not to be disappointed by the recent turn of events. It had seem ordained by heaven—or perhaps by Mr. Tobias Lacey, in his wisdom—that Miss Chloe and the new master would end up going down the aisle arm in arm.

Dawlish scowled. Everything had gone wrong since Mr. Stone had found the lady who looked so much like Lost Lenore. Not that he believed it one whit. It was only a matter of time, he was sure, before it turned out the Thornes were behind it all, as he'd heard Miss Chloe say. The butler had come to the same conclusion on his own. After all, why had no one come to claim the woman? No, no, it was sure to be some trick.

He was so caught up in regrets he almost forgot. "Miss Chloe, there are some packages come for you from London. Agnes and Biddy took them up to your room."

"Oh, those must be the gowns Lady Albinia had sent down. I'll go up and see."

There was a time when she would have been so overjoyed to have new, elegant clothes. Now they had little importance in the scheme of things. When she opened her door, she was in for a shock. Her room was unrecognizable. The bed and chairs and wardrobe were hung with all manner of fine feathers: traveling dresses in leaf green and bronze; day dresses in muted natural hues; evening gowns like deep-toned jewels. Shoes and hats, shawls of silk and cashmere, and gauzy spangles. Boxes filled with yards of lace, ribbons, and flowers for trim.

Agnes and Biddy were glowing with excitement. "Look how this silk flows, Miss Chloe!"

Lady Albinia stood by the dressing table. "I believe the ivory crepe de chine is my favorite. Do you approve, child?"

"They are exquisite!" Chloe joined her. "So many lovely things! But why did you not have them delivered in London, ma'am?"

"What, and have you arrive at Exton House with all your worldly goods in a valise?" Lady Albinia feigned horror. "Now *that* would cause a scandal."

She dismissed the maids, who went below stairs to spread the news of Miss Chloe's elegant new wardrobe.

"What do you think of this?" She gestured at a handsome traveling case of pale green leather, open on the table, fitted cunningly inside with cut crystal jars and bottles. Lotions and perfumes and powder enough for any gilded boudoir. The lids were solid gold and studded with topaz.

She lifted one out in wonder. The crystal facets caught fire in the light. It was extravagantly beautiful. And costly. "But this! Ma'am, I cannot accept such an expensive gift. Why it is worth a king's ransom."

"No, only a marquis's pocket change." Lady Albinia lowered her voice discreetly. "And see, he has even left room for the crest and your monogram, to be put on after the engagement."

Chloe looked at her sharply. "Both you and Lord Exton seem very sure that I will accept his offer."

Gideon's godmother looked pointedly out the window, to where he was sketching Lenore by the willow pond, and then back at Chloe. "You would be a fool not to accept. And I do not think you are a fool."

TWELVE

§§

THE DAYS RAN QUICKLY INTO ONE ANOTHER, AND BEFORE they knew it, Lord Pulham's exhibition was upon them.

Gideon went up to town in Lady Albinia's traveling coach, with his paintings in enormous crates. They took up almost the entire interior of the vehicle. He could not believe the difference his time as Lacey's Folly had made, both in the quality and the quantity of his work. Whatever mad genius had possessed him, it was gone now, replaced by an almost empty calm.

Chloe watched him drive away from her window. A tear trembled on her lashes. It would likely be the last time she would ever again stand here like this and watch him pull away. It was very possible that she would not return from London to Lacey's Folly. If she accepted Exton's proposal, she would stay in town for the rest of the season, to be introduced into the highest circles of society.

The prospect was daunting.

The alternative would be to move with Lady Albinia to her town house, and let Gideon's godmother try to arrange a less unequal match.

Chloe leaned her head against the glass pane. Oh, if only she could stay at Lacey's Folly until Perry went away to school! Or even just until after Christmas. She had always loved Christmas here.

He would like London, though. The museums and theaters.

The Tower of London. If she accepted Exton, Perry would have the best of private tutors before going off to Cambridge, where the marquis had endowed a college. They could have a good life—safe and comfortable and protected.

Suddenly, the sunny day was hidden in a blur of tears. *It is only that this has been my home for so long,* Chloe chided herself. *That I thought to end my days here beneath this roof, and Perry after me.* She blew her nose.

Her own things were packed and ready to go on the morrow. She looked at the trunks and bandboxes, the elegant travel case with its hand-cut crystal. A new life was beginning, for good or for ill. Whether she accepted Exton's offer, or another's, it didn't matter. As long as they understood that Perry was part of the package, it didn't matter at all.

Exton was intrigued with her. For now. Perhaps because she resisted his lures. Whether it lasted was something only time would tell. He might be the kind of man who lost interest once he'd attained his goal. Life with him would not be dull, and she suspected he would be a skilled and knowledgeable lover; but she also suspected that he could be cold and cruel.

He vowed that he had changed, and Lady Albinia seemed to agree. She seemed determined that Chloe would be a marchioness.

There was one thing that Chloe promised herself: regardless of whom she married, it would be in the church at Lesser Barnstable, where Tobias lay in the little churchyard. She would have Mrs. Osler and Mrs. Linley there for support. Dawlish and Cook, Agnes and Biddy and Netty, Henry and Rendulph, and the others, there to wish her well. Lady Albinia would be her only attendant.

Except for Perry, they were all she had.

The following morning the entire household was assembled to see her be driven off to London in high style. How the servants all goggled at Lord Exton's carriage, its splendid fittings and magnificent coachman, its footmen and liveried outriders!

Perry was more excited than usual, and Newton barked and

carried on so, that he had to be locked up in the stables. Mrs. Osler had taken over as Perry's unofficial tutor and promised to keep him well occupied.

The boy asked the question that was most on his mind: "If you marry Lord Exton, do you think he would let me drive his horses?"

She kissed his cheek. "I will not have you listen to servants' gossip. I have made no plans to marry anyone," she told him. "And in any case, you are far too young to manage a team. For one thing, your hands are not big enough to handle the ribbons."

He looked down at his fingers and grinned. "I hate it when you're right, Chloe."

A footman lowered the steps and opened the door for the ladies to enter. Chloe was very aware that Exton's servants were observing her from the corners of their eyes with great interest. She was glad she had on the bronze traveling dress and matching bonnet. It made her look sophisticated—and feel like a sham.

Lady Albinia whispered in Chloe's ear. "Now it begins, child. You shall have every luxury at your command during your stay in London. And perhaps, in the very near future, it is I who will have to bow to *you*."

"I have not made my decision," Chloe replied in a low voice, so the servants would not hear.

"Oh, my dear. You have no idea how persuasive Exton can be! And once you see Exton House—only one of his many properties, you know—why, the state dining room can sit upwards of sixty for dinner!"

Chloe was appalled.

"Are you so anxious for me to wed him?" she asked, when they were safely ensconced in the carriage.

Lady Albinia cocked her head in that birdlike way she had. Her blue eyes twinkled with mischief. "My dear, I am only anxious for your happiness."

Sixty for dinner is not a prospect to make me happy in the east.

All the way up to London, Chloe had visions of herself sitting stiffly at formal dinners, looking down an endless table glittering with crystal and plates of gold. Listening to statesmen and peers, and their bejeweled ladies, discuss politics and current events and whisper gossip about people she didn't know. She would infinitely rather be back in her parlor at Lacey's Folly with a good book, or out in her garden tending to her roses.

No, neither my parlor nor my garden. They belonged to Gideon now.

And to Lenore.

Exton House was as beautiful, as daunting, as Lady Albinia had told her. Chloe looked up at the imposing marble facade as their carriage drew up. "If I did not know better, I would think it museum, or a temple."

Lady Albinia laughed. "It is a museum of good taste, and a temple of wealth and lineage. But it is also a home, Chloe. You must remember that. The public rooms are princely, but I assure you the private apartments are more intimate and furnished for comfort, as well as beauty."

She put her gloved hand on Chloe's arm. "And his country seat is fabulous. You must see it in the spring! The gardens are extensive, and it requires an entire platoon of gardeners and undergardeners just to mow the lawns and clip the hedges." Leaning close, she whispered in Chloe's ear, "And you could have acres of roses, if you choose."

"If you mean to encourage me to favor Exton's suit, you are going about it wrong. With a platoon of gardeners, I would have nothing to do but arrange the flowers. Although there is likely a platoon of servants to do that, also."

"My dear, as Exton's wife, there would be so much to occupy your time, you wouldn't care. Breakfasts and balls and dinners and receptions every night! Entertaining his friends in the country, or at his hunting box. Never a dull moment, I am sure."

Chloe had no words to express her dismay; in any case

there was no time for further talk. The steps were let down, and a liveried footman helped them descend the carriage. Lady Albinia swept up the imposing steps arm in arm with Chloe. More footmen flanked the open doors. She took a deep breath and went in.

They entered a dramatic hall that was floored in black marble, streaked with white, and walled in white marble, streaked with black. It rose three stories to a huge glass dome. Enormous double doors of black lacquered wood flanked the wide reception space, and a magnificent sweep of stairs with ornate black rails curved gracefully to the upper floors. The rest was an overwhelming impression of gilt and crystal and ebony furniture lacquered to a high gloss.

"What do you think?" her companion said in low tones.

I think it is beautiful and elegant and cold as Dante's seventh ring of hell. But Chloe couldn't say that aloud. "It outdoes your descriptions by far," was the best she could come up with.

"Yes, is it not splendid?"

I had rather be back in the cozy parlor at Lacey's Folly, Chloe thought. "Splendid is not the word for it."

They were greeted by the housekeeper, a crisp woman, with skin so white and hair so black, Chloe wondered if she'd been selected to match the decor.

"Lord Exton is gone out," the woman said, after dropping a curtsey, "but everything is in readiness for your visit. I will show you to your chambers."

"Very proper of him," Lady Albinia said to Chloe, as they went up the staircase. "He does not mean to single you out and cause you embarrassment."

It was apparent, however, that the housekeeper already knew which way the wind was blowing. Her deference to Chloe, as potential mistress of the house, was equal to that accorded to Lady Albinia.

"If there is anything you require, Miss Hartsell, *anything* at all, you have only to ring."

Chloe thanked her, endured an hour of fussing by the maids

who brought refreshments and unpacked her clothes, and was finally glad to be alone in her wrapper, in the suite of rooms.

Books and candy were set out for her in the high-ceilinged blue sitting room, with soft divans and gilded mirrors. There were more in the rose and white bedchamber, and scented soaps in the dressing room and bath fit for a princess. Everything she could possibly want or need. Except one. Chloe lay down on the bed for a nap, wishing she had a packet of Dr. Marsh's headache powders, and a large vial of his strongest nerve tonic.

Her fears were unjustified. There were only Lord Exton, Lady Albinia, and herself for dinner. Her gown of white silk was shot with silver, to match the ribbons twined with pink silk roses in her hair. Lady Albinia had loaned her a gold necklace spaced with small diamonds. Chloe felt very elegant and quite at ease.

They dined in a lovely little parlor in the family apartments and retired to another afterward. It held family mementos and a marvelous painting of Exton's late wife, with their son, on the overmantel.

A good strategy on Exton's part, Albinia thought, listening to their easy conversation. *Chloe is nowhere so skittish as she was earlier.*

Exton looked across the room and smiled. He could still read Albinia's mind after all these years. While Chloe leafed through an album of engravings of Exton's country seat, he strolled over to her companion.

"There is something I wish to ask you, Albinia. I fear Chloe still feels a tendre for Gideon Stone. He is your godson, but am your longtime friend. I have been wondering whose side you are on?"

"You are under a misapprehension." She opened her fan and toyed with the ivory sticks. "There was never any sort of understanding between Miss Hartsell and my godson."

"Give me credit for some intelligence! She was enamored of him. I have no idea if he returned her regard. If not, he more of a fool than I thought. It is evident they had a falling out.''

"Their friendship is strained. I can say that much.''

"I am delighted to learn it.''

He looked back at Chloe, and a small smile played about his lips. She looked up, as if realizing they were talking about her, and flushed. Exton turned back to his companion. "But you have not said, Albinia. Whose interests are you trying to further?''

She closed her fan with a snap. "Chloe's interests, of course!''

The marquis frowned. "I see. I appreciate your honesty.'' He strolled back to Chloe's side in a brown study.

Evidently, he didn't know Albinia quite as well as he'd thought.

They went to the theater to see a new comedy. Chloe had never been to the theater and enjoyed it immensely. Until she spied Gideon in the box opposite.

He knew she was coming to London as Exton's guest, over his protests; but seeing her there beside the marquis was a shock. She looked extremely elegant and not at all like the Chloe he knew—and had almost loved.

By God, she has done well for herself! He thought angrily. *Sitting there as if she already wore a tiara.* Instead, her hair was entwined with silver ribbons and tiny silk roses to match those on her bodice.

Suddenly, he thought of Exton reaching up to unbind her hair, watching it cascade in shining curls down her back and . . . *Oh, that lecherous scoundrel!*

"Shhhhhh!''

Gideon looked around with a start. People were staring at him. He must have said it aloud.

Jack Rathburn turned in his chair. "Good Lord, Gideon, have you lost your mind?'' he hissed. "That is the hero, not the villain. And this is not the kind of theater where the audience is encouraged to shout things and throw rotten fruit!''

Gideon crossed his arms over his chest and glared at the other spectators until they turned back to the play.

The curtain came down on the first act, and Rathburn tapped his arm. "Who is that young beauty with Lady Albinia in Exton's box? I haven't seen her in town before."

"If I have my way, you won't see her in town again." Gideon rose so abruptly, his gilt chair tipped over.

Rathburn was shocked. "Damn it, Stone, you're foxed! I should have never let you finish that last glass of wine."

"I am not drunk, you fool. And that beauty is Chloe Hartsell, the young woman for whom I am supposed to supply a husband!"

"Well," his friend replied. "I would say that you're doing a bang-up job of it. By the way Exton is hanging over her, she has him in her clutches already."

"Damn your eyes, Rathburn. She shall not marry a cur like Exton. I will not let her!"

"Now I know you're foxed. Sit down, Gideon, for God's sake, and stop making an ape of yourself."

But Gideon was already on his way out. He forged his way through the crowd until he worked around to Exton's private box. "I would like to speak to Miss Hartsell alone."

Chloe started to rise. Albinia kept her in her chair by touching her arm. Exton rose languidly. "That, my good fellow, depends on Miss Hartsell entirely."

While Gideon simmered, the marquis turned to Chloe. "He appears to be in a ferocious mood. My advice would be to remain safely here, my dear."

Chloe swallowed. "I would like to hear what Mr. Stone has to say."

"Very well."

Exton pulled out her chair for her. Albinia watched as Chloe and Gideon left the box together. "Was that wise of you?"

"I am not perturbed. There is nothing like a man in a jealous rage to get a woman's back up. Anything Stone has to say while he is in such a mood is sure to rebound upon him." Exton smiled. "It will only serve my cause."

Gideon hustled Chloe past the throng, looking for a private corner. He finally found an empty box and thrust her inside. She knew he was in a fury, and seeing her with the marquis had to be the cause. She waited with her heart in her eyes. What did he mean to say to her? *I'm sorry Chloe. I was wrong, Chloe. I love you and only you, Chloe.*

Nothing so loverlike came out of his mouth. He clamped his hands down on her shoulders. "I had hoped that you would listen to reason, and stay in the country."

"I had far better reason to come to London, sir."

"Yes, I see that full well. I hope you are happy now that you have snared yourself a nobleman!" he said bitterly. "Exton may be a cheat and a lecher, but his rank and wealth outweigh that in your eyes. How glad you must be that you avoided any further entanglement with me, so that you are free wed him."

She trembled, and he fought the urge to sweep her into his arms and crush her mouth with kisses. But she was as false as all the rest.

Chloe wrenched herself free. A silk rose came off in his hand.

Now she was as furious as he. "I am delighted that our relationship went no further than it did! Exton has treated me with respect and every courtesy—which if more than I can say for you, *Mr. Stone!* I rue the day you ever came to Lacey's Folly. Had I known then what I do now, I would have packed my bags and fled the place the day Tobias was buried!"

"Ah, but you hadn't met Exton then! There was only myself, a fool of an artist who had stolen your inheritance. Or so you thought. And you meant to get it back, by any means necessary."

Her hand came out in a stinging slap to his cheek. He touched his face. *"By God, you little fiend, you've split my lip!"*

"And you, Gideon Stone, did far worse. You broke my heart! I loved you, and you broke my heart."

Gideon was staggered. There was such bleakness in her

eyes, such stark truth in her anger, that it convinced him. He'd been a blind and jealous fool. It was Chloe, only Chloe that he loved. Had always loved. The emotion overwhelmed him. He tried to speak. She wouldn't let him.

"No, you have said quite enough. Without giving me a chance to explain, you thought the very worst of me. The things you said were unforgivable."

"For God's sake, Chloe!" His voice was ragged with passion. What had he done? "Chloe, please. Listen to me!" He held his hands out to her, but she backed away, shaking her head.

"I have done listening to you." Her slender body shook, and her eyes were dark as a moonlit river in the candlelight. "You have seen the last of me. I would rather live in a hovel or sleep in a ditch than to spend a single night under the same roof as you again."

Turning, she ran straight into the wrathful dowager whose theater box they'd usurped. Untangling her brooch from the woman's satin-swagged bodice, she wrenched herself free and ran out to the corridor.

Gideon plunged past the woman in pursuit of Chloe, without a by-your-leave. "Young people," the dowager said scathingly. "No manners or sense of decorum. I wonder what the world is coming to!"

By the time Gideon made his way down the hallway, he'd lost Chloe in the crowd. Exton's box was empty. She must have convinced him to take her back to Exton House. He muttered an oath. With his high-handed tactics, he had sent her straight into Exton's arms!

Gideon leaned up against the wall beneath a gas lamp and cursed himself beneath his breath. Through pride and folly and vanity, he had thrown away the most precious thing he'd ever possessed: the love of a good and honest woman. *Oh, Chloe, you little wretch! What have you done to me?*

Rathburn found him there. "You look like death. Didn't I warn you against so much champagne?"

Gideon looked at him grimly. "You were right, Jack. I was

foxed. I didn't think it, but I must have been. Either that or I was out totally out of my mind." He rubbed his temples. "Now I've ruined everything."

"Yes, but listen to this!" his friend said, not paying him the slightest attention. "Some madman just made his way into Lady Yardley's private box and was berating some poor young woman at the top of his lungs! By the time the dowager sent for help, he'd escaped to Lord knows where. He might still be lurking about in the shadows, ready to pounce."

Gideon ran his fingers through his hair. His other hand still clutched the rose from Chloe's gown. "I know where he is, Jack. The poor devil is in hell! One of his own making."

Rathburn eyed him closely. "Now I know that you are foxed!"

Chloe was in no shape to hear Lord Exton's declarations when they returned to his mansion. She watched helplessly as Lady Albinia left them alone in the crimson drawing room, on the pretext of looking for an earring she'd dropped.

"Dear Albinia, always so tactful," the marquis said when she left. "Miss Hartsell . . . my dear Chloe, I have heard of your argument with Mr. Stone this evening. I wish, with all my heart, that I stood in a position to prevent you from ever undergoing such unpleasantness again. If you accept my offer of marriage, Mr. Stone will not dare come near you again."

Chloe twisted the bracelet on her arm. "It wasn't like that, my lord."

"I see." He looked grave. "A lover's quarrel, was it? In a public place, where it could only hold you up to ridicule? How touching! Am I to wish you happy then?"

She went white. "That is cruel. If you know what transpired, you know he does not return my regard."

"Then marry me, Chloe. You have nothing to lose."

It was true. Her resolution wavered. "My lord, I am an orphan, with nothing to recommend me. Your friends would be scandalized."

"You forget I am a great lord, my dear. I can give you

anything you wish—any past that you choose. No one will question it. And, as my wife, you will be one of the greatest ladies in the land. No one will dare risk offending you.''

Chloe was overwhelmed by it all. ''Why do you want me? You can have any woman in the realm. You don't *need* me.''

Exton stopped and turned to face her, taking her hands in his. ''Since our first meeting, you have become an obsession with me. I spend the nights lying awake, thinking of you. I want you, Chloe. And I mean to have you.''

''Ah, you see. You *don't* need me,'' she said disconsolately.

''Neither does Gideon Stone,'' Exton said sharply. ''They say he is brilliant. A man of genius. Some people believe that artists are more than human; personally, I believe that some are less.''

Chloe was indignant. ''How can you say such a thing?''

''Do you know how selfish, how totally consuming the creative passion of a brilliant artist or writer can be? Nothing else matters to him but his work. You cannot hope to compete with it. The stroke of the nib on paper or the brush on canvas can be far more seductive than any lover's caress.''

Chloe looked at him, and then away. Everything he said was true.

The marquis pushed his point. ''You are blinded by your feelings. Yes,'' he held up a hand. ''I know that you fancy yourself in love with him, despite everything. You think he needs you, that in time he will turn to you. But all he needs is his art—a handful of brushes, a palette of paint, and whichever woman has caught his current fancy.''

She took in a breath that was almost a sob. Exton sensed victory. ''Preferably a woman who is ready to take her clothes off at the drop of a hat and pose for him, and when she is done, warm his bed. That, my dear, is the life of an artist. They will parade through his life, while you fetch and carry and grow old. You were gently raised, Chloe. Can you learn to tolerate that sort of life?''

''No.'' Her voice was very small. ''I am not so tolerant as that.''

"And can you bear to spend the rest of your days being urged by him, being *required* almost, to tell him how wonderful he is, when the world has bruised his spirit with insufficient praise? Can you bear to listen to him gloat when he is on top of the world with success, and your mundane matters are like lint, to be brushed away with a flick of his hand?"

"Good Heavens, you paint a dreary· picture!"

Exton smiled. "That is my talent. To portray the truth."

Chloe refused to be taken in by his words. "I know he can be selfish and self-indulgent, but he is not the monster you deem him to be." Despite their estrangement, she knew Gideon's heart too well. "His temper is quick, his judgement hasty, but he has been kinder to me than you know. If there is any fault," she said, with quiet dignity, "I believe it to be mine."

The marquis raised her hand and kissed it. "Loyal to the end. Very well, my dear. I will not distress you further." His green eyes flashed as yellow as a cat's. There was still an ace up his sleeve, metaphorically speaking.

"Nor," he said softly, "will I accept your answer as final." Rising, he made her an elegant bow. "We will speak of this again. *After* the exhibit."

When he was gone, Chloe sat and played with the tassel on the end of the sofa cushion. *What a perverse creature I am. I was devastated when I lost Lacey's Folly, worried over how I would keep a roof over my head.* She looked around the room with its gilt furnishings and fabulous paintings. *And I have turned this down. I must be mad.*

Or hopelessly in love.

The door opened, and she looked up as Lady Albinia slipped in. "Should I curtsey?" the older woman asked, with a small smile.

"Only if you wish the practice," Chloe said. "I am not going to be a marchioness, if that is your question. I suppose that I shall still be plain Miss Hartsell when they plant me in the ground."

"Now, what foolishness is this?" Lady Albinia took her

hand. "I thought I was playing matchmaker all this time, and Exton did not come up to scratch again?"

"Oh, he did." Chloe blushed. "I told him I was not inclined to marry."

"Good God! Have you lost your mind?"

She looked away. "I like him well enough. I do not love him."

The other women looked at her straightly. "Love can come in time. I know Exton . . . quite well." She fanned herself rapidly. "He would be an interesting companion and an ardent husband. Best of all, child, you seem to have captured his fancy quite genuinely."

Those liquid silver eyes surveyed Lady Albinia. "Do you think so? Or is it merely because I do not throw myself at his head like the other women?"

There was a long pause while the older woman chose her words. "A few days ago, I should have said a bit of both. And the chance to wreak a little havoc with my godson. Exton suspects there was some entanglement, and he would love to do Gideon a mischief."

She paused to collect the exact words she wanted. What she had to say could very well alter Chloe's life. "They say rakes do not reform. That isn't always true. Some mellow with age. I think you have done something, Chloe, that many have tried and none—including myself—have accomplished. The 'Wicked' marquis is in danger of becoming tamed by a quiet little country miss, and all London is agog."

"Surely not!"

"Dear child, I have it on good authority. Everyone who matters knows that he means to make you his wife. Why, bets in the club are all called off for lack of takers."

Ah, Chloe thought, *perhaps that explains why Gideon was so angry to see me in town.* Her heart gave a little leap of hope. Could it be that he was jealous?

Lady Albinia saw that small, pure flame in Chloe's eyes. Poor girl! If she came out of this with a whole heart, it would be a miracle.

*   *   *

Lord Pulham's townhouse was thronged for the reception. Those who had not received their engraved invitations had retired early to the country, to save face.

"Are you sure you want to do this?" Lady Albinia asked, as they waited their turn to dismount from the carriage.

"No. I am not sure at all," Chloe said. "But it is something that I have to do."

The carriage rolled forward toward the steps, and they descended to the sidewalk. Like Exton House, Pulham's mansion was in one of London's most exclusive squares, built around a large park. Inside it was a shrine to extravagance.

Guests entered a hall supported by columns of green stone streaked with rose, and the walls were hung with ruched silk. Chloe counted six crystal and gold chandeliers, before she realized she was gawking and stopped.

The double stairway was thronged with eager guests moving to the next floor, where the exhibit was to be shown. By ones and twos they glanced her way as she waited below with Lady Albinia, and she was aware of the many whispers amid the din.

"Where has Lord Exton gone to?" Chloe looked around. "He was beside us a moment ago."

A footman materialized out of the crowd and whispered in Lady Albinia's ear. She smiled and touched Chloe's arm. "Now you will see the advantage of friends in high places."

The footman led them into a library, where the marquis awaited them. A small side room disclosed a hidden staircase to the upper floors, and they were whisked up to the ballroom in a trice. Exton smiled down at Chloe. "You see how easy life can be. I might have had a footman clear the stairway to let you ascend, but I thought you would not like it."

"Indeed I would not!" Chloe exclaimed.

They came out into a lovely gallery, with paintings and mirrors down its length, and sets of large windows along the wall overlooking the square.

The footman opened the doors, and they entered the ballroom. It was so large, Chloe thought that Lacey's Folly might be dropped into it whole. She had an impression of mirrors and marble and glass, of sparkling crystals and gilded sconces, and cloth of gold draperies tied back with red velvet swags.

Somehow, she found herself in the center of the room with a glass of champagne in her gloved hand. She sipped at it nervously. A distinguished man eyed them with interest from the dais and made an elegant bow.

Lady Albinia smiled and inclined her head. "That is the Earl of Wendle. A noted connoisseur of beauty. My dear, your success is assured."

"At the moment I would gladly trade it for a cool breeze."

Then she spied Gideon across the room, and her heart stood still. She took a deep breath. There were shadows beneath his eyes, and his curls were tousled as if he'd been running his hands through his hair.

How nervous he must be. Any moment now he would know if his painting of Lenore was a success or not. Exton leaned down. "Let me put you out of your misery, my dear. Mr. Stone has won the commission."

Chloe was startled. "Do you know it for a fact?"

"I do indeed. I was here yesterday when Pulham made his choice." His eyes glittered in candlelight. "I had to agree with him. It is superb."

Her emotions were so mixed, she didn't know if she should be happy or sad. "I see. This is why you spoke to me of an artist's life and the dangers of failure, or success. You thought that perhaps he and I had merely had a lover's spat, and might make it up. It is too late for that."

"Forgive me if I say I am happy to hear you say it."

She examined her heart. Yes, she was glad for Gideon. Whatever way the paths of fortune led them, she had helped him in some small way. Let that be enough.

She watched Gideon over the rim of her glass. "He is all the things you said, my lord. Hasty and selfish and hot-tempered. But he is also good and generous and kind. It is not on the surface, but goes deep to the core of him. There is no evil in Gideon Stone.''

Her face was so filled with emotion as she spoke that Exton felt a chill. ''What of his work? How will you feel when you are neglected, while he paints?''

''You speak as if he and I had an understanding. There is none, nor will there ever be.'' Her voice trembled just a little, then grew stronger.

Exton was no longer so sure. Her words said one thing—and she meant it sincerely—but her eyes said another. Gideon Stone might still win her away. He would have to count on pride—Chloe's as well as Stone's—and pray that it had built so high a wall, neither could find a way over it.

But would the victory be worth it, for what it would cost to Chloe? Exton was startled by the thought. *I am too old to become altruistic,* the marquis told himself. *But God Almighty, she has gotten under my skin!*

''Gideon Stone is a hot-headed young fool,'' Exton said viciously.

She misunderstood the war raging in Exton's breast. ''Do not fault him for the passion he puts into his work. He can no more turn his back on his art than I can change myself from a woman to a man. It is not something that he does, but something that he *is*.''

Exton looked down at her. He wished there were some woman who would defend him as passionately. He had one last, thin hope. ''We will talk again, my dear. After you have seen his painting.''

Something about the way he said it put a cold hand around Chloe's heart. His obsession with Lenore must show in every brush stroke. Someone claimed Exton's attention, and Chloe found herself alone in the crowd. The crush was so intense, there was scarcely room to move through the press of bodies. Somebody trod on her toe.

Chloe looked up to find Gideon at her side. ''I wish you would not stay,'' he said quietly. ''I do not want you to see the painting. Under the circumstances, it will only cause you pain.''

She lifted her chin. ''I have come all this way. I won't turn back now.''

''You will when it is unveiled. Would that I could take it back!'' Gideon was beside himself. ''Devil take it, Chloe! I never meant to hurt you. Believe me when I say that.'' He looked distressed and humbled. ''Believe me when you see what I have done!''

He would have said more, but Lord Pulham stepped upon the dais, where the painting was hidden behind a gold curtain. His name was called, and he left her reluctantly, to forge his way through the crowd.

Albinia materialized at Gideon's side. ''I have a riddle for you. Tell me, If there were one wish, one thing in the world you could ask for at this exact moment, what would it be?''

''Chloe's happiness,'' he said quietly.

''What? Not fame or fortune?''

He shook his head.

Albinia put her hand on his arm. ''But rumor says she is to marry Exton.''

''Yes,'' he said, looking away. ''Little Chloe to be a marchioness. She will have everything a woman could desire: rank, wealth, security. An apparently doting husband. At least there is a happy ending to that fairy tale.''

''It that what you believe?'' Albinia frowned. ''Do you truly think he will make her happy?''

Gideon's hands clenched. ''By God, he had better, or he will answer to me!''

''Exton will not make her happy, although I believe he will try. But she does not love him.''

''No?'' he said bitterly. ''She will learn. She loved me once, but now she loathes me. The unhappiest day in her life was the day I entered it.''

''*You* say that she loathes you. My impression is quite opposite.'' Albinia's voice was soft as a summer breeze. ''What are your own feelings? You must put them into words, Gideon. What is Chloe to you?''

"To me?'' Gideon was thunderstruck. "She is *everything* to me!''

Without Chloe he was hollow. A sham, a shell of a man, who would grow more selfish—less complete—less human, with every passing day. A parody of all that nature had intended him to be.

And as surely as his spirit would shrivel, his talent would petrify. Everything was entwined, and it was Chloe—only Chloe—at the heart of it all.

And now it was too late. Lord Pulham was making his announcement. After calling the crowd to attention, he thanked them for coming—and without further ado, pulled the cord that held the curtain.

A gasp went up from the assembly when the painting was revealed.

Chloe stood as if turned to stone. It was a masterpiece, there was no doubt of that. The colors were exquisite, the composition sublime. The woman in the portrait ethereally beautiful.

And, except for the flowers in the foreground that gave her some modesty, she was also totally nude.

She was also totally *Chloe.*

Chloe stared at the painting, thunderstruck. Now she understood why Gideon had wanted her to go, and why Exton had wanted her here.

"*Perfect Love,*" Lord Pulham intoned. "*Perfect Trust.*"

When the murmurs and comments and applause died down, she cleared her throat. "Who . . . who titled the portrait, my lord?''

"Why, the artist himself, Mr. Gideon Stone.''

Chloe gazed at her life-sized image. Everyone else was looking at it too. Except for Exton and Gideon, who were watching her. Gideon averted his head. He couldn't bear to see the disgust in her face, the shattering embarrassment that would follow. She would never understand what that painting meant to him, or what he wished it to convey to her.

She stepped closer. No one recognized the elegant young lady as the woman in the portrait. Not yet. Gideon had painted her face perfectly, but it was shaded by a leafy frond. But when had he done it? It had to be that day in the garden, the first time they'd made love.

As she examined the painting, she saw what he had not seen at the time: the tenderness, the care with which he had rendered her portrait, almost as if he were making love to her through the touch of the brush on canvas. There was her breast, where his mouth had touched, ripe and engorged. Her lips, parted in sleep with remembered passion. Her limbs rosy with lovemaking, relaxed and graceful in the bower of flowers.

Tears stung her eyes. She lowered her lids and made her way through the throng and out into the gallery. Exton watched her go, but stood frozen to the spot. Albinia had noticed, as well.

Chloe didn't look around once until she was in the gallery, with the sunlight pouring through the window like gold. No sooner was she through the door than Gideon was there at her side. She had known that he would follow her.

His face was ravaged with emotion. "I cannot blame you for hating me now. I can only hope that someday you will forgive me, Chloe. For everything!"

She looked up at him, her face shining. "Oh, Gideon! If you think I hate you, then Exton is right, and you are a fool."

Her voice was ragged whisper. "I know why you painted it. And why you chose it for the competition. But I must hear it in your own words. You must say it aloud!"

He stood before her, humble and sincere, with hope glowing in his heart.

"I wanted the world to see your beauty, as I see it. I wanted to show the world how much I love you." He lifted her trembling hand and kissed it.

"Oh, Chloe! My Chloe. Like Rossetti with Elizabeth Siddal. I wanted to make you *immortal!*"

She raised her face for his kiss and was pulled roughly into his arms. Gideon covered her mouth with hot kisses, and she returned them, every one.

His arm wound round her even more tightly. His blue eyes blazed with light. "I will make you a terrible husband."

"I know."

"I will be distracted and roar like a bear when I am interrupted from my work."

"I know."

"I have a vile temper . . ."

She was laughing now. "Oh, yes. I know."

"But I'll work like the devil to change it. And I will love you, Chloe, my dearest darling! I will love only you, and keep and cherish you until the day I die!"

She leaned her head against his shoulder and listened to the strong beating of his heart. "Oh, I know, Gideon. I know!"

He crushed her to him once more and kissed her passionately. Then he released her all at once. Taking her hand, he pulled her along the gallery toward the staircase. "Come along. Hurry!"

She was laughing and crying all at once. "But where are you taking me?"

He paused on the topmost step and scooped her into his arms for a lingering kiss. Then he lifted his head and smiled down at her.

"Ah, Chloe, my love. I am taking you home!"

THIRTEEN

⌘

GIDEON STOOD IN THE WINDOW OF GIOVANNA'S TOWER. Shadows lengthened in the glimmering world. He held his breath, waiting. And at that exact moment, just before the sun set, *she* stepped out of the shadows at the foot of the slope, insubstantial as a spirit in her fluttering white gown.

In the crystalline light, her fair skin was luminous as pearl, and her unbound hair shimmered like a wedding veil against the dark trunks of the trees. He knew now that he *had* been waiting all his life for this moment.

Waiting for *her*. He was afraid to move, to breathe. Afraid that she was a figment of his longing, and that she would vanish before his eyes.

For the span of a few heartbeats, she hesitated, and he thought that she would surely turn and bolt back into the safety of the sheltering trees. Then she came forward and stopped full in the moon's clear glow. In the golden light, he could see her with almost magical clarity.

Her beauty was so remarkable it robbed him of breath. His chest ached.

Then, raising her head slowly, she looked up at the turret where he stood framed in the arch of the open window. There was such yearning in her face, in every graceful line of her body, that it hit him with the force of a physical blow. He gripped the cool stone of the sill to keep from staggering backward. He was certain she couldn't see him in the shadows of the turret window, yet she lifted her arms, reaching out to him.

To *him!*

He remembered all the times that this had happened before, how he misread it completely, and laughed aloud.

Gideon ran down the tower stairs and burst out the door.

Chloe stood in Giovanna's garden, waiting for him. She still wore her wedding dress, but it was her hair, silvered by moonlight, that still gave the illusion of a veil.

"I have been waiting for you," he whispered. "All my life."

She stepped into his arms, knowing she belonged there. He held her tightly, then lifted her in his arms and carried her up the stairs.

Her discarded gown puddled like moonbeams on the floor. She stood naked and perfect before him, gleaming like ivory. Gideon snuffed the single candle, leaving them cocooned in lavender shadows. Lifting her in his arms, he carried her to the divan. Moonlight filtered through the open shutters onto her naked body.

It seemed fitting that they should spend the first night of their marriage in Giovanna's tower, where it had all started.

He stripped off his own garments and stretched out beside her. Cupping her breasts in his hand, he kissed their tips, then took one into his mouth. Chloe arched up beneath him, as he covered her with his length. She was ready for him, beginning to move urgently, as his hand moved down her ribs, along the sweet curve of her hips and thigh. He touched her lightly, heard her soft moan of pleasure, and retreated.

"Gideon," she murmured in protest.

"Patience, you little pagan. We have all night." He stroked along her inner thigh again. "And all day tomorrow. And the next."

"I hope you don't mean to wait until then," she laughed, and bit his ear lightly.

"Oh, is it that game you want to play?" He nipped her lower lip, her throat, the rosy aureole she offered him. "I know a hundred others," he promised her. "And you will like them all."

He roved his lips down her body, nipping the soft swell of her belly, the silken inside of her thighs, and all the way down to her toes. She writhed and reached for him. "Gideon, for the love of God!"

"No, for the love of my sweet Chloe." Again his hand brushed her intimately, but this time it lingered. She was slick and hot with passion. His fingers moved gently, persistently, then lunged deep, until she arched against him and cried out in sheer joy.

Then he held her close until the shudders ceased. And began again. Her mouth roved over his skin, touching the sensitive places. Her teeth were sharp against him. She was no longer the softly pliant lover, but elemental woman, calling to her other half. Her nails raked his shoulders and down over the muscles of his chest and arms, until he was as wild as she.

"You," she said breathlessly. "I want you, Gideon. All of you. Now."

Her voice, her need, shot through him, igniting his blood to the point of no return. He plunged inside her, thrusting deep, until they were both soaring on the clear silver light, dizzy with delight, shaken with the sudden, wracking release of passion.

When it ended, they lay entwined. Body to body, heart to heart, and soul to soul. Sapphire eyes looked into silver. "If you ever leave me, Chloe, I will die. It would tear such a hole in me, I'd bleed to death."

She smiled and snuggled against his shoulder. "I will never leave you, Gideon. I am yours for time and eternity."

As she nestled near his heart, he thought of how he'd almost ruined everything, first with his pride, then with his brief, hollow infatuation for Lenore. She read his mind.

"We must still decide what to do about Lenore."

"We'll think about it later," he said. "Much later . . ."

Perry tiptoed into the parlor quietly early one evening. His leg had healed miraculously, Dr. Marsh said, and he no longer even used a cane.

Lenore was sitting alone, staring into the empty hearth. She didn't look up at his entrance. Perry shook his head. She was very thin, and the gowns that Chloe had taken in for her, hung loose. Her skin was so pale, so translucent she looked as if she might vanish before his eyes.

"He's here," he said. "He's come for you."

Lenore jumped to her feet. "Are you sure?"

"It's him all right. You'll know when you see him." The boy looked at her worriedly. "Are you sure nothing passed your lips but water?"

"I am." Lenore glanced down at Newton, waddling along the floor. "Thank you. I hope your pup will soon work off all the food I fed to him."

"I'll see to it." He held out his hand. "Come with me. He's in the drawing room with Chloe and Gideon."

As he started out, Lenore stopped him. She bent down and whispered in his ear. "When I am gone, look behind the drawing room door. And on the shelf beside the buhl cabinet. Show them to Mrs. Osler. And there are others in the rockery," she added mysteriously. "I have no need of them."

Perry's eyes widened, and he nodded solemnly. "Thank you."

Meanwhile, Chloe and Gideon were in the drawing room, entertaining the stranger, while they waited for Perry to fetch Lenore.

His name, he told them, was LaFey. He was quite handsome, with eyes like autumn leaves, and long golden hair clubbed back in the old way, held by a black ribbon. It made him look exotic and rather dashing. His skin was windburned and tanned, yet held an odd, darker tone for which even Gideon's artist's eye could not account.

"We were staying at an inn near Eddlesfield, en route to our home. There was illness in the village, and we were both stricken with the fever within hours of one another," Mr. LaFey told them. "I lost consciousness, and rambled in feverish dreams for days. They feared for my life. When I came out of the delirium, my wife had been missing for the better part of two weeks.''

''Eddlesfield!'' Chloe exclaimed. ''Why that is quite far. Little wonder our inquiries never reached you. But . . . however did she walk all this way in her bare feet?''

Their guest shrugged. ''She may have taken a shortcut overland and lost her shoes in the woods. Or perhaps someone gave her a ride in a wagon, then thought she was demented, and abandoned her along the way.''

''Let me assure you, she came to no harm, other than the shock and cold,'' Gideon said, anxious to reassure him.

''How very odd that her name *is* Lenore,'' Chloe said.

''Not when you know her history.'' LaFey reached inside his jacket and pulled out a small leather case. His right hand was bandaged, and he had a little trouble removing it.

''You see, we were traveling through the area on our way to Wales and thought to stop and make inquiries of a place called Lacey's Folly. Since you are both aware of the legend, this will explain it all.''

Gideon took the case and opened it. Chloe gasped. ''Why, it is Lost Lenore. Even to the same gown and earrings.''

''My wife was a Dacre,'' he told them. ''She grew up with this miniature, which was a family heirloom. She was so taken with the legend, I even had earrings made up for her to match. An anniversary gift.''

The door opened and Lenore came in. She stood stock still. Then, as Gideon had seen once before, it seemed as if a ripple ran through her, as if she were a reflection on water.

Then the illusion passed, and for the first time, her lovely face was truly animated, full of light and life. ''John! Oh, John!''

She started toward him, then stopped. Reaching up, she undid Chloe's little gold and silver cross and handed it to her. ''I thank you again for the loan of it.''

Then she went across the floor and was swooped up in her husband's embrace. There was no doubt of the love they had for one another, or that Lenore's memory had come back in full.

The happy couple were invited to stay on for dinner, but

were in too much of a hurry to leave. "We have been separated too long," John LaFey said, after thanking them, "and we have a long journey ahead on the morrow. I've taken rooms at the inn in Greater Brampton for the night, and we must be on our way."

He shook hands with Gideon, awkwardly because of his bandage, and kissed Chloe's fingers. "I can never repay you for the care you showed my wife in her time of distress. You already have my thanks. I will give you my blessing as well."

Holding out his right hand formally, he spoke in the same liquid language that Lenore had done, then translated it into English:

> May you and yours live out your days
> with happy hearts and peaceful ways.
> May all your fondest dreams come true
> with never a breath of sorrow and rue.
> I bless you with this, three times three,
> in love and plenty. So mote it be.

Although a bit startled, Chloe and Gideon thanked him. A fond embrace from Lenore, and they were gone.

"That was rather strange," Gideon commented.

"Perhaps it is a Welsh blessing," Chloe said, as the door closed behind Lenore and her husband.

Gideon took Chloe's hand in his. "So, that is the end of our mystery," he said lightly.

"Not a plot of the Thornes to trick me out of Lacey's Folly, nor the return of a woman who vanished over a hundred years ago. Merely a descendent of the Dacres who bears an uncanny resemblance to Lost Lenore. A poor creature and her spouse, who wanted to learn more of her family legend, but were stricken with fever and delirium before they ever reached the village."

"Yes," Chloe said slowly. Had Gideon noticed the small red spot on Lenore's throat? Like a tiny cruciform blister, where her gold and silver cross had lain.

Gideon frowned to himself. He'd glimpsed the wound beneath the man's bandage. A curious burn across the flesh of his palm, round as an iron ring.

They looked at one another. "We are imagining things," Gideon said firmly.

"Of course we are," Chloe said. "They are as human as you or I."

But they both rushed to the window to watch the LaFeys drive off. They were gone, as if they'd vanished into thin air.

Not a minute later, Perry burst in the door behind them. "I've found it! I've found the Lacey treasure. It was where Tobias hinted to you, Chloe. If you hadn't been so besotted with Gideon, you would have guessed for yourself."

Gideon turned around first. The boy was lugging a mottled grayish stone the size of his head.

"Oh, no! Another great stone from that infernal collection."

Chloe laughed. It was round as a melon, and just as dull looking. "Perry, that is the rock I was using for a doorstop in the parlor."

"No," he said. "Well, yes it is. But it isn't a rock at all. It's a star sapphire. And there's five or six of them in the mineral collection. *Chloe's* mineral collection," he said pointedly.

He set it down on the hearth rug and turned it over to expose where the dull skin had been polished away. As he turned it, a ray of light flashed across the dark blue surface, like a moonbeam on a midnight sea. "And there are two jade boulders in the rockery, half buried beneath the creeping thyme. One lavender, one like cream. Mrs. Osler said they are worth a fortune!"

"Fabulous jewels from the earth's four corners," Chloe laughed. "No one ever said they were polished!"

Gideon wrapped one arm around Chloe and the other around the boy. "Don't worry, Perry. I'll lay no claim to it. I have all the treasure I want within the span of my two arms."

EPILOGUE

§§

"Is YOUR HAND VERY BAD?" LENORE ASKED, KISSING HER husband's fingers.

"It wasn't the burn that kept me," he told her. "But that fool boy! He put two iron rings across the door, along with some St. John's wort and a vial of holy water. It took time to clear it away."

Lenore looked up at him. Already her short stay in the mortal world was fading away into a dreamlike memory. Love shone in her eyes. "O my heart, why did you ever let me leave you?"

"My sweet love, a hundred years and a day had passed. I am as bound by the laws of Faerie as mortals are by the laws of gravity."

He tilted his head closer. Already she could see the silver circlet of kingship forming on his noble brow. His eyes had darkened and stars shone in their depths.

"Even so, Lenore, I would still have had to let you leave the rath. I would not keep you there against your will, even though you were my queen." He smiled. "And I would know, if you came back to me, that your love for me was true."

She leaned her head upon his shoulder, where the jacket had turned back into his favorite blue and silver tunic. How handsome he was, her fairy king.

Her husband and her love.

He gave a crack of his whip and the coach-and-four dis-

solved into sparks of light—hundreds of golden fireflies dart-ing on the warm night air. He said the words of command, and instantly, they were transported to the threshold of the rath beneath Pucca's Hill. His whip had turned into a jeweled scepter.

He touched it to the lichened rock, incised with runes, and a door opened in the hillside. Bright candlelight spilled out, and music so beautiful that Lenore wept for sheer happiness. The fairy castle had never looked more lovely, glowing like the moon.

Lenore and her fairy husband went through it eagerly, her hand clasped in his. Inside were her boon companions of the past hundred years, laughing and feasting in the full splendor of fairy glamour. Beyond the golden walls, she could glimpse sunlight and sapphire waters through the open windows. The Isles of the Blessed were green and misty in the far distance.

Her heart lifted with joy. The world of human affairs wisped away in her mind, like gauzy fragments of a scarcely remem-bered dream.

This was where she belonged now.

Her husband stopped her on the threshold and spoke the formal words of invitation: "Lady, will you come inside and join the feast with me?"

"Aye, I will sir. For this is my own, my only home." She twined her arms around his neck. "And here I will dwell with my own true love, forevermore."

The door to the fairy rath closed to the sound of flutes and harp, and the woods of Pucca's Hill were dark and silent. Hand in hand with her fairy king, Lenore Lacey stepped out of the shadowy mortal world, and back into glittering legend.